CW01214215

SEASON OF FEAR

SEASON OF FEAR

Emily Cooper

**SIMON &
SCHUSTER**

London · New York · Amsterdam/Antwerp · Sydney/Melbourne · Toronto · New Delhi

First published in Great Britain by Simon & Schuster UK Ltd, 2025

Copyright © Emily Cooper, 2025

The right of Emily Cooper to be identified as author of this work has been asserted in accordance with the Copyright, Designs and Patents Act, 1988.

1 3 5 7 9 10 8 6 4 2

Simon & Schuster UK Ltd
1st Floor
222 Gray's Inn Road
London WC1X 8HB

For more than 100 years, Simon & Schuster has championed authors and the stories they create. By respecting the copyright of an author's intellectual property, you enable Simon & Schuster and the author to continue publishing exceptional books for years to come. We thank you for supporting the author's copyright by purchasing an authorized edition of this book.

No amount of this book may be reproduced or stored in any format, nor may it be uploaded to any website, database, language-learning model, or other repository, retrieval, or artificial intelligence system without express permission. All rights reserved. Inquiries may be directed to Simon & Schuster, 222 Gray's Inn Road, London WC1X 8HB or RightsMailbox@simonandschuster.co.uk

Simon & Schuster Australia, Sydney
Simon & Schuster India, New Delhi

The authorised representative in the EEA is Simon & Schuster Netherlands BV, Herculesplein 96, 3584 AA Utrecht, Netherlands. info@simonandschuster.nl

www.simonandschuster.co.uk
www.simonandschuster.com.au
www.simonandschuster.co.in

Simon & Schuster strongly believes in freedom of expression and stands against censorship in all its forms. For more information, visit BooksBelong.com.

A CIP catalogue record for this book
is available from the British Library

Hardback ISBN: 978-1-3985-3579-4
Trade Paperback ISBN: 978-1-3985-3580-0
eBook ISBN: 978-1-3985-3581-7
Audio ISBN: 978-1-3985-3780-4

This book is a work of fiction. Names, characters, places and incidents are either a product of the author's imagination or are used fictitiously. Any resemblance to actual people living or dead, events or locales is entirely coincidental.

Typeset in Baskerville by M Rules
Printed and Bound in the UK using 100% Renewable Electricity
at CPI Group (UK) Ltd

*For my mum, who does feel fear,
but moves forward despite it.*

PROLOGUE

A human wall stretches around Heulensee. Women and girls kneel shoulder to shoulder in terrified reverence, linked together by white-knuckled hands. Their mouths hang open. Viewed from afar, you might imagine they are singing – that this is a celebration, or some benign folk ritual.

The scene is about as benign as the tumour which killed my papa. The women aren't singing; they're screaming.

They wail, heads tipped back, eyes red and white with terror. The wall of bodies sways and buckles with the weight of collective emotion. Some wear their fear proudly with unwavering falsetto screams; others are quieter, and the terror shudders free from their mouths in gasps.

My silence makes me an outlier. It makes me a target.

I stand behind Mama as the sole missing brick in our feeble defence. Beside her, my sister, Dorothea, wails. Terror twists her face. It wrinkles her forehead and makes her pretty eyes bulge from her skull.

Mama turns to me, eyes wild. 'Scream, Ilse!'

An apologetic smile is all I can offer. I want to render them in my image, even if just for a moment. Rid them of the fear that pains them. They are so determined, so full of horror – but their bodies are fleshy and easy to break. Secretly, I don't think their efforts will do much to protect us when the monsters come.

The looming threat of our demise sparks a realization: if I am going to die, I would like to do so by my sister's side. I nestle between Mama and Dorothea, perched awkwardly on my knees. They grasp my hands, knuckles popping. Something feral touches their eyes. They begin to howl. The sound runs through my bones.

From this angle, I can just make out the inky smear of the Hexenwald on the horizon. The sky above the trees blushes crimson. It's the only warning we receive before the forest overflows. On any other day, the forest seems almost benevolent. The Hexenwald's deceitful appearance is perhaps its most lethal trait. Whispering boughs mask a multitude of sins.

The trees serve as a breeding ground for all manner of monsters. Perhaps today will be like the summer when colossal serpents, *Lindwürmer*, emerged from the forest and swallowed four children whole. Maybe I will smell the same decay as the night an entire family was drained by bloodthirsty *Nachzehrer*, vampiric creatures who only know thirst.

While I cannot predict what will spill from the trees, one thing is certain. No matter how hard I try, I will not feel afraid.

'Please, Ilse,' Mama begs, my obvious distraction triggering desperation in her eyes.

I part my lips, hoping that Mama's own fear will leap down

my throat. That it will dig its claws into my heart or my brain – wherever I am *supposed* to feel it.

I begin to groan. It's a hollow sound. There is no weight behind it, no driving force. My heart thumps steadily, blood meandering through my veins. I think the absence of my terror must be glaring, but my performance seems to fool Mama and Thea. They relax their grip on my hands.

'Yes, Ilse!' Mama presses a fervent kiss on my cheek and goes back to screaming. The shock of her lips on my cheek is bittersweet. I cannot remember another time she's kissed me.

The ground shakes beneath my knees.

'It's coming,' Thea shrieks. 'The Saint is coming!'

The vibrations in the earth rattle my kneecaps and travel up my spine. They grow and grow until they're so close that they mirror the steady beat of my heart. *Thud, thud, thud.* Heat billows behind me – the displacement of air by something huge beyond comprehension. Moist, rotting breath grazes my nape.

The screaming stops.

Mama's grip on my hand tightens. Thea's, too. The air which hung heavy with terror moments ago is now totally still. I swallow. It sounds like a gunshot in my ears.

The next breath is so close that it makes my hair flutter.

'Are you afraid?' A deep, echoing voice asks from behind me. It sounds like the rumble of thunder which precedes the worst of a storm.

'Yes,' we shout. I am the only one who is lying.

A rush of air almost topples me; a shadow briefly blots out the sun. The beast lands in front of us, more macabre than I remember it. The Saint of Fear. It is a disgusting patchwork: its body is that of a wolf, but ten times the size; at the crown of its head, a deer's antlers branch out, reaching for the sun; its skull is that of an overgrown ram. I say skull, not head, because there is no flesh or fur to cover its awful maw. There is only bleached bone, deep hollows for eyes, and a permanent, toothy sneer. Heretics call it the *Untier*. The monster.

I strain to keep my gaze pinned to the floor, the way it wants me to – but I cannot stop my eyes from drifting upwards. Caves call to children, and the pits in the Saint's skull call to me. Deep in the socket, eyes the colour of blood flick to meet mine. The Saint falters mid-stride and releases a breath, more of a growl than an exhale.

I stare back into my lap, focusing on the pinch of Mama's nails against my palm. Rancid breath moistens my cheek. One of its bloody claws pins the edge of my dress to the dirt.

'Are you afraid?' it hisses into my face, each syllable echoing unnaturally.

Lie, my brain orders. 'Yes.'

A rumble comes from deep in its chest. 'You will be.'

A distant wail echoes. A chorus of whispers rise from the women. I let go of the exhale caught between my throat and lips, stealing a furtive glance at Thea. When she looks back at me, there is more white than blue in her eyes.

The wind dies down. The birds cease to sing. The Saint swings its colossal head towards the trees of the Hexenwald. Mama grips my hand so tightly that my skin blanches around her fingers. Anyone privy to this spectacle, unaware of Heulensee's macabre traditions, might believe that the monster before us is our foe.

No, this bloody-mawed creature is our *saviour*. The worst is yet to come.

An amorphous cloud of white floats free of the forest. Not

the serpentine Lindwurm, nor the insatiable Nachzehrer. As it glides over the lake, it separates into three distinct entities: three women, floating just above the water. Their arms and legs dangle, motionless as corpses. I watch them in the way I might ogle a snake before it strikes.

'The *Hexen*,' Mama whispers, her voice cracking. 'This is the end.'

Through all the eight years of my life, monsters have poured from the Hexenwald like blood from a wound. But never – *never* – have the Hexen shown their faces. They are the root of all the evil that has preceded them. They orchestrate; they do not bloody their hands.

Until today.

The Hexen reach our shore, gliding over the pebbles, then the grass, then the cobbled street. They hang just in front of the ancient Saint, staring it down with pupil-less eyes. One is grey-haired, her face weathered by time; one is maternal in her beauty, soft of cheek and hip. Between them, they clutch the youngest – no older than me, perhaps eight years old. She does not levitate so much as she hangs.

'We have come for the Saint of Fear.' They do not open their mouths, but they speak in discordant harmony.

I know their presence should stir something in me. They are predators, and I am their prey. Our relationship is the basis of life in this isolated valley; the creatures of the Hexenwald hunt, humans flee. But rather than fear, I feel anticipation. It is the same sense I get just before a storm breaks.

The eldest of the Hexen floats forwards. She cocks her head at an unnatural angle, eyes boring into the Saint's skull. The imposition of her gaze enrages the beast; it snarls, raising its hackles.

'Leave this place,' it barks. 'Do not folly with a Saint. I have slain the beasts you sent to terrorize this village; I will slay you just the same.'

The women's jaws fall open in unison; laughter tumbles out. It is flighty, girlish. Utterly strange from their cold, unsmiling faces.

'I will tear you, limb from limb,' the Saint growls, incensed. 'Then you shall see.'

The Hexen stop laughing. A wind whips around them, lifting the muddied hems of their dresses. The eldest turns her back and glides away, drawing level with her companions. I think they might be retreating – until her head rotates a half-circle atop her spine.

Eyes burning white hot, the woman says, 'Feast.'

The Hexen plunge through the air, jaws hanging open. The oldest smiles so widely that I think her cheeks might split; the middle adopts a rigid face so uncaring that I think she must be made of glass; the youngest screeches, a sound that makes my teeth ache. Gauzy, iridescent ether fills the sky, pulsing around them.

The beast roars. It leaps forward, plunging serrated teeth into one of the Hexens' legs – the youngest of the brood – and slams her to the ground. Her spine snaps at an angle, mimicking the staccato peaks of the mountains beyond the Hexenwald.

Mama screams. This time, it holds more than just terror. Her pupils narrow; tears stream down her cheeks, unbridled. The young Hexe's death snaps something vital inside her. It snaps something in the remaining Hexen, too. They wail. It's a magnetic sound, wrenching my focus away from Mama. Ether rolls off them in waves – the same way it seeps from the Hexenwald on a clear day. Their fists harden at their sides, and their assault resumes.

The eldest howls, anguish pinching her features; the other

laughs so shrilly that my eardrums begin to ring. Their outburst infects the Saint of Fear. Its eyes begin to water, and it moans with grief; its colossal heart beats so loudly I hear it at a distance, mirroring the maternal Hexe's erratic laughter. The Hexen set upon the weakened beast, tearing out great hunks of its flesh with their teeth.

The Saint swings its head, and I swear it looks directly at me as it bellows, 'I need *more*.'

My feigned scream is blunt. Powerless. Foaming at the mouth, the Saint breaks free from the Hexen and turns on us. The women shriek, clutching each other in desperation. The Hexen cackle as the Saint lumbers towards our ranks, one paw dragging limply behind.

At first, I think the Saint is coming for me – that it plans to punish my heresy once and for all. I throw myself in front of Thea, desperate to shield her from what comes next – but then the Saint diverts. It stalks down the line.

I look to the right just in time to see Klara Keller's head torn from her neck. The stump of her spine spurts blood. I gawk at the empty space where the girl's head should be, unable to comprehend her metamorphosis from person to corpse. My lungs calcify, denying me the breath I'm desperate for.

The Saint stares at me. It wants me to see Klara's lifeless eyes staring out from between its teeth. Her mouth is still ajar, as if she might reanimate at any moment and tell us not to worry. Slowly, slowly, the Saint grinds its jaws shut. Her face compresses and distorts and—

Mama uses our conjoined hands to shield my eyes. It does not stop me from hearing Klara's skull crack between the Saint's teeth.

By the time Mama removes her hand, what's left of Klara

kneels limply. She wears her best *dirndl*: a white apron, now bloody, with a dress the colour of forget-me-nots. How proud she must have been putting on that dress this morning, never anticipating it would be the last thing she'd wear.

Klara's mother and sister do not move; they maintain their grip on her hands, keeping her headless body upright. Even in death, Klara steadies the wall.

'Now,' the Saint roars, 'are you afraid?'

The women around me rally. They think the Saint is addressing us all. I know the truth: it has seen me. It knows the steady absence in my heart. Klara Keller died because of *me*.

Spittle flies from Mama's mouth. Further down the line, Klara's mother clutches her daughter's corpse and bellows. Terror becomes a tangible force, exploding from the women's feeble bodies, shrapnel feeding the Saint.

The beast changes. It rears up to stand on two legs, not four. Its antlers branch out, skeletal prongs sharpening. It walks like a man, not a beast. Teeth longer than the rest drop from its bony jaw.

The Hexen levitate, retreating to the lakeshore, and begin to chant. The Saint pursues them but gravity itself seems to be working against the creature. The Hexen's faces contort; they chant louder, louder. Groaning, the Saint collapses to the floor, body pressing into the earth.

The scream that Thea lets loose is the closest I have ever felt to fear. It is an urgent plea – a call to action. She scrabbles against me, anchoring our bodies. Her panic brings the reality of our situation into sharp focus: if the Saint of Fear dies, so do we.

And it will be my fault.

My chest shudders with guilt, blending with my longing to save

Thea and my desperation to be fearful, to be the way a girl *should* be. I let my mouth hang open, begging Thea's terror to inhabit me. Something else rises from my depths. *Fury.* A sound erupts from deep inside, somewhere primal.

The Hexen scream. I look up just in time to see them thrown across the lake, their limbs flung out like rag dolls. They crash deep in the Hexenwald. Trees collapse in their wake. There is the cracking of wood, the settling of leaves, and then there is silence.

The Saint turns to face us, panting. Thea draws me tighter against her, as if she can shroud me in the folds of her dress. I drop my eyes to the floor and whimper – the image of a subservient, fearful girl.

The Saint of Fear draws its maw level with my ear. My hair flutters as it whispers, 'Do not disappoint me again, Ilse Odenwald. It will be your sister's head next time.'

Without hesitation, the beast leaps over the wall of our bodies and retreats to its den. The villagers call after it, offering thanks and shaky prayers. Klara Keller's mother blows it a kiss. *A kiss.*

Thea collapses into a flood of tears. I kiss her cheek and turn to Mama to do the same, but her expression shows no relief. Mama stares at me with cold calculation, her eyes caught somewhere between suspicion and loathing.

She sees the absence in my heart. The glaring, angry silhouette my fear should occupy. It is a void – a hungry black hole that will consume everything she holds dear.

We both know the clock is ticking.

CHAPTER ONE

Ten years after Klara Keller's death, my sister goes missing. The village does not mark Klara's passing, but I cannot forget the date. No matter how frantically I try to distract myself, it's seared into my brain. Each anniversary I wake in the early hours, plagued down to my bones with the feeling that penance is coming. So much so that when Thea's husband begins throwing stones at my window mere minutes after midnight, I am already awake. Waiting. My fearlessness got Klara Keller killed. Now, it must be my turn to suffer.

I've bitten my fingernails down to stumps. It's a nervous habit I should have grown out of. I lick their blooded edges clean as I stagger downstairs, pre-emptive grief taking root in my stomach. It winds across my ribs, my lungs, my throat. Makes it so I can hardly breathe. Heat presses against my eyes. I try to stifle it – to not let my anguish show on my face. My stoicism is a defence mechanism, the same way injured animals attempt to mask their wounds.

Hans stands at our front door bleating that 'she was in the bath, and then she was gone.' I can barely hear him. Macabre images of Thea devour my consciousness: her wading into the lake, lips turning blue; her slipping down the impassable mountains, flesh tearing on jagged rocks. Or worse, her staggering into the Hexenwald.

The old Thea would never dare venture into the forest. But the new Thea – the one who took her Rite and came back different...

There's no telling what *she* might do.

My ears whine as I tune back into conversation. I rarely listen to Hans, but tonight I need to make an exception.

Hans braces one arm against the door frame. 'I didn't want to worry your mother, but I wondered if Thea might have come here—'

'No,' I interrupt, blinking loose the haze of tears that have settled over my vision. 'She's not here.'

His pulse flutters against his throat like a trapped bird. 'Please help me find her, Ilse.'

I like Hans about as much as I would like an adder in my boot. He and I exist in a strange purgatory – our relationship unchanging, yet fraught. Hans is nauseatingly pleasant; I rebuke his every attempt at friendship. I'm not sure whether my main gripe is his effusive nature or the fact that he took my sister away from me, even before the Rite did.

But with Thea's life at stake, there is little I won't do. For every foul word spoken about me in this village – and let me tell you, there are many – my loyalty to her cannot be denied. I retrieve my cloak from its hook and close the door quietly, so as not to wake Mama. 'Let's go.'

We descend the steep track from the Odenwald house in silence. Mist casts a gauze across the village. Our family's occupation as fire-watchers supplies us with little by way of fortune, but we do have Heulensee's finest view. Our house perches above the village like a falcon ready to take flight. We enjoy unspoilt views across the lake, all the way to the Hexenwald.

Tonight, moonlight spills across the water in a ream of silver silk. Swollen storm clouds writhe on the horizon, threatening to break. A bone-white lightning bolt forks down. It strikes somewhere deep in the trees beyond.

'She wouldn't go there,' Hans says quietly, eyes fixed on the violent bristles of the Hexenwald. There is an unspoken question mark at the end of his sentence.

'No,' I confirm, though I'm not sure I believe it. I'm not generally in the habit of dishonesty, but for both of our sakes, I think it's the best course of action.

The threat of the Hexenwald is sewn into us from childhood. On a clear day, when the fog lifts from the lake and you can see all the way to the forest, a lilting song rises from the schoolyard:

> *Blood spills from veins, skin starts to crack*
> *Ignore the forest; turn back, turn back*
> *Eyes become sockets, flesh melts to bone*
> *The forest is hungry; go home, go home*
> *The Hexen won't rest 'til your blood is shed*
> *Ignore the warning; you're dead, you're dead.*

The appearance of the Hexen ten years ago sparked a renewed desire to purge the forest – once and for all – but still, evil persists. Wildfire cannot singe it; fences cannot contain it; axes cannot fell its trees. Signs erected in warning are swallowed by the forest, and those who trespass either do not come back, or wish they hadn't.

I shut my eyes and send a plea out into the night. *Please let Thea be in the village.*

We enter Heulensee's central cobbled street. By day, it's a riot of colour; the mint-green apothecary, the rose-pink bakery, and vibrant flowers spilling from baskets on every window. The night has stripped away the colour, leaving behind a liminal husk like a bird's nest abandoned in winter.

'We should split up,' I say. 'You go towards the lake. I'll head for the hillock.'

Hans looks at me in abject horror. 'You can't go by yourself! You'll be terrified.'

The certainty of his assertion almost provokes me to laughter. I half-believed that Thea would've divulged my secret to Hans. At least, it seems this sacred relic of sisterhood lives on. Over the years, she has helped me compile a mental catalogue of things I should fear – men who claim to be lost, spiders with brightly-coloured carapaces – but the vigilance doesn't come naturally. Hans's dismay at my suggestion proves that.

I affect a shudder, running my hands across my arms. 'I'd feel so much better with a big, strong man by my side.' Hans puffs himself up, shoulders squared. He reminds me of a working dog: there's nothing he likes more than to be useful. With a saccharine smile, I add, 'Do you know where I might find one?'

Hans deflates, bottom lip jutting out. 'I'm going to ignore your childish humour and accompany you anyway, because I'm a gentleman and—'

'No need,' I interject. There are few things I'd like less than him dogging my steps, pushing his foppish hair out of his eyes and breathing too loudly.

He narrows his gaze. Accustomed to the good, fearful ladies of Heulensee, my insistence to go alone is a glaring disparity. Fumbling in the pocket of my cloak, I produce the penknife Papa gifted me when I was just a girl. I brandish the blade in front of Hans.

'I'm scared, but I'm not defenceless. Besides, if we separate, we can cover twice the ground. We'll find her quicker that way.'

Hans nods slowly. He doesn't seem entirely comfortable, but we part without another word. I watch as his form disappears into the fog.

Overhead, the clouds tear in half. An ocean falls in slow motion from the heavens, forming minute rivers in the seams of the cobbles. Thunder cracks like a whip and I remember to shriek, just in case someone is watching. I keep my charade stapled to my skin.

Fear is a permanent force in the village. It does not fade or wither. In fact, we cultivate it. We stare into shadowed corners and will monsters into existence; we look to the sky and imagine the stars crashing down to earth, raining hellfire.

I dream of knowing what it is to truly shudder.

I have devoted the years since Klara Keller's death to coaxing fear into the hostile expanse of my heart. At night, I scream and scream into my pillow until my vocal cords give out. Hands clasped tight, I pray for divine terror to inhabit my body – but it does not come. At fifteen, I risked my life for the cause. With bricks tied to my ankles, I waded out into the lake, praying that the last gasping moment between life and death would make me feel something.

I felt nothing at all until the ropes came loose, by design. Then I just felt disappointed at my steady pulse.

Even now, with Thea's life at stake, I do not fear for her. There is a feeling of apprehension – of knowing that I am on the cusp of the worst suffering of my life – but there is no terror. No matter how desperately I wish there was.

Hands cupped against the glass, I peer into the bakery window, wondering if a mischievous streak I don't think she possesses may have prompted Thea to steal *Krapfen* in the dead of night. The shop lies dormant. As does the apothecary, and the butcher's, and the tailor's, and the blacksmith's forge. One by one, I patrol each dead-end alley, each shadowed corner.

There is only one place left to check.

I follow the street to its end, where the cobbles turn to dirt. In the suffocating dark I can barely make out the bog: acres of waterlogged soil and sucking mud pools, grafted to Heulensee's heel like a festering blister. Slender willow trees fringe the mire, their branches skeletal in the darkness.

I shuffle forward, one foot in front of the other, until the planks of the boardwalk whine beneath my feet. The wooden path snakes all the way through the marsh – all the way to the Saint's den. Somewhere beneath the earth, our saviour lays dormant. Perhaps it can feel my footsteps now.

Driving rain stirs the wetland pools, giving the impression of a knotted mass of snakes writhing just beneath the surface. Bulrushes hiss in the wind. If I hold my breath, I can hear something else: a dull thud. A heartbeat, but not my own.

The entrance to the Saint's den comes into view, drawn out from the marsh like a boil on the skin: a misshapen hillock whose mouth is a howling abyss. I stare into it, narrowing my eyes against the darkness.

Something moves.

There, amid the infernal black of the Saint's burrow, there is movement. *Thud.* Fog swirls within the tunnel. *Thud, thud.* A fleck of white grows bigger and bigger. *Thud, thud, THUD.* I walk backwards, unafraid, but feeling deep in my flesh that nothing good can come of this. My fingers curl around the woody stem of a bulrush, which will serve as the only barrier between me and whatever is coming. A form takes shape. Something shrugs free of the burrow, lumbering towards me with intent . . .

Dorothea.

The beating stops. Maybe I imagined it all along. My sister stumbles out of the hillock's mouth. Thea's nightgown is torn and muddied; her eyes drift lazily to mine, seeing me, but not *seeing* me. Her hair is wet, plastered to her face in thick, golden strands.

'Why are you here?' Her voice is a flat monotone. 'Are you looking for me?'

Incredulous, I close the distance between us and sling my cloak around her bare shoulders. The rain is starting to sputter out, but the frigid air persists. 'What on earth are you doing?'

'I wasn't ready,' she says distantly. 'I'll come back soon.'

I drop my voice to a whisper. 'What do you mean, Thea?'

She stares back at me. Stares for so long, unblinking, that I think she might be experiencing some sort of seizure. But then she cocks her head to the side. Runs her tongue across her lips. She leans in, her breath scented with something nauseatingly saccharine. I see myself reflected in the endless black of her pupils. There is no recognition – no understanding.

These are the eyes of a predator.

'Thea?' I whisper.

Something snaps – or knits back together. Warmth floods into her face. She shakes her head as if waking from a deep slumber.

'Ilse?' She frowns, rubbing at her eyes. 'What are we doing here?'

A knot forms and tightens in my stomach. 'You were inside the Saint's den.'

'Was I?' Thea looks around us, fear mingling with confusion on her face. She seems distraught, exhaustion written in the bags beneath her eyes, the sagging of her lids. 'I don't understand. All I remember is getting into the bath.'

'You disappeared. Hans came to get me.' I speak slowly, but she doesn't seem to comprehend; the furrow in her brow deepens. 'We were both worried. How did you get here?'

'I don't know.' Her voice trembles.

Silence stretches between us. I study her; she studies me in return, tears welling in her eyes. 'Let's get you home,' I suggest. 'We can talk in the morning.'

Hand in hand, we retreat along the boardwalk. It groans beneath our feet – mine in boots, hers bare. Usually, when my chest echoes with the absence of terror, it makes me angry. Sometimes at the situation – at the man following me down a dark street, or the thunder spoiling a fine summer's day – but more often, I am angry at myself. Angry that I cannot feel the way I should.

But now, with the pressure of Thea's clammy hand against mine, I do not feel angry. I feel *sad*. A seemingly endless weight presses down on my shoulders, and my throat feels as if it's been caught in a vice. I have not known grief like this since Papa died – and even then, it was tinged with relief. Papa was a cruel constant.

If my sister is here, holding my hand, why do I grieve her? Why does my heart feel as if it's about to drop through my stomach and slop onto the floor?

As a child, I was never without bloodied knees or bruised arms. Thea was comparatively flawless – since her body warns her of danger. A quickened pulse coaxes her away from high ledges; a feeling of dread tells her not to touch the snake writhing in its burrow. Why, then, did she stumble into the Saint's den in the middle of the night? Why didn't her body *stop* her?

Ahead, Hans emerges from the fog. The knot at his brow dissolves; the muscles in his jaw loosen. It's as if he is seeing the first tentative rays of sunlight after a cruel winter. He breaks into a sprint and sweeps Thea into his arms, burrowing his nose into her hair.

'Dorothea.' His voice breaks on the final syllable. 'I'm so glad you're all right.'

Thea lets her weight sag, knowing that Hans will catch her. They exchange a series of whispered assurances. Only once Hans has verified that Thea is unharmed does he look in my direction.

'Thank you,' Hans murmurs. 'We'll walk you back.'

I shake my head. 'Take her straight home.'

'I left you alone once,' he replies. 'I won't do it again. The streets are frightening at night.'

In the nook of his shoulder, Thea stares back at me with wide eyes. She is the only one who knows my fatal flaw – my fearlessness.

'Thank you,' I relent, the words forced out between gritted teeth.

We make the homeward journey in silence. Hans waits for me to enter the house before scooping Thea into his arms, carrying her as if she weighs no more than a babe. She rests her head against his shoulder. They disappear into the fog. I am left alone, with nothing to contemplate but the itching beneath my skin.

I may not feel fear, but I can sense when something is wrong. A fight about to erupt. Ice about to crack underfoot. A rabid dog about to lunge.

Tonight, I know that something is wrong with my sister.

I do not sleep for even a moment. Deep in the marrow of my bones, I believe Thea's Rite changed her. She is colder than she was. Quicker to anger, easier to confuse. Sometimes, she has moments of brilliant clarity. For five minutes, or maybe ten, my sister emerges resplendent. It's as if she has found the strength to kick off the bottom of the lake she's drowning in. We laugh and talk the way we used to – but as quickly as she comes, she leaves.

She *always* leaves.

I've seen the blight which afflicts women after their Rite play out a hundred times. Frau Schmidt disappeared for a week and could not remember where she went; Frau Albrecht smothered her own mother but could not recall doing so; Johanna Fischer was found wandering around the Saint of Fear's den at four in the morning, just like Thea.

I'm not sure why I believed Thea would be spared.

If we lived in another time, or another place, it would be different – but we live in Heulensee, where the Rite is woven into our society. When a man turns eighteen, he leaves his childhood home to start a family. When a woman turns eighteen, she goes beneath the earth to the Saint's den and presents her fear as an offering. Some scream. Others simply tremble. It's this sacrifice – the Rite – that keeps the Saint fed, keeps it loyal, so that when bloodthirsty creatures spill from the Hexenwald, we have a monster of our own to defend us. Sorry, a *Saint*.

I often wonder what life was like two centuries ago, when the Hexenwald was just a forest. Before the earth tore open, releasing the infection that turned the land into something sordid. Something hungry.

Our scripture describes the origin of the rift as 'a manifestation of sin'. That explanation has always troubled me. If sins are given physical form, my every step should be dogged by a dark spectre, a signpost for my divergence. Whether the tear was borne of sin or not is impossible to verify.

There are some commonalities between the recollections of that day: there was an almighty roar, as if the mountains themselves were collapsing; the earth trembled; birds scattered; dogs began to howl. A crevasse tore through the forest, spewing a poisonous magic that changed Heulensee for ever.

Monsters sprung up where deer once roamed. Foul, eternally hungry creatures, in every shade of evil. The hunters and herbalists who once lived in the forest barely had time to raise arms. Some perished before the beasts had their chance at them, torn apart by magic, or swallowed by the crevasse. A select few *became* beasts, the dark power taking root in their bodies, stripping away their humanity. These were the first Hexen: immeasurably powerful, immeasurably cruel.

Once the beasts of the Hexenwald had picked its bones dry, they streamed towards Heulensee, attracted to the hum of flesh and blood like moths to a flame. The only warning Heulensee's townsfolk received was the sky turning red.

The villagers cried out for their Saints. One by one, they came; one by one, they were slain. They were lesser Saints, used to delivering small miracles – not to fending off bloodshed on this scale. A Saint cannot die permanently, but once they are reborn, they bear none of the loyalties, none of the memories forged in their former life. Heulensee was abandoned. Left defenceless.

By dawn, a third of the town had escaped or bled dry. In the aftermath, drawn by the atmosphere of heady terror, a final Saint descended. Unlike those which had come before it, this Saint took the form of a beast. The creature introduced itself as the Saint of Fear. It offered the townsfolk a deal: their lifelong worship in exchange for its protection from the Hexenwald.

It simply wouldn't do to have the entire town incapacitated by fear, the men reasoned. A compromise was struck: women alone would offer their fright, allowing men to retain their agency. I wonder if the women resisted, whether with their words or their fists. I suppose it doesn't matter.

Men argued that fear was a woman's gift – something to be held sacred. We become intimate with it throughout our lives: bearing children who may kill us on their way out, judging within seconds whether a stranger is friend or foe. Any resource the men had to offer paled in comparison, or so they claimed.

The men of Heulensee signed the scripture that would consign women to an eternity of terror. *We* are the ones who feed the Saint by taking our Rite. *We* are the ones who bolster the Saint with our horror each time the Hexenwald overflows. *We* are the blockade that stems the tide of monsters. Thea's Rite, therefore, is a brick in our defences. The nobility of it doesn't make her transformation hurt any less.

I emerge from my reverie as morning rolls across the lake in a sheet of apricot light. Beyond my bedroom window, the

Hexenwald seems to swell on the horizon, the crest of a dark wave which will surely swallow Heulensee whole.

Despite the threat, there is something intoxicating about the forest. It's the same way fresh paint invites errant fingerprints. I often find myself transfixed, wondering what lurks between the trees. Everyone must feel it, mustn't they? The pull, the allure of the forbidden. Sometimes, it grips me so strongly I can barely sleep for my longing to stare out at the Hexenwald.

I wrench my eyes away.

After donning a blouse and a skirt the colour of cornflowers, I head for the front door. There is no need to stay and watch for fires today – not when the entire valley is still drenched from last night's downpour. Late spring is my favourite time of year: it's warm enough to spend time outside, but wet enough to stave off the fires. Thea and I used to cherish these days. We'd spend hours swimming out into the lake, or chasing hares around the hayfields. She doesn't much care to spend time with me anymore.

No matter. I can occupy myself perfectly well. It's not as if I've spent my *entire* life living in Thea's shadow. When she started wasting time with Hans, I unearthed my personality. The things she never wanted to do turned out to be things I love doing. Turning over logs and inspecting the writhing insects beneath; prodding at animals who died frozen in motion after falling into the treacle-thick marsh.

I chronicle my finds in the first drawer of my dresser. It's divided into segments, each housing a wonder of my small world. Tiny bird skulls bleached by the sun; inky feathers that glow blue or green when the light hits them; red-and-white spotted mushrooms. I used to keep them on my shelf, but last spring Mama decided it was 'unsightly' and threw everything away. Thea managed to save my most treasured specimens, hiding them in her skirt pockets until she could smuggle them back to me.

The memory provokes a fresh pang of grief. I resolve to head for the marsh in search of snakeskins or glittering insects. Something to distract me. Just as I reach for the front-door handle, Mama emerges from the kitchen. I press a hand to my chest, feigning shock. She narrows her eyes. The Hexen's fateful visit long ago drew her worst fear into focus: the absence of mine.

'Did you want something?' I ask, each word clipped.

'Where did you go last night?'

My formative years were spent lying for Thea, covering the tracks of her trysts with Hans. It began when Papa sent her to the smithy. He told her to commission a set of iron traps to maim the wolves that were snatching our chickens. There she met the blacksmith's affable son: Hans.

I constructed an entire web of lies to veil her continued visits to the smithery, where Hans has worked since he was old enough to operate the forge. It's hard to maintain the same sense of sisterly loyalty when Mama insists Thea has not changed since her Rite. Perhaps the truth will finally convince her.

'Looking for Thea,' I explain. 'She went missing.'

Concern deepens the lines in Mama's brow. 'And you found her?'

'No.' I say drily, shrugging my shoulders. 'Perhaps she's in the forest by now!'

Mama fixes me with a scathing look. I probably deserve it. 'Where was she?'

'I found her coming out of the Saint's den in the early hours.'

Mama's jaw ticks involuntarily. She blanches, then runs her

hands across the front of her dirndl, smoothing out the dress if not her nerves. 'Perhaps she wanted to feel closer to the Saint.'

Sometimes, in my weaker moments, I wish Mama would love me the way she loves Thea. But for her to hear that her own daughter was inside the Saint's den in the dead of night and react with nonchalance...

Perhaps the way she loves Thea is sadder than the way she tolerates me.

A chair scrapes across the flagstones in the kitchen. Oma's leathery face appears around the doorframe. Her hair is swept into silver braids, which curl against her temples like a dove's wings.

'As long as Dorothea is safe now, that's all that matters,' Oma says, each word scraping up her throat like gravel. A lifetime of fighting fires has left its imprint on her lungs.

I nod, unconvinced. Mama retreats into the kitchen.

'Come, Ilse.' Oma takes her wicker basket from its place next to the door. It's stuffed with flowers, fruit and small loaves of bread. 'Help an old woman make her offerings.'

Oma doesn't really need my help – but she's adept at defusing the tension in our home, and knows that distance is the best remedy. With little else to occupy my time, I accept.

She clings to my arm as we descend the trail to the village. We make slow progress. Last night's deluge slickened the mud, and navigating Heulensee's cobbled streets takes twice as long as it should, because everyone wants to speak to Oma.

Eventually, we're able to wind our way around the lake. The warming air of late spring has coaxed crocuses into a purple halo around the water. We pause briefly at the graveyard on the village outskirts. Oma places fresh flowers at her sister's grave. I know little about my grand-aunt Hilde; she succumbed to pneumonia when she was barely a woman. It affects Oma more than she admits.

As soon as tears spring to her eyes, Oma wipes them fiercely with her sleeve and says, 'The Saints won't wait all day.'

I feel like I should say something meaningful. Tell her that it's okay to still mourn Hilde. Maybe wrap my arms around her – something not typically done in the Odenwald family – so she can cry into the nook of my shoulder, away from prying eyes. By the time I've summoned up the courage, she's marching off ahead.

The shrines lay on the lake's western shore, translocated from their original home in the marshland where the Saint of Fear now resides. The lesser Saints lived among us until the Hexenwald overflowed and they sacrificed themselves in our defence. I wonder where they are now. If they escaped this valley to form allegiances with humans who do not worship Fear. If they care about humans at all.

When the scripture was signed, we decentred our traditional Saints at the Saint of Fear's demand. While Fear is now the predominant faith in Heulensee, the townsfolk offer what little devotion remains to the now-lesser Saints. Even though our lives are punctuated by terror, people find ways to express hope.

And unlike me, Oma is *always* hopeful, always searching for something. Even though the lesser Saints no longer bear physical presence in the village, Oma – like many others – believes they will grant her boons in exchange for trinkets and soft words. In a hushed voice, she asks Henrietta, Saint of Fertility, to grant Frau Friedel the babe she so desperately wants; Adalwolfa, Saint of Retribution, for justice against the wicked husband of a dear friend; Felicie, Saint of Luck, for a summer without wildfire.

I help her kneel at Saint Henrietta's shrine. Oma groans, her body protesting the motion. She sets to work arranging sprigs of lavender at the Saint's stony feet, finding small gaps between plentiful offerings. Henrietta is the most revered of the lesser Saints; infertility runs rampant in Heulensee. Mama is the only one of Oma's four daughters able to have children. You'd think that might make her appreciate me more. No such luck.

Oma clears her throat. 'It upsets me to see you and Dorothea drifting apart.'

I hand her a bunch of rosemary, but do not meet her eyes. Eye contact has always felt like an unnecessary interrogation. 'It upsets me, too.'

'You should go to see her. I'm sure she's feeling out of sorts after last night.'

'She has changed,' I mutter, 'and I have stayed the same. Everyone changes after their Rite.'

'*I* took my Rite,' Oma says, leathery brow furrowed, 'and we're close, aren't we?'

Heat rushes to my cheeks. I don't like it when people pick holes in my hypocrisy. 'That's different.'

Oma stares back at me, and it only exacerbates my embarrassment. She chews thoughtfully on her lip. 'Have you ever wondered if the change you sense in Dorothea is something else entirely?'

I stare back at Oma, unsure what she is implying – or perhaps unwilling to acknowledge it.

'Maybe the change you attribute to the Rite is just Dorothea becoming a woman.' She takes my hand between her own and squeezes it. Quietly, as if breaking the news of a loved one's death, she says, 'Sisters can't stay the same forever, Ilse.'

'If womanhood is the cause, I hate it.' Oma's eyes widen at my petulance. Attempting to lighten the mood, I add, 'Perhaps I shall abstain. Remain childlike forevermore.'

Oma lets out a wheezing laugh. 'Now, wouldn't that be a fine thing?'

She releases my hand and goes back to preening her offerings. I think of Thea's pale face emerging from the Saint's den; of Frau Schmidt's unexplained disappearance; of Frau Albrecht stealing her mother's breath with a goose-feather pillow ...

None of those things seem like markers of womanhood – but who am I to pass judgement? This village has broken women stronger than I. With no chance of escape and not a semblance of power, men have us at their mercy. Herr Albrecht is a sloppy drunk, and I've witnessed Frau Albrecht on the receiving end of his ire; Herr Schmidt took the bakery Frau Schmidt's parents left to her, annexed her dreams and made them his own.

Perhaps I have something in common with them after all. This village made us sick. Stuffed us full of trauma until it had nowhere to go but out.

'I lost Hilde unexpectedly, Ilse. You never know how long you have left with the people you care about.' Oma rubs a sprig of rosemary between her forefinger and thumb, her expression blurring the line between contemplation and melancholy. 'Besides, your Rite will come around soon enough. Do you believe *you* will change?'

I wince. I have spent so long repressing the reality that my Rite will take place this autumn. Hearing it spoken aloud feels like a dagger plunged into my chest. It is possible to fail the Rite, despite the fact that fear is meant to be a woman's innate talent. I have seen it happen to perfectly fearful women.

The *Pfarrer*, our loathsome priest, acts as a mouthpiece for the Saint of Fear, separating the wheat from the chaff before the Saint tastes their terror. Sometimes a woman will scream with absolute commitment, only to have her fear deemed uninspired by the Pfarrer. Failure results in banishment to the meadow huts east of Heulensee, where the condemned live out their days in isolation.

Other traitors are bolder in their transgression. Rather than fearing the Hexenwald, they worship it. They see the Hexen not as witches, but as holy women. As *Saints*.

My crime is worst of all: a girl born without fear.

Keen to dull the pain, I busy myself beside Saint Adalwolfa. Her stone-rendered fist clutches a sword, held triumphantly to the sky. Even carved from granite, there is a defiant spark in her eyes.

Adalwolfa's shrine is scantly adorned. A desiccated flower in a vase; a cluster of shimmering quartz; a blackbird's oily feather. There is little room for defiant women in Heulensee, even if they're Saints.

'She's so human,' I murmur, a question forming on my tongue. 'They all are. Why is the Saint of Fear so ...' I falter, struggling for the words to describe the Saint without toeing the line of sacrilege.

Oma glances at me, one brow cocked. 'Have you lost your tongue?'

'The Saint of Fear looks more like a creature of the Hexenwald than a Saint.'

The soft line of Oma's back stiffens. She gestures for me to help her to her feet. 'The Hexenwald corrupts, Ilse. Do you recall the Webers' little boy, who stepped into the forest two springs ago?'

I nod, his tiny casket still fresh in my mind. He was only in the trees for a matter of seconds. Over the course of the next week, he grew quiet and cold. Medicine made no difference. When he died, spruce needles erupted from beneath his skin. I remember thinking, darkly, that he looked like a macabre hedgehog. Blood coated each spine, trickling down his tiny, milk-white body.

I have always harboured a preoccupation with the forest – drawn to the trees the way moths are lured to a flame. After the Webers' boy died, I dared not even look at it for the better part of a month, lest the Hexenwald infect me. Not everyone is tainted by the Hexenwald, but the boy's death reminded us all that trespass is not worth the risk.

'The Hexenwald tainted the Saint of Fear, too – but where the child's body perished, the Saint's grew stronger. Some of the forest's power lives inside the Saint. Its appearance is testament to that.'

Beneath my breath, almost hoping she will not hear me, I mutter, 'Is that why it's so cruel?'

'Do not speak ill of the Saint.' Oma's voice is sharper than usual as she parrots the Pfarrer's sermons. 'It is holy in all it does.'

Shame knots in my throat. Oma rarely scolds me – that honour is typically reserved for Mama. We do not speak for the rest of the trip.

When we arrive back at the house, I ask to accompany her on her next venture, whether to the markets or the shrines. There's pity in her eyes – recognition that I am desperate to cling onto the only person who still seems to care about me. But the next morning I watch from the window as she hurries down the street, having made no effort to request my companionship. She heads east, away from the shrines and the markets. Whatever Oma is doing, she does not want me as her witness.

CHAPTER TWO

Oma's prayers for a summer without wildfire fell on deaf ears. All too quickly, summer burns spring to the ground. Fire tears across our drought-stricken fields. Smoke billows so thickly I feel as if I could curl my fingers around it. We haven't seen wildfires this fierce in years. They used to constrain themselves to the outskirts, always doused before they got a hold of our houses, our crops. This year is different.

Against the advice of the doctor, Oma takes up the helm to fight the fires. The whole family work shifts to support her. Our time is divided into segments: one to sleep and nurse our burns; one to attend to the necessary chores and keep our house running; and one to fight fires as if we've never been burned.

Thea, ever the pragmatist, creates a rota. I notice a pattern. She has ensured our paths never cross. I try not to let it wound me – after all, she is different now, and there is no sense longing after something I believe extinct – but one morning, she bemoans the fact we never get to see each other anymore. I blink back at her, chewing on the remnants of my breakfast.

She raises an eyebrow, pilfering a slice of bread from the counter. *Does Hans not feed her?* 'Why are you looking at me like that?'

I swallow noisily. '*You* made the rota, Thea.'

'Why would I create a rota where we never got to see each other?' A knot forms between her brows. 'Spending time with you is the only thing that makes summer tolerable.'

I'm so bewildered by the compliment that I almost let it lie, but I can't. I push back from the kitchen table, taking the schedule from where it hangs above the fireplace.

'This is *your* handwriting,' I tell her, flapping the piece of paper in front of her face.

She fixes me with a withering stare, preparing to protest – but then her eyes focus on the script. Thea braces one hand on the kitchen table. Quietly, she says, 'I wouldn't keep us apart.'

'But you did.' Incredulity heightens my pitch. 'You have.'

Thea's lip wobbles. She opens her mouth, only to close it again. Her eyes grow glassy and I know tears aren't far behind.

'Thea,' I groan, ready to apologize, or back down, or whatever it will take to not be the reason she cries – but she's already on her way out the door.

I retreat to my bedroom, my breathing matching the swaying of the Hexenwald beyond my window. I open the top drawer of my dresser and graze each artefact, dipping my knuckle into the vacant eye socket of a crow, brushing my fingertips against a peregrine's feather. My splendours cannot erase the sour shame in my stomach. Even though I do not understand the ways in which Thea is changing, upsetting her makes me feel monstrous.

Maybe Oma was right. Maybe Thea is becoming a woman,

and there are things going on in her life that I don't understand. Maybe this will all make sense, in retrospect. Maybe I'll pass my Rite, and we can laugh about the period we stopped speaking the same language. *Maybe, maybe, maybe.*

I spend so long dissecting mine and Thea's faults that I almost miss the beginning of my firefighting shift. I ease my drawer of treasures shut and fling myself into action. My uniform assaults me with the stench of smoke as I pull it on. It consists of a woollen tunic and leggings, paired with thick gloves and a scarf I can pull up around my mouth. It affords me anonymity of gender. I can walk the streets without men's eyes lingering on my breasts, my waist. It's freeing.

My destination is marked by the black smoke that curls up into the air. Silent, unsmiling Thea prepares to switch with me. Ash stains her brow; her cheeks are ruddy, scalded by flames. My guilt reawakens.

'I'm sorry,' I tell her, shoving aside what little pride I have. 'I didn't mean to upset you.'

She shrugs and does not break stride. Desperate to knit back together the wound I dealt, I attempt a conversation.

'It's just as hot as the summer the barn caught fire,' I remark.

Her brow furrows, the lines emphasized by the soot. 'What?'

'You saved me,' I say slowly. 'Remember?'

Thea looks back at me, her expression caught somewhere between confusion and disgust. It doesn't make any sense for her to not remember. The barn burning down is an integral thread in the tapestry of our childhood. We reference it constantly – a pillar of the shared language of anecdotes and inside jokes that only *we* understand.

That summer was suffocatingly hot, just like this one. Thea

and I were too young to fight the fires, so we occupied ourselves – often in ways our family would label precarious, if they knew. One day, while the elders were out risking their skin to snuff out an approaching wildfire, we decided to play in the barn downhill from our house.

By the time we realized the wildfire had reached us, it had eaten away at the barn's structure. I distinctly remember looking up as a plank of burning wood fell from the hayloft. It would've crushed me, had Thea not pushed me out of the way. She got struck in the process, clipped by the detritus. To this day, she bears a scar on her calf. A physical testament to the bond we shared.

Despite the pain, Thea's first concern was me. It was always me. Even as a child, she stepped up to fill the doting role Mama failed to occupy. She'd brush my hair each evening, singing while she worked; she'd stand in my defence when other schoolchildren called me strange; she'd sit with me for hours in silence, knowing it was my preferred state. She was the perfect big sister.

Today, that perfect big sister looks at me blankly. 'Oh,' she says distantly. 'That.'

Irritation sparks like the fires I'm supposed to douse. All of a sudden, I cannot understand why I felt any guilt at telling her *she* is the one who wrote the schedule that keeps us apart. That *she* is the architect of our distance. 'You don't remember? No matter. I'd hate to intrude upon the significant mental space you reserve for cataloguing Hans's every sigh and glance.'

Immediately, Thea softens. Her eyes round. Back comes the girl who could not recognize her own handwriting. She reaches out to touch me, but when I pull away, her fingers curl around thin air. 'Why would you say that, Ilse?'

I keep my lips pressed together. When my temper erupts as it's threatening to, I'm prone to saying things I later regret.

'I'm sorry if I've seemed distant, but things are hard for me at the moment.' She swallows. 'I don't need you turning on me as well.'

Thea waits – waits for me to acknowledge her, or to apologize, or to strike back like the venomous little creature I can be. When she realizes I'm not going to grant her a response, she turns and walks away. I stand there, torn between two seemingly impossible wants: to retrieve the version of Thea that existed before her Rite, and to punish her for what she has become.

Oma's voice curls through smoke to reach me. 'Ilse, I need your help!'

I cannot pause to linger in my emotions – the fires won't wait. I soak my scarf in water, pull it up over my mouth, and plunge through the smog. The fire licks along golden fronds of wheat, leaping from one row to the next. Oma is mere metres from the blaze. She guides a panicked horse to plough a thick margin of the crop into the dirt.

Knowing the famine Heulensee suffered last winter, my heart beats out a frantic rhythm in my chest. 'Oma!' I scream, my voice rising above the roar of the blaze. 'What are you doing?'

She offers me a grim look and forges onward. I close the distance between us, pulling the draft horse to a stop.

'We'll starve,' I shout. 'We have to save the harvest.'

Oma swats me away, not unkindly, and urges the horse on. Though her shoulders have narrowed with time, they remain strongly set. She carries herself with the air of a much younger woman, even as her body threatens to give out.

'If you cannot stop the fire,' she pants, sweat dripping from her brow to her lip, 'take away its fuel.'

The conviction in her voice is enough to change my mind. I shadow her, deepening the ploughed margin with a shovel to create a firebreak. Errant sparks burn freckles onto my cheeks.

We spend the rest of the afternoon ferrying carts of water to the field, dealing the fatal blow to its embers. Eventually, the fire admits defeat.

That night, I wash the ash from my skin, the dirt from beneath my nails. As I'm slathering a salve onto my burns, I wonder whether Oma's wisdom can be applied in other ways. If I cannot stop my sister changing, maybe I should stop loving her. Stop the pain from spreading. If only sisterly bonds could be extinguished as easily as fires.

※

After three months of incessant wildfire, September sees autumn arrive in a hurry. Oma throws a dinner party in celebration of fires beaten into submission. Thea and Hans join us, along with my Tanten and Onkel Lars. I've been dreading this – the charade of what our family used to be – but something unexpected happens. Everything feels ... normal. It's like slipping back into a favourite dress, long since outgrown, only to find that it magically fits again.

Thea wears the matching dirndl Oma got us two years ago, and I happen to be wearing mine as well. Skirts sewn in meadow-green fabric brush our calves; pale bodices embroidered with wildflowers hug our chests. It might just be a coincidence, but it feels like a patch being sewn over torn clothes. Something once broken now mended, made stronger.

Thea laughs as she steals a *Knödel* from my plate, using it to soak up the dregs of her stew. I laugh with her. While Mama is busy serving dessert, Thea kicks me beneath the table and secretes something in my hand. I steal a glimpse and find a perfectly polished snail shell between my fingers. Oma smiles at us from across the table. My heart swells – hopeful, despite everything.

In the throes of winter, you'd be forgiven for believing it might never be sunny again – but the sun does come back, because it has to. In the same way, there is a part of me that believes Thea and I *must* return to normal – because that's how the world works. And as she rests her cheek on my shoulder, sleepy from good food, I think this might be it. The sun coming back.

With the food devoured, we light a bonfire in the garden. When a family's vocation is fighting fires, there is a special joy in seeing one contained – declawed and blunt-toothed. Hans watches Thea from across the flames, his eyes glossy with awe. I've never coveted romance, but I am suddenly struck by the feeling that I would like someone to look at me that way.

I almost wish I could find fault in the way Hans loves Thea. That I could point out inconsistencies in his behaviour, or that he would let her down – not badly enough to hurt her – but enough to show that he is flawed. That love itself is flawed.

Which it is. Love is Herr Schmidt publicly acquainting his wife with the back of his hand after she drops a loaf on the floor; it's Onkel Lars, Tante Beth's husband, threatening divorce if she does not bear a child by the end of the year; it's Papa, grey and sweating on his deathbed, yet still berating Mama.

In my experience, love is a woman giving and giving until she is nothing but someone's wife. An incubator to be filled; a maid to be assigned duties; a nurse, and a cook, and a seamstress, and a sage.

Hans and Thea aren't like that.

When she cries, he is there to soothe her; when she is happy, he shares in her joy; when she feels hopeless, he reminds her of the good in the world. Even now, three *Mass* of beer down, he is unwavering in his tenderness. Onkel Lars speaks over Thea as she attempts to explain her plans to open a shop. She trails off, always ready to shrink herself down – but Hans lifts her up.

'What was that, Thea?' he says.

Chagrined, Lars falls silent. We listen in rapture as Thea explains how she will breathe new life into Heulensee's fashion. While she speaks, she wraps her arms around her chest, bracing against the cold. Hans sheds his jacket and places it across her shoulders. They are a perfect team, tackling an imperfect world together.

The knowledge that a love like that exists should reassure me; the fact that my sister has found it should delight me. But all I can feel is envy. I don't think I will ever get to experience what they have.

Part of the fault lies with me. There is nothing wrong with the way I look: unruly auburn hair, hazel eyes, a build which is softer than it is lithe. But whenever a man approaches me, I see it in his eyes. The minute I begin to talk, he feels uneasy. He can never pinpoint why – but it doesn't matter.

The rest of the fault lies with men. I cannot imagine binding myself to someone who takes no issue with my subjugation – who hides at home while I'm on my knees, howling to protect our village. On a shallower level, I've never looked at a man and felt something stir in me – and it should, shouldn't it?

As midnight draws near, Oma throws a bucket of water over the bonfire's embers. Onkel Lars narrows his gaze at me. I've been lost in thought for the past half hour, and I may have missed a question directed my way.

'You're the last one standing, Ilse,' he says, slurring his words.

My eyes fix on a particularly vibrant fly agaric mushroom nestled against the stump of a tree. 'What do you mean?'

'You're the only girl here who hasn't yet taken her Rite.' Lars brings his cup to his mouth, rivulets of beer running down the sides of his face. It makes my skin crawl. 'Almost your turn, isn't it?'

Retorts leap to my tongue. *Isn't it 'almost your turn' to be quiet, Onkel? Your turn to brush your yellowing teeth? Your turn to attempt pleasantry for the first time in your Saints-forsaken life?*

Before I can vocalize any of my rebukes, Thea says, 'There's only a few months left.' She smiles. 'You must be excited, Ils.'

My mouth drops open. I stare back at her while an uncomfortable silence settles over our gathering.

'What?' Her eyes dart to my Tanten, to Mama, to Oma. 'We've all done it. It's a rite of passage.'

The urge to vomit almost knocks me to the floor. She knows why the Rite will be different for me. I mutter an apology and take off towards Heulensee. Oma calls after me, but I cannot make myself turn back. Only when I feel the pebbled lakeshore beneath my feet do I slow. My emotions come all at once – anguish, rage, petulance – but not fear. Never fear.

I throw myself to the ground. My fist closes around a scattering of pebbles. With a grunt, I launch them into the water. Crystalline droplets explode into the air. I fasten my fingers around another handful, ready to pelt them.

'Are you all right?'

I freeze mid-throw, letting the stones clatter back onto the shore. Embarrassed, I drag a sleeve across my face and hope it will mask the fact that I've been crying.

'Ilse.'

When I do not turn to face my sister, she kneels between me and the lake.

'Talk to me, Ilse,' Thea says, gently. 'Help me understand.'

Anger ripples across my skin. How dare she ask me to help *her* understand? She is the perpetrator. I turn wild eyes to her, an argument brewing on my tongue – but the sight of her wrenches the breath from my lungs. Her eyes are clear and sincere. There is no trace of the cold predator I found in the marsh that night, or the withdrawn stare I've seen on so many occasions since. This is my sister.

My voice trembles as I murmur, 'You're back.'

'What do you mean?' She pulls a face, lower lip jutting out. 'I never left.'

I do not bother to challenge her assertion. It's all I can do not to cry.

Thea shuffles closer, pebbles crunching beneath her knees. 'What's going on, Ils?'

'You were supposed to be my person.'

'I am your person,' Thea insists. 'And you are mine.'

'Liar,' I hiss, hideously aware of the break in my voice. 'You've changed, Thea. And the worst part is you don't even see it.'

At that point, she huffs and crosses her arms. It is an expression so utterly Thea that I almost believe she is unchanged. 'Is that it, then? You're no longer my sister, and I no longer yours?'

'Stop being cruel.' Her voice bristles with the older-sister authority she so rarely uses against me. I open my mouth to respond, but she silences me with an upheld hand. 'You have treated me differently ever since my Rite. How do you think that makes me feel?'

'It changed you! I found you coming out of the Saint's den, for goodness' sake—'

She throws her hands up in exasperation. 'I *sleepwalk*, Ilse. It's a curse. Ever since I left home, I cannot sleep through the night. How ridiculous is that – I've moved five minutes down the street, and I'm so homesick that my body tries to find its way home in its sleep!'

I swallow. That would explain the dullness in her eyes that night. It would also explain her short temper, her easy confusion, the faraway looks. My conviction falters.

Still, I insist, 'You *are* different.'

'Ask me something, then. If I've changed, surely I will have forgotten our memories. Our secrets.'

I shake my head and fix my eyes on the Hexenwald. It seems to beckon. I wonder if it does the same to Thea. She ducks to the side, placing herself again between the trees and I. Counting on her fingers, she rattles off facts.

'My name is Dorothea Odenwald. You are Ilse, my sister. We – you – live with Mama and Oma. I live with Hans, who I love' – she blushes, laughing at how easily those words come to her – 'You ate all the *Obatzda* Mama was saving for Oma's birthday. I was the one who broke your pocket mirror, and I'm not sorry, because *you* are the one who tore the skirt I was going to wear on *Hexennacht*.'

'None of this means anything, Thea.'

'It means everything,' she whispers, her eyes filling with tears. 'It's our life, Ils. *Our* life. I remember you as a babe, following spiders to their webs while I screamed, not understanding why it made Mama cross; I remember you as a girl, how desperately you wanted to be like me; I remember when you tried to drown yourself in the lake and pretended it was an accident—'

My cheeks tingle. 'It *was* an accident. I—'

She launches to her feet. 'I saw the rope burns at your ankles!' Tears stream freely down her face; she wipes at them furiously, as if her own emotion is a stumbling block to be overcome. 'I have watched you torture yourself, curse yourself, turn yourself inside out in hopes that it will make you belong. I know exactly what you're doing. You believe that you will fail your Rite, so you are severing our bond before someone else can. You think that if you are in control, you can stop it from hurting.'

At that moment, I realize I have been lying to myself. While I *do* believe that there is something rotten in the Rite, that comes secondary to my real grievance: Thea has gone somewhere I cannot follow. She has joined the ranks of women who know what takes place inside the Saint's den. She belongs. The way I never will.

Next year, when my Rite inevitably exposes me, banishment is the best I can hope for. I will be torn from Thea. From Oma. From everything I have ever known.

I do not realize I'm crying again until tears land in fat blotches on my blouse. Thea moves to comfort me, but falters. I am best consoled from afar. She chews on her lip, caught somewhere in her mind, searching deeply for words that will soothe me.

'This place is not meant for people like you, Ilse,' she murmurs.

'I don't know what to do,' I whisper. 'I've tried so hard to become—'

'I know,' she interjects, her eyes darting across my shoulder. Even here, she is afraid on my behalf. 'I know, Ils. But I want you to keep trying.' Thea pauses to squeeze my hand. 'For me.'

My stomach drops. My own sister is asking me to nurture a dead plant in the hopes that it will spontaneously revive.

She must see the disappointment plain on my face, because she steals a furtive glance around us, leans in close, and whispers, 'But if it were up to me – if we lived in a different time, or a different place – I would keep you just as you are.' Thea swallows thickly. 'And even at this time, in this place, I love you. Fearing or not.'

The words hang in the air between us. I wish I could clasp my hands around them and keep them pressed up against my heart. Grip them so tightly that they would finally meld to my flesh and become a part of me. I could live in this moment forever: the lake hushing against the shore; the silver moon reflected in the water; the smell of bonfires and spruce. Two sisters and the understanding that flickers between them.

She draws circles on my palm with her thumb. 'In another land, you might be revered for your lack of fear.'

Revered. The weight of the word is enough to force my eyes back to her face. She's as serious as she's ever been. The earnestness in her expression makes my throat ache.

But then Thea's face changes. Her pupils dilate, blown out so fiercely that I cannot see the blue of her irises. She clutches at her chest, frantically scrabbling at her blouse.

'Thea?' Confusion rattles through me. I take her by the shoulders, bidding her to meet my gaze. The inky black of her pupils glints back. She grows so pale that I think she might faint. I brace to receive her weight, but then the moment passes. Blood returns to her cheeks; breath returns to her lungs.

The pulse at her wrists is rapid, panicked, like a moth caught against a windowpane. She draws her knees up to her chest and drags in three deep breaths before she is able to look at me again.

'I've had too much to drink,' Thea murmurs, pressing one hand to her now-clammy forehead.

'Is that all?'

She struggles to her feet; I grip her elbow tightly, lest she crash back to the ground. 'I ought to get back. Hans'll be worried.'

When I do not release her elbow, she tips her head back and laughs.

'I'm fine, Ils. Let's go home.'

Home. It's a foreign concept for a girl who has always felt out of place. Thea beckons me towards her, unaware that she is the closest thing to home I have.

My sister hums as we walk back to the house. It's almost enough to lull me into believing that nothing has changed. That she is still Thea, and I am still Ilse. That sleepwalking is her only ailment.

But I cannot dispute the way my stomach knots at the sight of her, the same way it used to when Mama forced me to sit by Papa's deathbed. My body is convinced that there is something terribly wrong with my sister. I just don't understand what.

CHAPTER THREE

My attempts to claw back the version of Thea that existed on the lakeshore are futile. Over the next few weeks, I invite her out for tea; Hans comes with her, unannounced. I ask for her help painting my room; she doesn't have time. Most desperately, I weave false accounts of conversations with boys who don't know I exist – if only to render myself in her image. To build a bridge by which we can still understand each other.

Thea listens to my tales with cool amusement. She is not cruel. A spectator unaware of the devotion we shared might perceive our interactions as normal. A tight smile in passing, a half-hearted wave, curt remarks on the weather. They might look at Thea, too, and think she has always been muted, forgetful, apathetic.

But she wasn't. She was brilliant. Smarter than me by far, with a whip-like wit that she often wielded in my defence. The strength of her wit only surpassed by her fists. I still remember the day a classmate interrogated me about why I didn't scream when lightning struck in the playground. Thea swiftly punched him between the legs and asked if *he* was going to scream.

Despite my failed attempts to get her back, there is a spark of hope. My fearlessness binds us together. It's a secret shared by us alone. One morning when she visits the house, I dig my claws in.

'I don't want to take my Rite,' I admit.

Thea looks up from the drawer she's ransacking. She has begun apprenticing under the tailor, and practises by taking scissor and needle to her old clothes. 'Why not?'

'You know why.'

She pauses to nibble her bottom lip, then looks away again. 'You'll be fine.'

'I am unfearing, Thea.' The words leave my mouth as an incredulous exhale.

Her back stiffens. Ten torturous seconds of silence pass between us. Eventually, she insists, 'It's just a phase. Your fear is just quieter than others.'

It seems absurd that *this* is how I lose her. No blood will be spilled, no bones broken. I will sit here on my bed, and with each day that passes, our bond will diminish. The truth of me only exists in our two brains, in whispered exchanges and knowing looks. Without her, I am unknown.

☠

I am so busy grieving Thea that I barely register my own life progressing. Summer has fully yielded to autumn now. Fires rarely spark, and when they do, they're quickly snuffed out by passing rainclouds. I spend hours watching the Hexenwald from my bedroom window, lulled into a stupor by the swaying of the trees. I often find myself struck by a desperate urge to run to them. Let them consume me.

As the leaves on the trees brown, Heulensee hums with excitement. Hexennacht arrives: a night of rituals meant to steel us against the Hexenwald's horrors for another year. Usually, I adore Hexennacht. Today, it doubles up as the eve of my Rite. I struggle to feel festive with my inevitable banishment looming.

Before the Hexenwald changed, our traditions were based around the now-lesser Saints. These ancient events are scantly documented: the Saint of Fear demanded we forsake our old ways when we became its patrons. Oma, however, has a book detailing the old festivals. I'm not sure if she squirrelled it away as an act of defiance, or if she simply forgot it existed.

I used to borrow it at night to read it greedily beneath the covers. To celebrate Felicie, Saint of Luck, people would leave coins in hidden caches across the village; Mathis, Saint of the Hunt, was honoured with a theatrical retelling of his victory against a colossal bear, allegedly the size of a house.

Now, our traditions revolve around the Saint of Fear and the monsters it protects us from. Where merriment and celebration once reigned, warding off Hexen has taken centre stage – masked in bonfires, bright colours and intoxicating drinks.

I dress in plain black skirts and a matching bodice, layered over the top of a white blouse. Many girls wear special dirndl for Hexennacht, embroidered with crescent moons or sewn from richly coloured fabric. I prefer to blend into the night. As I lace the bodice, the door flies open, ricocheting off the wall.

Thea shoulders into my bedroom as if she'd never left. I feel my heart seize at the sight of her. She smiles at me, light and sincere.

'Ready, Ils?'

I swallow my shock. 'You want to go together?'

She snorts. 'Of course, silly. We always go together.'

I'm so desperate to preserve the moment that I dare not move. If I shift, even slightly, I might break whatever has knitted back together inside my sister.

'Here.' Thea takes the laces from my hands and works deftly to fasten them. 'Let me.'

She pulls the strings tight, the way she always has. I prefer to wear my bodice loosely, but Thea says that a small waist and pert breasts are powerful weapons when wielded against men. I don't think she realizes I have no interest in capturing a man. I suspect she would find this even stranger than my fearlessness.

Thea flashes a devilish smile. 'I shall call you Elke.'

I groan. Folk tales claim that if you do a favour for a creature of the Hexenwald, they are honour-bound to repay you. Giving them a name before they fulfil the debt binds them to you, compelling their obedience to your commands. I'm not sure anyone has ever tested this theory, as monsters are more prone to eat you than to enter into a contract – but the lore persists.

'Put your apron on,' Thea says, still smiling.

Begrudgingly, I rifle through my wardrobe. My fingers brush against the ivory skirt I will wear tomorrow for my Rite. It saps all the warmth from me. Thea, perhaps sensing the change in my mood, takes over. I suggest a black apron with scalloped edges, but Thea voices her discontent. We eventually choose an emerald-green one, which I tie with a bow on the right side of my waist.

'You're not married,' Thea remarks, 'and we're not going to fix that if you keep pretending.'

She unfastens the apron strings, retying them on the left side.

The bow's placement is a subtle method of communication: on the left, it means you are not yet spoken for; on the right, it means you are married. Men leave married women alone, more respectful of another man's claim than they are of the women themselves.

'It makes me feel like livestock,' I grouch.

'Live a little, Ils.' Thea squeezes my cheek. 'Who knows – you might even enjoy yourself!'

Before we leave, Thea insists we adorn the house with juniper, as is tradition. She busies me with hanging the foliage around the house. 'This'll ward off the Hexen,' she explains, as if we haven't clutched at the same hapless rituals our entire lives.

Just as we're about to go, Thea pauses beside the mirror in the hallway. She inspects her face as if it's foreign, running a hand across the curve of her jaw, then pulling down her lower eyelid with one finger.

'Stop preening,' I mutter.

She locks eyes with herself in the mirror. Tilts her head to the side. 'Is that really what I look like?'

I freeze. 'What do you mean?'

We stand there for five seconds, ten, without speaking a word. Her hurried breaths fog the glass. In an instant, she snaps out of her stupor, flashing me a smile.

'Shall we go?'

Before I can answer, she takes my hand and leads me through the door, humming beneath her breath as we descend into the town. I am more willing to forget the strange moment in the hallway than I perhaps ought to be. I clutch her fingers tightly between my own, desperate to hang onto this reawakening of our sisterhood.

The men have returned from their expedition to find a suitable *Maibaum*. Thea and I trail them as they carry a spectacular spruce, stripped of its branches, towards the lake.

Sunset stains the water bloody as the townsfolk carve their family shields into the Maibaum. Onkel Lars whittles ours under Oma's watchful eye. Hans's father, the blacksmith, attaches a wreath to the top of the tree. Townsfolk flinch with each clang of his hammer. Women move in like sparrows, long colourful ribbons clutched in their fists.

The Maibaum is erected in the same place the Hexen stood ten years ago – the little meadow between the town and the lake. Its ribbons flutter like their hair. Off to the side, the men construct a bonfire. One of them fixes a straw effigy of a faceless Hexe to a pyre at the bonfire's heart.

'A Hexe will burn tonight,' he bellows.

I roll my eyes. Claims like this are a source of pride for the men. We all live in fear of the Hexenwald, but men harbour an added layer of animosity. They craft and burn effigies; they dress as huntsmen, swords strapped to their backs; their drunken discussions devolve into detailed accounts of how they'd flay a Hexe alive.

Men use our fear to discredit and to diminish us. But it is our fear – our 'hysteria' – that sates the Saint and keeps us safe. Our terror is a lantern against the darkness. They clutch it tight during the endless night, but come daytime, they question what use our light serves.

Hans looks almost embarrassed as he arrives clutching mugs of *Maibowle* – wine punch flavoured with sweet woodruff – for Thea and I. Thirst bids me to accept his offering. He averts his eyes when the other men look to him for support. Where they are brash, he is gentle, introspective – but it doesn't stop me from wishing he'd do more to keep them in check. Maybe Heulensee constricts him just as it does me.

The Maibowle slips down my throat too easily. It makes everything lighter, funnier. I even start to detest Hans less! He makes a mildly funny joke and I find myself laughing, though I do my best to mask it with a cough. Still, that doesn't stop him from making another, and another, in an attempt to win my favour. I smile despite myself. Thea looks as if all her dreams are coming true.

Another mug of Maibowle – Hans will bankrupt himself at this rate – and everything starts to spin. Thea commands me to dance with her, and for the sake of tradition I acquiesce. She wheels me towards the bonfire, and I almost feel like we're us again. We dance in ever tighter circles, shrieking and singing off-key to the music. I catch glimpses of the lake in my peripheral vision.

The church bell tolls – an insistent, whining sound – and the mood changes. Women and girls descend upon the bonfire. Thea drags me along with her, slotting us into the circle forming around the flames. Hands linked, we drop to our knees, just as we do when the Hexenwald breaches. While the first part of the evening serves to ward off the Hexen, the second half pays tribute to our bloodthirsty saviour.

A hush falls across the town. There is a collective intake of breath. And then we scream.

With alcohol simmering in my belly, I stare into the fire and howl. I expect it to come out weak, uninspired, like every other time. Instead, a primal sound rips free of my throat unbidden, leaping into the night air with claws extended and teeth bared.

I stare down the fact that my sister is drifting away and there is nothing I can do about it and the fact that tomorrow, when I fail my Rite, I will be cleaved from Heulensee for ever. My anger is so visceral that Thea flinches, causing her own scream to falter.

Girls across the bonfire turn horrified eyes to me. My scream is borne of rage, not terror, but they eat it up all the same. How I wish the Saint could be so easily fooled. Some try to outdo me – to raise their voices louder or open their mouths wider. While they excise their fear on a regular basis, my anger has been left to grow septic. It overflows.

My rage is so white-hot I hardly register that the other women have stopped screaming. Echoes of my fury ripple through the night long after my lips have fluttered shut. The women stand on shaky legs, and the men pulse around us.

'That was incredible,' Thea whispers.

I do not respond. Furious tremors wrack my body.

Just past midnight, when my wrath and the Hexennacht bonfire are reduced to embers, Hans and Thea walk me home. I slink into the house and feel hollow. There is nothing left but the anticipation of my Rite.

Once I have shed my clothes and scrubbed the scent of smoke from my hair, I stumble into bed. Oma's weary-shouldered silhouette appears in the doorway to my room. She enters wordlessly and tucks me into bed, a beloved routine abandoned years ago.

'Are you going to try, Ilse?'

I know she's talking about tomorrow; I don't respond. A confession claws its way up my throat. I press my lips together, teeth clamped shut. *Don't tell her*, something inside me hisses, each word dripping venom. *You'll lose her, too.*

Oma continues, 'You just need to give them your fear, Ilse. No more, no less.'

'I cannot give what I do not have.' A weighty confession, delivered on a whim. Gravity anchors me to the bed. My family knows I'm different, but not a heretic. My fearlessness goes against everything Heulensee believes. Against human nature.

Oma sinks her face into her hands. A deep sigh rattles through her chest. Her breaths often rattle these days. I keep my own breath pinned inside my chest, sorrow poised to overflow as I wait for her disownment.

'You're not like the others, Ilse. I know that.'

Tears cloud my vision as I blink back at her. She *knew*? The hollow in my chest rings out, the hopeful pealing of a bell.

'I remember the day you were born. I went into your mama's room, and there you were. Fresh as a daisy, pink as a thistle head. You didn't cry. Just looked at me, looked around the room, looked at your mama. You were so small, but it was as if you ... understood. As if you had nothing to fear, and knew that crying would serve no good. I knew then. I think she did, too.'

My breath comes out in shaky puffs as I ask, 'Why did you keep me?'

'What would you have me do – abandon you in the Hexenwald?' She huffs. 'It never even crossed my mind. I love every part of you.' Her aggressive affection dissipates; she chews on her lip thoughtfully. 'But in Heulensee, your fearlessness makes you a target. Remember: if you cannot stop the fire, take away its fuel. Do not give them a reason to banish you.'

My façade is so tightly bound to my flesh that I cannot imagine myself without it. It is convincing enough to fool the townsfolk – but to fool a Saint?

'If you fail the Rite, you will be banished. You'll watch from a distance as Thea's future unfolds. You will see her grow older, have children – but only through glimpses. No real closeness. One day, she will look at you and there will be no recognition in her eyes.'

My stomach aches. Even though our bond has changed, losing Thea entirely is the greatest threat Oma can level against me. 'Don't say that.'

She takes my hands between hers. 'If you want to avoid it, you have to *try*.'

I swallow, but the lump in my throat persists. 'I will.'

Oma melts off ten years of age in a breath; the worry lines on her face fade and her shoulders drop. I sometimes forget that there are people other than Thea in this world who care about me.

CHAPTER FOUR

Thea wakes me – a ghost of our childhood birthday rituals, reanimated for my Rite, which she holds in greater esteem. She plants a kiss on my cheek and whispers for me to place my hands over my ears. I understand why moments later – Oma bursts into the room to sing '*Zum Geburtstag viel Glück*'.

When I emerge into the kitchen, still dressed in nightclothes, the air is thick with powdered sugar. Golden light filters in through the window. A heaping plate of *Kaiserschmarrn* – fluffy hunks of pancake dusted with sugar, served with applesauce and plum compote – awaits me on the table. Oma whistles as she washes up dishes. My eighteenth birthday is as glorious a morning as I have ever known.

I wash the final bite down with a mug of spiced, sweet coffee. The front door clicks open and a sea of women pour in. My Tanten Beth, Lena and Ida see Thea and me as their chance at children of their own, and celebrate our milestones with zeal.

Tante Lena was divorced by her husband when they failed to conceive; Tante Beth is on thin ice with Onkel Lars, whose rage grows each day her womb does not ripen; Ida has forgone marriage entirely, perhaps afraid that she bears the same curse. Mama – her womb, specifically – is envied by them all. She follows their procession, noticeably less animated. The whirlwind which is Thea emerges from her old bedroom.

Mama pulls me to my feet. There is a strange sensation when she touches me, and I realize it is because it's such a rarity. She keeps me at arm's length – not in the way that Thea does, mindful that I prefer affection from afar. Mama's distance is that of prey fearing a predator. I gobble down what little tenderness she has to offer, even if I know it is manufactured.

My relatives descend on me like crows on the summer corn, punctuating silence with the flutter of linen and clatter of trinkets. Oma braids my hair into a crown. Tante Beth plucks my unruly eyebrows; Ida strips me of my gown and pulls a white blouse over my head; Lena laces me into a matching ivory bodice and skirt, then ties a scarlet apron at my waist as if I am a gift to unwrap. Thea paints my lips rosy, forces a blush into my cheeks and dusts shimmering powder across my eyelids.

Within minutes, I am transformed. In their eyes, they are facilitating my metamorphosis from misshapen caterpillar to lace-winged butterfly. I feel more like the winning sow at the annual *Herbstfest*. No matter how well-groomed I am, it won't stop the village devouring me for supper.

My family speaks in hushed euphemisms, tiptoeing around the monster in the room. Women do not discuss the events of the Rite overtly. While our fear is a spectacle to be stuffed greedily down the town's collective gullet, the Rite is something we're expected to suffer alone.

When Thea returned from her Rite two years ago, I expected us to convene beneath the shroud of our quilts, the way we always did. I thought we'd speak in hushed voices, picking apart every aspect of her Rite, scheming how we'd ensure that I would pass, just as she did. Instead, she went straight to her bed and locked the door. We never spoke of it again.

Thea and I make idle small talk on the way to the church, pretending not to feel the entire town's eyes tracking our every step. I falter on the threshold, staring up at the church spire shaped like a bulbous thorn. It might be less painful to scale the steeple and jump.

As if sensing my thoughts, Thea places a hand on the small of my back and propels me through the doors. Any hopes I had of one last conversation with my sister evaporate.

It's probably for the best. It would only disappoint me.

'Ilse.' The Pfarrer's voice echoes through the church. We are alone. He watches me from the lectern with a lazy leer on his face 'You know, I had my concerns about you,' he continues, placing a hand against his heart. 'But I see you're taking after your sister. You are a fine young woman now, terror-stricken and pure.'

Woman. I do not wish to be reminded.

The Pfarrer turns his back to me, and pours wine into two waiting chalices with shaking hands. I wonder if this is part of the ritual, or if he just wanted an excuse to imbibe. He tips back his balding head and takes a deep swig. Handing me my cup, he flashes a smile. I'm sure it's supposed to be charming, but the wine has stained his crooked teeth red.

'Thank you, Pfarrer,' I murmur, disdain barely hidden.

He downs his drink and smacks his lips together. 'Will you be celebrating this evening?'

I have spent years imagining my celebration. The image is hazy in my mind, like looking through the glass bottom of a milk bottle. White-clad girls are daubs of ivory against the inky smear of the lake at midnight. I feel the warmth of the fire's glow; I hear the chime of laughter, the clink of glasses; I smell the smoke rising from the bonfire. The images swirl together, and I drown myself in them.

Nebulous, half-formed dreams are the closest I'll get to such a happy Rite. Celebrations don't belong to girls like me.

Lie. 'I have decided to celebrate with my family.'

'Sensible,' the Pfarrer says. Somehow, his approval makes it even sadder. He gestures for me to finish my wine; I try not to grimace as I down the dregs.

The church doors swing open. My family leads the charge, sliding into the frontmost pews. Behind them, the benches fill with eager-eyed women. Lambent candlelight dances against the stained-glass windows, painting the congregation blue and red and green. Beyond the windows, men emerge from the shadows, drawn to the church's glow like flies to overripe fruit. For them, this is a spectacle. A rare glimpse into our world – a realm of terror and weighty responsibility that they do not bear, but benefit from.

Bile rises in my throat as the Pfarrer wraps a clammy hand around my shoulder. By the time I register that he has been talking, he is looking at me expectantly. His fingers coil around the ceremonial bone crown. The oldest bones are those of the women who defied the Rite's initial creation; the newest are those of the women who failed their Rite and defied banishment. Defiant women, whittled into a crown to adorn those who bend the knee. Women who *know* their consent does not matter.

I've seen the crown a hundred times before. Up close, it's different. I am suddenly aware that each of these bones belonged to someone. The finger bones which will rest on my temples might have whittled wood, or sewn dresses, or played an instrument. The vertebrae which will skirt my scalp once held someone upright. The jawbone which will sit flush against my forehead once formed words.

I am struck by the urge to take the crown between my hands and smash it against the floor. Or maybe I'll use it to bludgeon the Pfarrer, leaving fragments of bone embedded in his face.

Instead, I submit, dampening down my anger. I dip my head to accept the crown, willing the memories of dead women to surface and share their horror with me. Their bones are cool and hard against my skull.

Numb, I lead the procession to the marshland where the Saint festers beneath the earth. My consciousness separates from my body. I am a detached observer, watching someone else stagger towards their unavoidable banishment.

I snap back into my flesh just as the Pfarrer clears his throat.

'Saint of Fear,' he calls, voice trembling, 'please accept our offering. Ilse Odenwald will volunteer her fear in exchange for your continued protection from the Hexenwald. We are eternally grateful for your guardianship of this town.' The Pfarrer pauses to look at me, eyes darting to the peak of my breasts. I'd like to wrench his eyeballs from their sockets. 'Are you ready, Ilse Odenwald, to accept the Saint's blessing and demonstrate your fear?'

Dazed, I look around me. Women kneel on either side of the

boardwalk, their feet dangling off its edge. I suck in a breath between gritted teeth. With it comes the smell synonymous with Heulensee's faith: sweat, copper and iron. *Fear.* A stale breeze jostles the bulrushes, coaxing them to hiss like snakes.

The Pfarrer clears his throat again. Time is running out.

I spread my arms, palms turned to the sky. Something bids me to search for my family, hoping for a sign that I will be missed – but Thea blinks back at me, her expression indifferent. It wrenches me back to the Hexennacht bonfire last night – to the rage that erupted from deep within.

It doesn't take much to summon it back. After everything we've been through, how can Thea react to my imminent demise with such apathy? Rage comes easily, salivating at the opportunity to be let loose. Wrath seeps from my pores, oozing from my lips and my nail beds and my tear ducts. I am about to be torn from my sister, from the only life I have ever known, and she *doesn't care.*

I scream.

The women clasp their hands in front of their chests – worshipping me as some sort of petrified deity. I force the air from my lungs, screaming and screaming until I suffocate.

My faux terror lives on even once I shut my mouth. It ricochets off the stagnant water; it rattles between sedge and grass, a frightened bird trying to escape; it courses along the boardwalk, reassuring Mama that I am fearful in the holiest of ways.

The women cannot speak, but I know what their glossy eyes are saying. *Beautiful Ilse. Beautiful, terrified Ilse.*

I have never felt more loved than I do in this moment. Nobody expected this from me. *I* didn't expect this from me. I blink at my family, studying the segments of their faces: wet eyes, wobbling lips, cheeks flushed with pride. This is what it feels like to be adored. To be revered.

The Pfarrer beckons me down the boardwalk, between the avenue of enraptured women. I am half-inclined to believe this is a maladaptive daydream. That the real Ilse has already been banished, and this is my brain's effort to lessen the pain. But then I press a hand against the cool earth of the hillock, and there is no disputing the way the soil yields beneath my fingertips.

I passed.

They worship a false deity. My fear is a lie.

I did not prepare for this eventuality. The Pfarrer's hand is on my lower back, propelling me towards the howling mouth of the Saint's den. I dig in my heels; he pushes harder. No matter how hard I squint, I cannot make out what lies within. I am about to come face to face with the Saint who singled me out all those years ago, the beast who killed Klara Keller.

'Good luck, Ilse,' the Pfarrer calls as I stumble into the shadows.

My foot catches on a gnarled root. Flinging my hands out in the darkness, I scrabble for something to keep me upright. My fingers close around a hunk of moss, which is as much use as a hay cart with no bottom. I hit the ground with a resounding *thump*.

Thighs aching, I stagger to my feet. I extend my arms and place a palm on each wall to steady myself. I inch my way forwards. In just a few steps, the walls have constricted enough that my arms are bent at the elbow; in a few more, they are tucked up against my side. The tunnel continues to narrow.

A realization prickles at me as I sidle along the wall. Viewed from the outside, the hillock cannot be more than ten metres at its widest point. I have been walking in a straight line, without ascent or descent, for ten minutes. I cannot process this impossibility with as much focus as I'd like; the walls press against my ribs, demanding that I give all my energy to breathing.

In the next gasp, I'm falling again. Sideways, this time. I land awkwardly on my shoulder and roll onto my back with a groan.

'Ilse Odenwald. I have been waiting for you.'

I sit up, searching for the voice. It echoes around the cave, causing strange-looking bats to scatter. They fly with staccato beats, as if time skips and distorts under the pressure of their leathery wings. Damp drips from the ceiling. A fire burns in the centre of the hollowed-out space. Stretched-out shadows dance across my body.

I blink, and a sea of bodies flicker into existence. Women – *all* women – hover just above the ground in a macabre circle. Their lifeless heads loll forward, chins tucked up against breast bones. It is as if they're suspended by their napes, hanging from an invisible thread in the clouds.

And then the women wake up.

Heads snap upright. Jaws drop open. Their skin is pallid, waxy. I walk along their ranks, bile searing my throat. Some moan as I pass them, dull pupils tracking my movement. Others have glassy eyes, covered with a thin film, and don't seem to register my presence at all. It's like a gallery of decay. Shin bones peek through rotting flesh. Ribs glint beneath peeled-back skin. Distended stomachs bulge.

I stop in front of a woman who moans with particular urgency. I narrow my eyes, blurring the scabs on her cheeks until I can believe she's just blushing. The bruising around her eyes becomes vigorously applied eyeshadow, the blood at her throat a ruby necklace. It's the birthmark on her temple that makes her face click into place.

It's Johanna Fischer.

Her long, golden hair has dulled, clinging to her scalp in matted knots. Her once-full cheeks are gaunt. She parts her lips, and for a moment, I think she's about to say something – but then she just lets out a rattling breath, laced with the scent of decomposition.

I'm struck by the urge to do something. I reach out to take Johanna's hand, if only to offer some meagre comfort – but she extricates her rotting fingers from mine, panic flashing in her eyes. She quiets when I step away.

With a headache pressing against my temples, I continue down the line of women. I pick out recognizable features in the sea of decaying faces. Mia Koch, who used to sing in the church choir, is only familiar for the fact she has two differently coloured eyes: one brown, one green. Everything that surrounds them is foreign: a toothy grimace, sunken cheeks.

I can hardly separate one tortured expression from the next. The faces blur into one another. The pain scrawled in the tense lines of their mouths, their brows, is translated directly into my own body. My heart aches for them. I feel so helpless, so useless, unable to do anything but silently cry as I walk past them.

One of the women hisses as I pass her. I almost avert my eyes from her suffering – knowing there's nothing I can do to ease her pain – but then I pause. Double-take as my brain places her face.

It's Thea.

My stomach drops so violently it almost brings me to my knees.

Her skin is pale, and as I close the distance between us, I

realize that her right eye is missing. Maggots fill the cavity, giving the impression of a white eyeball which shifts and writhes.

A sob erupts from my lips; I clamp a hand over my mouth to stop it. This is my sister. The girl who used to sing while she braided my hair. Who punched a boy in the face for touching my breast. The girl who had beautiful, clear eyes, a smile never far from her face.

I reach for her hand as I say, 'Thea?'

Her entire body shudders and she turns her head to meet my gaze.

'Ilse . . .' she groans, just before she flickers out of existence.

My desperate hands fasten around thin air. She's gone – they're *all* gone.

A gust of air surges through the cave.

'You saw them,' the disembodied voice says. *'You saw them!'*

The earth begins to rumble. Before I can catch my breath, the Saint explodes from the shadows on my left. It smashes into my side and I fly across the cavern. There is a loud snap as I collide with the wall. At first, I cannot discern where it came from – until pain screeches through my torso. I realize then that the sound was my ribs breaking.

The taste of copper fills my mouth; I probe with my tongue, finding one of my teeth shattered, the jagged root clinging to my gums. I try to steady myself, to breathe through the pain, but each time I drag in a breath, it's as if my lungs are being lanced by a knife.

By the time I have shaken the stars from my vision, the Saint stands over me. Tendrils of steam creep from its nostrils and the gaps between its teeth – teeth which I notice are red and wet.

'Little Ilse Odenwald,' it hisses, though its mouth does not move. 'You do not belong here.'

Tears bead along my lower lash line. My lip trembles of its own accord. Faking fear is easier when you've got broken ribs and a missing tooth. I am suddenly aware of just how small I am – just how breakable. The pain overwhelms me, so blinding that I cannot think of anything else.

'I am here for my Rite,' I whimper.

It leans in, letting a growl loose from its chest. A long, prehensile tongue slips free from its mouth. I grit my teeth as it licks the blood running from my nose. The Saint bellows, rearing up onto its lupine hind legs. Its clawed feet land inches short of my flesh.

'Where is your fear?'

I screw up my eyes and turn my face to the side, hoping that disgust and fear are similar enough. 'In my heart.'

'Lies,' it hisses. Again, its sandpaper tongue rasps across the scarlet staining my face. 'No fear, no flavour.'

'The Pfarrer deemed me fearful,' I protest.

'You fooled a man, silly girl. You do not fool a Saint.' It shudders with rage, then seems to compose itself, growing deathly still. 'Back to where you came from,' it says decisively. 'Back to the town you have damned.'

It uses its horns to force me to my feet. Like a sheep driven by Lars Pfeiffer's collie, I am channelled towards the tunnel. I scuttle backwards, faster and faster until the walls close around me.

The Saint waits at the mouth of the tunnel, its blood-red eyes luminous as darkness descends. My foot catches on something, and then I am falling. My head cracks against the floor, and just before I lose consciousness, the Saint's skull seems to grin.

'I'll meet you there, Ilse Odenwald.'

CHAPTER FIVE

I wake to dark skies and the sound of screaming.

My time inside the hillock felt like a span of seconds, not hours, yet the sun has disappeared and the air has begun to cool. I push to my feet, surprised to find that my ribs no longer ache. My nose has stopped bleeding, each of my teeth are where they should be, and I am completely clear-headed.

If I'd suffered the attack I dreamt up, my body would be bruised, bloodied. And I saw Thea mere hours ago; there's no way she could've been strung up in the Saint's den without me knowing. It must've been a nightmare. An illusion. Something the Saint implanted in my brain.

But when I look down at my dirndl, I notice the fabric has been sullied. A splash of blood across the ivory bodice, dirt gathered along the hem, unmistakable claw marks through the apron. It's vital evidence – but if my clothes bear the memory of the attack, why doesn't my body?

Another scream comes from the village.

I set off at a jog, darting in between the trees. By the time I arrive at the foot of the main street, my brow itches with sweat. I pause, squinting through the evening for the source of the noise. Everything is as it should be: the street is quiet, the torches that line the paths burn softly, their dancing flames illuminating the cobbles – slick and wet after a bout of rain.

Rain, though the sky is cloudless.

I lean down, touch my hand to the stones, and examine my palm under the light of a torch. My fingers glisten with something dark and viscous. *Blood.*

I pick my way across the cobbles, bracing against the slickness underfoot. The moon guides me to the few dry patches scattered across the street like grisly stepping stones.

'Come, Ilse,' a disembodied voice calls from every direction; it rumbles through the cobbles beneath my feet, radiates from the heavens and leaps through half-open doors. 'You won't want to miss this.'

I hasten my pace and follow the street to its end. There is no sign of life. Shutters are drawn and doors bolted shut. In the distance, the lake is an ominous, inky black.

'Hello?' I call. There is no response; only the flutter and snap of the colourful ribbons on the Maibaum. I hold my breath and listen again.

Flutter, flutter, snap. Flutter, flutter, snap.

The slender trunk of the Maibaum stands stark against the horizon. This year's tree is particularly tall, tapered to form a point. The wreath at its peak is thicker than I remember and there are more ribbons than I can count. They whip in a frenzy around the pole, rising and falling with the breeze. There is no sign of the voice. Just me and the wind.

'Where are you?' I shout into the darkness.

The Maibaum groans, 'I'm here.'

The Maibaum cannot speak – but even if it could, I am certain it would not sound like Oma.

And that's when the jumble of shadows become clear in my mind. It's not the ribbons I heard flapping in the breeze; it's Oma's hair. The Maibaum juts straight through her stomach. She faces the sky, head lolling back. Her legs hang limply, arms flung out to the side like the broken wings of a greylag goose.

'Ilse,' she cries. 'Make it stop.'

I clamp my hand over my mouth, a futile attempt to hold back the nausea that threatens to overflow. Fat tears press against my eyelids. I'm reminded of a morning I spent with Papa. We kept pigs, back when he was alive. One morning, he led me out into the stye and pointed out that my favourite sow was ready for slaughter. I started to cry, and he placed a firm hand over my mouth. *'Don't cry,'* he said. *'We can't let her know that anything is wrong.'*

As I watch Oma impaled on the Maibaum, the back of my throat aches with a sob I know I cannot release.

'It's okay,' I lie, my voice cracking. 'I'm here now, Oma.'

My hands itch to do something – *anything* – to save her. The rational part of me knows she is already dead.

Beneath my feet, the earth shudders. Hot breath grazes my nape. I do not give the Saint the satisfaction of turning my head. My grief distils into something sharper, more acidic. I rely on my peripheral vision, through which I can see the tip of its snout drawn level with my cheek. Blood drips from its teeth. A globule lands wetly on my shoulder.

'She's marinating,' the Saint hisses.

My nostrils flare. I clench my fists tighter, *tighter*, until I feel that my emotion is somewhat bridled. I stride away from the creature, placing myself between it and Oma. The moon hovers between the Saint's horns. Something about the image reminds me who I am talking to: a Saint.

I open my mouth and close it. Take a deep breath. Remind myself that if I let my anger overflow, things will only get worse. I remember how it tore Klara Keller's head from her neck.

Through gritted teeth, I manage to grind out a single word. 'Why?'

The Saint tosses its head. 'She will taste better once she has soaked in her own fear.'

Another deep breath. 'Why *her*? Why now?'

'A warning, Ilse Odenwald.' A rattle sounds from deep in its chest. 'I am older than you can comprehend; more powerful than you can dream; hungrier than you can imagine. I am a Saint, and you are just a girl.'

'Woman,' I snarl back. The word which disgusted me as it left the Pfarrer's mouth has taken on a certain power. It's imbued with the wisdom of my Oma, with Thea's forgotten brilliance.

'Woman or girl, whatever you are, you cannot feed me. I could eat you,' – it smacks its tongue – 'but it would not sate me. That is not the way of this land; nothing is given for free. I warned you once before, and you did not listen.'

The Saint stalks over to the Maibaum. With one swing of its horns, it breaks the pole, brings it to the ground. Oma and the Maibaum fall together. Two cracks – wood and bone splitting.

'Stop!' I shout, each fibre of my being telling me to *stop this*. To take my fleshy fists to the beast until it is left bloody and broken. I want to reach into its sockets and pull the glowing eyeballs from within; to tear the antlers from its head and plunge them through its chest.

But my adversary is a Saint, and I am just a woman.

With its teeth hovering just above Oma's limp form, the Saint pauses. 'Do you know why I wait until eighteen to perform the Rite?' I shake my head numbly. 'That is when a girl's fear is most potent. Childlike innocence dissolved, she knows the horrors of the world. At the same time, she has yet to acquire the nerve of women that I so abhor. Today, I will make an exception.'

Before I can protest, the Saint slides Oma free from the Maibaum like a spit-roasted hen. She hangs from the Saint's mouth, barely clinging to life. In the darkness, all I can see is the terrified whites of her eyes. She opens her mouth, forming words behind broken teeth—

The Saint throws its head back and swallows Oma whole.

Dizziness washes over me, forcing me to my knees. My vision cracks into a kaleidoscope of grey and scarlet. The night sky and blood, and the cobbles and blood, and the lake's surface and blood, blood, *blood*.

Grief leaves my body as an animalistic howl. There is no body to hold, no corpse to weep over. Oma is gone. Irretrievable. I could've stemmed the bleeding, bound her broken bones – but now everything that made her *her* is dissolving in the Saint's stomach.

My Oma is dead, and I have nothing left.

I heave until my stomach muscles ache. Agony rips through me, gripping my lungs, my throat. A stabbing pain radiates through my chest – my anguish so intense that I think it might kill me.

'You killed her!' I sob.

The Saint lumbers towards me. '*You* killed her. It is your transgression that spelled her end. I warned you all those years ago.'

The glaring absence that I have spent my life concealing is torn open, rot and decay spilling out for all to see. Had I died in the lake, it would've been a mercy, a correction. Oma would still be alive. Wild-eyed, I look to the water now, wondering if the cold would be enough to drown me—

'I require something of you, Ilse Odenwald.'

I spit onto the cobbles, a hysterical half-laugh-half-sob ripping from my lungs. 'You murder my Oma and seek *favours?*'

The Saint pauses, unnatural in its stillness. Its bony jaw creaks open in a grimace. 'In thirty days, I will return to this street. When I do, I want to taste your fear. *Real* fear.'

My voice is a broken snarl. It is all I can do not to throw myself at the beast. 'Do not ask for what I cannot give you.'

'"Cannot",' the Saint parrots. 'Such a human condition. In my realm, there is only will, and will not. I offer you a choice, Ilse. Find your fear, or I will reduce your dear sister to blood and bone. Thirty days.'

My diaphragm aches with a howl I do not have the strength to let loose. An abyss opens inside me, maw flung wide. Not Thea. *Anyone but Thea.* The macabre illusion in the Saint's den pained me enough. She might be a distant memory of the sister I loved – but I will not see her hurt.

The Saint stalks away, leaving me alone with what remains of Oma. A bloody imprint; a lock of silver hair; a tooth, jerked loose when she hit the floor. I crawl over to the silhouette of her body and press my palm against the space where her hand would've been. Her presence is so recent, so visceral, that I feel as if I might be able to will her back into existence by concentrating hard enough.

Oma would know what to do. She would know how to save Thea.

I scramble to my feet and leave the town behind, aiming for the lake for which Heulensee is named. *Howling lake.* The lake does not howl, but I will.

I collapse on the shore and scream. My body releases emotion in violent, shaking waves. The pain doesn't truly leave, though; it cloys in my throat and tangles around my lungs like ivy. My nails chip and break as I claw myself across the pebble shore and into the water. I surrender myself to the cold, letting it numb every part of me that hurts.

Oma's blood washes from my body in long, scarlet ribbons. It winds through my fingers and around my calves. The lake magnifies my crime. A cloud of crimson radiates from me – growing and growing until I am a tiny dot at its centre.

I will die here, I think, *and I will be grateful.*

I lose the strength to keep myself afloat. The survival instinct I didn't know I possessed momentarily convinces me to thrash my limbs, but then serenity takes hold. I see my end. There are worse deaths than in the belly of the lake. Perhaps fish will feed on my corpse. At least then my existence might be meaningful.

But Heulensee has other plans. A current cradles me, lulls me into a stupor, and spits me out on the shore. I try to crawl back in, but the lake pushes me onto land. For the second time in my life, the lake refuses to grant me respite.

I lay on the shore, pebbles digging into my back, until the rising sun stains the sky red.

Red was my favourite colour, once. I do not think I like it anymore.

I regain consciousness in my own bed, with no sense of how I got there. A halo of lake water stains the sheets around me. My skin smells like copper and earth.

I heave myself out of bed and listen. The house is silent. A steel tub of water waits in the kitchen. I submerge myself, willing the lukewarm water to numb the ache Oma left behind. I use a coarse-bristled brush to scrub and scrub and scrub until I break skin.

I still feel dirty.

By the time I have dressed, the sun has reached its summit. There's still no sign of Mama. I prepare bread and cheese on lunch plates, one fewer than usual, and arrange it in pretty little patterns.

Mama does not come home, and I do not touch my food.

I should stay and watch for fires but by evening, restless legs drive me from the house. Pausing in the half-light, I cast my eyes east, where the banished women live somewhere beyond view. It would've been better if the Pfarrer had deemed my fear impure. Sent me to join the mad women. At least then Oma would still be alive.

I take the trail down from our house to the cobbled street. The stones have been scrubbed clean. All traces of Oma's blood have washed away into the gutters.

Against my better judgement, I pause in front of the church. The doors are barely ajar, but the sliver of holiness that I can discern sours my stomach. A sea of white-clad backs linger in the pews. At the altar, the Pfarrer stands in silence.

And he is staring straight at me.

CHAPTER SIX

The Pfarrer slowly raises a hand and beckons me into the church. Half of me contemplates running away and surrendering to the Hexenwald. The other half knows I deserve the Pfarrer's judgement.

A hundred pairs of eyes singe into my skin as I walk the aisle. Within the bowels of the church, I am reminded of my strange recurring dreams where I have accidentally let myself into someone else's house. I feel that same sense of unease now; the deep-rooted knowledge that I do not belong here. As if the Saint of Fear might burst through at any moment. Perhaps it will turn me to ash where I stand. Perhaps that will be a mercy.

The Pfarrer smiles, arms spread wide, a shepherd welcoming home a wayward sheep – but when I walk into his embrace, it feels more like a spider's pincers snapping shut.

'Oh, Ilse,' he breathes, lips grazing my ear. 'What happened?'

'I do not know,' I murmur.

'Do not lie to me, child.'

My back stiffens. I may not feel fear, but I can sense a threat. Something pulses beneath my skin, hot and rippling. *Get out*, it tells me. *Run while you can.*

'You have always been different. Now, I think I understand why.'

I swallow so noisily that it must echo across the pews. My body hums, frozen between fight or flight.

'Tell me, Ilse. Do you feel fear?'

I pull back from the Pfarrer and turn my head to the crowd. Thea stares back, white-faced, a warning caged behind her eyes. Perhaps if I was more like her, I would be able to interpret her fear – to sense the scale of the threat held just beneath the surface of the gathering, a whirlpool rising from the depths.

But what use is my charade? I thought that if I dug out everything that makes me *me*, I could survive here. Despite contorting myself into ever smaller boxes, there is no safety for me here. The congregation salivates, waiting for my confession.

Let this town be damned. Let *me* be damned.

'I do not.'

A collective gasp shatters the silence. The Pfarrer sways on his feet, overtaken by horror or some divine spirit. Thea lets out the breath she's been holding and screws her eyes shut. Mama burrows her face into her hands. Beside her, Oma's empty pew is a hungry abyss. My Tanten cling to each other with blanched knuckles, but the emotion doesn't reach their eyes.

'In the history of our beautiful town, never have our doors been darkened by someone like you. An abomination.' The Pfarrer blanches paler than usual. 'Those outcast to the meadow have never been so bold in their disrespect of our ways.' He turns serpentine eyes to Mama, who can hardly meet his gaze. 'Something must be done.'

'Kill her.'

The command rings clear. Herr Schmidt, the baker who used to slip Thea and I *Brezeln*, stares back at me. There is no recognition in his eyes – only bloodlust. A rabid dog.

'*Kill her*,' he insists. 'We cannot risk the Saint of Fear's wrath. It has shown us what it thinks of her transgression.'

My jaw drops open. This man watched me grow up, and now he looks at me as nothing but a doe to be slain.

Whispers rise from the crowd, ghosts rising from graves. 'Kill her,' they murmur. 'Execute her before she damns us.'

Fists tightening at my sides, I bite the inside of my cheek until I taste copper. I dare not open my mouth, lest years of anger spill out like wasps from a disturbed hive. Beneath my skin, something boils. I feel as if one flick of my wrist, one pointed glance, could reduce this church to rubble. Let the bastards claw their way out.

'You cannot spill the blood of a woman who passed their Rite.'

The crowd's attention snaps to Thea. Mine does, too.

My sister stands on shaky legs in the pews. Her face is drawn and white. Hans clutches at her hand. 'You *cannot* spill the blood of a woman who has taken their Rite,' she repeats, gaining control over her trembling voice, 'which means that Ilse cannot be killed.'

'She did not pass her Rite,' Herr Schmidt argues.

'The Pfarrer deemed her fear worthy of conversing with the Saint of Fear. She entered the Saint's den and returned. That is the only requirement. She *passed* her Rite.'

Thea's attentiveness to our scripture has paid off. She has found a loophole, which will permit my survival. The guilt inside me burgeons. No matter the rift between us, Thea is attempting to save me. If the Saint's threat is true, I am the only one who can save her in return. But how?

'Semantics aside,' Herr Schmidt says with a sneer, 'I would argue that her crimes—'

'Do you claim to know better than the old ones?' Thea protests.

I never believed that Thea could be wrathful, but she summons every iota of rage in her body and channels it towards Herr Schmidt. 'The ones who first brokered the deal with the Saint of Fear, and kept us safe from the horrors of the Hexenwald? Do you believe the scripture that keeps Heulensee safe is *flawed*?'

The congregation turns to look at Herr Schmidt. Thea has used his own piousness against him. He shrinks beneath their gaze, retreating into his seat the way a snail retracts into its shell.

'Something must be done,' the Pfarrer says, reclaiming the attention of his herd.

'Let us not be hasty.'

Mama's voice comes as a shock. Thea's defence of me was predictable; Mama's is unprecedented.

'I would ask you to honour the debt we Odenwald women have paid over the years. Not one of our women has failed their Rite. Trace our lineage back a hundred years; you'll find fear through and through.' The Pfarrer seems unconvinced, his brow wrinkled. Changing tack, Mama hurries to add, 'Fertility blooms in my line, Pfarrer. Ilse is an asset.'

An asset. She may as well have called me a broodmare.

The Pfarrer concedes with a bob of his bald head. 'The Odenwalds have been reliable. But Ilse's transgression is dire, and—'

'It's a family matter,' Mama interrupts. 'By sunrise, we will have a solution.'

'The solution lies in her blood,' Herr Schmidt snaps.

'By sunrise, we will deliver a solution,' Mama repeats, voice strained. Then, more quietly, 'If not, we will let Ilse go.'

My sentimental hopes – that after all these years, Mama *does* care – sink into the earth. Thea turns to her, enraged. For the first time, my sister sees the monster beneath Mama's skin. Hans reaches out for Thea's hand and pulls her back into their pew.

The Pfarrer's eyes flick to me, then to Mama. 'You have until sunrise.'

'Go, Ilse,' Mama commands.

I do not hesitate. Numb legs carry me out of the church, along the street and up the tortuously steep track to our house. The sun is beginning its descent, sapping away warmth and colour.

I slip inside the house, slamming the door shut behind me. Only in the comfort of my bedroom do I indulge emotion. I scream into my pillow, raging and grieving all at once, until it's sodden with tears and the heat of my breath.

By the time the front door clicks open, dusk has fallen – sucking the light and warmth from my room. Footsteps ascend the stairs, coming to an ominous stop outside my bedroom. The door whines open.

'Stop it.' Mama stands in the doorway, hands on hips. She looks disgusted. I have rarely cried in front of her – even as a child. Her reaction in this moment reminds me why. 'Selfish, self-pitying girl. You knew this would happen eventually.'

Furious, I right myself and hiss, 'These tears are not for *me*.'

'Crying will not bring her back,' she snaps.

'This isn't about Oma!'

Mama stares at me, calculating. The pieces fall into place. She draws a sharp breath. Even from a distance, I see goosebumps race to stipple her arms. If my tears are not for Oma, she knows there is only one other person in this world that I would mourn so deeply.

'*Dorothea.*' Her voice comes out as a ragged exhale. She sinks to the floor, back braced against the door. 'Tell me what happened.'

'The Saint of Fear told me that I must become fearful.'

'And if you fail?'

My bottom lip trembles. 'It will kill Dorothea.'

'No,' she protests weakly. 'Not Thea.'

'Perhaps it's best if the townsfolk kill me,' I reason. My inner child prays that she will correct me.

'No.'

'My death is no huge loss.' My desperation breaks in a sob.

'*No*, Ilse.' Mama ploughs straight through my statement. She heaves herself to her feet and paces about the room, muttering under her breath. 'The Saint asked for your fear; it will not take kindly to being short-changed.'

I curse myself for expecting anything other than cold logic from her.

'What, then?' I urge, my voice cracking. 'What can I do?'

'You find your fear.'

I stare back at her, brows raised with incredulity. 'Don't you think I have *tried*?'

'There is a frontier you have not crossed,' she murmurs. Her eyes drift to my bedroom window, out over the lake. Beyond, the forest seems to grin with bloody teeth.

My voice comes out broken. 'The Hexenwald?'

Mama hesitates, torn between barely restrained terror and her desire to save Thea. Slipping out into the kitchen, I hear her haul one of the kitchen chairs across the flagstones. She clambers up onto it – I can tell from the way she groans.

Mama is pale when she comes back into the bedroom. There is a roll of parchment clutched in her fist. She unfurls it, blows a flurry of dust from its surface and spreads it on my bed. Ink winds across its surface, drawn to resemble the expanse of the Hexenwald. An illustrated scrawl at the forest's heart reads, 'The cuckoo'. I do not recognize the handwriting.

'Here,' Mama says, breathlessly.

'What is "the cuckoo"?'

'It's a . . .' She swallows, eyes pinned to the map. 'A being of the forest. If anything can help you find your fear, this is it.'

It makes no sense for Mama – the most fearful woman I know – to be familiar with creatures in the Hexenwald. 'But you have never entered the Hexenwald,' I continue, noting the irritation sparking in her eyes. 'How can you know what lies within?'

'There is no time for telling stories, Ilse.' Mama's head snaps to the side. I follow her gaze to the window. Fire flickers in the half-light beyond. A sea of meteoric light creeps across the land, staining the earth amber. 'They're coming.'

Torches lit against the encroaching dark, the townsfolk approach. Their fury, or perhaps their terror, has driven them to ignore the Pfarrer's decree, this once.

Mama flings herself into action. She grabs me by the wrist and tows me into the kitchen. Before I can question what we're doing, she begins stuffing supplies into a hazel-green knapsack. My heart aches.

Mama gave me this knapsack when I turned thirteen. She said it was purely practical – that I needed to be more independent, and the knapsack would permit it. Later, Thea told me offhandedly that when Mama picked the backpack, she said it was because the colour reminded her of my eyes. To imagine her standing in the tailor's shop seeing the colour green and thinking of *me* made me believe she might care for me. For a while, at least.

'I'll give you enough food to last a week. You remember how to hunt? How to snare?'

'Of course I remember,' I snap. Hunting – watching animals bleed out on the forest floor, mewling and helpless – was one of Papa's favourite things to do with his girls. He'd make us lay snares for velvet-snouted deer, and shout at us when we couldn't find the strength to finish the job.

Mama gives a curt nod, satisfied.

'That's it, then?' I utter, childlike in my dismay. She disappoints me at every turn, and I let her. 'The Hexenwald will kill me.'

She continues rifling through the cupboards without a backward glance. 'And does that scare you?'

Quietly, I admit, 'No.'

'You're the lucky one. The fear of death is worse than death itself.'

I stare at the back of her head, wondering how she can love Thea so wholly and me so little.

Thea bursts through the front door, Hans trailing behind her. She falters as she enters the kitchen, her eyes darting between me, Mama and the knapsack. The warning she had hoped to give is futile. Hans lingers on the threshold.

'Where are you going?' Thea asks me, eyes glossy with tears.

'To Flussdorf, across the southern mountains,' Mama replies before I can answer. Her withering look silences the protest forming on my tongue. 'We have distant cousins there. They will give her shelter.'

'The mountains are impassable!' Thea balls her fists at her sides. 'Let alone in the dark. This is a death sentence, Mama.'

'I could take her to the foot of the mountain,' Hans offers. 'Let me.'

'That won't be necessary,' Mama interrupts. She crafts a spectacular show of guilt on her face. 'I . . . anticipated this. That there would be a complication with Ilse's Rite. I sent word to my cousins days ago. A shepherd will meet Ilse on the pass.'

Hans nods. Thea narrows her eyes, just a fraction. She looks between us, suspicion rolling off her in waves. Her gaze lands on the map, still spread open on the kitchen table. The corner of her mouth quirks up. I do not have time to study her reaction before Mama snatches the paper away, stuffing it into the knapsack. She thrusts it into my arms.

Beyond the window, the mass of flickering torches grows ever closer.

'Say goodbye to your sister, Thea,' Mama says.

Thea's lip trembles. She throws herself against me – a crisis hug – and sobs into the nook between my shoulder and my neck. 'I love you,' she cries. It's the first time she's said that out loud in a long time. Perhaps it will be the last time, too. 'I'll visit. I swear it.'

Leaving her with a lie – that I am bound for Flussdorf, not the Hexenwald – makes my heart twist. I give her a truth to assuage my guilt. 'I love you, too.'

Thea pulls back to look at me. Tears bead along her lashes, tiny crystals. There is something different in her eyes – a depth that I have never noticed until now. Before I can examine it, she turns and plants a kiss on Hans's cheek.

'Stay here,' she says breathlessly. 'Keep them safe.'

Before he has the chance to respond, Thea darts towards the door. She dons a cloak, pulls up the hood and bursts out of the house.

I watch from the window as Thea runs across the path of the oncoming horde, cloak pulled tight around her face. Distantly, I hear her hollering for the townsfolk's attention. The torches switch course, following my sister as she bounds through the night. We barely look alike; whatever time her charade affords me is slipping away with every breath.

Mama nods to the knapsack in my hands. 'Gather anything else you want to take.'

I retreat into my bedroom, hoping Mama will not see the effect her indifference has on me. She and Hans exchange tense words in the kitchen. My ears drone so loudly I cannot decipher what they're saying.

Hands steady, I stuff my personal effects into the bag. There is no logic to it: I grab a fistful of juniper, leftover from Hexennacht; Papa's penknife – three dull, rusted inches of metal, which are my only means of staving off the Hexenwald's horrors; a silver barrette studded with green stones, gifted to me by Oma on my fifteenth birthday.

Just before I let the barrette fall into the backpack, I curl my fingers around it. Despite Oma's insistence, I have never actually worn it. As I fasten it in my hair, it feels like I'm taking a piece of her with me.

'What's really happening, Ilse?'

Hans stands in the doorway, face tense, as if he's not sure he really wants the answer.

'I'm going to Flussdorf,' I insist, fumbling with the straps of the knapsack.

'The route to Flussdorf has been impassable since the avalanche last winter.'

I freeze, fingers stilling. My brain races to come up with an adequate explanation. Mama slams cupboard doors in the kitchen.

Hans casts a hurried glance across his shoulder. He takes another step into the room and drops his voice to a whisper. 'Where are you really going?'

'It doesn't matter,' I snap. 'Leave it alone, Hans.'

'Maybe I can help you,' he offers. 'I could walk you part of the way to wherever—'

'You can't help.'

'Don't be so stubborn—'

'You *can't* help,' I repeat.

'Why? Is independence more important to you than survival?'

'Because Thea is going to die, unless I do something about it.' If he's so desperate for answers, let this be his burden too. Teeth gritted, I ask, 'Do you want that?'

Hans blanches. 'No,' he says, voice shaking. 'I don't.'

'Time to go, Ilse,' Mama calls from the kitchen.

I shoulder past Hans, and do not meet his eyes, nor Mama's, as I shrug on my cloak. Hinges rusty from years of disuse, the back door groans as I shoulder it open. The Hexenwald will probably kill me, and I do not want to leave any questions unspoken. Knowing my demise is imminent, Mama will be bound to answer me. I pause in the doorway, face half-turned to her.

'What did I do wrong?'

I do not need to elaborate – we both understand the implication. Emotion flickers across her face, ephemeral as the dancing shadows of a candle. She smooths it out. Channels whatever she is feeling to her fists, which clench and relax at her sides.

'Now is not the time, Ilse.'

'The forest will kill me,' I choke out, a knot tightening in my throat. 'When is the time, if not now?'

'You need to leave,' Mama says, refusing to meet my gaze.

I cross the kitchen in three short steps and take Mama's clenched fists between my hands. She flinches as if *I* am the perpetrator of the war between us. Even though we're touching, the gulf between us is bigger than ever. Insurmountable.

'Why couldn't you love me?' I bleat, hopelessly childish. 'What did I do wrong?'

I need this closure, this catharsis – even if it hurts. She finally stares back at me, eyes darting across my face. Mama swallows once, clears her throat.

She responds, 'You were born different, Ilse.'

And isn't that the sum of it? That I am divergent, and that is wrong.

CHAPTER SEVEN

I bolt for the lake. Clumsy feet snag beneath me, catching against each undulation in the earth. My ragged breaths are shards of glass pressed to my throat. It's not enough to distract from the uproar in my mind. How could my own mother love me so little? How could the town that cooed over me as a babe want to tear me limb from limb?

I swallow my anger and run.

A glance over my shoulder confirms the mob have switched course, hot on my trail. Thea's distraction has crumbled. The townsfolk must've caught up to her, finding an Odenwald, but not the one whose blood they crave. Their torchlight is getting closer.

Meadow grass gives way to the rocky lake shore. I keep to the water line, hoping the inky depths will conceal my presence. I look into the lake's heart, which – even in daylight – is a dark, ominous blue, starkly contrasted against the turquoise shallows. Tonight, its depth is infernal.

A dark mass of trees looms on the horizon. The forest is a paradox, promising death and sanctuary at once. A crack sounds from within the woods; flocks of crows take to the sky, lit up against the moon. I pass signs warning to turn away from the Hexenwald. The temperature drops and my breaths leave my mouth as shuddered plumes of steam. Snippets of the macabre nursery rhyme echo in my ears.

Blood spills from veins, skin starts to crack
Ignore the forest; turn back, turn back.

A thousand warnings. A thousand indications that danger lies ahead. I storm past each of them. I *know* that this forest might kill me. Courage is seen as the opposite of fear – but I have always considered myself lacking in that, too. Today, though, I must try. For Thea.

I pull my cloak tighter, bracing against the biting cold. A scream rises from the Hexenwald, visceral in its horror. Behind, the sea of torches pauses. They must have reached the first warning sign. Held back by the invisible barrier of their fear, they linger in an uneasy line.

In an instant, their torches wink out.

The light takes my breath with it. When I turn back around, the forest bears down. Caught between the wrath of the townsfolk and the Hexenwald's siren call, I falter. It's not fear that causes me to baulk. It's that same sense that has followed me my whole life: the sense of *wrongness*. The trees are too tall, too conspiratorial. The birds within their boughs sing just off-key. The breeze is violent yet stale. It's a canvas of inconsistencies – stark enough to notice, benign enough to write off.

Eyes become sockets, flesh melts to bone
The forest is hungry; go home, go home.

'Ilse.'

I spin around. Hans stands just behind me, chest heaving, damp, dark hair clinging to his forehead. I swing my rucksack to my front and withdraw Papa's penknife. Brandishing the blade, I hiss, 'If you are here to stop me, I wish you luck.'

Hans stifles a laugh. His amusement heightens my ire and it must show in my expression, for he holds out his hands the way one might fend off a hungry wolf. 'I'm not here to stop you.'

'What, then?'

'I told you I want to help.'

I scoff incredulously, gesturing to the looming mass of the Hexenwald. 'This is my final stop.'

'I gathered,' Hans says, matching my dry demeanour. 'I don't know what you have planned, but I'm coming too.'

'You can't help me,' I snarl. 'I am the only one who can save her.'

Hans raises his voice. 'But you aren't the only one who loves her, Ilse.'

'Go home, Hans. This is no place for a man like you.'

'A man like me?' He snorts. 'You barely know me.'

'You'll slow me down.'

Beneath his breath, he mutters, 'You've always been stubborn.'

I glare at him. 'Go home, Hans. She needs you there.'

Three measured breaths pass between my lips before I turn on my heel, bound for the forest. The pines seem to bend and yield, a mouth opening to swallow me whole. I break their ranks, the sky flashes crimson ...

The trees turn bloodthirsty. They tear at every inch of exposed flesh, and when they cannot find it, they rip open my garments in search. I feel the warmth seeping from me, each branch a leech suckered to my flesh. Ice springs up where their needles brush my skin. The pain is too much, too overwhelming. I try to turn back, to find another way, but wherever I go the trees rise up to meet me, herding me forward, deeper into their gullet.

The Hexen won't rest 'til your blood is shed
Ignore the warning, you're dead, you're dead.

Bracing my arms around my face, I plunge in.

My boots sink into increasingly waterlogged ground. Hungry trees claw at me, leaving behind fingerprints of sap and bark. Hans calls after me; the forest eats his voice. The air grows cold and thick, stuffed into the atmosphere like cotton, stinging my throat with each inhale.

Something howls, desperate and pained – or perhaps it's me who is howling. Time bends and stutters. It takes ages to move even one step, yet in the next breath, I look back and see an ocean of trees separating myself from Heulensee. Mocking laughter rattles between branches.

The trees lunge with renewed hunger. Suddenly I see with clarity: this is where I was destined to die. I will become a sad, tattered legend. The cautionary tale of the girl who fled into the Hexenwald and never returned. A new nursery rhyme will spring up in my wake. Thea will die, too, and it will be my fault.

I recall the day the barn set on fire. The way Thea threw her body in front of mine, shielding me from the flames. It's my turn to protect her. Fists held close to my face, I strike back at the trees. Their boughs snarl as I break them. One whips me across the cheek, leaving behind a welt which sings with pain but does not bleed.

'I have no quarrel with you!' I shout. 'I am here to save my sister!'

And then everything stops. A preternatural stillness falls across the forest, thick as a down blanket. The laughter and the snapping of teeth cease; the air sweetens to a gentle midsummer breeze. The trees straighten, confined to regimented lines which seem as though they would never dream of misbehaving.

I don't dare to think my quarrel with the forest is over, but in that moment of silence, a realization buds. If I return from the Hexenwald triumphant, having snatched my sister from the jaws of death and shunted my missing piece – my fear – firmly into place, what will the village think? No one has entered the Hexenwald and left unscathed, much less victorious.

Maybe this is why I've always felt a pull to the forest. Because this is where I am made whole. This is where I find the key to belonging.

A thrill races through me. I subdue it with a handful of steady breaths. After assessing the damage to my cheek – irritating, but hardly fatal – I push deeper into the forest. Trees moan their growing pains into the wind.

Something else moans, too. Something human.

'Help me.'

Frozen mid-stride, my eyes dart from spruce to spruce.

A shuddered exhale, not my own. *'Help me.'*

There, among the trees. Ropes hang from four evergreens, coiling like snakes with each hint of a breeze. A body is attached to each rope. Necks red-raw with rope burns, oozing with pus, some barely held by a thread of ligament and sinew. Flies hum in great swarms – living plumes of smoke with flashing wings and hungry mouths.

Three of the men are beyond saving. They are alive, but any movement will hinder more than help. I think of Thea's favourite hen, Olga. The way Papa tucked Olga under his arm, stroked her back and broke her neck in one fell swoop. *'She would've died slowly otherwise,'* he told me. *'It's better this way.'*

I don't think I have the strength to break a grown man's neck.

Nauseous, I look to the man whose lips are still parted around the words *'help me'*. With one limp hand, he gestures for me to come closer. 'Please ... Let me down.' Blood gathers in the seams of his mouth with each word.

Wrong, my body sings. I feel it in my bones and my chest. But he is so pained, so helpless. How can I defy his pleas?

I unfurl my fingers, examining Papa's penknife in my forest-scarred hands. Time and disuse have dulled the blade.

'Hurry.'

Fingers curled around the knife's hilt, I cross the clearing. The air I disturb sends flies wheeling into the sky, only settling once they've determined I'm not a threat to their meal.

The smell – heavens, the *smell* – of decay fills my lungs. Sour enough to make my eyes water, yet saccharine at the same time. I wrestle with my throat, begging myself not to gag. Imagine that: you're dying, *rotting*, and your rescuer gags at the smell of you. The man reaches out, bloody fingers curling around thin air, and utters another moan.

'It's okay,' I murmur, trying desperately to look *anywhere* but the rotten scabs at his neck, the gaunt hollows of his cheeks, the bulging of his milky eyeballs. 'I will help you down.'

Spruces are notoriously difficult to climb, and this one is made near-impassable by the lack of any lower branches. I'll have to shimmy up it, but that will also mean brushing against the man's fly-ridden limbs.

Knife clenched between my teeth, I turn my head and inhale one last gulp of fresh air. Breathe in. *Hold.* I grip the tree trunk, jump, and pin my knees around it. The bark gnaws at my skin. I hoist myself up until I'm able to reach the rope. His hands twitch as they graze me. I begin to cut through the rope and my elbow rings with pain. Each snapping thread reminds me of the other men's necks.

I saw faster—

the man falls to the ground.

I follow, throwing myself to the earth. My lungs ring with the inhale I have been denying myself. My teeth clack together, blood blooms on my tongue. Crawling on bruised knees and hands, I press my knife to the rope at his throat.

'It's okay,' I pant. 'Nearly there.'

Wrong, my body screams. But of course it's wrong; he's dying, and I am tasked with saving him, equipped only with a dull penknife and what little medical knowledge I can remember.

'Ilse.' A hissed warning, somewhere behind. I know that voice: it belongs to Hans. 'Don't move.' My eyes blur, focusing only on the rope at the man's neck. 'If you move, it will kill you.'

Another voice. Closer, rasping with death. 'Look at me.'

I keep my eyes fixed on the rope.

'Look at me!'

From behind, Hans commands, 'Don't look at it, Ilse!'

'LOOK AT ME!'

And then my eyes start to move. I wrestle with them, begging them to stay down – but they move of their own accord. 'I can't help it,' I say, voice ragged. 'I'm going to look at it.'

'No, Ilse!' Hans shouts.

'LOOK. AT. ME!'

My gaze slides up the man's throat. Grazes the crooked line of his jaw. Passes his mouth, where jagged, inhuman teeth have dropped from his gums. I meet his eyes.

His eyes.

They are black. Endlessly, hopelessly black. They stretch all the way from his cheekbones to his hairline. He bolts upright and fastens his hands like a vice around my throat.

'Aren't you beautiful?' he hisses, voice wet, blood dripping from his teeth. 'I'm going to keep you for ever.'

The man presses our foreheads together, the void of his eyes inches from mine – now I cannot see.

Stripped of my sight, I scrabble against the hands at my throat. He grips me so tightly that I cannot draw even the slightest of breaths. The man – monster – barks a falsetto laugh. Rotting breath moistens my cheeks.

'Got your eyes!' he taunts, affecting a mocking sing-song. 'I can't wait to taste them.'

Liquid splatters my face. I *feel* the colour red, caustic and macabre, a dampness across my cheeks. I hear a blade strike flesh, flesh, bone. A wet thud. My fingers bunch in the grass, dirt gathering beneath my nails. The hands at my throat loosen.

Slowly, my vision returns. The picture forms gradually; the gloom of the sky, the dark threat of the trees. Before me, scarlet. The man is still there, hands limply curled around my neck, but there is a glaring absence where his head should be.

His head rolls across the grass, leaving a trail of black blood behind it. When it comes to a stop, the jaw lolls open, eyes shrinking back to human size.

Hans stands to the side, chest heaving, cloak speckled crimson. Warring emotions overwhelm me: gratitude for his intervention, irritated disbelief that he followed me in the first place. For all his faults, I am struck by his bravery.

The perception in the village is that men, by nature, are brave. But the fact that they do not scream and cower the way we do doesn't make them courageous. It just means they wear their terror differently. Hans is an exception. He faced these monsters as if they were inconsequential. Followed me into the Hexenwald as if it's a normal forest. I do not tell him this, of course, but I find myself viewing him from a new perspective.

I rub my throat, where the memory of the creature's hands lingers. 'What was that?'

'A hanged man. They were strung up for some foul crime, many years in the past when the Hexenwald was a fraction of the size it is now. To escape eternal hanging, they have to convince someone to get close enough and steal their life force.'

I narrow my eyes. 'How do you know so much about a creature of the Hexenwald?'

His expression tightens. '*How* I know doesn't matter. What matters is that this trap' – he points the bloody tip of his sword at the carcass – 'is exactly why you need me.'

'I don't *need* you,' I rebuke, the penknife suspended between my numb fingers. 'Your intervention was ... convenient, but I can deal with it from here.'

'Most people just say thank you. Whether you can "deal with it" or not,' he says, his lips curving with a hint of sarcasm, 'you shouldn't have approached him in the first place.'

'I thought I could save him.' The words sound weak even as they leave my mouth. I stare down at my lap, reeling in the stupidity of what I just did.

My fearlessness has led me astray more than once. Most of my life, Thea has acted as my compass. Her nervous system works twice as hard, compensating for what I lack. But she isn't always there. Alone, I cannot sense that the man in the tavern doesn't have my best interests at heart, nor that the sound coming from a darkened alleyway is a sinister one. Being born with a missing piece is one thing; the traumas I have suffered as a result are worse.

Hans pauses, his expression pitying or bemused – I cannot tell. 'Do you know why humans feel fear?'

I have spent my life pondering this very question. But I cannot say what I suspect. I cannot let him know that I believe myself to be as defective as everyone else does. 'Because humans are weak.'

He shakes his head. 'Fear is a gift. It keeps us alive. You need me.'

My eyes dart back to the beheaded man. I am reminded of Klara Keller – of the fact that it was *my* fearlessness that spelled her end. Oma's murder, too. Thea will be next if I cannot save her. The awful truth is that Hans is right. I do need him. He could be my compass – the one that will guide me through the Hexenwald with minimal bloodshed.

But he is made of flesh, just as I am. He can bend and break.

Quietly, I say, 'If you die, Thea will never forgive me.'

'If *you* die, Thea will die.' Hans kneels beside me, his face sincere. 'I know we haven't been the best of friends, but we can put that aside. For her. What are you here to do, Ilse?' he says, voice gentle as the ripple of water through a brook. 'You can tell me.'

At the mercy of the bloodthirsty forest, Hans is the closest thing I have to an ally. A breeze whisks between us, bringing with it the scent of the hanged men and something sweeter. Honeysuckle – one of Thea's favourites. I take it as a sign.

I cannot meet his eyes as I make my confession, too ashamed to read the disgust I will no doubt see there. 'I have thirty – now twenty-nine – days to find my fear, or the Saint will kill Thea. I think the Hexenwald is the key.'

Finally, I look up. There is no judgement on Hans's face. He watches me with sombre understanding and a tense jaw.

'Okay,' he breathes, slapping his thigh. 'Then let's go.'

CHAPTER EIGHT

Hans is the human equivalent of a songbird. A songbird who insists on chirping directly into my ear. I've always found his boyish optimism tedious. But here, with sinister boughs pressing down around us, a very small part of me is glad for his lightness. There is something about him that makes me believe. Believe that I can find my fear. Believe that I can save Thea.

I tuck my penknife into my backpack. Hans dispatches the remaining hanged men, which takes little more than a kiss of his sharp sword. There is use in having the blacksmith's son by my side.

Hans looks to me expectantly, awaiting instruction, but I don't have much to give.

'We need to find the cuckoo,' I say, with an inflection that I hope conveys authority.

Hans cocks an eyebrow. 'A bird?'

'Yes, Hans. We came to the Hexenwald to find a bird,' I say

drily, with a roll of my eyes. 'It's a being of the Hexenwald. We will find it at the forest's heart.'

'Manners cost nothing,' he mutters.

Still grumbling, Hans withdraws a compass from his pocket and sets about plotting our course. The needle whirrs, spinning round and round the compass face, unable to strike north.

Hans must feel unease at this, but he doesn't let it show. 'Right,' he says, pragmatic as ever. 'We'll have to orient ourselves a different way. It's late, but we ought to make some progress before we rest.'

He scales the sturdiest-looking spruce he can find and swivels around until he spots the barbed mountains beyond the Hexenwald. I thought they were at our front, but somehow, they've sprung up behind us. We must have gotten turned around without realizing. Hans leaps down, grinning, and instructs me to follow him.

It takes a lot to sap this man's enthusiasm. We trek through bogs, knee-deep in mud; we accidentally disturb a hornets' nest and have to flee with our cloaks over our heads; a downpour strikes from the dark sky, soaking us to the bone. Through all of this, he whistles merrily. Until we arrive back at the corpses of the hanged men.

Hans stops in his tracks. He reaches up, runs a hand through his hair. We have been walking for at least a couple of hours – my feet won't let me forget. But despite setting our course, despite pausing every half hour to orient ourselves around the mountains, we are right back where we started.

'That's strange.' Again, he rakes a hand through his hair. This time, the action is more frantic than reflexive.

Stars peek out from the haze above us. We must be approaching midnight. 'What should we do?'

Hans drums his fingers against the tree he leans on. 'We'll set up camp. I'm sure it will make more sense in the morning, once our heads are clearer.'

A thicket of unease sprouts between us. We exchange a look, the impossibility of our mission felt, if unspoken. We're unwilling to share a clearing with dead men, so we venture into the forest.

The night air is warmer than it should be. A boon, given that Mama only thought to pack me a light blanket. Hans constructs the bones of a campfire and instructs me to gather firewood. Thankfully, there is no shortage of that.

Staring into the flickering embers, I ask, 'Did you speak to Thea before you left?'

'Only briefly,' he says quietly. 'With all the chaos, there wasn't much time.'

'What did you tell her?'

Hans looks up from the campfire, his face curtained by shaggy hair. 'About why I was leaving?' I give a curt nod. 'I told her I was going to help you get to wherever you were going. The roads are dangerous for a young woman on her own.'

'Not really a lie, then.'

'No,' he agrees. 'I don't think I could lie to her.'

Guilt curdles in my stomach about leaving my sister with a lie. But before I can self-flagellate, my attention is stolen by a rustling in the undergrowth. A pair of amber eyes peer out from the grass, serrated teeth glinting in the half-light. It's the size of a small child, and there is something vaguely human about it – but its ears are pricked like a dog's and grey fur coats its body.

Hans immediately pushes to his feet. He finds a sharp stone amidst the detritus and hurls it at the creature. It yelps, scurrying off into the undergrowth. I am struck again by his willingness to shield me from danger.

I wrinkle my nose. 'What was that?'

'An *Alp*. Don't you remember when they invaded the village a few years back?'

I do remember. Fifteen at the time, I can still recall the bitter cold. Oma woke us at midnight. We joined the other nightgown-clad women, hand in hand, and wailed our terror at the stars. The Saint slew the Alpe before dawn.

Hans grimaces. 'Alpe wait for people to fall asleep and straddle their chest until they suffocate. They prefer women.'

'Don't all monsters?'

His mouth opens and closes, the words he wants to say forming and evaporating on his tongue. 'I'm sorry.'

'For what?'

'For – for the way men are in Heulensee. I suppose I'm one of them. I don't absolve myself of that. There is more I could do – *should* do. But I do not take the women's sacrifice lightly. I hope it doesn't seem that way.' He takes a breath and dips his gaze. 'I tried to convince Thea to leave with me once.'

My heart stutters. 'And she refused?'

'She was quite put off by me even asking. Said that all the Odenwald women passed their Rite and she didn't think herself above it.'

To think that *duty* kept Thea in Heulensee makes me want to retch. My head spins and I am struck by the same vertigo that befalls me after overindulging in mead.

I pivot the conversation away from Thea, away from the knowledge that my sister could be living an ordinary, unremarkable life when instead she is staring down the barrel of a horrible death.

'How do you know so much about them? The Alpe, and the hanged men?'

He chews on his lip, considering his next words. 'Have you heard of my mother?'

I pause to think and realize that I don't. His father, the blacksmith, is well-known in Heulensee but I cannot conjure an image of his mother. It's as if Hans spawned as a fully formed child. I shake my head.

'They say she died when I was a few years old,' he says, swallowing uncomfortably. 'But she lives. I know she does.'

'How do you know?'

'Father told me when he got roaring drunk. Admitted that he was the catalyst in her banishment.'

My brow furrows. 'He caused her to fail her Rite?'

'She passed her Rite,' Hans says. 'The Pfarrer likes you to believe that once you pass the Rite, you're safe – but you're not. She passed, and he banished her anyway, several years later. He would've done the same to you, had the townsfolk not taken matters into their own hands.'

Hans's face is open and sincere, as it tends to be. There is no trace of deceit. This revelation ought to shock me more, but it doesn't. Not really. I've seen how the Pfarrer looks at women. He sees us as problems to be solved.

'Why did he banish her?'

He grimaces. 'She was obsessed with the Hexenwald. Had a whole field diary filled with observations about it. Father found it and told the Pfarrer – in hopes he'd set her straight. He didn't do anything. Not that father knew at the time, anyway. But they must've been watching her, because a few weeks later, the Pfarrer came back.

'Someone had reported Mother for spreading misinformation

about the Hexenwald. The Pfarrer banished her that night. The public announcement was that she drowned.' Hans sucks his teeth. 'The Pfarrer told my father it was better for people to believe that. That it would be better for *me* if people saw her as a tragic memory, rather than a heretic.'

I braid strands of grass between my fingers. 'Do you miss her?'

He thinks about it, face pensive, and shrugs. 'I miss the idea of her.'

'The idea?'

Hans looks at me strangely. 'You know, the idea of having a mother. Someone who would've told me my drawings were perfect, even though they weren't. Someone who would've soothed me through thunderstorms. Someone who would've wanted more for me than just survival.'

My fingers tighten around the strands of grass. I have been so blinded by Mama's apathy that I didn't realize what a mother *could* be. The way Hans explains it ignites an ache deep in my chest. A childish, plaintive longing.

I wonder if, had Mama been different, *I* might be, too. Once I arrived into the world, unloved and unwanted, perhaps my body sensed that there was no reason to fear anything else; the worst had already taken place.

☠

I do not recall falling asleep – but when I open my eyes, a hazy sun peeks above the trees. It is not a pleasant awakening; I think I would've slept for another hour, were I not wrenched into consciousness by the sound of Hans gagging.

I fly into a sitting position, brow wrinkled in disgust. 'Is that strictly necessary?'

He wipes his mouth with the back of his hand. With the other, he gestures incredulously to the clearing around us.

Something foul happened overnight.

Carcasses bake beneath the morning sun. I cannot discern their origin, or anything other than that they are fleshy with bony protuberances. A low hum rumbles beneath the trees. Only when Hans shifts, disturbing a rotting ribcage, do I realize that the humming is the sound of a million flies. Sheets of them ripple through the air.

As quickly as the flies appeared, they vanish. The carcasses, too. They sink into the ground, flesh melting into earth. The forest consumes. Hans and I exchange a queasy look.

'What's happening?' I whisper.

'I don't know,' he admits. 'Maybe the forest is trying to scare us.'

I'm not scared, but the forest has successfully spoiled my appetite. Hans is somehow able to conjure up a desire to eat. I watch as he chews thoughtfully on a hunk of rye bread.

The sun sheds a hazy light over everything as we set off. Trees cast long, skeletal shadows along our path. Hans spends several minutes deliberating how best to move forward. The mountains cannot be trusted to stay in one place, nor can we rely on the sun. It moves at a strange speed, gliding to the east in one moment and pivoting north the next.

'Water,' he declares, so loudly that I might be startled if I had the propensity for it. 'We'll find running water and follow it. It might not take us to the cuckoo, but at least it will take us away from here.'

Over the course of the morning – I *think* it's morning – the sun loses its milky glaze. Once that hint of the supernatural disappears, I find that if I squint, I can almost believe that the Hexenwald is an ordinary forest. But there is a strange ether in the air, shifting and glistening among the trees. The intrusion of my gaze stirs it, whirling between the trunks in ephemeral coils.

By the time my stomach starts to rumble, we track the dulcet babbling of water to its source. A river winds through the undergrowth. I let out a triumphant laugh, but it dies in my throat as I look closer. The water flows against the confines of gravity, moving steadily uphill.

This realization troubles Hans more than any that have come before. He faced the hanged men with grim determination and chased off the Alp with calculated anger. But now, as he throws a stick into the river and watches water drag it uphill, his façade slips.

'Impossible.' His throat bobs. He kneels and places a hand in the water, as if his will alone can right the flow. 'That doesn't make sense.'

'Nothing here does.' I wait a span of breaths for Hans to compose himself, but he doesn't. I gently prompt him. 'Shall we keep going?'

'Yes.' A weary sigh passes his lips. 'Let's keep going.'

Traversing the Hexenwald is torturous, even for the unfearing. There is nothing to indicate that we've made any progress; each tree is a carbon copy of the one beside it. Every now and then, we notice a pond or a fallen branch identical to one we spotted hours – or perhaps days – earlier. At first, we make note and convince ourselves of small discrepancies. On our third time passing the pond, we cease to mention it. Subconsciously, we both know we are stuck in a loop that we're powerless to escape.

I cannot remember how many times we set up and dismantle our camp. The only way to mark the time is by the rapid vanishing of food in my knapsack. This morning, I finished the last aniseed-infused slices of *Schüttelbrot*. One stale hunk of rye bread remains. Hans has largely been subsisting off his own supplies, so I wager that we've been in the Hexenwald a week. I'm not sure if it feels more like thirty minutes or a year.

Twenty-two days left. Twenty-two days to save my sister, and our efforts have thus far been fruitless. I express this to Hans, my hands shaking at my sides. He likens the Hexenwald to quicksand; the more we struggle, the deeper we'll sink. On his advice, I try to nurture optimism – until I notice that his hands are shaking, too.

There *is* change in the Hexenwald, even though we are stuck traversing the same trail over and over. There is a cyclical passing of seasons – but not seasons as we know them beyond the forest. Hans and I name the seasons we observe, believing that it might tip the scales in our favour.

We realize the rancid carcasses that appeared on our first morning form the Rot season, a time of sordid decay. Dark corners fester, insects hum. Next comes the False season. Mewling and innocent, the forest plays clement. Fawns stumble and nose at our pockets. Birds perch on our shoulders and sing the most beautiful harmonies. Handsome men and women beckon, begging us to stay a little longer. I watch them roll on soft beds of clover. Hans shuts his eyes.

Though he detests the False season, what comes next is worse. During the Fear season, the birds begin to scream. *Everything* screams. The trees we chop for firewood bleed scarlet, moaning at each swing of the axe. Hans claws at his throat, so consumed by terror that he can barely breathe. My chest cavity echoes with silence.

A shimmering, iridescent Ether season finishes the cycle. The air thickens, cloying in my throat with each breath. It tastes like blueberries and spun sugar. The sun and moon hang central in the sky, never rising or falling. We lose track of time, walking until we can't any longer, or sleeping until we can barely remember our names. Sometimes, it makes us laugh until our ribcages ache; other times, like this morning, it robs us of the ability to think clearly.

'What are we doing?'

Hans's voice distracts me from my breakfast. Another four days have passed, I think, based on my cyclical hunger rearing its head once a day. Subsisting off foul apples and the sickly rabbits we're able to snare, Hans is a shadow of the man he once was: all sharp lines, gaunt eyes, a jaw full of stubble. Delirium has settled over the both of us, spurred on by our empty bellies and the depths of the Ether season.

'What do you mean?'

'This.' He gestures at the clearing around us. We have tried walking upstream, downstream and abandoning the river altogether – but no matter what, we end up in the same place. We have revisited this clearing at least five times. 'What are we *doing*?'

My eyelids flutter. I try to summon a response, but the words are like treacle in my throat. 'Saving Thea.'

'But we're not, Ilse. We're walking in circles!' Hans stands and flings his half-eaten apple to the floor. I think that's the last of our fruit, but I don't dare mention it. 'Why aren't you bothered? How is this happening?'

I shake my head, disturbing the ether which gauzes the clearing. My tongue feels too large in my mouth. 'I'm not sure.'

I try to think past the uncanny fog as it coils around my temples. I start with easy things: what is my name? I say it aloud, *Ill-zuh*, but it feels awkward and heavy once it's hanging in the air. Why am I in the Hexenwald? To find my fear. Why do I need to do that? To save my sister. I'm quite pleased with my clarity until realization settles over me: I can't picture Thea's face.

I can conjure up the shape of her, but not the colour of her eyes, the profile of her nose, the tilt of her lips. Nausea builds in my stomach.

'Hans,' I whisper, the word scratching up my throat, 'I can't remember what Thea looks like.'

Hans looks at me, wild-eyed. 'That's impossible.'

'What colour are her eyes?'

He scoffs. But then he opens his mouth to tell me that they are blue or green or brown – and the words don't come. He swallows hard. Clutches at his head. 'I'll remember in a moment.'

'What colour are they, Hans?' I ask, urgency heightening my pitch. The fact that neither of us can summon the answer makes my breaths unsteady.

'Her eyes are . . .' He pauses, clutching at his head. 'No, no, *no*. Why can't I picture her face? Her voice?'

I can only watch as Hans blunders round the clearing, eyes wild. He squares up to one of the spruce trees, chest fluttering. 'You will not take her from me!'

'Hans, stop—'

'What will it take for you to let us go?' A vein in his temple flickers. He wraps a hand around one of the spruce's lowest branches and tears it from the trunk. The splitting of wood rumbles like thunder through the atmosphere. Before I can stop him, Hans takes the jagged branch and drags it across his palm.

'Is it my blood you want? Will that sate you? Take it. Go ahead, drink up.'

The flash of red jerks me into action. I fling myself across the clearing and wrench the branch from Hans before he can do any more harm. Ether swells around us, pulsing at our feet in a blanket of shimmering mist.

'Stop,' I say weakly, exhaustion hitting me all at once. A cuckoo calls out somewhere overhead.

Cu-ckoo.

'Stop?' He fastens one hand around my wrist and pulls me through the trees, laughing hysterically. 'We can't stop now, Ilse.'

Cu-ckoo.

Hans clenches his fist, letting scarlet rivulets drip, drip, drip onto the forest floor. As soon as they land, the earth absorbs them – hungry strands of grass pulling apart like teeth, then reforming around the blood. We watch them, silently.

'I think that helped,' he whispers, although his eyes are still clouded. 'I feel clearer, now. You should try it.'

A breath rattles past my lips. 'I don't think you should've done that, Hans.'

'The forest likes me now,' he argues. 'Here – let me help you.'

He reaches for the branch to pierce my skin. I swat him away. 'Not yet,' I protest weakly. 'I'm too tired.'

My desperate attempts to fight the exhaustion are futile. It feels like an impossibly heavy blanket has been slung across my body. My feet are unsteady beneath me. I sink to the grass with my rucksack still on my back. Moss compresses beneath me.

I whisper, 'I think . . . I think I'm going to rest now.'

Cu-ckoo.

'What do you mean *rest*? We need to find' – I hear Hans hit the floor, his teeth clacking together – 'Where am I?'

Cu-ckoo.

'Such a nice sound,' I muse. My eyes grow bleary. The leaves above stir in a shimmer of green as the cuckoo takes flight.

Leaves. Not needles. An ash tree spreads its boughs above me. It's the most beautiful thing I've ever seen. I'm not sure if it's just because it's different – a deciduous sentinel among evergreens – or if there's something more to my infatuation. Emerald leaves whisper sweet nothings to the breeze. I'm struck by the sense that I want to spend my life in its shade. To have it shed leaves on me in autumn, to drink raindrops off its boughs in the spring.

'Do you see that tree?'

'See what?' Hans raves. 'All I see is this Saintsforsaken fog!'

I register the distant call of *cu-ckoo* and the gentle rustling of leaves above. I stand, not of my own volition, and cross the clearing to my sister's soulmate. The look on Hans's face reminds me of the wolves Papa caught in his snares. Dangerous and terrified all at once.

I place my hands around his jaw. For a moment, I think he might snap and plunge his teeth into my hand. Instead, he softens under my touch. I guide his head until he looks straight at the ash tree. His pupils dilate. His pulse thrums steadily beneath my fingers.

'I see it.'

I tilt my head. 'We haven't encountered that before, have we?'

'I don't think so.'

I release his face and turn on my heel. He calls after me, but I cannot make sense of his words. Inexplicably, I am consumed by the tree. I want to feel its leaves brush against my face, to trace the contours of its bark with my fingers. Hans's protests grow louder, more insistent, but I don't care. I am driven by a force I cannot comprehend. If I can just touch it, everything will be better. Everything will be *safe*.

There is a distortion in the bark – barely visible, a welt risen from the skin. Breath caged, I approach with a hand outstretched. My fingers brush the trunk, wood warm beneath my fingers.

Wrong. Wrong, wrong, wrong.

Bark sloughs from the tree. The distortion – the *figure* – separates from the trunk. It towers over me, eyes the colour of ivy bearing down. All the ether in the clearing surges towards it, drawn to its body like moths to a flame.

'Ilse!' Hans shouts from behind me. I hear the warning in his voice but cannot heed it. I am a fly, intoxicated by the scent of a carnivorous plant which is bound to swallow me whole.

'A visitor,' the being croaks, voice as coarse as the bark lining its skin. 'The first in many years. Come to steal my boughs?'

I hold out my arms in an attempt at mediation. The being matches my pose, their woody fingers sprout leaves and lengthen into tendrils. They wrap around my wrist, anchoring me to the spot. Steadfast as the tree it came from, the being is unfazed by the weight of me. It lifts me into the air. My legs dangle helplessly.

The creature draws a deep breath, inhaling all the ether. As it clears, so does my head, and I suddenly realize what a mess I've gotten myself into.

'Fight, Ilse!' comes Hans's frantic voice. 'For Thea!'

Thea. Her face fills my head, and I suddenly understand why I cannot feed this ancient beast. Without my flesh and bone, I cannot save my sister.

'Hold on, Ilse!'

I turn just in time to see Hans lunging, sword extended. A sapling bursts free from the earth and coils around his leg like a snake, rooting him to the spot. So much for my knight in shining armour.

With my spare hand, I reach for my knapsack, searching for my penknife. All I can find is the sprig of juniper. If it repels Hexen on Hexennacht – and Thea desperately believes it does – maybe it will protect me from this beast.

I brandish the bouquet. 'Back off. Let me go.'

The creature falters. It lowers me until I am level with its eyes. They are beautiful and dangerous; molten pools of green, deep as the swamp west of Heulensee that swallows children whole.

'An offering?' it creaks.

I nod fervently, if only because I'm not sure what else to do. The tendrils around my wrist loosen. Tentative relief buds inside my chest.

'Give it to me,' the creature demands.

I extend my clenched fist and open my hand. The sprigs of juniper rustle in the wind. More tendrils burst from the creature's midriff; they snake around the juniper and absorb it. My palm is left bare.

'It has been so long . . .' the creature whispers.

Bark gives way to dark skin – *human* skin – and the tendril limbs disappear. My knees crack as I hit the floor. Above me, the creature continues to change; dark, tightly coiled hair sprouts from its head, its features become human, and its eyes mellow to a mossy hue.

The woman looks down at me, her naked chest rising and falling heavily. She is still much taller than me, with a slender frame and toned abdomen. I try not to look any lower than that, on account of her nudity. She inspects her hand beneath the sunlight and uses it to graze the skin on her arms. There is something otherworldly about her, even in human form. Being in her orbit makes me feel utterly inadequate – as if I should apologize for my banal existence.

'Human,' she sighs, voice like a summer's breeze. 'Almost human.' The air ripples around her, shimmering and dancing with each shift of her body. She leans down and traces the line of my jaw with a long fingernail. Goosebumps raise in its wake. 'You're quite beautiful, aren't you?'

It takes a moment to register that she's speaking to me. My heart lurches against my chest so suddenly I think it might break the skin. I've never looked in the mirror and seen beauty – just all the ways I differ from Thea. My untamed copper waves against her poker-straight blonde; my round hips compared to her lithe frame; my common hazel eyes, the muddied waters to her crystal blue.

I am so busy taking the woman in – *all* in – that I have to force my gaze to meet hers. Those emerald eyes threaten to consume me whole.

'Cat got your tongue?' She cocks her head to one side. 'I hardly believe that someone with the knowledge, never mind the guts, to liberate an *Eschenfrau* would be lost for words over a simple compliment.' The woman exhales, amusement playing at her lips. 'How did you know?'

Eschenfrau: ash-tree woman. I recall the word whispered over bonfires as a child. Eschenfrauen are creatures said to live in the Hexenwald: women whose bodies and souls are fused with an ash tree.

My words come out as a stuttered cacophony. Something other than fear makes me lose my grip on language. 'Kn-know what?'

'You offered me a gift. You *released* me.' She reaches for me again with a willowy hand, but stops just short, as if she senses a danger I cannot. 'Now I am in your debt. What would you have in return?'

Bargaining with a creature of the Hexenwald seems ill-advised. From what little I know, they are experts in manipulation and half-truths. But what choice do I have? This creature – this woman – is the first progress we've made. If I want to save Thea, I need to be reckless. To be the sort of person the village would welcome with open arms.

I cast a wild-eyed glance over my shoulder to see Hans caught somewhere between intrigue and horror. I need to soothe him, somehow. Perhaps if I can humanize this creature, learn her origins and name, it will ease his fear. Papa always told me not to name our animals because it made them too familiar. I never listened, of course.

'Do you have a name?'

The woman frowns. 'You do not need my name.'

She doesn't intend to make this easy. I drag in a deep breath. If she will not familiarize herself, I will do it for her. The ash tree she blossomed from fresh in my mind, I name her aloud. 'Then I will call you Ash.'

Heat explodes through the clearing. Before I can react, Ash's hand is at my throat. She hoists me up against a tree, my weight inconsequential. Her stare burns. She sees past all pretence – straight through my mask and right to the core of my being. Behind her, Hans has used his sword to saw through the roots that snared him. He creeps forward, breath bated, ready to strike.

Ash flicks her free hand towards Hans. Roots burst from the earth, knocking him out cold. If nothing else, at least he will die peacefully.

'I agree to help you and you *bind* me?'

I scrabble uselessly against her fingers, regretful I didn't take a deeper breath before she pinned me. 'Bind you?'

'Do not play the fool,' she snarls.

'I only gave you a name!'

She fixes me with a hard stare. My limbs turn to liquid. Her grip at my throat tightens, tightens, and then releases. Ash distances herself with a tut. She looks down at me as if I am an insect she cannot decide whether to ignore or step on.

'I thought you were malicious,' she drawls, 'but you are merely stupid. I do not know which is worse.'

I rub at my throat, where the imprints of her hands join my marks from the hanged man. I am not sure what my neck did to deserve a repeated wringing. 'What did I do wrong?'

'You released me from imprisonment,' she says, affecting a mocking sing-song one might use when conversing with a particularly dim child, 'and I offered you something in return. But before I could make good on our bargain, you decided to name me, and therefore bound me.'

'That's real?' It's the same reason Thea named me Elke on Hexennacht. I knew the tradition was related to the idea of tethering creatures of the Hexenwald – but I didn't think the act held any true power.

'Of course it's real. Go on, then,' she says drily, eyes narrowed.

'Go on what?'

She throws her arms up. 'Our binding needs terms. What will you ask of me?'

'Can't I just . . . un-bind you?'

She blinks back at me, long lashes fanning across her under-eyes. 'Unless you're doing a particularly good job of concealing innate magical ability, then no. You cannot unbind me. If you refuse to set the terms of this bond, I will be compelled to follow you wherever you go – though I can assure you I won't make for pleasant company.'

I consider our predicament, though quiet contemplation is difficult when the woman – Ash – is looking down at me, her agitated breaths whisking across my face. She might be able to help me find my fear, but I don't know if that's specific enough. I could ask her to help me save Thea – but I don't trust her not to misconstrue my terms.

'A bloodthirsty Saint lives in my village,' I tell her, picking delicately over each word. 'I need your help to stop it from killing any more girls.' This, I decide, is my best chance of a catch-all solution.

Ash grits her teeth. 'The task you have assigned to me might take weeks, or months, or years.'

'It can't,' I tell her. 'We only have eighteen days.'

This seems to appease her; she irons out the furrows of her brow. 'Very well, then.'

I relay everything I know – that I was born unfearing, that I must alter myself to save my sister, that the cuckoo is the key. She tilts her head, one dark brow raised in question.

'I know nothing of a cuckoo,' she says. The optimism exits my body in a great wave. 'But there is someone who might. He understands the back roads of this forest better than any.'

An unsteady breath rattles my lungs. 'Will you take us to him?'

She considers it, green eyes roaming hungrily across the clearing. One bare foot extended, she wriggles her toes. 'You have bound me, but I am not a chaperone. If you can keep up, you may follow. Do not expect me to slow to your human pace.'

Ash shakes her hair. Leaves fall from her tresses. One lands on her shoulder and multiplies, forming a natural woven fabric that unfolds to cover the contours of her body. The resulting outfit is not unlike the dirndl we wear in Heulensee, except hers is rendered in shades of forest green, of teal, of jade. A gossamer blouse lies beneath a tight-fitting bodice with a lace-up front. A loose skirt skims her calves.

Behind us, Hans stirs with a groan. Ash considers him with a grimace.

'This is my friend,' I explain, gesturing to Hans as he hauls himself to his feet. My claiming him as a friend catches us both by surprise. 'His name is Hans.'

'Well, tell Hans to hurry up. We need to make progress before nightfall.'

I help Hans gather his belongings and shoulder my rucksack. We scurry behind Ash as she stalks off into the trees.

'Fantastic,' Hans mutters. 'Now our only hope is to follow this tree-demon into the forest and—'

'Tread lightly, boy. My time as an Eschenfrau left me with some useful tricks.' Ash half-turns to face us and flexes her hand, prompting her fingers to lengthen into jagged shards of wood. 'I can think of a few awfully inconvenient places for a splinter.'

Hans flushes scarlet. He hastens his pace, keener to keep up with Ash than he'd like to admit. His gait is more fluid than mine; I move as though I'm wading through waist-deep water.

'It feels easier now,' he says brightly, perhaps hoping Ash will overhear. 'Less like the forest is trying to hold me down.'

I nod in agreement, though secretly, I feel just as burdened by the forest as I did before. That feeling takes physical form:

despite walking at the same pace, Ash and Hans grow smaller and smaller as they gain distance. The forest pins me in place. My legs move beneath me, but I cover no ground.

'I can't move!' I shout.

Hans and Ash turn back to face me. The former jogs to my side, the latter rubs an exasperated hand across her face before sauntering over. Ash studies me, eyes flicking across each of my features. Suddenly, she takes my wrist between her fingers. My skin alights, heart cavorting inside my chest – no doubt the impact of the mystical power she possesses.

Attempting authority, I tell her, 'I do not appreciate you using magic on me.'

Ash pauses, a smirk tugging at the corner of her lips. 'I only touched you, Ilse.'

My cheeks flare. The feeling does not subside as she inspects my forearms, my biceps, my calves. Her inspection comes to an end on my palms, where she traces the joints of my knuckles with a sharp nail. A shiver courses up my spine.

'Of course you can't move.' She tuts. 'You haven't made your sacrifice.'

I let my hand fall back to my side, slightly breathless. 'Sacrifice?'

Ash draws a deep breath and pinches the bridge of her nose. I stare at her blankly; she rolls her eyes. 'The forest charges a toll. If you hope to traverse it, you must sacrifice something.'

'But Hans didn't sacrifice anything. Why can he move?'

'Yes, he did.'

Ash takes his hand. She holds it up to us.

'Was it before or after cutting yourself, Hans,' Ash says, lips drawn tight, 'that the forest let you advance?'

'After.' His throat bobs as he swallows. Ash stares at him, deadpan, until he realizes. 'The blood was my sacrifice. It actually worked...'

Ash drops his hand like a lead weight. 'Correct.' She glances my way. 'If he is the shrewder of you two, we are truly damned.'

I reach for my penknife. 'So I, too, should give my blood?'

'No,' Ash snaps. She takes a deep breath before continuing. 'Something else.'

'Why?'

'Offering your blood can invite the forest in,' she explains. 'If it gets into your wound, it can infect you. *He* was lucky. You may not be. Pick something else. Something meaningful.'

If anyone would have the good fortune to avoid infection, it would be Hans. I don't need to rifle through my rucksack to know that I possess nothing of any value. My hand drifts to Oma's barrette where it's fastened in my hair.

No. Not that. It's the last piece of her I possess. Instead, I look at the penknife in my hand. A lump builds in my throat.

'Is that important to you?' Ash asks.

'Yes.' I curse the way my voice breaks. 'It belonged to my papa.'

Ash's gaze softens. It's the most human she has looked.

Gifting me this penknife was the only affection Papa ever gave – and even then, it was more of a practicality. That act represented everything worth knowing about Papa. A knife for a girl so emotionally stunted she did not know how to love or be loved – but at least she could make people bleed. There is so much anger, so much power, pent up in that little blade.

Leaving the knife tucked against the trunk of a spruce should feel like catharsis. Instead, all the violence seems to leach from the blade, back into my blood.

Ash twists the ball of her bare foot against the earth. 'The forest is pleased.'

With that, she sets off again. I barely have time to give the penknife a backward glance before I shoulder my knapsack and run after her. Hans follows close behind, clutching his belongings beneath each arm.

Ash sets a torturous pace. Her legs are impossibly long, and she covers the ground like a draft horse. I follow her with bated breath, ready for her to disappear into the trees while the forest keeps me rooted in place, patrolling the same stretch of haunted land until the end of time – but suddenly, I'm moving.

Our surroundings change. For the first time the Hexenwald takes us somewhere new.

CHAPTER NINE

We walk until the forest grows so dark that I can barely make out my own feet. I ask Ash if we can rest for the night; she's irritated by my request, but acquiesces. Ash promptly lays down in the grass while Hans and I spread out our bedrolls. She and I end up face to face, separated by mere feet.

She studies me, but not in the way people usually do. Whenever people look my way, it's a dissection. A futile attempt to decipher why I unsettle them. They venture stolen glances, afraid of what I'll do if I catch them. Ash, on the other hand, observes me without shame. Her stare is blatant and intrusive.

'What is it?' I whisper, my voice barbed in anticipation.

'Even though you did something awfully stupid,' she murmurs, 'I find myself intrigued by you.'

The honesty of her response softens me into laughter. I stifle it with the back of my hand, lest I wake Hans up.

She props herself up, one arm braced against the earth. 'Why are you laughing?'

'I didn't expect you to be so frank,' I explain. Then, self-indulgently, I ask her, 'Why are you intrigued?'

Ash twirls one of her black curls around her fingers. 'Well, you already know I find you beautiful.' This reaffirmation makes me draw my cloak up around my mouth, self-conscious and giddy at once. 'But there is something else about you. Something other than your lack of forward thinking. I can't put my finger on it.'

'Well,' I release a shaky breath, 'I suppose I'm intrigued by you, too.'

'Is that so?' Her lips curl into a smile. 'Just as well, given that we're bound together for the foreseeable future.' She lowers herself back down onto the grass, stretching her arms above her head until the joints pop. 'Goodnight, Ilse.'

Almost immediately, her chest rises and falls with the even tempo of sleep. Rest does not find me so easily. I toss and turn, unsettled by the sudden tightness of my chest. The night passes in flashes: I wake once to a blood-red moon, then to Hans sitting upright in his bedroll, then to utter darkness.

The next time I open my eyes, I am floating on the lake's surface. Thea calls for me from the shore, but I can't find the strength to swim back to her. When I look down, there are ropes tied to my ankles. I sink like a stone. The light dissipates, leaving nothing but cold, black water. Even as the lake invades my lungs, I do not feel fear. I hate myself for it. *Let it end*, I scream into the black, my rage a storm that I will not surface from. *Let me—*

'Ilse!'

My body jerks into consciousness. I inhale raggedly, if only to prove that I can, and bolt upright. How I *wish* that my skin was glazed with sweat after the nightmare. A raised heart rate, a singular goosebump, the prickle of hairs at my nape – any of these tells would be rapturous. But I am hollow, save for the residual rage from my dream.

Unaware of my inner turmoil, Hans stands with a knife in one hand, the other cupped to his brow, staring at the sky. Light filters through the trees above in a way that suggests it's daytime, but the clouds are stained red.

They always are before the Hexenwald breaches.

'It's been like this for hours,' he muses. 'Nothing's happened.'

I am struck by the casualness of his observation. Thea would be shrieking, Mama swearing, Oma...

The image of her limp body between the Saint's teeth guts me. I lock her memory away somewhere distant, where I am not responsible for her death. Where I was a good granddaughter, and Oma died peacefully of old age.

Hans's nonchalance should not shock me. Men have never been expected to lay their fear bare the way women do. We present ours proudly; theirs festers beneath the surface until it ruptures.

'You let me sleep in,' I accuse, dragging my eyes away from the clouds.

'You needed it.' Hans shrugs. He begins grinding the dagger he holds against a whetstone. 'This blade is for you, by the way. I know it's not your father's penknife, but it's helped me in a bind. Better than nothing.'

I eye him warily, the way a doe eyes a wolf – though we both know I'm the one with sharp teeth. 'You didn't need to.'

He raises a brow, glances at me, then back to the knife. 'Why does my kindness offend you?'

'No one is kind to me. Not without a price.'

'Thea is,' Hans protests.

'She pays the price of being my sister. Having to spend her entire life hiding my true nature.'

He stops sharpening and stares back at me, contemplating. 'You're a funny sort, Ilse Odenwald.'

I scowl. There is little to pack into my knapsack, but I make a great show of it. Before long I am finished my task and forced to face Hans again. He presses my new dagger into my palm. I notice he's bandaged the self-inflicted wound on his hand. Scarlet bleeds through the gauze. My stomach clenches.

'Ilse,' he says softly. 'I am not giving you this because I want something, or because I pity you. I am giving it to you because I care about you. We're the only ones we can trust in here.'

I avoid his gaze in my emotionally stunted way, even though my heart stirs at his words. He is a difficult man to be cold to. 'Thank you.'

'Now, you can carry my courage with you.' He grins lopsidedly.

'I'll need it,' I tell him, and I mean it. The dagger's weight is a comforting presence in my hand. I'm concerned Hans might say something else heartfelt so I quickly change the subject. 'Have you seen Ash?'

'She's ...' – he wrinkles his nose and points into the trees – 'over there.'

I raise a brow at him and trudge across the clearing. For a minute, I think he has me fooled until I spot Ash, spread out in the grass. Entirely naked.

Her rich brown skin is perfectly smooth and unblemished. Tight coils of dark hair spread out in a halo around her head, and her chest – heavens, her chest – flutters with gentle breaths. Her hands rest on her navel, just above the line of her hips.

'What are you doing?' I splutter, heat racing through my body.

'Photosynthesizing,' she murmurs, voice gentle as the rustle of leaves.

My cheeks redden. I turn my eyes to the sky, focusing on the patchwork of branches overhead. Keeping my gaze upwards is a battle. 'Can we depart?'

Ash turns her head and closes her eyes. 'Mm.'

I wait for her follow-up, but it doesn't come. My eyes drift away from her face, grazing the sharp line of her collarbone, lower—

One eye peeled open, Ash asks, 'Do I *intrigue* you this morning, Ilse?'

I choke, cheeks flushing. 'We really should leave."

'You seem flustered.' She sits up, stretching her arms in a wide arc above her head. The muscles of her torso pull taut. My breaths grow erratic, beating their way up my throat. 'Is something the matter?'

'It's just that I am constrained for time,' I explain, 'and I really need to find the cuckoo.'

'A time frame to find a cuckoo,' she says dreamily. 'What a strange thing.'

'It is not a real cuckoo,' I remind her, though as the words leave my mouth, I'm struck by the fact that it *could* be a cuckoo. Nothing makes sense to me in the Hexenwald. 'It will help me discover my fear.'

Her gaze wanders languorously up and down my form. A mischievous smile wrinkles the skin by her eyes. 'Self-discovery has no time limit.'

I pause, feeling as if her words have a double meaning that I cannot discern. Agitation ripples through me.

'This is not a matter of self-discovery. If I do not change myself – if I cannot find my fear – my sister will die.'

I wait for her to fix me with a strange look, or to make some trite comment about fear being human nature. Instead, she simply smiles. 'You should have said so.'

Ash yawns, stretches, and clambers to her feet. She is utterly at home in her skin. I envy that. I have always seen my body as something shameful. Even when I'm on my own, my naked form feels clandestine. Her willowy form is what I've always aspired to. I trace the soft curve of her calves, the expanse of her thighs – I screw my eyes shut.

Don't look, I tell myself. *Do. Not. Look.*

But why must I wrestle my eyes from her frame? Perhaps it's the fact that this is forbidden. My being here, conversing with her. I cannot explain it any other way. She must sense the pressure of my gaze, for she flashes me a crooked smile.

I flush an even deeper shade of scarlet.

Ash once again magics clothes into existence, which is probably for the best. This time she wears a long, sage-coloured dress with sleeves that billow as she leads us through the forest.

We walk for the whole morning, and most of the afternoon. The Hexenwald's treasures make my collection back home look dull. I find a nest strewn with bright turquoise feathers; a geode which cracks open the second I touch it, revealing a molten interior; a tiny bird's skull with spiralling horns attached to it. I'm desperate to pocket at least *some* of these wonders for my collection, but each time I go to touch a specimen, Hans hisses at me like an exasperated mother.

When he's not monitoring my every move, Hans struggles through the trees. Thorns tear at his cloak, and rogue breezes cause branches to whip across his cheeks. He throws foul looks my way each time he catches me snickering, though secretly, I think he likes making me laugh.

Ash occasionally summons my attention, showing me beetles the size of my fist with glittering carapaces; snakes that wear rabbit fur rather than scales; flowers that smell like *Apfelstrudel*. She doesn't explain why she is showing me these things – simply watches me with a burning intensity, as if there's a specific response I'm supposed to exhibit. I think our dynamic mimics a cat dropping some poor deceased prey at its human's feet. An aloof display of affection. Or perhaps that's my wishful thinking.

As evening begins as a pinkish suggestion in the sky, Ash comes to a screeching halt. I have been following her quite doggedly, which I convince myself has nothing to do with the fact that her dress is ever so slightly see-through when the light hits it, hypnotic as a crackling fire. My proximity means that I have to veer to the right to avoid colliding with her back. Just as I pass her she flings out an arm, blocking me from taking another step.

When I look down, I understand why: a large, serrated fissure of indiscernible depth spits ether inches from my feet.

'Is that the tear?' Hans asks, voice hushed. 'The origin of the infection in this forest?'

When Ash doesn't answer, I glance up at her, only to find she's already watching me. More specifically, she's staring at her own fingers where they're hooked tightly around my waist. Now that I've noticed them perched there, it's all I can think about. Something *stirs*. A tickle of heat beneath my blouse. A whisper of goosebumps across my arms.

Ash meets my eyes, a hint of a smile at her lips. I manage to hold her gaze for all of a split second before my eyes dart away of their own accord.

'Hello?' Hans snaps his fingers. 'Has the ether addled your brains?'

Ash clears her throat, peeling her fingers from my skin. It's like she's thrown a cold bucket of water over me. 'It is the tear, yes. And you'd do well not to fall into it.'

She clears the fissure in a nimble leap and offers me her hand. I take it gladly, placing far too much stock in the way her hand curls around mine. Hans makes the jump by himself, landing with a grunt.

We continue through the trees, eventually emerging into a meadow. The air tenses around us as we cross its boundary. Impossibly green grass shimmers with each touch of the wind. Wild-eyed hares sit to attention against a backdrop of ivory anemones with butter-yellow hearts. Beyond, the mountain peaks are dusted white. Everything is quiet; even the breeze seems to whisper. It's a scene so serene that I begin to wonder if we've entered the False season, but it seems as if the microclimates that grip the Hexenwald do not touch this place.

Ash looks at me expectantly. 'It reminds you of home?'

Despite its splendour, there is something unnatural about the meadow. Something that screams *not home*. 'It doesn't feel like the Hexenwald.'

She seems pleased with my observation; a slight smile curves her lips. When she directs it towards me, I swear my heart falters. 'This place is protected from the worst the Hexenwald has to offer.'

'How are *you* here, then?' Hans asks, half-teasing.

Ash rolls her eyes. We traverse the rocky track that winds across the meadow. A wooden hut emerges over the hump of a hill. Planters hang from each window, overflowing with red and white flowers. The garden is similarly wild, only stifled by the picket fence at its edges. Many years ago, someone must have painted it bright blue. Time and rain have sapped the colour, but the hut's white door and shutters look to have been freshly painted. The air is sweet, almost cloying, all wildflowers and cut grass.

'Thea would love this,' Hans says softly.

When I look over to see him soft-eyed and sentimental, his emotion infects me. Suddenly, there's a lump in my throat, and I think I'm about to cry on account of a house. But he's right: she would love this. She'd paint the shutters emerald green or rosy pink, and grow sunflowers in the garden. I can almost see her smiling back at me from the windows, beckoning me inside.

Mustering up all my optimism, I tell him, 'You'll have to build her one just like it when this is all over.'

He smiles. I see the image taking root behind his eyes. 'A reminder of our time in the forest.'

'Are you going in,' Ash says, 'or do you plan to waste the last of the light on sentimentality?' She yawns, a sound more groaning tree than human, and lowers herself into the meadow grass. 'I need more sunlight before it's all gone for the day. He's inside the house. Bring him out here once you're finished; I'd like to speak with him.'

Hans clears his throat. 'What exactly are we walking into?'

'A house,' Ash replies.

I stifle a laugh. Her honesty is a double-edged sword.

He throws her a sullen look; Ash returns one twice as foul. 'Let me clarify: what, or *who*, is inside the house?'

Her lids flutter shut. 'A man.'

'Ash,' I say, gently.

She peels one eye open, flashing a smirk that makes me splutter. 'A Hexe. He has—'

Hans wraps a hand around the hilt of his sword. 'You are sending us into the den of a *Hexe*? Did you not think to mention the risk of impending death? I knew you weren't to be trusted!'

The fear on Hans's face quickly distils to anger. I press a hand to my temple, trying to push down the pain budding beneath my skull. Of *course* the solution to our problems is a Hexe. It couldn't be easy, could it?

Ash sits up and wrinkles her nose. She finds amusement in Hans the way a cat plays with a mouse before it bites its head off. 'What do you know of Hexen?'

'I know that they are bloodthirsty, murderous creatures with a penchant for human flesh,' Hans spits. 'I have seen them descend on Heulensee's shores, poised to deliver destruction.'

Ash barks out a laugh devoid of humour. 'How typical of a human to hate something they have never seen. Hexen cannot leave the Hexenwald. I do not know what you saw, but it was not a Hexe.'

Not a Hexe? I study Ash's expression and find no trace of deceit.

Hans folds his arms across his chest, similarly confused. 'I . . . we' – he points emphatically in my direction – 'saw three women, levitating above the ground, eyes white as milk. What is that, if not a Hexe?'

She shrugs. 'I am not omniscient.'

'You promise . . .' I ask, stepping forward. 'You promise the creatures on our shores weren't Hexen?'

'Hexen cannot leave the forest,' she repeats. 'They are part of the Hexenwald. The minute they leave its bounds, blisters consume their skin – a withdrawal symptom brought on by the lack of ether. They would be dead long before reaching your inconsequential little town.' When the tension does not leave Hans's face, she turns to me and says, 'We are bound, Ilse. Your goal has become my goal. Lying to you serves me no purpose.'

It's true. Despite Ash's 'intrigue', I cannot imagine she wants to remain bound to me eternally. Beginning our working relationship with deceit wouldn't make any sense – not if she wants to dissolve this bond as quickly as possible.

Tentatively, Hans says, 'So, we have never laid eyes upon a Hexe?'

'Well ...' Amusement returns to her face, cheeks dimpling, 'You have now.'

It takes three seconds for the realization to sink in. '*You're* a Hexe?'

Hans's expression tells me I'm not as unsettled by this revelation as I should be. For me, it is a welcome explanation. Everything falls into place: the way Ash moves, the power her eyes exert, the aura she radiates. *This* is why she sets me on edge. Why I am simultaneously bewitched and intrigued by her.

'Oh, come now,' Ash mutters. 'You thought I was human?'

Hans huffs, drawing a hand through his hair. His other hand tightens around the hilt of his sword, and though I don't think he'll use it, I hurry to defuse the tension. 'Perhaps our fury towards Hexen is misplaced,' I say. 'Besides, if Hexen can help us save Thea ...'

Jaw clenched, Hans stares me down. Thea is his weakness, just as she is mine. 'Fine.'

I let out the breath I have been holding. 'Let's go, then.'

Ash smiles sweetly at Hans. 'Don't let the Hexen bite.'

CHAPTER TEN

I push open the garden gate and wince at its long, drawn-out *creeeeak*. A trail of stepping stones lead me to the front door. Unsure of the etiquette for visiting powerful supernatural beings' homes, I rap the lion's-head knocker tentatively three times.

After seconds of silence from within the house, I turn to Hans for guidance. He twists his mouth and gestures for me to try again. Once the second knock goes unanswered, he shimmies past me to try the handle.

The door swings open.

Hans stumbles back, shrinking from whatever he fears lies within. His reaction is out of character, and we both sense it. He swallows loudly.

I try not to let concern show on my face. 'Are you okay?'

He begins to nod his head, then shakes it. 'I'm . . . scared.'

I almost tell him 'that isn't like you' – but I don't think he needs me to emphasize the obvious. Maybe the impacts of the last Fear season linger in his blood.

Hans hurries to add, 'And I don't trust Ash. Neither of us should.'

Sensing a resolution for his obvious trepidation, I suggest that I go in by myself. 'You should guard the entrance. Keep an eye on Ash.' Hans likes to be useful. To feel needed.

'I can't let you go in there alone,' he mutters.

'I'll be fine.' I produce his dagger from a pocket sewn into my skirt, wiggling it in front of his face. 'I've got your protection with me.'

He hesitates for a long moment, but then smiles softly, eyes lingering on the blade. 'The second you sense danger, shout for me. Promise?'

I shake his hand. 'Promise.'

I cross the threshold into the cottage. I am in a living room, but it's unlike any living room I've ever seen. It's like stepping into a greenhouse; steam heavy in the air, everything distorted by an orange haze. Honey lingers on my tongue. The wooden floorboards are worn from use, with a distinct line tracing the route from the front door towards the back of the house. Stairs lead up to a second floor but I don't dare traverse them: the darkness at their summit is a threat even *I* can recognize.

'Hello?'

My voice thuds against the amber walls, not echoing but *absorbing*. It's as if they're hewn from beeswax. I study the coffee table in the centre of the room. It's littered with all matter of treasures from the forest, but none of them are quite as they should be. A raven's feather that seems to breathe, expanding and contracting at even intervals; a toadstool whose spots contain tiny, blinking eyes; a clump of moss that squeals when I brush my fingers across it.

Something raps against the window. I turn to see Hans's incredulous face framed there, mouthing the words 'don't touch it' alongside a string of expletives. I grin back, which only serves to exasperate him further. Ducking beneath tendrils of ivy that hang from the ceiling, I tiptoe across the room. At the end of the worn-wood path, a closed door leaks molten light from its outline. I place a hand against the door frame and pause.

Before I can push the door ajar, the light flees the room as if someone snuffed out the sun. The door swings open.

A man – or a being in the shape of a man – towers over me, eyes sharp as topaz even in the murk, skin dark and glowing. Curls of black hair graze his forehead. I cannot tear my gaze away from him. He is unnatural in his stillness, unblinking and unbreathing. I am struck by the promise of an onslaught – of teeth and claws that will tear me in half.

'What are you doing in my house?'

'I am searching for the cuckoo,' I say. He frowns at the steadiness of my voice. 'I was told to seek your help.'

'Consult an ornithologist,' he snaps, 'and get out of my house before I remove you myself.'

I do not back down. 'Not a real cuckoo.' I withdraw the crumpled piece of parchment from my backpack and unfurl it, tracing the scroll with my finger.

He grimaces at the crude map. 'Well, this will never lead you there. The Hexenwald has no landmarks. It shifts and changes. Nothing has a permanent place.'

I stare back at him for three long breaths. The imposition of my gaze seems to make him uncomfortable; he shifts his weight and lets out a murmured sigh.

'Do you know where I can find the cuckoo, or not?'

'Not,' he says. And then, after a dramatic pause, 'But I am curious – what exactly are you hoping to achieve by finding the cuckoo?'

I am half-inclined to be withholding, thinking that it might give me some semblance of power. But the man radiates an aura so strong, so tangible, that I think there is little I could do to best him. 'I was born without the capacity to fear.' The confession that used to go unspoken comes easily now, though I am no less ashamed. 'I need to learn how to feel fear – to sate the Saint of Fear, lest it kill my sister.'

His brow arches. 'The Saint of Fear?'

The man is slow, it seems. I nod. He narrows golden eyes and gives his head another shake.

'Perhaps it was born before your time,' I say, with more bite in my voice than I intend. 'It is ancient.'

'*I* am ancient.'

'You don't look it.'

He grins, showing brilliantly white teeth. 'You flatter me.'

I scowl and direct my gaze to the room behind him. The walls are lined with tomes and alchemical diagrams. My sentence comes out broken. 'Could you ... would you help me to fear? I was told the cuckoo was my best hope, but perhaps ...'

He takes a step back into the room he came from. A fire burns in the grate behind him, illuminating the sharp line of his jaw. 'Would you ask me to harness a rainbow? To whittle wood into gold? To weave life from death?'

I lift my shoulders, hold my chin defiantly. 'To save my sister, I would.'

He stares back at me, pitying or loathing, I can't tell. 'I can make someone dizzy with love when they feel only indifference; I can provoke all-consuming rage over mild annoyance. But I cannot conjure emotion where there is none. I cannot grow a plant without a seed.'

'There must be something,' I argue, voice tight with desperation. 'A potion, or a spell, or a—'

He holds up a hand in a bid to quiet me. 'I cannot make you fearful.'

'You are lying.' I step into the room. The fire's heat flares across my face. After everything I have endured, everything Hans has endured, this man cannot simply turn me away. 'There must be a way.'

His nostrils flare. 'What is more important to you? Finding your fear, or saving your sister?'

'Why does it matter to you?'

'It doesn't matter, as such,' he says, a calculated smile at his lips. 'I simply find it amusing that you've identified your difference as the tumour to dig out.'

'If not my *difference*,' I bite out, heat sparking in my stomach, 'then what, pray tell, is the problem? It is my fearlessness that put my sister at risk.'

'To be clear: a Saint threatens to eat a young woman lest it get what it wants, and you believe yourself to be the problem?'

I open my mouth to retort, but I am taken aback by his statement. His words were not a kindness. He did not intend to soothe me or assuage my guilt. But somehow, he has. I am not the problem.

I tuck away my disbelief. 'If I cannot fix myself, my sister will die.'

'No.' He presses a hand to his temple, as if my statement physically pains him. 'If the Saint eats your sister, she will die. Cause and effect.'

'What are you suggesting?'

He sighs, seeming to weigh up whether to help me or not, but then retreats further into the room. 'Follow me.'

I hesitate to follow. 'What's your name?'

'Torsten,' he calls back. 'Torsten Nachtnebel.'

Nachtnebel. Night fog. Feeling each syllable of his name against my throat finally gives me a sense of power. It's enough security for me; I follow him deeper into the room. Bookcases stretch all the way to the ceiling, wooden shelves sagging. Curios are tucked between stacks of books: desiccated toads, flowers with butterfly wings for petals. I'd quite like to add them to my dresser-drawer collection.

Torsten hums beneath his breath, running a finger across the spines of tomes as thick as my thigh. He slides one from its place and throws it onto the desk. Dust leaps from the crevices.

I move to touch the book, whose title – *A Compendium of the Hexenwald* – is emblazoned in gold across the spine. Torsten stops me with a glare. His eyes exert their own gravity, forcing me to retreat. The speed with which he flips the pages prompts nausea to bud in my stomach.

'Look.' He flicks through the section on Saints. I recognize the lesser Saints of our village illustrated in crude detail: Henrietta and her swollen belly, Adalwolfa and her sword. We enter a section on the major Saints, and he lands on a double-page spread titled 'The Saints of Pathos'. Three figures stand with hoods drawn tight to their faces. One is shorter than the others, with a lithe frame that suggests adolescence. Beneath them, elegant script reads: 'The Saint of Sadness, The Saint of Love and the Saint of Fear.'

The Saint of Fear.

'That's not right,' I murmur, drawing my thumb across the women's shrouded faces. 'The Saint of Fear is a beast, not a woman.' Torsten stares back at me, waiting. I continue, 'I have seen it with my own eyes. I have felt its breath on my face, heard the grinding of its teeth and smelled the rot from its maw – and you expect me to believe that it does not exist?'

He tuts. 'Don't be so obtuse. The Saint of Fear exists, but it is not the creature you describe.'

Something acidic ignites in my stomach. I wonder if I might retch all over the ancient tomes. A memory comes to me so violently it nearly knocks me off balance. Oma and I are kneeling at the shrines, Adalwolfa holding her sword above us. I ask her why the Saint of Fear looks like a creature of the Hexenwald. Her back had tightened, her lips pursed—

'If not a Saint . . .' I pause, fumbling around the sudden dryness of my mouth. 'What is it?'

He fixes me with yellow eyes. 'What does it look like?'

'A patchwork.' Words spill from my mouth. 'It's made of stolen parts from other creatures. A wolf's body, pronged antlers. When it grows stronger, it walks on two legs . . .' My voice trails off as I realize that Torsten is no longer listening. He grasps the book and flicks back through the pages. We bypass the section on Saints entirely, and turn to a new section: *Untiere.* Monsters.

The red-eyed Alp hunches over a sleeping body; three *Kobold*, mischievous sprites, set fire to a house; a thirsty Nachzehrer leeches blood from the neck of a woman. Torsten comes to a decisive stop on the letter P.

There, on the page, the Saint of Fear stares back at me. It's much smaller, less formidable, but the resemblance is undeniable.

'Parasite,' he says, breathless. 'You are dealing with a parasite.'

A series of annotations explain that the parasite does not always manifest in the same way – rather taking on a form that aids its parasitism, in one way or another. My eyes lose focus; the letters blur into a charcoal smear across the page. I am knocked hopelessly off axis. The shelves spin around me. I grab the edge of the desk, using it is an anchor.

There is a commotion somewhere behind: the front door opening, boots compressing floorboards. Hans appears at my side.

'Ilse?' Hans takes me by the arm, bolstering my unsteady legs. 'You were gone too long. Is everything . . . '

His eyes land on the book, darting between the unmistakable illustration of the Saint, our Saint, and its contradictory title.

'What do you mean?' I choke. 'The Saint has ruled Heulensee for centuries.'

'Parasites steal. They latch onto the image of an existing creature and use it to bolster themselves. It seems this one has stolen the identity of the *real* Saint of Fear and used it to reap what it wants from your village. Blood and fear. For all a parasite drains, they become more powerful. Saint-like, even.'

'It protects us,' Hans argues. 'Why would it do that if it was just a parasite?'

He shrugs broad shoulders. 'I suppose it keeps the livestock – that's you, by the way – amenable. And alive.'

'I don't believe you,' I tell him, even as I feel my conviction wavering. 'This must be a mistake—'

'I do not make mistakes.'

I stare back at Torsten, chest heaving with each of my breaths. I desperately want him to be lying.

'He's not telling the truth.' I glance sideways at Hans. 'Is he?'

Hans turns slowly to face me, features suspended in a mask of terror. 'I think he is, Ils.'

Without asking for permission, I sink into the chair in front of me. That bastard creature. It has oppressed us for years, and we have allowed it. How could we question a Saint? How could we desecrate something holy?

It was never a Saint at all. Let me call it what it is: a monster. I don't care if that makes me a heretic. Agony courses through my veins. I bend at the waist, resting my forehead against the desk. We believed the girls' suffering *meant* something. That their pain and terror was a sacrifice to a higher power. All that time, we were feeding a parasite.

I lost my Oma to the Untier; might yet lose my sister, too. I coil my fingers around the edge of the chair, nail beds bleached white. There are no martyrs. Only prey.

Torsten braces his forearms against the desk, attempting to peer beneath the curtain of my hair that has fallen loose of Oma's barrette. 'You understand what this means, don't you?' His breath is cool against my cheek. 'Your fear, or lack thereof, is not the problem. You do not need to sate the creature. You need to kill it.'

My blood pumps sluggishly, then all at once. Each heartbeat spurs a tidal wave through my veins. The resounding hollow in my chest taunts me. *This* is when I should fear. Yet all I feel is desolation. The impossibility of the situation sits heavy on my shoulders.

Hans splutters beside me. He attempts to form words, but his throat is so constricted by fear that he cannot speak. I stare into my lap, reckoning with this task of upending a centuries-long tradition. The task of killing a monster.

Angry hot tears spill over the edge of my lids, and before I can stop myself, I'm sobbing into the sleeves of my blouse. I thought there was a remedy in this forest. Hans clutches hopelessly at my arm.

'Goodness,' Torsten mutters, watching me with a mix of revulsion and intrigue. 'Giving up so soon?'

I turn on him, flashing hopeless eyes and bared teeth. 'What else would you have me do? Kill the beast with my bare hands?'

'Such dramatics.' He rolls his eyes. 'There is always a solution. What better to kill a false Saint than a real one?' His gaze flicks between us. 'You need to find the *true* Saint of Fear and convince it to fight alongside you.'

CHAPTER ELEVEN

My brain drones. Dark shapes fringe my vision, and I feel the sudden urge to sink to my knees. How fitting that I must gain favour with the Saint of an emotion I do not possess.

'Our only chance is a Saint?' Hans asks from beneath a furrowed brow. 'Heulensee's Saints left long ago.'

'Having seen them with my own eyes, I can tell you this: the Saints of Pathos are very much alive, and they reside in the Hexenwald. Your Saints were torn apart when they acted in Heulensee's defence, and abandoned Heulensee as a result. The Saints of Pathos were, ironically, saved by their apathy. Rather than attempting to quell the Hexenwald's magic, they *absorbed* it. And isn't that a lesson?' Torsten's eyes twinkle. 'Empathy will get you nowhere.'

'Hypothetically,' Hans begins, voice trembling, 'how would we convince the Saint of Fear to aid us?'

I look at him in disbelief, shaken by how quickly he has warmed to this absurd plan.

Torsten blows out a breath. 'It will be more a matter of forcing, with a little bit of alchemical help . . .' A fervour strikes him at that second. He rushes to his bookshelf and loads his arms with tomes. He's hardly set them down before he starts rifling through the pages.

'I'm not much use with alchemy,' Hans says, 'but I can work a forge. If weapons will help, I can return to the village and—'

'You're not seriously considering this, are you?'

Hans's eyes snap to mine. He shrugs his shoulders, sheepish. 'I think we need to consider it. It might be the only way to save her—'

'There must be another way.'

Torsten cocks a brow. 'Why are you so opposed to this?'

Because it makes my skin itch. It feels wrong. There is something in me saying this is the worst possible route we could take. That only death awaits us on this path.

Deep down, I think I know why. Hans has spent his life spectating our rituals; I have been moulded by them. While I never believed the way Mama and Thea do, our worship of the Untier is sewn into my flesh. I thought it was a corrupted Saint – not another species entirely. Not a *monster*.

Despite what I now know, killing the Untier seems like sacrilege, a betrayal against our kin. But I can't say that aloud; they'll think I'm mad.

'Why are *you* so keen to help us?' I say, after a long pause. Turning it back on him buys me time to articulate precisely why I'm so reluctant.

Torsten lets out an exaggerated sigh. 'Do you doubt the goodness in my heart?'

'Absolutely,' Hans and I reply at the same time.

'To tell you the truth, I'm bored.' He purses his full lips. 'I've been alive for a very long time. The things that brought me joy in my youth have lost their charm.'

There is a certain sadness in his voice – a melancholy that makes me wonder if his sardonic nature is a shroud for something much darker.

'I have to find ways to entertain myself. Watching two humans attempt to win a Saint's favour will be funny, if nothing else. Besides, I do love a challenge.'

With Torsten's motivations clarified, his and Hans's attention returns to me.

'I still don't feel comfortable,' I say. 'The idea that a fearless girl must win over the Saint of Fear is no less perverse than the hanged men begging for help.'

Hans cocks his head, strands of hair falling across his forehead. 'Is it perverse, or is it serendipitous?'

'Serendipity?' I snort. 'How could it be—'

'Think about it, Ilse,' Hans urges. 'People worship Saint Henrietta because they believe she will help them bear children. So, the Saint of Fear . . .'

His voice trails off, waiting for me to connect the dots. Where moments before my skin itched, now it sings. A thrill races through me. A possibility – that this is destiny. I can save my sister and cure myself in one fell swoop. Once Thea is safe and the Untier defeated, I could ask the Saint of Fear for something more. For my own terror.

My heart brims with anticipation. The feeling that struck me when I entered the forest might be more than fanciful. I could return to Heulensee a saviour, my missing piece finally slotted into place. I could walk the streets, head held high. Those who wished me dead would look upon me, at my goosebumps and wide eyes, and know they were wrong. That I am the same as them.

My chest flutters rapidly – the double-time tempo of my heart and each eager breath.

'See, Ils?' Hans grins. 'It's meant to be.'

In his eyes I see the tender snowdrops that push up from the snow after Heulensee's seemingly endless winters. I see hope, but just barely.

My tongue is dry and heavy in my mouth. 'I suppose it is.'

Torsten claps his hands together, startling Hans. 'Fantastic. You should lead with non-violence, of course, but just in case ...' He throws another book onto the desk. *Alchemical Warfare* lands beside *Bonds: a Beginner's Guide to Making and Breaking Them*. Hans gulps as he reads the first title. 'A talented Hexe might be able to weaken the real Saint of Fear enough to bind it to someone temporarily, so you can compel them to aid you. Not me, mind you; I have better things to do.'

Torsten must expect me to throw myself at his feet, for when I shrug, he looks quite perplexed.

'We already have a Hexe helping us,' Hans explains.

Torsten freezes. His eyes dart between us; his chest flutters with hurried breaths. 'You already have a Hexe,' he repeats slowly.

Hans nods earnestly. 'She's outside.'

Torsten stares back at us, jaw clenched and rigid. He storms out of the room. The front door ricochets off its hinges. I scuttle after him, Hans at my heels.

Torsten stands in the garden, his entire body drawn taut. He whips round to look at me, his eyes even more ferocious in the evening light. 'Where are they?'

I raise a hand and point to the patch of meadow grass we left Ash in. The tip of her nose and the swell of her breast is just visible above the grass. Torsten hesitates, drawing his cloak tighter around himself. He squints at Ash, an attempt to decipher her. Sensing the pressure of his eyes, she sits up and grins, sharp canines glinting as the sun catches them.

'Hello, brother.'

The realization clicks into place. They share the same watchful eyes, though Ash's are green where Torsten's are yellow; their ears have the same slightly pointed ends; their skin is the same warm sepia, though Ash's is flushed with excitement and Torsten's blanched with fear.

Immediately, he turns to run. Ash touches a languid finger to the earth. The soil shudders beneath my feet. Her smile widens as a root bursts from the ground, ensnaring Torsten's ankle. He hits the dirt and rolls onto his back.

In a wicked sing-song, Ash says, 'Trees are wonderfully powerful, Torsten. Do you like my new magic?' She stands, cracks her neck, and advances. Her gait is fluid and assured. Predatory.

'Forgive me, sister,' Torsten urges. 'I was wrong.'

'Forgive you?' she hisses. 'You imprison me for a decade and dare ask forgiveness?'

Torsten kicks at the vines tightening around his ankle. 'It was ... a miscalculation.'

'You foul, insipid creature,' she spits. 'I will take great delight in stripping your flesh from your—'

'Ash.' My firm voice is a harsh contrast to Torsten's pleading. Ash's eyes snap to meet mine. 'I don't think you should hurt him.'

'Had you not freed me, he would've left me to rot in that tree for the rest of my days. That is not the act of a brother.'

'And he should repent,' I add hurriedly, 'but he cannot do that if you kill him.'

Ash seems briefly enamoured by the idea of her brother's penance. I turn my attention to Torsten, whose eyes are wide, skin taut. 'You trapped your sister inside a tree?'

Torsten twists his mouth. 'Technically, I turned her into a Eschenfrau. They spend the first few decades of their lives immobile, unless someone makes an offering to liberate them. She would've been able to free herself, eventually—'

'Now is not the time for technicalities,' I snap. Hans snorts behind us. Ash's hands clench to fists. I ask, 'Why would you do such a thing?'

Torsten will not meet my eyes as he responds, 'We had a disagreement.'

My eyebrows shoot up. 'A disagreement so bad that you thought imprisoning her for years—'

'A decade,' Ash interjects.

'... imprisoning her for a decade was the best solution? That's some quarrel.'

'It was,' Torsten says, face sombre. 'Ash ruined a family heirloom of great sentimental value.'

'*A family heirloom*?' Ash cackles, maniacal. 'It was a bottle of wine, Torsten! You were just sour that I drank it without you.'

I massage my temples; Hans attempts to mask his resulting laugh with a cough. 'You imprisoned your own sister ... for a decade ... over a bottle of wine?'

'It was a really gorgeous vintage,' he says earnestly. 'As you can imagine, it's difficult to source well-made wine in the forest.'

A vicious smile plays at Ash's lips. 'I poured half of it out.'

Torsten glares at her, nostrils flaring. 'Take that back.'

My heart seizes. Seeing the siblings' rivalry drives home just how much I miss Thea. I miss bickering with her like this. Our sisterhood was intense in both directions: we would've killed for each other, certainly, but we also came close to killing each other on several occasions.

Our spats never lasted long. They were over the most mundane things – clothes believed stolen, food believed pilfered. We didn't argue because we hated each other. Quite the opposite: sometimes conflict was the only way we knew how to engage with one another. Our bond was so strong that even most minor provocations felt worth picking over.

Ash feigns disinterest, inspecting her nails. 'No. It tasted like pond water.'

'You are a menace, Amalia Nachtne—'

'Ash,' she says. 'My name is Ash now.'

Torsten's eyes flick between Ash and I, putting the puzzle pieces together. 'Ash – as in, an ash tree?' He turns up his nose at me. 'Couldn't you have been more imaginative?'

'My thoughts exactly,' Ash laments. 'She bound me and didn't even have the decency to choose a good name.'

Fortunately, their shared mockery of me seems to defuse the tension. The vines recede from Torsten's ankles.

Rubbing at the raw lines left behind, he says, 'I happen to be excellent at dissolving bonds, should the need arise.'

My stomach drops. The idea of facing the task ahead without Ash makes my head spin – not only because we need her expertise, but because I am incurably curious about her. *I want more time with her, not less.*

Torsten continues, 'I am glad to see you well, sister.' He approaches Ash carefully, poised to flee at any moment. Assessing the threat she poses as dire but not immediate, he gingerly wraps his arms around her.

Hans sidles closer to me and whispers, 'Is it over?'

Suddenly, Ash stiffens. Her limbs take on the hard lines of a tree's boughs. Her fingers are the Hexenwald's branches, ready to snatch and tear. 'Get off me. A decade, Torsten!'

'A decade is nothing! We've barely aged in the last two hundred years. We'll live for centuries more! The decade of your imprisonment will seem infinitesimal, in retrospect.' His excuses only act to further incense Ash; the earth begins to shift beneath her feet as roots writhe to the surface again. 'Let me make it up to you.'

'I will not give you the chance.' She shoves Torsten away. Her emerald eyes flick to me. '*She*,' she says, with such gusto that Hans flinches, 'She is a *human* who has ventured into the Hexenwald to save her sister. I could only dream of a sibling willing to throw themselves into the fire to save me. I am departing to aid her in her quest. When I return, I do not want to see you here.'

'I shall accompany you,' Torsten says earnestly. 'That shall be my penance.'

Nostrils flared, nails clenched so hard into her palm that she must be drawing blood, Ash stares him down.

I step forward, one arm outstretched in a plea for peace. 'Your brother claims the Saint is in fact a parasite we must slaughter. We'll need to enlist the help of the true Saint to kill it. We could use him for all this.'

Ash's eyes flick to me. Back to her brother on the floor. Back to me. Her chest heaves with the effort of a deep sigh. 'Fine. But do not expect me to be sisterly.'

'You?' Torsten scoffs. 'Never.' His cockiness is belied by the rest of his body language: that of a dog with its tail between its legs.

Ash stalks away, letting the door bang as she enters the house. Torsten follows closely behind. Left alone in the meadow, Hans and I share the weight of the evening's revelations in a single glance.

'It was never a Saint,' I murmur.

He nods numbly. 'In a strange way, this almost makes sense.'

I turn his words over in my head. He's right. The now-lesser Saints were depicted as selfless heroes, their stories interwoven with acts of kindness and self-sacrifice. The Saint of Fear was an obvious outlier, in retrospect.

'I don't know if we can do this, Hans,' I admit, voice quivering.

This seems to shake him more than the revelation about the Untier. He quickly takes my hand between his, rough and calloused from years spent working the forge.

'How on earth are we going to win the favour of a real Saint?' Tears blur my vision; I try to blink them away, but they cling to my eyelashes. 'How on earth are we going to kill the Untier?'

My despondence only strengthens Hans's resolve. His expression is antithetical to my own. Colour returns to his face. Grim determination tightens his mouth. 'I know it feels insurmountable now, but you aren't alone, Ilse. You'll never be alone. We can do this.' He squeezes my hand. 'Together.'

In that moment, I understand completely why Thea loves him. He is strong when I fail to be, optimistic when I am overrun by desolation. The rare sort of friend who constantly compensates for what you lack.

Before I can thank him, he suggests we go inside. This time, he does not hesitate to enter the cabin. Ash and Torsten are silently packing supplies into knapsacks. When Ash sees me, she takes the rucksack Mama gave me, murmuring, 'Not fit for purpose.'

Sentimentality echoes through me, sour and aching. The threadbare bag is one of the few things Mama ever gifted me.

Ash must notice my reluctance, for she cocks an eyebrow and asks, 'It means something to you?'

'My mama gave it to me.' It sounds even more pathetic out loud.

Ash nods slowly and disappears into Torsten's study with the rucksack – presumably to dispose of it. Hans must notice my hurt, for he moves to hover beside me.

'How long will it take us to find the Saints?' I ask Torsten, Thea's countdown a constant presence in my head.

From the other room, Ash calls, 'How many spruce needles are there in the Hexenwald?'

Hans and I stare blankly at each other.

'What my sister *means* to say is that our journey will depend on the Hexenwald itself,' Torsten explains. 'It could lead us to the Saints tomorrow, or it might do everything in its power to stop us.'

Hans's face drops. 'So if the Saints don't want to be found, we might never find them?'

'The Hexenwald is not controlled by the Saints. It acts in its own best interests. It can be spiteful, playful, morose . . .' Torsten makes a flippant gesture with his hand. 'But I happen to be particularly good at talking to it. The forest likes me. Most of the time.'

'We only have seventeen days.' I emphasize the impossibility of our situation.

'Seventeen days.' Torsten grins. 'Humans have such a strange preoccupation with time.'

'Perhaps you might too,' I hiss, 'if you cared for the safety of *your* sister.'

Ash emerges from the study with eyes wide. She is either impressed or amused. Winning her favour feels more important to me than it ought to be.

Torsten feigns hurt, a hand pressed to his chest. 'You are so quick to anger, Ilse. It must be exhausting.'

Maybe he's right. I am so full of ire these days that I've forgotten what it's like to feel much else.

Ash thrusts a rucksack into my hands, heavy with supplies. No – not *a* rucksack. *My* rucksack. She has fortified the tears and snags with patches of shimmering green fabric. I look between her and the bag in disbelief, rendered speechless by her kindness.

'You fixed it for me,' I whisper, once I've summoned the wits to speak.

She shrugs noncommittally, a flush creeping across her cheeks. 'It didn't take long.'

'That's uncharacteristically compassionate of you,' Torsten mutters.

Ash spears him with a glare and shoulders her own bag before leaving the house. I clutch the repaired rucksack to my chest as I follow her, my heart performing uncomfortable little somersaults in my chest. Torsten and Hans scurry dutifully behind.

'Shouldn't we wait until first light?' Hans asks, his voice tight.

'The Hexenwald is dangerous no matter the time of day,' Torsten says. 'Besides, I recall Ilse giving me some *very* stern words about your timeline.'

The meadow successfully lulled us into a false sense of security. Within its bounds, everything is blissfully, torturously unremarkable. Beyond the divide, the Hexenwald is wild.

'Well,' Torsten says with a sigh. 'Here we go.'

He leads our motley procession between worlds. Shattering the boundary between the two realms is as simple as walking. With one step, we are swaddled in the bucolic charm of the meadow. In the next, we are at the mercy of the Hexenwald. The air chills and stills; a metallic taste blooms on my tongue; the birds shriek rather than sing.

Ash and Torsten bicker relentlessly as we walk. Hans and I are glad for the distraction from what's happening around us in the foulest depths of the Rot season. When Hans attempts to rebandage the wound on his palm as we walk, droves of flies are drawn to the now-inky blood slick. He resolves to deal with it later. My stomach twists each time I look at the soiled bandages.

We walk until my hips ache, until my knees protest at each step. It feels like an eternity before we set up camp for a late supper, or perhaps an extraordinarily early breakfast, though Ash claims we've only been walking for a couple of hours. I find it hard to muster an appetite when rotting carcasses keep rising from the ground around us. Hans has no such trouble; he eats three slices of rye bread in quick succession and devours the apple Torsten throws to him. I liken Hans to a dog – he is none too pleased.

Ash sits with her head tilted towards the fire's heat. The amber flames make her skin glow. When she peels one eye open and catches me staring, she winks. I almost choke on thin air. In an attempt to save face, I offer her my apple.

'I do not experience hunger,' she murmurs, lips curling up into a smile although she refuses to meet my gaze.

'It seems my sister has forgotten her manners after . . .' Torsten breaks off, unwilling to reference his crimes. 'We don't eat. Or rather, we don't *need* to eat.'

Hans clears his throat. 'But you feed on blood, don't you?'

Torsten barks out a laugh. Ash tries to push down the wry smile which springs to her lips. 'Do you also believe that Saint Nikolaus brings you gifts each December?'

'I don't appreciate your mockery,' Hans says, his cheeks turning red. I stifle a smile, sensing that Hans believes in Saint Nikolaus more than he would care to admit. 'But I know of the Hexen's bloodlust.'

'Do you know what a Hexe is? Truly?'

Hans stares back at Torsten stubbornly. I answer in his stead. 'Were you human once?'

Ash nods, eyes still shut. 'Until the tear. We lived in the forest. Many people did, back then. Hunters. Soothsayers. Herbalists.'

I nibble on a corner of bread. 'And when the earth tore open, it turned everyone who lived in the forest into Hexen?'

She shakes her head. 'Not everyone survived. Most didn't, in fact. Their bodies ruptured, torn apart by the shockwaves of magic.' Ash swallows. The motion jerks loose a bead of moisture clinging to her lashes. 'That's when we lost Mother.'

'We tried to go to Heulensee for aid, but the minute we stepped out of the forest, blisters consumed our skin,' Torsten adds. 'We lingered on the forest's edge, hoping the villagers – people we'd known our entire lives – would help us. They tarred us with the same brush as the other monsters once they saw how we'd changed.'

When he notices the slight depression of my brow, he elaborates, 'We weren't always this preternaturally beautiful, you know. And back then, we struggled to control the magic that had taken root. Errant sparks flying from our fists, fog rolling from our mouths. Nothing serious,' – Hans interrupts with a snort, perhaps thinking that Torsten's description sounds very serious indeed – 'but it scared them. They called us Hexen.' Torsten spits out the word bitterly. 'The term stuck. I take it as a compliment now.'

'The tear gave us magic,' Ash says, 'but it took something away from us, too. Our humanity.'

Torsten lets out a deep breath. 'It's been so long since we were human.' He pauses, thinking. 'But not long enough to develop a thirst for human blood.'

Hans's cheeks dimple. 'In that case, I apologize.'

Torsten waves a hand. 'There are plenty of creatures in the Hexenwald to fear. Hexen aren't one of them.' Ether rolls across his fingers, a storm playing out in miniature. 'Unless you anger us.'

By the time we resolve to settle down for the evening, the False season sweeps in to replace the Rot. Ash and Torsten disappear between the trees, creating wards which will keep us concealed, just as the meadow is, masking our scents and sounds. A crackle of energy chases up my spine. I question it when the siblings return: Torsten tells me I must have felt their magic.

As I relax onto the bedroll, a mattress of downy clover sprouts beneath my body. I roll onto my side, brushing away the tuft-eared squirrel which nuzzles at my cheek. In the clearing beyond – a glowing, dew-kissed parting in the trees which I swear did not exist a moment ago – a man and woman beckon. They are both naked as the day they were born, and so beautiful that I feel indecent just gazing upon them. I cannot tell which draws my attention more. Troubling.

I stuff the thought down, roll onto my back and focus on the sky as it blushes pink above us.

'If you won't approach them,' Ash murmurs, padding past me, 'I will.'

In my peripheral vision, I watch her slink into the clearing beyond. The man holds out his arms. My stomach knots inexplicably.

Torsten coughs, and I am glad for the distraction. 'It seems my sister's imprisonment ridded her of shame.'

A butterfly lands on my shoulder as I turn over, placing my back to the clearing. An ugly feeling brews beneath my skin – one which I do not recognize. I make a clumsy attempt to change the subject. 'Why does the Hexenwald have seasons?'

'They're not seasons, so much as defence mechanisms,' Torsten explains. 'If there were rats in your cellar, you might try to starve them. If that didn't work, poison. If the rats persisted, you might flood the cellar to drown them.'

I think about it for a moment. 'So we are the rats,' I say with a frown, 'and the Hexenwald is the cellar?'

He points at Hans and me. 'You are the rats.'

CHAPTER TWELVE

I sulk until Ash returns, hair tousled and cheeks flushed. I cannot fathom why that makes me even more irritated. She drinks greedily from a waterskin, her throat bobbing hypnotically. When she notices me watching, she swallows a final mouthful and runs her tongue across her lips. Heat swirls low in my stomach.

Ash offers me the waterskin, the corners of her lips curled upwards. Our skin grazes during the transfer. I pull back with a hissed inhale. Ash takes no stock in my reaction, clearly accustomed to conjuring fear.

But for me, it's not fear. So why does her proximity make my heart lurch against my ribs? Maybe it's a reaction to her earlier kindness, mending my rucksack to soothe my cheap sentimentality. Out of sorts, I down greedy glugs of water in the hopes it will clear my mind. I'm on my third gulp before I realize that it's not water, but a potent alcohol.

'Blackberry wine,' Ash says through full lips, which I now notice are stained purple. 'Delicious.'

Torsten gestures for me to hand it over, and I do, but not before taking two more sips for myself. He sinks half of the remainder, and Hans sheepishly consumes the dregs.

'I won't sleep otherwise,' he says.

Ash demands the empty waterskin. The loose leather burgeons beneath her fingertips. Hans reaches greedily for the now-full vessel, eager to taste the spoils of Ash's magic. Plum-coloured wine trickles from his lips.

The wine coaxes out the optimism that I had stuffed deep into my bones. Similarly, the alcohol, or maybe the *encounter*, seems to have improved Ash's mood. As I watch my companions laughing around the campfire – though Hans's laughter is more nervous tittering than exultation, fuelled in part by the never-ending supply of blackberry wine – I start to believe that we can do this. We can harness a Saint's power and use it to save Thea. Perhaps even fix me in the process. Mould me into something the village could love.

It doesn't take long for Torsten and Hans to become suitably drunk. They are crooning out a song we used to sing back in Heulensee. I join in for the falsetto, if only to stop them from attempting it. Across the campfire, Ash watches me with a strange expression on her face. Her cheeks are flushed, her lips slightly parted. It brings goosebumps to my arms.

The song dies in my mouth. 'What?' I ask, more accusatory than I mean to be.

She shakes her head, dark curls bouncing, and redirects her attention to the flames. 'Nothing.'

After filling the air with my voice, its absence is jarring.

Torsten and Hans, unaware of the stand-off, quickly break the silence with a spirited conversation on blacksmithery, which has advanced quite significantly since Torsten last left the forest.

In Heulensee, I wondered if I would feel more at home in the Hexenwald: an aberration in comparable company. But here in the forest of blood and terror, I still feel strange. Ash senses it, too.

I drag in a breath of smoke-laced air – that smell will never lose its malice – and stand. It becomes apparent at once that the wine has unsteadied me. Were I sensible, were I fearing, I would stay within the bounds of the campsite. But I am rarely sensible and never fearing, so I drift into the thick cover of the trees.

A stagnant pond, thick with algae, festers at the heart of the next clearing I come across. Before I can investigate, fog wafts across the pond's surface in great plumes. Its tendrils reach out, desperate to consume.

Senses dulled by the wine, I watch through bleary eyes. The fog dissipates as quickly as it arrived. But it leaves something behind – some*one*.

Dorothea.

She sits on the banks of the pond, legs dangling into the fetid water. A twig snaps beneath my foot. Thea whips around. A smile explodes onto her face – sun returning after rain.

'I hoped I would find you here,' she says.

'Thea?' My voice cracks.

To see her alive, unharmed, brings tears to my eyes. I am suddenly buoyant, lighter than I've felt since entering the Hexenwald. I step forward, flinging out my arms, and then I pause.

My sister shouldn't be here. In fact, her being here is impossible. The forest may have abstained from my flesh, but she is too appetising, too fearful. The Hexenwald would sooner consume her whole than ferry her to my side. 'What are you doing here?'

Thea sniffs and looks around us. She pulls herself to her feet. The stagnant water leaves a ring of foam around her calves. 'It's not very nice, is it?'

I swallow. In the silence that hangs between us, it sounds like a curse. 'What are you doing in the forest, Thea?'

She pouts in a way that I have never seen. Almost reluctantly, she drags her gaze to meet mine. 'Well, I'm not *really* here.'

'What do you mean?'

'I'm dead, Ilse.'

My heart gives one anguished beat. After that, I am not sure it beats at all.

Straight-faced, Thea drags a finger across her throat. 'Gone.'

My tears blur Thea into spectral watercolour. The ghostly white of her skin; the shocking blue of her eyes; the blood-red of her lips. I open and shut my mouth, torn between defying her and telling her that I love her. She cannot be dead. If Thea is dead, this has all been for nothing. If Thea is dead ... I'm not sure I can go on.

'And the worst part?' She points her finger at my chest and I feel its impact deep in my heart. 'My own sister killed me. You couldn't find it in yourself to fear, and now I'm dead. Do you know how it feels to be eaten alive?' I stagger backwards, shaking my head, palms clammy. Thea stalks forward, relentless. 'Pure torture. The Saint's teeth in my bones. The sound of my skull cracking. The smell of—'

'*Stop it,*' I cry, clutching my own chest as if I can stop the grief from taking root. 'You can't be gone. The Untier promised me time.'

'"The Untier promised,"' she repeats my words in a mocking singsong. 'It doesn't matter what the Untier said. If I just had a penitent sister, I'd still be alive.'

'You can't be dead,' I protest, my eyes watering. 'You can't be.'

She snarls, baring her teeth. 'Yet here I am. We all wish you were born fearing, but perhaps it would have been better had you never been born at all.'

'Please, Thea,' I sob, holding out my hands, begging for forgiveness, 'I'd trade my life for yours ten times over.'

'That's sweet. But it won't stop me dissolving in the Saint's stomach while you gallivant around the Hexenwald. I hate you, wretched girl. I will hate you until my soul festers, until the last time my name is ever spoken. I wish you weren't my sister.'

I fall to my knees. Her eternal resentment is a fate worse than death. My secret keeper has confirmed every foul thought I've ever had about myself. All of our memories are tainted. They are not of two sisters, two friends – they are of a pathetic girl who cannot see the poison in her own sibling's eyes.

'And even though my life hung in the balance, that was never your only motivation, was it? You came here in search of belonging. You really, truly believed you would emerge a victor! Did my life ever matter to you, or was it just a convenient by-product?'

Shame sinks like a stone in my stomach. My own foolish desire to belong never should've entered the equation – but it *did*. I was so enamoured with the idea of belonging. How could something so shallow factor against my sister's life?

Thea moves closer. She smells different, like moss and earth. Lips drawn to my ear, she snarls, 'I'd wish you out of existence.'

'Stop.'

A hand closes around my shoulder. Numb, I look at the fingers curled there. Ash's. Thea stares up at her with panicked eyes.

'Shed that skin,' Ash commands, teeth bared. She extends a hand and clenches it. The air shifts around her fist, forming a shimmering cord that wraps itself around Thea. It squeezes tighter, *tighter*, and Thea explodes into steam.

I scrabble at my mouth, my chest, desperate to stem the anguish. My sister was here, dead but present, and now she is gone entirely.

Ash closes her free hand around my wrist. The pressure of her fingers against my veins is the only thing keeping me upright. 'It is an illusion,' she murmurs. 'That was not your sister, but a Nix.'

Ash walks me closer to the pond, pausing to accommodate my unsteady legs. She draws in a breath and blows the steam away. There, just visible above the algae, two inky black eyes blink back at us.

'Wretched Hexe,' it snarls, showing serrated teeth. 'Spoiled my meal.'

'You will never eat again,' Ash bites back, just as venomous.

Sensing the threat, the Nix dips below the surface. Not quick enough; Ash plunges an arm into the pool and takes the Nix by its throat. Its withered, humanoid body dangles, water dripping from clawed toes. Ash's fingernails lengthen, sharpen, twisting into shards of wood. She swipes them across the Nix's neck.

The Nix writhes, letting out a bloodcurdling scream – and then it goes limp. Black blood pours from the creature's throat, darkening the pond. Ash tosses the Nix to the side, her breaths coming thick and fast. Ether pulses across the surface of the pool. The algae retreats, leaving behind clear, fresh water.

The wrath melts from Ash's face as she turns to me. Her eyes soften, lashes half-lowered. 'Are you okay?'

Those three words, a simple question, should be easy to answer. Yes or no. But instead, they open a floodgate. All of the sadness and anger pent up inside my soul comes pouring out like pus from a wound gone septic. I sink to the ground as every emotion flees my body in an exodus.

'I wish I was like the rest of them,' I half-cry, half-rage. 'I'm so sick of this.'

My words hang in the air, somehow leaden and weightless at once. I have felt it keenly my whole life – the desire to be like the other girls – but I have never said so aloud. I thought that if I kept tamping it down, the longing might dissolve entirely. But all I have done is let it blister and decay. It rots me from the inside out.

If I could dig it out, I would. I'd root through my chest cavity, nails scraping flesh and bone. Bloody-fingered, I'd hold it up to the sun and let it burn. With cardiac muscle pulsing between my fingers, I'd scream. *What will you hate me for now?*

The day I bound rocks to my ankles in the lake, I told myself that it was because I wanted to *feel*. I'm not sure that was the truth. I think I wanted to *stop* feeling. The shame, the self-hatred. I wanted it all to stop. For ever.

Ash, who has rarely been anything but blunt, hesitates. Her lips flutter open and shut before she can form the word, 'Why?'

It seems like a strange question, given the circumstances. 'Because if I was fearing, Thea would be safe.'

She shuffles closer to me, purposeful yet stiff in her movements. It's as if, just like me, she doesn't know how to be close. 'I think you have always felt this way. Am I correct?'

I replay the times I begged fear to inhabit my body. The weights at my ankles, the cold of the lake invading my lungs. The distinct absence of fear, even when faced with death. 'Yes.'

'So Thea is not the root of your pain,' she says, her voice barely a murmur. 'You abhor your differences for another reason. What is it?'

I hesitate. 'No matter how exacting my charade, I will always be *other*.' I sink my head into my hands, unable to carry its weight. 'I'm exhausted, Ash. I do not want to pretend anymore.' Disclosing this to her feels safer than it perhaps should. I barely know her, and yet I feel comfortable divulging my most shameful secrets. Perhaps it's because we are bound to one another – at least for as long as it takes to save the girls in Heulensee.

Ash swallows thickly. 'I spent the first two decades of my life as a human, then had that humanity stolen when the tear opened. I understand what it means to be different. To feel, in your bones, that there is something wrong with what you are.'

I stare back at her, dumbfounded, incapable of forming the words I'd like to give her. I've never been able to vocalize the fact that I feel utterly foreign – but Ash understands without any explanation.

'What I mean to say is that you don't have to pretend,' she whispers, eyes dipped. The scent of blackberry wine lingers on her lips. 'Not with me.'

Her assertion almost knocks me breathless. I fret with my hands, picking at my fingernails. A hysterical laugh escapes my lips. 'Don't you see something strange when you look at me?'

'No. I see a girl who was able to enter the Hexenwald without so much as a goosebump. I see a girl who talked me down from killing my own brother. I see a girl who is driven not by fear, but by love.' She pauses to draw breath, the taut line of her shoulders giving the impression of treading uncharted territory. 'Fear is reflexive. It is blind and unfeeling. But to have love as your compass? To grit your teeth and follow it? That is something to be proud of.'

If those words came from anyone else's mouth, I would not believe them. But Ash, who seems loathe to deceive or pretend, stares me dead in the eye and tells me to be *proud*. We study each other, but looking at her is like looking at the sun. Her beauty has to be seen in stolen glances, knowing the next might rob you of your vision entirely.

I direct my attention to the forest floor and let the tears spill there. She moves in, one hand brushing my arm, and I do not recoil. In fact, being touched by Ash does not feel like such a bad thing. Her skin trails static across mine.

I steal another glance at her. To catch her looking back at me sparks something quite unknown. It is not grief, nor the anger that has become background noise in my brain. It's an awareness that stretches from the tips of my fingers to the soles of my feet. An electric hum, settled deep in my bones, whose origin I cannot discern.

'There is one thing I don't understand about you, Ilse.'

Breathless, I ask, 'What is it?'

She tucks a strand of hair behind my ear. 'For a girl who cannot fear, you seem awfully anxious around me.'

Convinced I am on the brink of fainting, I lurch sideways, bracing myself against a tree. Ash watches me with a bemused smile. My heart drums an offbeat rhythm, matched by the piecemeal breaths I'm able to drag down my throat.

Once I've gathered myself – or perhaps not – I blurt out, 'You repaired my rucksack.'

For Saint's sake, Ilse. All the things you could've said, and that's what you chose?

Ash cocks a brow. 'Is that all?'

I wipe a hand across my face, in disbelief of my own fumbling. 'What I mean to say is that to be seen,' – I swallow, working around the tension in my throat – 'to be *known*, is alien.'

'You'll have to get used to it,' she murmurs. 'I don't wish to simply look at the surface, Ilse. I want to know the depths of you.'

My heart stops entirely. Ash raises her hand, fingers curling just short of my face. I lean forward, consenting to her touch. She trails her nails along my jawline, sending sparks through my body. Never have I felt so bare, so vulnerable, yet so willing to fling my arms open and let myself be seen. Her other hand drifts to the small of my back. She leans in, close enough that I can smell the wine on her breath –

'Ilse!' comes Hans's voice. 'Help me show Torsten how to dance the *Schuhplattler*!'

Ash pulls back. I could kill him. A muscle ticks in my jaw, and I fight to stop my hands curling into fists.

'Come on, Ilse,' Ash says, a laugh held behind her lips. 'This sounds like it could be good.'

She leaves the clearing. I stay rooted to the spot, paralysed by my desire to know what would've happened without Hans's interruption. Ash casts a glance over her shoulder, beckoning with a curled finger. We walk back through the trees together, our hands grazing.

CHAPTER THIRTEEN

By the time Torsten wakes us the next morning, it feels like I haven't slept at all. I must have, because Ash is dousing the fire's embers and my head is pounding with the after-effects of the wine. Torsten assures me that we slept far longer than he intended, as if that should remedy my fatigue. When I ask how he knows this, he simply taps his nose and says, 'That's between me and my forest.'

Hans and I exchange an exasperated look. Nevertheless, when Torsten sets off, we follow, sheep to our shepherd. Ash magics herself a new dirndl, this time in the deep purple of a copper birch. When she catches me watching, she winks, long lashes fanning, and disappears into the trees. I watch her go, feeling as if a songbird is caught in my chest.

Torsten navigates the forest with equal parts intuition and artistry. He whispers to the trees beneath his breath, asks questions of the crows, and understands what each shift of light and smell means. The Rot season continues, and Torsten pauses occasionally to inspect the festering corpses. He says they can be read like tea leaves, indicating the proximity of certain creatures, of the day's likely weather. He uses the information to steer us clear of a group of Nachzehrer, and informs us the day will be fair.

Hans is a different matter. I cannot tell if the forest loves him and wants to keep him, or loathes him and wants him dead. He is constantly stumbling against brambles that ensnare his limbs, or staggering into pools of mud that tug at his ankles. If it were me, my mood would sour. Hans, as ever, takes it on the chin. When a group of thorns conspire to tear the bandage from his palm, he simply grins and says fresh air will do the wound good.

'If Thea could see me now,' he says, a chuckle rolling up his throat, 'I wonder what she'd say.'

I smile. 'She'd probably scold you for being daft enough to deliberately slice your palm open in the first place.'

We reminisce on the time I fell into a particularly jagged patch of brambles. Thea wore a face like thunder as she picked each thorn from my cheeks. Her love is so fierce that she takes our injuries as a personal slight.

I look over at Hans as he laughs, recalling her tone when she told me to never, ever fight a blackberry bush again. Maybe this is my silver lining. Never did I think he and I would be able to share our love of Thea.

Every now and then, Torsten barks out commands to Ash, who lingers somewhere out of sight.

'Where is she?' I ask, with enough delay that my question seems nonchalant.

'Trailing behind,' Torsten calls over his shoulder. 'Masking your scents. A lot of the creatures in this forest have a taste for human flesh. I'm surprised you made it this far without being eaten.'

My mind lingers in the moment we shared last night. If I concentrate hard enough, I can conjure up the tingle of her nails on my jaw, her breath on my lips. I find myself smiling, unbidden. It's an effort to wipe the expression from my face.

Maybe Ash was just trying to be my friend. A friend, and nothing more. Perhaps that's why I felt so odd. Friendship is uncharted territory for me.

Deep down, I know it's not just that. Hans has become my friend, but I have never felt jittery in his presence. Slowly, something unravels. A spool of thought drapes across my consciousness. It cannot be ignored, but it cannot be explained either. My jaw aches from the pressure of keeping my teeth so firmly gritted; pain buds under my temples but still, I insist on frowning.

'Okay?'

Hans's voice shatters my revery. He watches me with a worried expression, dark brows drawn. I unclench my jaw and smooth the wrinkles from my forehead.

Voice distant, I say, 'I'm just thinking.'

'A problem shared is a problem halved.'

Perhaps he is right. I can't quite believe I am considering confiding in *Hans* – the boy I blamed for luring my sister away. His concern sparks a warm feeling in my chest. How embarrassing.

Each word sticking in my throat, I say, 'Something strange happened last night.'

He laughs, but masks it with a cough. 'I thought I might've been interrupting.'

'You didn't interrupt anything.' My denial is too quick, too sharp.

'All right,' he mutters drily.

'It's just ...' I pause, blowing out a breath. Vulnerability does not always come easily. 'Ash treats me very kindly, and I don't understand what it means ... nor how it makes me feel.'

'Ilse Odenwald struggling to interpret kindness? Colour me shocked.'

'*Hans.*'

He composes himself, scrubbing the amusement from his face. 'How does she make you feel?'

I cannot find the words to respond. Luckily, Hans doesn't make me.

'If it helps,' he says, feigning nonchalance, 'when I first met Thea, I was utterly on edge. I could hardly speak for the way she took my breath away.'

I pick at my nails, my heart thundering in my chest. 'But she's a woman ...' I pause, attempt and fail to swallow, then drag a frantic hand through my hair. Tears inexplicably needle at my eyes. 'And *I* am a woman.'

'That is no barrier.'

I consider his words. Perhaps *this* is why I've never looked at a man and had something stir in me: because I was never meant to be with a man at all.

Hans squeezes my shoulder. 'Go and speak to her. Perhaps she can help you decipher her intentions.'

I groan. 'That sounds torturous.'

'What's worse: asking her the impossible question, or spending the rest of your life thinking about it?' When I don't respond, he gives me a little shove. 'Go on, Ilse. Be brave.'

It doesn't take long to find Ash. She hums softly as she walks between the trees. Each of her movements is languorous.

'Ash,' I call, swallowing my pride. She doesn't pause, nor does she slow.

Ash glances at me, lips pursed. 'What is it?'

I rack my brain for the perfect words. I need to tell her that what she said to me last night means more than even I can understand. That I don't know why she is so kind to me, but I would like to. None of the sentiments I conjure suffice, nor does the silence which now stretches between us.

'I wanted to talk to you.' I blurt out the words as quickly as possible. 'About last night.'

That gets her attention. She stops abruptly; I almost careen into her.

'What about it?'

Her eyes burn into mine. As she looks back at me – lips full, slightly parted; high cheekbones dusted with sweat; emerald eyes sparking with intrigue – I regret ever opening my mouth. How can I stand before this goddess of a woman and bleat out that I am transfixed by her? I should be down on my knees, a supplicant at her shrine.

A hint of a smile curves her lips. 'You're awfully pretty when you're lost for words.'

The breath I'd intended to take gets stuck in my throat. I blink up at her, dazed.

'You're awfully pretty' – I falter, not entirely sure how I'd planned to end this sentence – '*always*.'

A low laugh rumbles through her chest. She reaches out, tucking a strand of hair behind my ear. The graze of her fingertips makes me shiver. I swallow, working around the lump in my throat, but then the light shifts. Her eyes change from emeralds to rubies; her skin turns red. I drag my gaze away from her, up to the sky.

The clouds are redder than ever. Ether rolls through the atmosphere, shimmering and pulsating. The air stiffens, no longer moving freely between the trees, but constricting. I reach for Ash, and she reaches for me. When our fingertips collide, neither of us knows what comes next.

'What's happening?'

Ash lets out a shuddered breath. Steam snakes into the air. 'They're here.'

A guttural, raw scream echoes around us. It's the scream of someone whose nails are being pried from their fingertips. Red descends all around, a fine scarlet mist which burns every inch of skin it touches.

If there is a hell, this might be its portal.

I press my hands over my ears and pull my cloak tighter; Ash draws me against her. The contours of her body become the sole focus of my existence, drowning out the bloodshed around us. Her hip bones press against my stomach, my heart *pounds*. It seems foolish that I didn't immediately realize my response to her was romantic. How could anyone not want to kiss her?

Torsten runs up beside us and Hans follows closely behind, facial muscles pulled taut. Hand still curled around my wrist, Ash steps back. The distance between us swells like an ocean.

'They're close,' Torsten says, eyes awed or terrified – I cannot tell. 'Closer than they've ever been. We should—'

Torsten's sentence dies in his mouth. The earth rumbles beneath our feet.

There are times when the Hexenwald is silent and watchful,

the way forests should be. There are stranger times when the trees scream and groan in pain, lashing out with hungry boughs. But I have never seen the trees uproot and travel.

I watch in disbelief, breath stuck somewhere between my mouth and lungs, as the trees make haste. I once saw a mole breaking earth. Papa stabbed it with a pitchfork shortly thereafter, and the image that remained with me is the mole's blood on the prongs. But now I remember the way it coursed a track of freshly turned soil. The trees move the earth in the same way.

'Is that,' Hans falters mid-sentence to swallow the nervous saliva no doubt pooling in his mouth, 'ordinary?'

'No,' Ash murmurs, fingers tightening around my own. 'It is not.'

Torsten crouches, placing a hand to the soil. He rubs the earth between his thumb and forefinger. He looks up, opens his mouth ... and then he's gone.

A tree strikes him from the side. The force sends him flying into the forest. The exhaust from his enormous gasp is the only sign he was ever here.

'Ilse,' Ash says, voice panicked. 'Don't let go.'

And then the forest takes her. Hans and I share eye contact for a split second, and then he's gone too. The Hexenwald is picking us off, one by one.

Before I can form a plan, a tree strikes my back. The impact rings through my vertebrae. I cannot pause to discern whether the pain is life-changing or merely agonizing before the spruce ushers – no, herds me through the forest. Trees blur on either side.

'Ash!' I cough, still winded. 'Hans! Torsten!'

Let them be okay. Let them survive this. Tears bead along my lashes; I howl my companions' names into the wind.

The tree picks up speed. Bracing myself against it seems wiser than attempting to break free. My nails bend and snap as I dig them into the thick trunk.

Just as quickly as it started, the tree comes to a halt. I fall face-first into the dirt. Nose wrinkled, I turn my head to the side and spit out soil-specked saliva. I push myself up to my feet, noting the ache in my thighs which portends plum-coloured bruises come morning. If I survive that long.

When I look around, the forest is utterly still and silent. There is no sign the trees ever moved. The earth is smooth, unmarred. To be hoodwinked by a forest is a whole new level.

I open my mouth to call the others, but a hidden instinct bids me to stop. My entire body hums with the sense that I am not alone. That I am being watched, hunted. I feel like a deer surrounded by wolves. If I stay perfectly still, they might lose interest. One misstep and their teeth will be around my throat.

An elderly woman watches me from between the trees, her face cold and unfeeling. She bleeds from the mouth. Black, congealed viscera coats her fingers. I move to help her, thinking perhaps she is some poor, memory-addled grandmother who was snatched by the forest. Only when I squint do I realize that she is not bleeding.

She is *feeding*.

As she stares back at me, the woman's fingers loosen around the decayed organ in her hands. It slips from her grip and slops onto the forest floor, sprinkling muddy beads of crimson into the grass. Her mask slips; emotion bleeds into the cool plane of her face.

She draws a breath between gritted teeth. 'I *thought* it was you. She will be so pleased. You look just like her.'

My voice is steady as I ask, 'Like who?'

The mask descends again. Her skin is weathered by time, and it's as if her face is hewn from stone. There is no movement, nothing human. Eyes fixed on mine, she steps over the debris. No, not steps. Floats. Her feet skim the grass.

Why is she so familiar? Why does this entire scene – the floating woman, grass brushing the soles of her feet, a backdrop of trees – feel so familiar?

'Like *who*?' I insist.

She tilts her head to the side, contemplating. 'Like your mother.'

My blood halts in my veins. I do not look like Mama, in body or soul; she is lithe and blonde, where I am soft and auburn-haired. 'I am nothing like Mama.'

She stares back, emotionless, waiting. I do not break her gaze.

'Like your *real* mother.' Her voice is the hum of a thousand wasps; the rumble of mountains before an avalanche.

Amidst my disorientation, lost deep in the turgid waters of the sinkhole yawning open inside me, there is something else. Something which screams *wrong*.

I look up at the sky. The clouds are red. Crimson. Blinding scarlet. A freshly sawn wound, pumping blood. Realization snaps into place. *This* is the creature from my memories. One of the three Hexen who invaded Heulensee ten years ago.

Ever so slowly, I look back at the old woman, but she has disappeared. The space she occupied still hums with her energy. She is not present corporeally, but I can sense her. The temperature drops five degrees, then ten. My breath leaves my mouth in curling tendrils.

'Show yourself,' I demand.

A hand brushes my shoulder. When I whip around to clutch at it, there is nobody there. Crows land noisily in the trees. They caw, louder and louder, until I have to press my hands against my ears. Wolves stalk into the clearing, teeth bared and bloody.

I snarl, exposing my teeth straight back. 'Show yourself.'

Owls hoot overhead. The wolves press closer. Corvids descend, beaks aiming for my eyes. I bat them away.

'You ought to be scared.' The voice is close enough to whisk the hair from my face, but there is no source. 'You ought to be *terrified.*'

One of the wolves launches. Its jaws close around my forearm. Pain flares, forcing my lungs into gasping. I thrash against the wolf's grip. My movement is enough to startle the beast, but when it pulls away, my arm is in tatters. Blood pours to the forest floor, leaving my body so fast that I *know* this wound could kill me.

My survival instinct roars to life. Embers course through my veins. Adrenaline steadies my legs, but it cannot stave off the black halos forming around my vision.

My knees buckle. I lurch forward, hauling myself from tree to tree with my good hand. Jaws snap behind me. Crows' wings brush my cheek. An owl stares back at me from the canopy as if it knows who I am, what I will be, and how I will end.

'Do not delay the inevitable,' a disembodied voice echoes from the trees, from the sky, from the earth. 'This is the natural order.'

Each breath is shallower than the last. My vision narrows to a pinprick. I flail, searching for the next tree to brace myself against – but my fingers fasten around thin air. I take another step forward, and then I'm falling.

CHAPTER FOURTEEN

My jaw snaps shut as I hit the ground. I scrabble against the earth, trying desperately to right myself, but the decimation of my vision has left me completely unsettled.

'Ash!' I shout into the darkness – but she does not come. *Cannot* come, perhaps.

My sight returns at a fraction of its usual sharpness. I attempt once more to stand, but my limbs aren't strong enough to support my weight. Cold racks my body, worse than any Heulensee winter. I try to think of *Lebkuchen* and burning incense, but all I can smell is the copper of my own blood. A wolf eclipses my view of the scarlet clouds above.

'If you must kill me,' I grind out between gritted teeth, 'Do so with your own hands.'

The forest falls silent. The eyes of the wolf above me clear, and it lets out a high-pitched whimper and scatters. The birds cease their squawking. Ether fills the clearing, so thick and silken that I feel it brushing against my skin.

'*Show yourself,*' I hiss, the light fading from my eyes.

And then she does.

A face appears just above mine. She is reminiscent of the elderly woman, but appears forty, maybe fifty years younger. She is horrifying. She is *beautiful*. An ivory gown clings to her skin. Auburn hair falls around her face. Her skin is the gossamer wing of a butterfly, near translucent. Blue veins hum beneath the surface. Eyes white as milk stare back at me, unfeeling.

I have seen those eyes before. I *know* them. How can the Saints I need to save Thea be the Hexen – or whatever these monsters *truly* are – that terrorized Heulensee?

'You're a Hexe.' My tremulous recognition hangs in the air.

She smiles with bloody teeth. 'Saint.'

'Hexe,' I insist, dragging each syllable up my throat to conjure some conviction. Even as the word leaves my mouth, I realize it doesn't make sense. Ash and Torsten are Hexe, yet they are entirely different to the white-eyed woman in front of me. 'You cannot be a Saint.'

'You know nothing of Sainthood,' she growls, her eyes emitting white light, which scalds my face. 'You will learn.'

Aware that my next words may be my last, I search for something powerfully poetic. Something worthy of my headstone. But sifting through my brain is like wading through treacle. I cannot find the words that will save me. The words that will save Thea.

'I will worship you,' I splutter. 'In exchange for your aid.'

My croaked plea piques her interest. She tips her head to the side, calculating. 'You desire our *aid*?'

At first I think I'm seeing double, but now there are two of them. The elderly woman from before drifts into my frame of vision. Her face is an aged version of the Saint who currently kneels before me. They hum in a discordant harmony, one gravel-toned, one dulcet.

'A false Saint plagues my village,' I grind out. 'I require the help of a real Saint to defeat it.'

'A false Saint,' they echo. 'An imposition indeed.'

'It calls itself the Saint of Fear,' I say. 'You should not tolerate such imitation.'

The younger of the pair kneels beside me. There is a distinct noiselessness in her movement. Her feet do not stir the grass; her physicality does not displace air the way a body should. She brings a cold hand to my arm. Ice stings my skin as she traces the puncture wounds with her fingers.

My field of vision widens. The darkness subsides, chased off to the fringes. My body hums with the triumphant return of sensation after full-body pins and needles. I do not know much of magic, but this power to heal a life-ending wound . . . now *that* could slay the Untier.

'Thank you.' It feels like a shallow offering.

I do not blink, do not breathe. Any move I make could be the wrong one, the one which will get my neck snapped or my throat slit. 'Are you the Saint of Fear?'

'I am the Saint of Love.'

'And I am the Saint of Sadness,' the older woman adds.

They make no efforts to elaborate. I draw my own conclusion. 'The third of you must have been the Saint of Fear.'

'Yes,' they echo.

I saw the violent end the Saint of Fear met, but if these Saints grieve her, it does not show on their faces. Perhaps Saints are hardier than I believed. She might still live.

Ignore the forest, my brain rings. *Turn back, turn back.* 'Where might I find her?'

'She is here.'

I look around, but it is just the two of them, watching me expectantly. My blood stills, chilling in my veins. Time slows.

The forest is hungry; go home, go home.

'My cuckoo child,' the younger Saint coos. 'Come home to roost.'

Cu-ckoo. I try to swallow but my throat will not loosen. *Cu-ckoo.* My flesh sings with understanding. *Cu-ckoo.* I want to fasten my hands around time and stop it. *Cu-ckoo.*

'What did you call me?' I breathe.

She tilts her head at a strange angle. 'Do you know what cuckoos do?' I stare back at her, a buzzing in my ears. 'They find a nest and push the eggs out, then replace them with their own. The unsuspecting mother bird returns and raises the cuckoo baby as her child.'

Suddenly, she changes. The milky glaze to her eyes disappears, leaving behind hues of hazel and moss. Her hair falls in gentle waves of copper, the same way mine does. She possesses that unnatural stillness that people have always found strange in me. Freckles smatter the bridge of her nose. The truth is laid bare on her face.

Ignore the warning, you're dead, dead, dead.

Like the toll of a bell, an unshakeable realization tears through me, even before she vocalizes it.

'I am your mother,' she drones.

I blink back at her, heart rabbit-kicking at my throat not from fear but *grief*. The sister I have spilled blood to save was never my sister at all. The mother whose approval I coveted in vain was never my mother. I am alone in the universe. A sob rears up, but I claw it back. I brace myself against a tree trunk while my chest threatens to collapse.

My voice is barely audible above the wind. 'You are – you are my mother?'

'I am. You may call me Borbet.'

'But if you are not human,' I say, stumbling around the leaden weight of my tongue, 'if you are a Saint . . .'

'I am the Mother Sun, the Saint of Love.' Borbet gestures to the other woman, the sleeve of her dress billowing open like a bat's wing. 'She is the Grandmother Moon, the Saint of Sadness, Wilbet.'

Together, they hum, 'You are the Daughter Earth, the Saint of Fear.'

CHAPTER FIFTEEN

I stare down at my hands, mouth ajar. Dried blood forms crescent moons beneath my nails. I am not sure whether it is a relief or a tragedy to learn that I am not human. Perhaps it is neither – perhaps it's a comedy. The strange girl was never a girl at all.

This revelation should be my undoing. The fact that Thea is not my sister should be secondary – a fly-bite against an axe wound. But all I can think about is our broken bond. My Sainthood feels inconsequential, comparatively. It is an explanation for a feeling that has plagued me my entire life. A diagnosis for my ills.

'Did they name you?'

I look up. Borbet's eyes have returned to their strange, milky state. 'They called me Ilse.'

'Your ancestral name is Ambet.'

Ambet. I say it aloud, testing the way it feels against my tongue.

To have a name chosen by a real mother – by someone who might love me – feels like an opportunity, a new beginning, if nothing else.

'Stand up,' Borbet commands.

The order momentarily stuns me into silence. I do as she says, heaving myself up on strangely steady feet. Wilbet watches. I am struck by how much of me rejects her. My dear Oma is dead; she cannot be replaced. This woman is not my *grandmother*.

I think back to the day I first saw the Hexen, or rather the *Saints*. The way they drifted above the meadow grass. The way the Untier slaughtered the third.

Saliva pools in my mouth as I ask, 'If I am your child, who was the girl the Untier killed?'

'The sparrow child. I swapped you with the real Odenwald babe at birth. While you were raised to believe yourself human,' her lip curls at that word, 'she was raised to believe she was a Saint.'

The way Mama screamed that day has haunted me ever since. Now I understand the depth of her anguish. She might not have known that was her child, but mothers have a special sense for their own blood, don't they? She watched her own babe snapped in half while the cuckoo baby sat fearless beside her. No wonder she could not love me.

'*Why?*' Tears prick at my eyes, threatening to spill over. 'Why would you do such a thing?'

'We could not allow you to grow up in the Hexenwald,' Borbet says. 'You were fragile in your infancy. There are many creatures in the forest who would seek to harm you. To kill you. Allowing you to mature in Heulensee was a necessity for your survival. The sparrow child was a necessary decoy.'

She talks about murder as if it is inconsequential. As if the death of a *child* is no grounds for remorse. I still remember the sound of her spine cracking.

I think of the girl, Mama's birth daughter, trying to find a sense of belonging among Saints. She must've been so scared. So out of place, just as I was in the village. I wonder if she lingered on the edge of the Hexenwald, staring at Heulensee, wondering if the village might be a better home.

'You left me in a town with that *monster*.' The word tears across my lips. 'And you expect me to believe it was for my own safety?'

'The parasite would not have killed you.'

My brow furrows. 'How could you possibly know that?'

'We knew,' Borbet says. 'You do not need to understand it. Only to accept it.'

I get the sense that arguing with her is utterly fruitless. She and Mama are alike, in that sense. 'Did my mama know? Did she realize I wasn't her child?'

'She did not know, but she had suspicions. We made the swap surreptitiously, but human mothers have a connection to their kin.' I shudder.

Borbet pauses, watching my reaction with cool intrigue. 'This will be an adjustment,' she says, 'growing into your Sainthood after believing yourself ordinary.'

I almost laugh. If only she understood that I have dissected myself over and over, looking for the blight which taints me. My strangeness would've been easier tolerated had I known the word for it. *Sainthood*.

Before I can react, Borbet places a hand to my temple. Cold radiates from her fingertips, permeating my brain. I recoil; her other hand flies to my wrist and anchors me in place. The sensation is not painful but it is not pleasant, either. Like my mind is being tickled.

'Your power has begun to take root,' she says distantly. 'My touch will encourage it to flower.'

Floodgates tear open beneath my skull. I salivate uncontrollably, my eyes water in a steady stream down my face. Were I not held upright by Borbet, I would sink to the floor. Whatever she did unsteadies me – but then it bolsters me. My vision grows clearer, my hearing more acute. Something familiar sings beneath my skin.

'Promising,' she says. I might take it as a compliment were it not for the indifference in her voice. 'It seems we made the right decision by sending you to mature beyond the forest.'

My head spins. I force bile back down my throat. 'If you sent me to Heulensee for refuge, why did you terrorize the town? Why did you send monsters from the Hexenwald to bloody our shores?'

'I have existed for two centuries, and I will persist when this earth crumbles, when darkness returns,' Wilbet hisses, and I believe her. There is an all-knowing edge to her eyes. 'Do you think a village which will exist only as long as one of my heartbeats is a concern? Do you think I would sully my hands with the blood of commonfolk?'

'The Hexenwald overflows of its own volition,' Borbet interjects. 'It is not of our making. You saw us, the day the sparrow child perished. Did *we* spill a single drop of human blood?'

After a moment, I shake my head no. We were always taught that the Hexen – what we *thought* were Hexen – were the root of every ill that's ever befallen Heulensee. I truly believed that they languished in the forest, commanding their creatures to ravage our village whenever they so pleased. It was easier to blame our misfortunes on them than it was to dig out the truth: that suffering is random and cruel. That we worshipped a parasitic monster.

Borbet assesses me, her expression calculated. 'We have waited a long time for your return.'

'How did you know I would come back?'

'You are a child of the Hexenwald,' she says, voice unchanging. 'You belong to the forest. It called to you, did it not?'

I think of all the times I stood, bewitched by the inky mass of the Hexenwald on the horizon. The bone-deep feeling that I belonged there. 'Yes,' I confess, 'it did.'

'Once you matured, we knew the call would be too much to deny.'

'Now that you have returned, our triad is complete,' Wilbet hums. 'Maiden, mother, crone. The Hexenwald will bow to us.'

My eyes dart to the trees around us, half-believing they will strike Wilbet down where she stands. 'What do you mean?'

'The Saints of Pathos were never meant to be separated,' Borbet explains. 'Alone, our power is mighty, but together, it grows exponentially. As a triad, we have the strength to consume this forest and everything inside it.'

'The forest,' I repeat, Ash's face swimming through my mind, 'and everything inside it?'

Wilbet glides forward. 'So long as the forest persists, we must share the magic which wells beneath the earth. Not just with the trees, but with the Alpe, the Nachzehrer, the Hexen. Now that you have returned, the odds are finally in our favour. Once we bleed this forest dry, the magic will be ours for the taking. We will ascend. From Saints to Gods.'

'No,' I snarl before I can stop myself. If the Hexenwald

perishes, so will Ash. I cannot let them hurt her. *Will not* let them hurt her.

Wilbet draws herself up to full height, her posture that of a predator. Her eyes turn milky; she pulls her upper lip back, revealing sharp teeth. 'No?'

Sensing that I am not in a position to take on two Saints, I make myself small. For now, I will bite my tongue. 'I apologize,' I murmur, feigning chagrin. 'I have grown fond of the forest.'

Borbet moves past Wilbet. She opens her arms, a flower opening for the sun.

'Come,' she says. There is something intoxicating in her outspread arms. Like an unsteady fawn, I stagger and fall into her. The scent of spruce and edelweiss fills my lungs.

Hans once spoke to me about missing the idea of his mother. With Borbet's arms around me, I understand why.

'I dreamt of this,' I say into the curtain of her hair. 'Of a mother other than my own.'

The line of Borbet's back stiffens. 'I did not know she would be cruel.'

'She was not cruel,' I say, barely convinced of my own words, 'but she did not *love* me.'

My mother extricates herself from our embrace, chest heaving with a sigh. I reach after her, childlike. She watches me with her lips pursed. 'Do not ask for what I cannot give.'

My mouth drops open. 'What do you mean?'

'Do not ask me to love you, Ambet.'

The air vacates my lungs in one fell swoop. My knees weaken. 'But you are my *mother.*'

She takes another step back. A chasm yawns open between us. 'Yes, but first I am a Saint.'

'You are the Saint of Love!' My voice comes out weak, quaking with the threat of tears.

'I cannot love you, Ambet.'

I want to kick and scream. To throw myself to the floor, to indulge in the indignation I was never allowed. I want to hurt and howl and have someone care. Have my pain mean something.

The opportunity I briefly saw in her – the possibility of being loved wholly and truly – evaporates. Thea is not my sister, my fake mother resents my existence and my real mother is incapable of loving me.

A gentle breeze amidst the tempest of my rage, Borbet murmurs, 'My Sainthood means I cannot feel love. If I did, it would compromise my ability to deliver it unto others. You are the Saint of Fear, Ambet. That is why you cannot feel it.'

Another realization hits: if my mother cannot muster even an ounce of love for her own daughter, there is no hope for me to summon the real fear it will take to protect Thea. I will always be unfearing.

'I am truly cursed,' I spit, my words lost to incredulous laughter.

Borbet takes a step back; the chasm between us stretches further. Wilbet is similarly displeased; she does not open her mouth, but an echoing voice radiates from her. 'Why did you come here, child? It is clear you are not prepared to accept your calling.' I think of Oma and how different her reaction would've been.

My whole world has been upended, yet all they care about is my ability to aid them. Rage swells, but I tamp it down. Concentrate it into a fiery ball at the heart of me. 'I came here to stop the false Saint ravaging Heulensee,' I say. 'If we do not intervene, that parasite will kill Thea.' My voice is barely a whisper. 'I need your help.'

Wilbet and Borbet exchange a cool look. 'We do not interfere with matters beyond the Hexenwald.'

'But my sister—'

'You do not have a sister, Ambet. We are your family.'

My hands harden into fists at my side. I look between them, incredulous. 'She may not be my blood, but she is my *sister*.'

Wilbet's eyes harden. 'We were going to deal with the parasite. When we visited Heulensee to surveil your maturation the Untier got in our way, giving us reason to attack. But now you've returned here of your own volition and completed our triad. There is no longer a need for us to intervene.'

A sob carves a channel through my chest. 'So you won't help me?'

'No. But we will teach you to harness your power, to grow into your Sainthood.'

'Teach me *now*,' I plead, 'and I will slay the beast myself.'

Wilbet says, 'We will teach you, in time. First, you must understand what it means to be a Saint. To endure.'

The hope leaches from me, whisking away on the breeze. I am left cold and desolate. 'How can you care so little?'

'Caring is a human vice,' Borbet says, apathetic. 'When you've lived as long as we have, you will understand that nothing is permanent. Attachment is nonsensical. *We* are the only constants. *We* endure.'

'In time, you will forget,' Wilbet adds. 'This "sister" will perish and decay, but *we* will remain. Centuries will pass. The earth will continue turning.'

'I will not forget,' I hiss, tearful, 'and if you cannot help me, I must depart.'

I turn my back on the mother I thought I wanted and fix my sights on saving the sister I have chosen.

'We cannot allow you to leave, Ambet.'

I hesitate, my legs not responding to the conviction in my head. Borbet's words are a promise of bloodshed.

Wilbet calls out, 'You must complete our triad, willing or not.'

Half-turned to face them, I notice Borbet's fingers twitching at her side. I register too late the malice behind the gesture. She tugs, and my heart lurches in my chest. I cannot breathe, cannot think. Her hand makes a fist and pain explodes across my ribs. The ricochets send me to my knees, gasping and heaving into the dirt.

Suddenly I realize what's happening. This force is love. My mother has weaponized *love*. My heart beats like a hawkmoth's wings, each contraction blurring into the next. Dizziness strikes me so violently that I cannot tell where the sky ends and the earth begins.

'Stop,' I gasp. 'Stop it.'

Wilbet's shadow looms over me. She floats just above the ground, bone-white eyes boring into my soul. Her fingers flex; my stomach fills with misery. Anguish floods my body, so intense that I cannot think past it. Tears burst from my eyes in a torrent, thick and fast. Even when I tied stones to my ankles and waded out into the lake, I did not feel sorrow as biting as this. To be numb would be a blessing.

They are my *family*. Why does my defiance merit punishment? I stare up at Wilbet, praying she will see reason. I am her granddaughter, and she is torturing me. My heart seizes again, clenching tight as my fists. Stars expand and burst across my vision. Death lingers, unable or unwilling to claim me, but still salivating, purring.

'Am I interrupting something?'

The pain lifts. Borbet and Wilbet's frantic movements yield to statuesque calm. The only sign that they are made not of stone – but of flesh – is the wind whisking through their hair. I pant and heave into the grass.

Torsten strolls into the clearing, rolling a glass orb across his palm. Relief floods through me, a wave breaking first on my head then washing down my aching limbs. His gait is cool, collected. Our gaze meets for a split second, my laboured breaths an errant contrast to his measured ones. A purple contusion rings one of his eyes, dealt by the Hexenwald, no doubt. My heart aches. Please let Ash be okay.

'What business do you have here, Hexe?' Borbet spits, her feet lifting from the ground.

He shrugs. 'My friend seems to be in distress. I thought I ought to intervene.'

Wilbet levitates, too. Her skin turns translucent. 'Challenging Saints spells death.'

'*Usually*, yes,' Torsten drawls. 'But death and I have never gotten along.'

The two Saints turn to each other and say, 'A most insolent creature.'

'Superlatives so soon?' He flashes white teeth. 'As much as I enjoy your sweet nothings, I'm afraid Ilse and I will be leaving.'

'The girl is ours,' Borbet and Wilbet hum in unison. 'Touch her and perish.'

Torsten winks. 'Don't threaten me with a good time.'

Time distorts and slows. The Saints hurl themselves at Torsten. Something radiates from his body: tendrils of black, whipping and snapping in the breeze. He hauls back his arm, fastening his fingers around the orb. Spruces lean in, ready to witness the bloodshed, and then Torsten's gaze snaps to meet mine.

'Shut your eyes,' he shouts.

I shut them just at the moment the world explodes. Shrapnel assaults me, jagged splinters thrown outward by broken trees. The blast knocks me to my knees. A wall of heat hits me. Light, red and white hot, pierces the translucent film of my eyelids. Torsten's form is silhouetted against the inferno.

'What have you done?' I shout.

'It's an alchemical reaction,' he calls back. 'It will arrest them, but not for long. *Go!*'

My legs are rooted to the spot. I look around with wild eyes. Half of me wants to stay and fight; the other half wants to flee.

'*Now*, Ilse!'

I bolt into motion. Borbet and Wilbet's howls follow me as I stagger from the clearing. Torsten lets out an anguished cry. I falter, throwing a haphazard glance across my shoulder. Wilbet has him by his throat, hoisted up against a tree trunk. Smoke sizzles between her fingertips. Through the pain, Torsten manages to mouth the word *go*.

I should turn back. I should save him. But I am a coward.

When the smoke thins, I reorient myself and *run*. The Hexenwald claws at me. Any delusions I had of being embraced by the forest vanish as tree needles lodge into my skin. Roots erupt from the ground beside me, matching each of my steps. A howling wail builds behind, and I cannot tell if it's the Hexenwald or the Saints.

'Leave me!' I snarl, cursing the trees as they whip my skin.

Another root snakes up my leg. Before I can react, it winds around my torso and wrestles me to a stop. I swear and thrash against the restraints, an animal caught in a trap. In the distance, someone calls my name. But I am not Ilse. Not anymore.

My fingernails bend and tear as I scrabble at the roots. I am a Saint, yet an overgrown weed impedes me. Feverish, I dig through my inner workings for power. Borbet and Wilbet can wield it. Why can't I?

Hazy shapes drift in front of me. At first, I suspect I must have hit my head and compromised my vision, but the shadows are real. Ethereal cords of black light linger in the clearing, as easily dispersed as smoke. Driven by intuition, I reach out and curl my fingers around one. Something sparks.

Bone-deep. Instinctual. It's that same feeling I have possessed all my life; uneasy anticipation, the knowledge that something is wrong. Except now, I think I know what it is.

Magic.

CHAPTER SIXTEEN

The black light pulls away from me; I tug back. There is a shift inside my consciousness. Tentative and nearly imperceptible, like the first bubbles of simmering water upon a stove. But water boils gradually, and whatever sparks inside me is anything but gradual. It's tempestuous, bolting from a gentle hum to an aching howl.

'Ilse.'

The voice cannot cut through the haze of my power. I have inhaled the essence of Sainthood, and it is addictive. My eyes roll back into my skull. I hold the cord tighter, tighter.

'Ilse!'

My head snaps to the side. Ash stands next to me, her eyes wide and panicked. 'It's me,' she breathes. 'The roots are mine. I just wanted to catch up. It's okay. You are safe.'

Three more strangled breaths pass my lips before my brain fog dissipates. I centre Ash's face in my vision, focusing on each of her features in sequence. The same black cords lingering in the air extend from her body, curling in the breeze. Her expression makes it seem like she's seeing me for the first time.

'You're okay,' I breathe, collapsing into her arms before I can think better of it.

'We're both okay,' she murmurs, arms held awkwardly around me, as if she can't quite decide what to do with them, or with us. 'What happened?'

I open my mouth, but the words do not come. All I can muster is, 'Torsten.'

Ash's nostrils flare. She extricates herself from my grip, and I almost reach after her, despite myself.

'Stay here,' she says. There's a hint of hesitation, so subtle that I can hardly be sure it existed – and then she turns back and runs into the trees.

My ears whine. I pick out a low, moaning sound ahead. Shaky-limbed, I follow the sound to its source.

Hans. He cowers against a tree trunk, skin lined in goose-bumps so pronounced that I notice them from a distance. I breathe his name, the way you might announce yourself to a frightened animal.

'I don't know what's happening to me,' he chokes out, teeth chattering on each syllable. The whites of his eyes are a torch against the dark. 'Make it stop.'

The Fear season renders him horrified, just like this. But we're not *in* the Fear season. Cotton-tailed rabbits hop around us, hallmarks of the False season.

A spool of darkness stretches from his chest, pulsing. Breath held, I look to my hand, where the other end of it is still clenched between my fingertips.

'Do you see that?' I whisper, turning the thread over. 'The cord?'

'See what?' he asks, voice shaking.

I pull it tight. 'This.'

Hans screams. I drop the thread of shadows like a hot coal. The spell over him breaks; he draws in a sharp breath. His relief is instantaneous. I stagger back, so ridden with guilt that I cannot look him in the eye. The cord retracts into Hans's chest, swirling where his heart beats beneath his skin.

I did that. Made him so scared that he could hardly speak. I look down at my hands, expecting to find them sullied by the terror I just inflicted, but they look the same as they always have. If this is Sainthood, I'm no longer sure I want it.

The trauma of the afternoon crashes down on me. I wrap my arms around my own body, desperate to hold the shattered pieces of me together. I have spent my life in search of two things: a sense of belonging, and an understanding of the absence inside me. Now that I've reached the latter, I'm drifting even further from humanity than I thought possible.

Before I can register what's happening, Hans envelops me. He squeezes the air from my lungs, but I do not pull away. I sag into his embrace, letting my knees buckle, knowing that he will support me.

'I'm here now, Ils,' Hans murmurs, stroking the back of my head. 'Can you tell me what happened?' He pulls back, studying my face and counting each cut from the shrapnel. 'Are you okay?'

I clamp my lip between my teeth and shake my head *no*. I am not okay. He exhales, then guides my head to rest against his shoulder. The tears come easily. Their scalding heat is the only warmth in my body.

'Whatever happened, we can get past it. We can still save her.'

I sob and ache until there is no more to give. Until my chest shudders with the empty threat of tears. I extricate myself from Hans, look him in the eye, and confess the worst of it all.

'Thea isn't my sister,' I bleat. 'She was never my sister.'

'Oh, Ilse.' He studies me – my trembling lip, the hopelessness in my eyes – and decides that I must be held together. Hans crushes me against him once more, and I do not fight it. The pressure of his arms makes me think I might not crumble entirely. In that moment, I cannot believe I ever hated him.

His grip falters, just for a second. 'Who told you that?'

'My mother,' I splutter. 'My *real* mother.'

I stumble backwards. He reaches after me, but all of a sudden his proximity is too much to bear. I brace myself against a tree, chest heaving. I have discovered I am the Saint of Fear, yet Thea not being my sister troubles me more.

Ash staggers into the clearing, Torsten slung over her shoulder. Her mouth is set in a grim line; Torsten is worryingly quiet. Ash finally speaks: 'The minute the Saints regain consciousness, they will hunt us down. Our meadow is warded; they cannot follow us there, nor will they be able to sense us once we're inside – but we have to get there first.'

She spares one tense look at me and flees into the trees. I follow, Hans's heavy footfalls behind me the only indication he heard her. He is silent, contemplative. I turn once to look at him, and the whites of his eyes flash.

Fear, as I understand it, tells our body things that our conscious minds cannot sense. It tells us not to pass through the dark alleyway at night. It tells us that brightly-coloured insects should be avoided, and that sharp teeth and claws will draw blood.

When Hans looks at me now, I see it in his face. His body senses the threat his mind won't accept. He is afraid.

He is afraid of *me*.

☠

Torsten wasn't lying when he said the Hexenwald favours him. The trees yield as we run, branches pointing us towards the meadow. Staggering across the threshold is like pushing through a bubble of soap without piercing it. The boundary snaps back into place in our wake.

'They cannot follow us here,' Ash calls over her shoulder, relief softening her anxiety. Hans offers to help bear Torsten's weight, but Ash seems to take the gesture as an insult. Fiercely protective, she hauls Torsten to the cabin. His feet drag limply across the ground.

'Clear the desk,' she commands.

Hans and I sweep the contents of the desk – tomes, left out by Torsten before our venture; half-empty vessels of ink and worn-down quills; parchment scrawled with illegible notes – into a basket. With a grunt, Ash deposits her brother onto the wooden surface. His body is deathly heavy. There is no resistance, no tension in his flesh.

'Don't you dare die,' she hisses. 'If anyone is going to kill you, it will be me.' Torsten's head lolls back, lifeless. Ash draws a breath between gritted teeth. Panicked eyes dart to meet Hans's. 'In the garden, behind the cabin. Fetch me yarrow, lemon balm and a handful of the black berries that grow by the window.'

Hans sprints from the room, repeating the list of ingredients as he goes. I clear my throat and ask, 'Will he be okay?'

'I don't know,' Ash frets. Her skin pales; her hands tremble as she traces the red welts which bloom across his throat – the memory of Wilbet's suffocating hold. 'Torsten, you *idiot*. Who goes hand to hand with a Saint?'

Voice trembling, I say, 'He saved me. Held them up long enough for me to get away.' Guilt writhes inside me.

She pauses. Her next exhale comes out shakily. Emotion wells against her eyelids.

Hans returns with the ingredients; Ash snatches them from his hands and grinds them into a paste using a mortar and pestle. As a last step, she attempts to strip the black berries from their stems.

'Here,' I whisper, prying the fruit from her shaking hands. 'Tell me how many.'

She eventually loosens her grip. 'Just one.'

I drop one berry into the bowl and follow instructions as Ash stutters through measures of liquids held in amber bottles – two drops of the burgundy, one of the clear, five of the midnight blue. I mix the concoction until it forms a thick paste that sizzles with heat. Waves of ether roll off its surface.

'Don't touch,' Ash snaps. Then, with a softer voice, 'It's not good for humans.'

A hollow gapes open inside me. How can I tell her what I truly am? That my kin seeks to destroy the Hexenwald, her home, altogether?

How can I tell Hans? He could barely handle Ash being a Hexe. Now to find out that he has been aiding a Saint all this time . . .

I can't lose their trust. My stomach curdles as Ash drips the concoction into Torsten's mouth. After two torturous minutes, the butterfly-wing flutter of his chest grows stronger. Colour returns to his face.

Ash peels back her brother's eyelids and examines his pupils. 'There we go,' she says at last, the relief in her voice palpable. She addresses Hans and I. 'He'll live.'

A fraction of the weight lifts from my chest and I feel that I can breathe again, at least for a moment. I take Torsten's limp hand and squeeze it. He had no reason to risk his life for me, no familial loyalty or debt to settle, and yet he *did*. His bravery is a stark reminder of my own duty.

'He needs to rest, now.' Ash ushers us out of the study and follows, snicking the door shut behind her.

Hans sits down on the fainting couch in the amber-walled room, face pale. 'What happened out there?'

Ash looks to me, waiting. 'I was wondering the same thing.'

The events of the day catch up with me, rushing through my brain in a deluge. How can I explain that in the space of thirty minutes, I met my real family; almost died at the hands of said family; and discovered that I am in fact a *Saint*?

For years, I've felt a breakdown on the horizon. Perhaps this is it. If I spill everything, I might scare away Hans and Ash. But if I don't, I will combust. The truth of my Sainthood is a blister to be lanced.

Hans pats the seat beside him, beckoning me to sit down. 'Are you all right, Ilse?'

'I'm perfectly fine.' Ash and Hans exchange a worried look while I press a hand against my breastbone, searching for the dormant power surely stored there. My voice cracks when I say, 'What has plagued me my whole life has a name.'

Hans swallows, sensing the gravity of what I am about to confess. 'Tell me.'

I look at him, then at Ash. This could be our final moment of kinship. Maybe they'll brand me a liar. A deceiver. A *monster*.

'I am a Saint.' The weight of my words fills the room; the air crackles around me. At first I think I have imagined it, but Hans flinches in time with the static. A palpable tension swells between us. Belief and doubt intertwine on his face. Ash watches me with a measured expression.

'A Saint?' Hans frowns. 'Ilse—'

'Or rather, *the* Saint,' I bite out. 'The Saint of Fear – the one we've been searching for. Also, the creatures we thought were Hexen? The ones who bloodied our shores all those years ago?' I pause, barely long enough for Hans to process. 'They are Saints, too. I am the third of them.'

He shakes his head slowly. 'Ilse, that can't be.'

A feverishness strips away all my sense. I deliver the news the only way I know how: bluntly. 'It *is*, Hans.' I turn my eyes to Ash, knowing she needs to hear this, too. 'I am not human. Mama is not my mama; Thea is not my sister. I am a Saint, and *I* remain our only hope of saving Thea. Except I don't know how to wield my magic, and my real family will not teach me. In fact, they just tried to *kill* me. Torsten rescued me, and now he's—'

'Ilse.' There is a forceful concern to Ash's voice, enough to break my frenzied train of thought. I stare back at her, breathless from rambling. My entire body itches, as if I have outgrown it and need to shed my skin. 'You need to sit down.'

'You don't believe me?'

Her eyes flash at the frantic tone in my voice. 'I believe you, but I think you need to *breathe*.'

Suddenly, I realize that her face, Hans's face, the entire *room*, is bathed in blinding white light. Hans winces, too polite to shield himself. I turn, casting my eyes to my translucent reflection in the warped windowpanes. The sight is enough to make me heave. My eyes are milky white, devoid of pupils. Devoid of *humanity*. The maternal resemblance is uncanny. Power hums within me, thrashing against my veins.

I sink down to the floor. Ash rushes to my side, one hand wavering about my shoulders.

'*Breathe*, Ilse,' she commands.

I am not bound to her the way she is to me, but I obey her, nonetheless. Gasping, I suck in a breath. Hold it. Let it out. *Another.* Hold it. Let it out. *Another.*

I do not know how long it takes for my senses to return and my eyes to lose their ghostly pallor, but the next time I look at Hans he does not flinch at my appearance. Ash's hand lingers at my shoulder, never quite fastening, but never leaving either.

'How does it feel,' I mutter, 'to know that you have harboured a Saint?'

I wait for her to banish me from the house, but she simply twists her mouth and looks me up and down. 'I knew there was something different about you.'

'You knew?'

'Well,' she blows out a breath, 'I did not know you were a Saint, exactly. That would have given me pause. But I knew your aura was different.'

'Different?' I ask. 'How?'

She sniffs, eyes flicking between us. '*His* is the same as every human who wanders into the Hexenwald. Copper and salt.' Hans opens his mouth to protest, but Ash waves him off. 'You're rosemary and marjoram. I sensed you weren't entirely human.'

Hearing it aloud is enough to make me wince.

Ash senses my hurt; she moves in, squeezes my shoulder and says, 'Different is not such a bad thing to be.'

My muscles tingle beneath her fingertips. I cannot comprehend that my life has been altered so significantly, so irrevocably, without experiencing any material change. This thing – my Sainthood – has been a part of me all along, but now that I am aware of it, the breath is wrenched from my lungs.

'Can you sense it?' Ash asks. 'Your magic?'

I look inward to the squall at my core that awakened with Borbet's touch. As soon as I focus on it, the black cords reappear. They thrash about the room. Hans's body is lined so thickly with them that they tangle in the air. Ash is scarcely adorned, in comparison, but two shimmering ribbons of darkness extend from her heart and her throat. One ties her to Torsten in the other room; another stretches out towards me. I back away before it can make contact. I cannot bear to touch them.

I blink, hoping the threads will disappear. 'Will I ever grow used to it?'

'You will. My magic is an extension of me. It's no more distracting than the feel of my blood nurturing my muscles.'

I turn to Hans, who shrinks under my gaze. 'Are you afraid?'

'Yes,' he confesses, sheepish. 'Terrified.'

'I can *see* it,' I admit.

To see the physical manifestation of fear makes me relieved not to *feel* it. The cords constrict his throat and force his heart into an unrestrained cadence. Perhaps my curse is also a privilege; witnessing his suffering in such visceral detail makes me aware of that. I want to save him, to comfort him, but I'm not sure I am even capable. We are entirely different species.

Something tells me that unfurling the tightly coiled tendrils of my magic is a path from which I cannot return. Once I open myself to Sainthood, I will have crossed an irreversible boundary between the person I was, and the Saint I will become.

But if I stay at this crossroads, I cannot save Thea. Cannot be the saviour Heulensee needs. The one it will come to worship. I must dive into Sainthood, head-on. Let it try and drown me.

CHAPTER SEVENTEEN

'You are a fool, Torsten Nachtnebel! I knew you were slow-witted, but this level of stupidity is unprecedented!'

I'm dragged from sleep by Ash's voice. At first, I'm filled with relief at the fact that Torsten is clearly conscious, but then the reality of our situation sets in. The Saints who were to help us kill the Untier have no interest in our mission.

And *I* am a Saint.

'No one is coming to save us,' I whisper, as if speaking the words aloud robs them of their power. 'It has to be me.'

Hans asks, 'What's that?'

I didn't realize he was awake. Ash gave us the bedroom she and Torsten shared as children: two single beds, separated by a nightstand. She *also* gave me one of her nightgowns, which I read into perhaps more than I should have. Hans sits upright in bed, pulling at the bandages around his palm. Whatever he sees beneath them makes him grimace.

'Nothing,' I say. 'I was just daydreaming. Is your hand okay?'

'Fine,' he says, patting the bandages back into place.

'It doesn't *seem* fine,' I counter.

'I'm not good with blood.' He shudders. 'Makes me feel ill.'

I contemplate demanding to assess the wound myself, but then another shout comes from down the hallway. Ash is interrogating Torsten about his abject stupidity, stating that it 'certainly doesn't run in the family'.

'You'd better go and intervene before she finishes him off.' Hans laughs.

I slip out of bed, Ash's nightgown dragging on the floor as I tiptoe to Torsten's room.

Wide-eyed, Torsten is propped up against his headboard. The sight of him awake brings momentary relief, which dissipates as soon as I take in the full scene. He has one hand raised in what looks like surrender; the other curls, white-knuckled, around the quilt. Ash leans over him with her brow furrowed. Seeing her enraged stirs something in me.

'What happened?' I ask, still rubbing the sleep from my eyes.

Torsten's eyes slide to mine. 'I just . . . woke up.'

Ether seeps between the cracks of Ash's clenched fists as she says, 'It is what you did *before* waking that troubles me.'

'Did you expect the Saints to go easy on me?'

'I expected you not to fight with Saints in the first place!'

'I didn't fight them,' he argues. 'Technically,' – *always* with the technicalities – 'I made a failed attempt to bind them.'

Sensing that Ash might be about to polish him off, I intervene. 'He saved me, Ash.' My voice is a quiet protest, a gentle reminder of Torsten's sacrifice. 'He bought me enough time to run.'

Torsten flashes me a conspiratorial look. It says, *thank you, but your efforts are futile.*

'Had I died, you might have considered it a penance,' he says.

'Is that really what you believe?' she spits. 'That you would leave me on my own for the rest of this near-eternal life and I would be *grateful*?'

The corners of Torsten's mouth wrinkle. He is touched by her words.

Ash hurries to add, 'I have no interest in bearing the responsibility for your death.'

'I have free will. If I'd died, it would've had nothing to do with you.'

She scoffs. 'You were only searching for the Saints because *I* was.'

'And *you* were only searching for the Saints because I turned you into a tree, until you met Ilse and she bound you.'

'This isn't a game, Torsten!' The atmosphere in the room thickens, as if a storm is about to unleash. 'You are the only thing I have left from before. If you die, part of me dies with you.' She pauses and draws in a breath. 'If you *ever* do anything like that again, I'll—'

'Kill me?' Torsten grins.

I catch Ash's palm just before it collides with his cheek.

She turns to me, frantic. 'Let me go.'

'No,' I protest, fingers tightening around her wrist. 'Go outside and cool off.'

She looks between Torsten and me, eyes aflame. Five painful seconds pass before she shakes her hand loose and crosses the room in two strides, slamming the door on her way out.

I flop down onto the bed. 'That went well.'

'She'll calm down,' Torsten says, running his fingers across a particularly jagged cut on his arm.

Staring at the scar, I ask, 'Why *did* you save me?' Torsten stares back, perplexed. 'I'm a stranger. Why would you do something like that?'

'For her,' he admits quietly.

My heart seizes. I curl one hand around the quilt. 'What do you mean?'

He rubs his fist across his eyes. 'Don't be naive.'

'What do you *mean*, Torsten?'

He kicks a leg beneath the cover, forcing me off the bed. 'I'm pumped full of potions, Ilse. I don't know.'

My pride forbids me from asking him a third time.

☠

In the days which follow, Ash and Torsten's relationship does not entirely heal, but it scabs over. A minor provocation might cause it to tear open and bleed once more. She is preoccupied with his care, of course, but I can't help focusing on the fact that our time left to save Thea is slipping away.

I attempt to practise my magic, thinking that if I can hone it, that'll give me a sense of forward momentum. But despite Hans repeatedly bidding me to manipulate his fear, I can't bring myself to do it. I don't want him looking at me the way a deer looks at a wolf ever again.

The black cords dominate my perception. It's like suddenly becoming aware that you can see the tip of your own nose, and being unable to focus on anything else. Every time I talk to Hans, or watch Ash as she dotes over Torsten, all I can see is the shadowed tendrils. I have to actively distract myself to make them fade into the background.

Just as I'm about to combust from my desire to effect *something*, Ash helps Torsten downstairs. He takes the steps slowly, but the colour has returned to his skin and each movement doesn't make him wince anymore.

'My brother is going to teach you how to wield your magic,' Ash says, helping him through the front door. 'If the Saints won't help us, your own powers will need to suffice.'

The three of us venture into the meadow, leaving Hans to nap. It's a gloriously sunny day, thick with the sort of heat that's good for little other than sprawling in the sun. Torsten picks a flattened patch of grass and sits down cross-legged, gesturing for me to do the same.

Ash finds a seat on the stairs to the cabin's porch. She watches me with a furtive smile. It's the first time I've seen that look since Torsten was injured. I can't help but grin back at her, to which she waggles a finger at me and mouths 'concentrate'. The way her lips move around the word does *not* help my focus.

Torsten studies me. He grits his teeth as he rearranges himself in the grass. 'Well?'

I lift my chin. 'What?'

'Show me your magic.'

A singular black cord extends from his heart, tossed about by the breeze. I grasp it gingerly, the way one might scoop up an injured bird. Torsten's reaction is instantaneous; his golden eyes widen. I drop the tendril like a hot coal. The memory of Hans's fear is visceral.

'It's okay,' he insists. 'You need to practise.'

Reluctantly, I take his fear back between my fingers. Feeling it dance across my skin is like trying to read a book in a language I do not speak. I turn it this way and that, attempting to decipher the fear. No matter what I do, the idea of wielding it – forging it into something with teeth – repulses me.

I clench my jaw. 'I can't.'

'Come now, Ilse,' Ash calls from across the meadow, her voice teasing. 'You are a Saint. Patience is in your blood.'

'Don't distract my student,' Torsten shouts back. Ash sticks out her tongue. Dropping his voice so she cannot eavesdrop, Torsten says, 'You need to will something to happen. For the wind to surge, or fire to spark. Focus that energy.'

I exhale, letting my lungs empty. I fill my mind with a gentle humming sound, if only to muffle the noise of my thoughts. *I want the wind to pick up*, I think. A gentle fizz courses across my skin – Torsten's fear, flowing through my veins – and I want to retch. I clench the tendril tighter. My heart pounds, sweat gathers on my forehead, I shake—

'Stop, Ilse.'

My eyes snap open.

Torsten looks back at me, brow lowered. 'You were going to faint.'

'I don't understand,' I gripe. 'This is who I am. It should be as easy as breathing.'

I expect Torsten to comfort me, but the troubled look on his face serves only to heighten my angst. 'You have innate magic, as all creatures of the Hexenwald do. Fear simply amplifies it, if the other Saints of Pathos are anything to go by. Perhaps we should focus on innate magic first. The way fear interacts with it can come later.'

I sever the connection with Torsten's terror and feel immediate relief. Over the course of the day, we hone my innate magic. At first, I approach it with a sullen apathy, thinking I will be just as hopeless at this as I was at wielding his fear. But then I find a little flutter of a feeling, that creeping unease inside me. I nurture it into an effervescent spark, transforming a wrong feeling into something just right. It's like sinking into a pair of boots made just for me.

'Think of something you want,' Torsten reminds me. 'It helps channel the magic.'

I shut my eyes, my heartbeat a steady metronome.

'What are you thinking of, Ilse?' Ash teases. I peel one eye open to scowl at her, though I can't help but mirror the smile on her face.

'*Ash*,' Torsten chastises. 'Stop flirting.'

My eyes grow to the size of dinner plates and I blush; Ash skulks to a shaded spot in the meadow, laying down in the grass. Her impression lingers in my mind. The soft expanse of her skin; the shape of her hips; the fullness of her lips. I push those thoughts down, despite their best efforts to resurface. I exhale, willing the wind to stir, and it does.

'How is that possible?' I ask, giddy with excitement.

'How is it possible that water falls from the sky, that a tiny seed can grow into an oak tree, that I can rub rocks together and make fire?' Unsure if this is a rhetorical question or a riddle, I keep my mouth shut. 'Magic is a force of nature,' Torsten says. 'I can't explain it any more than I can explain why the sky is blue. It just is.'

Harnessing my magic feels like learning to swim. At first, I thrash wildly, expending fruitless energy, only able to keep my lips above the waves. By the end of the day, calling my magic – commanding it – is an effortless breaststroke through warm water. It is a far cry from the feral power I felt with Hans's terror bolstering me, but it is safe.

Eventually Ash wanders back over to sit beside us. She watches the flame flickering in my palm. Amber light dances across her cheeks, burnishing her skin.

Almost reverential, she whispers, 'Your magic is strong.'

I flush a deep shade of scarlet. Torsten rolls his eyes.

'Will it be enough?' I ask him.

His eyes turn serious. 'We are barely scratching the surface here, Ilse. These are parlour tricks. If you wish to defeat the Untier, we need to train. Hard.'

My pulse thrums against my throat like a butterfly's wings. 'How long will it take?'

'To get you to a level where I would feel confident sending you into battle against a false Saint?' Torsten looks to the skies, pondering. 'A year. But given that we have' – he carries out simple maths on his fingers – 'all of fourteen days, I'll make do with ten.'

Fourteen days feels like torture. 'A fish does not have the luxury to pause and learn how to breathe underwater,' I say in protest.

'But a bird knows the wisdom of waiting until its wings are strong before it fledges the nest,' he counters.

He always has an answer for everything.

By the time we return to the house, Hans is still deep in sleep. When he wakes, he doesn't seem rested. Ash wrinkles her nose at his bandaged palm. Upon further inspection, we find that the wound has turned septic. Once his flesh has been cleaned, Ash sends him again to bed with a belly full of medicine.

During the night, pre-emptive grief clutches my heart in a vice. I believe I will wake to find that spruce needles have erupted from beneath his skin. When morning finally comes, the wound is pink and healthy. I do not let Hans see my relief. He rests for the next day while I continue to train with Torsten. Sleeping eases his lethargy, but he still seems out of sorts. I don't have the capacity to discern exactly *how*.

Despite my worries about Hans, Ash proves an easy distraction. When Torsten goes for a rest of his own, still reeling from his encounter with the Saints, she asks me to show her what I've learned that day. We venture briefly into the Hexenwald, where a juvenile Lindwurm snakes across our path. Its strong front legs drag a serpentine tail, its head almost draconic. I fix it in my gaze, shout the word 'sleep', and watch as it falls into a slumber.

Ash is so impressed that I conspicuously perform a number of other feats: igniting and extinguishing a blueberry bush, felling an admittedly stringy sapling with a swipe of my fingers, summoning water to the cupped bowl of her hands. It's only when I look up that I realize she's far more focused on me than on the magic.

She's just about to speak when the sky darkens. Reddens.

Ash takes my hand. We sprint back through the trees, bursting across the meadow's threshold as scarlet churns overhead. Trees thrash hungrily against the boundary. They bend so fiercely that I think they might snap. Thunder roars; static fills the air, coaxing my hairs to stand on end.

'I thought they couldn't follow us here,' I say.

'They can't,' Ash breathes.

We stand just short of the boundary, close enough that I can see its shimmering fabric. My even breaths stir it into ripples.

Beside me, Ash's pupils twitch as she scans the forest. I follow suit, narrowing my eyes against the shaded spaces between the trees.

We needn't have bothered scouring. Our hunter has no reason to hide.

She is the apex predator of this forest; we are the deer. Wilbet glides through the trees towards us, her jaw hanging open. Her feet – bloodied or muddied, I cannot tell – dangle limply, shifting direction as she does. Wilbet flicks her tongue out, tasting the air. And then she looks straight at me.

Ash lets out a shuddered exhale. I cup a hand over her mouth. Wilbet glides closer, closer, until her face is level with mine. Her measured breath pierces the barrier, bringing the scent of rot and copper.

A brown bear once made its way into the village. It slaughtered two children before anyone caught it. Would've slaughtered me, too, had Papa not driven a blade into the broad space between its eyes. I do not remember the weapon – it could've been a spear, or a sword, or maybe even the penknife – but I do remember those hungry eyes.

I can find mischief in the gaze of a fox, or wisdom in that of a wolf. The bear's eyes were empty. It lumbered towards me, ready to spill my intestines across the grass, and its eyes gave away nothing. They were endlessly black, absent of colour and emotion. Voids that called and called and *called*. My grandmother has the same eyes, except rendered in ivory.

Wilbet presses both palms against the meadow's boundary. White bear eyes stare back at me. Scarlet teardrops well and roll down her face, gathering in the seam of her lips.

'I know you're close, Ambet,' she hisses, peering from side to side. 'You cannot hide for ever.'

I dare not breathe.

Ash fastens her hand around mine. She presses her thumb tight against my palm. The panicked thrum of her pulse races through my skin. Wilbet's nostrils expand as she inhales. Too late, I realize she can *smell* us. I know she possesses the power to tear this boundary to shreds. In a breath, the only barrier between her and her prey will vanish. *We* will vanish. Death will be quick, if we're lucky. If not . . .

Something snaps in the forest. Wilbet's head swivels a half circle. She glides away at breakneck speed, disappearing into the trees.

Ash and I stand in silence for what must be five minutes. My eyes do not leave the treeline.

Eventually, I break the quiet. 'She nearly found us.' My voice is a monotone, hardly the sound of someone who just stared into the eyes of their hunter.

'It was my fault,' Ash murmurs. 'I shouldn't have taken you beyond the meadow.'

When I turn to look at her, she's already staring back at me. My heart lurches.

'If anything happened to you, Ilse . . .' Her jaw tightens, lips pulling taut.

'We're safe,' I tell her. 'We're alive.'

'Alive,' she repeats, gaze darting between my lips and my eyes.

Thunder growls overhead. Swollen droplets of rain burst on our heads. A rivulet runs down the swell of Ash's cheek, dripping from her chin and onto her chest. It snakes between her breasts, beneath the maroon fabric of her blouse. My eyes track its path. I run my tongue across my lips, tasting rainwater when I wish I were tasting *her*.

Ash studies me silently, seemingly resolving to speak three times before she actually does. 'Let's get you inside,' she says hoarsely. 'Out of the rain.'

I reluctantly follow her inside the house, wondering if I have manufactured the tension between us. She retreats to her bedroom, and does not emerge for the rest of the day.

Each time I look at Hans, a knot forms in my stomach. Though his wound has closed and the infection has not returned, he seems ... different. Less vibrant. He sleeps too much and eats too little. He rarely laughs. A gnawing feeling tells me the forest has stripped something vital from him. I don't think it intends to give it back.

I spend as much time with him as I can, desperate to reawaken the optimism I know slumbers beneath his skin. Though I'm not actively avoiding Ash, I don't know how to be around her without my entire body humming, so my preoccupation with Hans is a welcome distraction.

I spend the morning after Wilbet's appearance in the kitchen with Hans. I'm helping him chop herbs when a question leaps to my lips unbidden. 'How did you know Thea liked you?'

He cocks an eyebrow. 'Why do you ...' Hans trails off as realization washes across his features. He leans in, grinning ear to ear, and says, 'Are you in lov—'

'If you say another word, I swear I will never speak to you again.' Heat rushes to my cheeks. 'Just answer the question.'

I stir the large pot of barley stew, our meal big enough to feed a small army. Although he doesn't eat much these days, Hans cooks enough to ensure that I'm fed like a prize pig.

He reaches over my shoulder, dropping a handful of herbs into the pot. 'Funnily enough, we bonded over food. I offered her some of the *Spätzle* I was eating, expecting her to use her own fork – but she took my fork instead.'

Delicious as it is, I'm not sure how spätzle constitutes an admission of attraction.

Sensing my confusion, Hans elaborates with a sheepish smile. 'I decided that if she didn't mind sharing saliva in that way, she might not mind sharing it in ... other ways.'

'Hans!' I shriek, mortified, grabbing the wooden spoon from the countertop to swat at him.

He dodges me, hands thrown into the air. 'You asked!'

'Well, just in case it's not yet clear, I never, ever, want to hear about you and my sister swapping saliva. *Ever.*'

Hans throws his head back and laughs so loudly that my ears ring. I make a great show of my disgust, though secretly it's a joy to entertain him. I ladle stew into my bowl and rush out to the meadow before he can say anything else.

On my way out, I nearly trip over Ash. She sits on the steps to the house, knees drawn up to her chest.

I stop dead in my tracks. She glances at me out of the corner of her eye. Her lips draw into a crooked smile. 'Care to sit?'

Fortunately, the day is warm enough that I do not think my flushed cheeks look out of place. I perch beside her, our thighs separated by mere inches. Though I would never confess it to Hans, I'm too distracted to even taste his stew as I wolf it down.

With the stew in my lap and Ash at my side, I sense an opportunity. Time to test Hans's hypothesis. 'Would you like to try some?'

Ash looks at the bowl, then back to me. She wrinkles her nose.

Purses her lips. *Oh heavens.* The thought of sharing a spoon with me disgusts her. *I* disgust her. Somewhere along the line, I've made a dire miscalculation. How could I interpret her closeness as anything more than the fact that we are magically bound together? She must think I'm mad, or foul, or unsettling.

I draw the bowl back onto my lap, blushing furiously.

Ash reaches out, curling gentle fingers around my wrist. 'I don't eat, Ilse. Remember?'

Ah. That explains it.

'You don't eat,' I echo, my voice hollow. I'm not sure what's worse, her rejection of my offer, or the fact that I forgot this about her.

'But I'll try it. I *can* eat, if I have to. I generally just ... don't.'

She uncoils her hand from my wrist and takes a spoonful of stew.

'You don't have to do that.' I attempt to take the spoon from her, but she holds fast.

'I want to,' Ash protests, trying to regain control of it.

She's got hold of the spoon, and *I've* got hold of the spoon, and our hands are overlapping, and I'm trying to pull back but she's guiding it to her mouth, and oh Saints, I'm feeding her, and her perfect lips draw shut around the food, and I have never been so jealous of a Saints-forsaken spoon, and I can't *breathe*—

'Delicious,' she purrs.

I once read a book wherein the heroine fainted at the sight of her lover. I didn't understand it at the time.

'You should tell Hans,' I mumble clumsily. *Why am I dragging Hans into this?* 'He would be pleased.'

She laughs uproariously; it makes me feel even fainter. 'I don't think I have ever pleased Hans.'

I spend so long debating what I should or should not tell her that by the time I've made up my mind, the moment has long since passed. She yawns and brings her cheek to rest on my shoulder.

'I like spending time with you, Ilse,' she murmurs.

My heart stumbles into an unsteady cadence. If I could live in this moment forever, I would. The weight of Ash's head on my shoulder; her soft breaths fluttering against my throat; the setting sun rendering the meadow in shades of bronze and gold.

Chest tight, I ask her, 'Do you think we might spend time together once this is done – after the Untier is defeated? After our bond is dissolved?'

She pauses. When she answers, there's a smile in her voice. 'I'd like that very much.'

CHAPTER EIGHTEEN

I eventually extricate myself from Ash, worrying that if I don't, I might end up saying something foolish. Hans asks, with a wiggle of his eyebrows, if she liked the stew. I tell him to mind his own business and wash the bowl in the sink. By the time I've placed it back in the cupboard, Ash calls for me from the porch.

'Don't keep her waiting,' Hans says drily. 'You must be riveting company.'

When I push open the front door, Ash is still sitting on the top step of the porch, her eyes fixed in the distance.

'What is it?' I ask.

She nods out into the meadow, where the midday sun beats down. A magnificent roebuck crosses the clearing. Illuminated against the light, its pronged antlers are skeletal trees. Ash watches in awe, her breath escaping in an unsteady whisper.

'It bypassed the boundary,' I say.

'The boundary protects us primarily from the unnatural beasts of the Hexenwald,' Ash explains, admiring the deer with glossy eyes. 'I think this fellow is ... normal. We don't often see animals here.'

'Beautiful,' I whisper.

The buck, sensing Ash's awe, stops still. It turns to face us, inky black eyes rounding. The deer's velvet snout twitches.

The wind turns cold. Every hint of happiness drains from my body. I am perfectly alert, perfectly still. *Wrong*, my brain shrieks. Magic drums at my fingertips. *Wrong, wrong*—

The deer rears up onto its hind legs. It shifts and contorts its body, standing the way only a human should be able to. Its forelegs jut out in front of its body. Ash's hand flies to mine. The deer's jaw drops open. Its mouth forms a yawning abyss.

And then it starts to talk.

'Ilse!' the deer shrills, speaking in a woman's voice. 'Help me, Ilse!'

It is not just *any* woman's voice. With dread coiled in my belly, I whisper, 'That's Thea.'

Even in my peripheral vision, the whites of Ash's eyes are obvious. 'It's a trick,' she murmurs, hand still tight against my wrist. 'This creature is a mimic. Don't listen.'

Behind us, the cabin door swings open, ricocheting off its timber frame.

'Thea!' Hans shouts. 'I'm coming!'

His frantic footfalls stop abruptly. He has no doubt pinpointed the strange, upright buck. Where an ordinary deer would bolt at the first noise, this one watches, daring us.

'Save me, please!' comes Thea's voice. 'I'm in agony!'

Delirious with sorrow, I bury my face in Ash's shoulder. She hoists me to my feet and drags me into the house, Hans following close behind. 'Torsten!' she shouts. 'We need your help.'

Torsten takes the stairs two at a time, wincing at each movement. He pauses in the doorway. With a trembling arm, Ash points to the meadow. Her brother rolls up his sleeves and strides into the cooling air.

Ash pushes Hans and I onto the fainting couch. She pulls the window shutters closed. With a flick of her hand, a cluster of snowdrops inexplicably sprouting from the windowsill begin to sing. Their harmonies drown out the noises from the meadow: Torsten grunting with exertion, the broken syllables of Thea's voice.

'It's okay,' she murmurs, voice softer than a bed of down. 'It wasn't real.'

'You said the deer was a mimic.'

'Yes. Someone enchanted the creature to repeat her words—'

'*Repeat.*' My heart drops down into my stomach. 'Meaning she said those words herself.'

Hans puts his head in his hands. Whispers a curse between his fingers.

I look to Ash, hoping my eyes convey the desperation burning in my heart. 'I need to go back. *Now.*'

'Ilse, you barely have a hold over your magic. If you wait, we could increase your training sessions—'

'There is no time left to waste,' I say, more tersely than I intend. Ash is the last person to deserve my razor edge. 'Besides, I am a true Saint. My power should be more than enough to slay a false one.'

'Ilse,' Hans says, voice quaking, 'I understand the urgency. *Believe* me, I do. But wouldn't it be better to hone your . . .' he swallows thickly, 'Magic?'

'I am sorry,' I say, and I mean it. 'But I have to go. This is my chance to save her. We don't have as much time as we thought.'

The front door rattles open. Torsten staggers into the living room, his palms slick with the same blood that stains his shirt. Sweat glistens across his forehead.

'It's done,' Torsten pants. 'The mimic is dead. Our boundary protects against creatures of the Hexenwald – not natural animals suffering from enchantment. We've never needed it to. Not until now.'

I cross the room, hoping he can read the urgency in my eyes. Of the three, I know he's most likely to be truthful with me. To place reality above the preservation of my feelings ... or my life.

'How would someone – *something* – enchant that mimic to repeat my sister's words?'

He stiffens, eyes darting between the three of us.

'Don't look at them,' I snap. 'Look at me.'

'The magic itself is simple. You take an animal and enchant its vocal cords. But to make it repeat *those* words ...' Torsten's throat bobs. 'They would've had to torture her, Ilse.'

Heat presses against my eyelids. I whirl on my companions as if this is their fault, and not the machinations of a monster. '*Torture*,' I repeat, my voice cracking.

Voice soft, Ash says, 'Do not let emotion make you act rashly, Ilse.'

'Emotion?' I spit out. 'If your brother was being tortured, would you not move to save him? Even if doing so risked your life?'

'I agree with Ash,' Hans says, for what might be the first and last time. 'We need to think this through.'

'While we're here "thinking it through", perhaps the Untier is pulling out another of her teeth, or prying her nails loose from their beds.' Rage steadies my voice. I'm glad for it; without that heat, I might sink to my knees and never stop crying.

'This might all be a trick,' Ash protests. 'It would not be below the Untier to manufacture the sounds somehow, to lure you back to the village—'

'Did it sound manufactured to you?' I look at each of them in turn. Slowly, they begin to shake their heads. 'Then let's stop wasting time.' I cross the room, bound for the front door.

Ash catches my fingers between hers. 'The Untier could kill you, Ilse.'

I almost move to shake her loose, but then I register the emotion swelling in her voice, the wetness lingering at the edge of her lids. It softens me, if only slightly.

'I think you're all forgetting something,' Torsten says quietly.

I expect to see a dry smirk upon his lips, some brilliant plan forming behind his eyes – but instead, he seems morose. He does not meet my eyes.

'In the rush to understand your magic, we've neglected to discuss one of the core tenets of your Sainthood, Ilse.' A long breath inflates his chest. 'You cannot die. Just like the other Saints, you can only resurrect. And if you do, you'll forget . . .' Torsten makes a sweeping gesture with his hand.

I'll forget Torsten, Hans, Thea, Heulensee, the Hexenwald. I'll forget *Ash*. Somehow, this is a fate worse than death. A life where my body persists, but my memories do not. The heart which once unsteadied at the graze of her hand will persist in the cradle of my chest, but my eyes will not recognize her.

No one moves to stop me as I stagger out of the room, out of the cabin. I throw myself down on the porch steps. Tuck my head between my knees, because it's the only position which doesn't make me feel like I'm about to heave.

Immortal. *Immortal.* The word is a drumbeat in my mind.

Discovering my Sainthood was a departure from humanity, certainly, but it felt as if I was walking a parallel path. One by which Thea could still understand me. One which Ash could walk with me. Now, it's as if they're walking off into the distance and I'm stuck like the animals that fall into the marsh. Mud sucking at my limbs, tightening its grip each time I struggle.

Soft footsteps compress the stairs. A warm body nestles against my side. The way goosebumps rise across my skin lets me know it's Ash.

'I don't know how it didn't occur to me sooner,' I whisper.

'You've had a lot on your mind.' Ash tucks a strand of hair behind my ear, fingers lingering on my temple. 'It's strange, isn't it? That your lifespan extending feels like something to grieve.'

'I don't know if I want to live forever.' A knot tightens in my throat. 'Not on my own. Not like this.'

'Hexen aren't immortal,' she says quietly. 'But we age very, very slowly. You won't be alone for a very long time, Ilse.'

I lift my head. It feels heavier than it should. Ash watches me, loose ringlets framing those exquisite eyes. I can't imagine existing in a body which doesn't remember them.

'I don't want to forget you.' The words leave my mouth in a gust of air, expelled with the force of my conviction.

Ash's gaze falls to her lap. 'I don't want you to forget me either.'

Without speaking, she entwines our fingers. Our hands fit together like two halves of a chestnut shell.

'I don't want to forget you,' I repeat, my words stilted, 'but I have to try and save my sister.'

'I know.' She squeezes my hand, drawing in a long breath. The door whines behind us as someone steps out onto the porch. I ignore the sound, not yet ready to rupture the sensation that she and I are the only things that exist. 'I wish I could go with you. I'll take you to the forest's edge, but after that, you'll be on your own.'

'No, she won't.'

We turn to find Hans stood behind us. His shoulders are set in a firm line, his jaw clenched.

'I may not be a Saint, or a Hexe, but I can help.'

'It's too dangerous,' I insist. 'You will be safer with Ash and Torsten.'

Ash grimaces, unimpressed by the prospect of being Hans's chaperone.

Hans shakes his head. 'If it's not too dangerous for you, then it's not too dangerous for me, either. If we're going to save Thea, we'll do it together. Face the monster side by side.'

There is a stubborn slant to Hans's brow that makes me realize he will not concede. Emotion threatens to spill over. I focus on the pressure of Ash's fingers curled around mine.

Not keen to let Hans see how much his support means, I say, 'Well, if you insist on accompanying me, you ought to stick to the shadows. I'm not going to be the one to tell Thea you died of obstinance.'

Hans grins and pushes his hair out of his eyes. The optimism I thought he'd lost resurfaces, if only for a second. 'Then let's go.'

We leave the cabin with what feels like finality, even if I don't admit it to my companions. Torsten waves us off. Ash masks our scents as we step into the trees. My family's intrusion is the last thing we need.

I'd assumed the forest would permit our passage, salivating at the bloodshed set to take place at its foot. Instead, it challenges our every step. Trees gather so tightly I have to turn sideways to squeeze between them; the Fear season takes hold so suddenly that Hans almost turns and runs back to the meadow. I take his hand between mine. We both know this is strange, but neither of us says anything about it.

Brambles grab at our clothes, tangling around our ankles. Something howls behind us – almost lupine, but slightly off pitch. If I could feel fear, I think it would possess me now. My brain assaults me with violent images: Hans torn open like a paper bag, his intestines spilled like sugared almonds; a Thea-sized lump making its way down the Untier's gullet; my blood spilling beyond repair, eyes glowing white as I resurrect. Ash waiting to welcome me back, only to be met with a total lack of recognition.

A lone Nachzehrer staggers across our path, prying me from my reverie. Dark eyes blink back at us, embedded in grey, waxy skin. *I want to kill it*, I think, my anger at the Untier, at what I stand to lose, directed squarely at the monster before us. *I want its bones to break. Its blood to drain. Its—*

The Nachzehrer explodes in a hiss of red mist. Ash and Hans look at me, eyes wide. I thought the display might reassure them. When I narrow my gaze, I note that the threads of fear extending from their bodies have multiplied. I suppose power that volatile scares people, even if the power is on their side.

Finally, snippets of Heulensee appear between the trees. Hans and I gawk at the town we left behind. Everything appears just as it was, but there is a profound difference I cannot pinpoint. It's in the curve of the church tower's spire, the shade of the water, the smell of the air.

Or perhaps we are the ones who have changed.

I left this town as a woman and returned as a Saint. Hans, rather than gaining, has had something stripped from him. There should be a twinkle in his eye, a witty quip on the top of his tongue, a hand ready to clap me on the back should I need courage. His spirit has suffered a wound. I cannot help but feel I wield the sword which dealt it.

'You do not have to come,' I tell him. 'I would think no less of you.'

He shakes his head, dark eyes sincere. 'I follow you gladly. Besides,' he says, his eyes filling with tears, 'I want to save my wife.'

My heart lurches. Where before I saw his endless optimism as a taunt, I now see the truth of it. Hans is *good*. There are few people in life whom I could say that about.

I force down the emotion welling in my chest and mouth the words 'thank you' at him. Turning to Ash, I find her features tight with anxiety. Black cords unfurl from her chest to her fingers. Her mouth opens, attempts a word, and shuts again.

After a breath of silence, she says, 'I will see you upon your return.'

'Come on, Ils!' Hans shouts, having broken the boundary already. He stands a few metres into Heulensee, a grim expression at his lips.

I commit the shade of Ash's eyes to memory. It's the green of summer leaves, of fresh shoots, of bluebell stems. Saying goodbye makes my heart twist; departing without ever speaking my feelings into existence is doubly torturous. I make an unspoken vow: I *will* see her again.

And when I do, I'll tell her what she means to me.

'Goodbye, then.'

'See you soon, Ilse,' she corrects as she squeezes my hand once. Breath held, I step out of the Hexenwald.

I expected a sense of relief. The release of pressure, the easing of discomfort. Instead, I feel like a trout pulled from the lake. The light glares, the air suffocates, the sound of ambient birdsong overwhelms. I recall the way I used to stand at my window, entranced by the Hexenwald's boughs. Perhaps I was always meant for the forest.

Catching up with Hans, heat itches at my skin. The fog which rolls from the forest seems to lodge in my throat – that, and something thicker. A smell most familiar. *Smoke.* We exchange a tense look. Autumn has deepened its grip on the landscape, draining it of colour and warmth. The earth beneath our feet is waterlogged. There's no reason for wildfires to rage.

I cast my gaze back towards the Hexenwald, where Ash lingers between the trees. She raises a hand before disappearing back into the forest. Instinct drives me forward, and I outpace Hans. I pause on the lakeshore, squinting out across Heulensee. When I cannot discern the smoke's origin, we continue towards the town.

Only when we arrive at the meadow that separates the lake from Heulensee proper do I pause. Something niggles at me. A foreboding. It's unlike Hans to stay silent.

A few paces behind, Hans sinks to his knees, clawing at his throat.

'It's okay,' I murmur. 'The Fear season never lasts long . . .'

My sentence breaks off. Blinking down at him, I am struck by the wrongness of it. That he is on his knees, unable to breathe, unable to talk – that the Hexenwald is controlling him . . . But we are no longer in the forest.

Crouched in Heulensee's soft meadow grass, Hans's lips turn

blue. His eyes glaze over, fixed on the lake just over my shoulder. I grasp him by the front of his shirt and pull him to me. 'Breathe, Hans.'

His eyes snap to mine and his cheeks hollow with the effort of a breath – but it's fruitless. He sags in my arms, a dead weight I cannot hold.

'Ash!' I scream, anguish poisoning my veins. 'Help!'

My eyes are caught in battle between watching Hans's throat for a pulse and inspecting the treeline for Ash's presence. Seeing her form between the trees is the only thing that could calm me, but she's not there. No matter how many times I shout, how hoarse I make my voice, she's not there.

But soon enough, someone else is.

Borbet levitates on the edge of the Hexenwald, her white eyes visible even at a distance. She watches Hans dying with cool composure. Knowing the threat she poses, I place myself, my flesh, between her and Hans – a shield she's certain to pierce straight through.

A shudder wracks Borbet's body. She floats towards us, free of the trees. Her feet stir the water as she glides above the lake. Waves of copper hair fall around her chest. The air chills as she advances, raising goosebumps across my skin.

Borbet stops just short of where Hans lies. Her milk-white eyes drift between me and him. 'You have been hiding from me, Ambet.'

I throw my arms out to the side in defence of Hans. Sorrow twisting my words, I shout, 'You almost killed me! What did you expect?'

'I would not kill you, Ambet,' she says, disregarding the assault she and Wilbet unleashed.

I shake my head, as if that will help clear it. As if that will change the fact that my closest friend is dying before my eyes. I search for a pulse at his throat and bring my ear to his mouth in pursuit of a whispered breath. I find neither.

'Hans,' I whisper, shaking him by the shoulders. 'Please come back.'

'He is human,' Borbet says. 'In seventy years, at most, he will expire. An early demise is inconsequential.'

'It's consequential to *me*,' I spit back, tears welling.

Borbet watches as I place my hands on his chest, his throat, and bid my magic to inhabit him. To solder together the fractures, to knit his life force back together.

'That will not work, Ambet.'

'Then tell me what will!' As I look down at Hans's blue lips, I'm compelled to lower my voice, almost reverent. 'I can't do this without you.'

A strange sound forces its way past Borbet's lips. Her face has changed. She wears eyes of hazel-green, not ivory, and an expression I cannot read. Borbet looks down at Hans. She wraps her hands around his ankles and *pulls*. Her fingers dig into his flesh, dimpling against the skin.

Borbet hauls him with the strength of a team of oxen, her feet not quite brushing the ground as she drags him through the grass, towards the Hexenwald.

She's *stealing* him.

I take off after them, willing my magic to make me faster, to slow her progress, but my powers are no match for my mother's. She's back at the treeline, Hans in her clutches.

The Hexenwald, either submitting to Borbet's influence or simply refusing to aid me, bears down. Branches whip past me on either side. I catch slivers of Borbet and Hans: her white gown, her muddied feet, his pale face and shock of dark hair. My magic surges, forcing the trees to bend and permit my passage.

Suddenly, she stops.

Placing Hans in the middle of a clearing, Borbet retreats. She watches from a distance, materializing to the south, then the east, then the north.

'What did you do to him?' I ask her, the tremor in my voice indicating that fresh tears are not far behind. I run to Hans. His chest is still. It's *motionless*. I rant incoherently, grabbing at the front of his shirt, demanding that he wake up. My knuckles turn white as I grasp Hans's hand.

Borbet watches. Hans turns bluer and bluer and—

His chest rises. It falls. And rises again.

Something jolts his lungs. Pink returns to his face and ruddies his cheeks. I look between him and Borbet, not understanding the miracle I just witnessed. He was dead, and now he is alive.

'Did you save him?' I ask, my voice barely competing with the wind that whips through the trees overhead.

Deeper in the forest, something stirs. It's in the thickening of the breeze, the swirling of ether at our ankles. Borbet's pupils narrow.

'Heed my advice, Ambet. Do not interfere with human matters.'

'Did you save him?' I repeat.

She stares back at me blankly. 'You are not like them. And never will be.' Her eyes range across my shoulder. 'Nor like *them*.'

I turn around, following her line of sight. Ash bounds through the trees towards us. Relief floods me, stilling my shaking hands, easing my hurried breaths. By the time I turn back around,

Borbet has vanished, leaving behind a cloud of ether that eddies in her wake.

Ash throws herself down beside Hans and me. She cups my jaw in her hand, green eyes scanning every inch of my face, my body.

'You're okay,' she whispers, the words slipping between her lips in an exhale. 'The Saint of Love didn't hurt you?'

'No. She . . .' My sentence trails off, not sure how to vocalize the suspicion taking root beneath my skin: that Borbet *saved* Hans, one way or another. It doesn't make sense for her to be altruistic, but she intervened, and now Hans is alive. Why would she do me a favour without bargaining for something in return? I can't summon an answer, so I tell Ash, 'I'm fine. But Hans . . . he was dead!'

'What happened?'

'He went to his knees. I don't know why, but . . .' I falter, realizing that Ash isn't watching me with shock, but with pity.

'What is it?' I whisper. Something tells me I don't want to find out.

'I watched you leave,' she says, her voice tight with melancholy, 'and I thought it was okay. I thought *he* was okay. But I should've waited longer. I should've made sure.'

My cloud of relief dissolves. 'What do you mean?'

'Hans offered the forest his blood,' Ash murmurs, her voice weak. 'He let it in, Ilse. The Hexenwald is a part of Hans now, and he is a part of the Hexenwald.'

My mind stretches back to that day in the forest. The slick of red on a jagged branch as Hans dragged it across his palm. His wound leaking pus only to heal in the morning. The optimism and light gradually fleeing his body. The forest dogging his every step.

'But he was fine,' I protest, tears blurring my vision. 'You said it could infect him, but it didn't. He was *fine*!'

She sinks her head into his hands. 'The infection is slow-moving. There were moments when I suspected it might be taking hold; Torsten and I told him as much. But we didn't *know*, and we didn't want to burden you with a possibility, Ilse.'

'What will happen to him?' I urge, each breath leaving my mouth in an anguished flutter.

'The infection means he cannot leave the forest,' she admits, her eyes glassy with tears. 'Not now. Not ever.'

I bite down on my fist. The cruelty of it all forces tears to my eyes. They burn. I can hardly bear to look at Hans head-on, so I steal glimpses from the corner of my tear-frosted eyes. Laid out in the grass, lids fluttering, skin flushed and lips parted, he is the image of coltish youth. He is kind. He is *innocent*. He had a whole life ahead of him, and it's been shattered into a thousand jagged pieces.

'He came here to save her,' I murmur, voice quaking.

Ash bites the inside of her cheek, attempting to subdue her own grief.

'He can have a life here,' she offers. 'Thea could visit him on the fringes. We will ensure her safety.'

We exchange a look, both knowing that it's a poor trade. 'The fault lies with me.'

Ash leans over and takes my hand between hers. The warmth of her palms brings heat to my tear-glazed cheeks. I do not want her to let go.

'It is *not* your fault, Ilse. Hans *chose* to help you. For Thea.'

My bottom lip wobbles. His sleeping face makes me want to sob. The wind picks up, and the scent of smoke infiltrates the Hexenwald. It gathers in thick plumes amidst the tree trunks.

'You should go,' she says. 'Don't worry about Hans. I will care for him as if he were my own . . .' – she falters, aware that caring for him as her own brother is perhaps not the standard of care that I desire for Hans – 'As my dearest friend.'

My eyes flick between them: Hans, blameless and boyish; Ash, sincere. Both vulnerable in their own ways. I push to my feet, guilt a lead weight upon my shoulders.

All this time, I've been dreaming of a return to normality. One where Thea and I are sisters again, taking walks by the lake and meeting every Sunday for lunch. It was always just the two of us – but now, as I will the image to surface, I realize Hans is there, too. He's stealing food from my plate, kissing Thea on the top of her head, smiling as he regales us with tales about difficult clients at the smithery.

But that's all it will ever be. A dream.

On the precipice of a fight I might not survive, and with Hans inextricably bound to this forest, I have to believe there is some version of the future where we can all be happy. Where Thea lives, where Hans is cured by a miracle, where the village sees what I have done for them and goes to its knees in search of forgiveness.

'When it's done, where will you go?'

Ash's words bring my eyes to her face. It's almost as if she read my mind. I realize, then, that my future does not feel right without her in it. It's all off-colour, dulled. But how do I reconcile my desire to belong in the village with my desire to be by Ash's side? Besides, she is magically bound to help me. I do not want to insist that she stays by my side for longer than she is contractually obliged to.

Rather than telling her this, I say, 'I don't know.'

Ash smiles tightly. 'We can talk about it afterwards.' She pauses, hinting that she might say more – and oh how I pray that she will. Instead, she simply murmurs, 'Now go.'

I force a smile and turn on my heel. When I have one foot in Heulensee and the other in the Hexenwald, Ash calls after me. 'Wait, Ilse.'

I turn, heart fluttering. I've started to grow so accustomed to the black threads of fear that I barely register them, but now I take notice of one which extends from her chest. My breath quakes in anticipation. She bridges the distance between us and presses her lips against my cheek. Up close, she smells like sweet woodruff and ripe blackberries.

Her lips linger on my skin. Is this the same kiss she'd leave *any* friend with – or is it something more? Heat ignites low in my stomach. I am struck by the urge to wrap my arms around her. To draw her body against mine.

'Be careful,' Ash says, after a moment's hesitation. The cords retract. 'Come back to us in one piece.'

An unspoken tension lingers between us. There is a very real possibility that I will die – that this will be the last conversation Ash and I have. Adrenaline courses through my veins. For a brief moment, I feel brave. I resolve to ask her the question that has plagued me since we met – does she feel it, too? Do I unsteady her the way she unsteadies me?

I open my mouth, ready to give life to this dizzying, bewildering *thing* that crackles between us – but all that comes out is, 'I'll see you soon.'

Ash smiles, though melancholy flits across her eyes. 'See you soon.'

A bittersweet ache rings through my body as I turn and cross the boundary into Heulensee. Hans's voice follows me and I cannot tell if it's real or another trick of the forest. Part of me wants to stay and comfort him as he wakes. The other part cannot bear to see his face when he realizes he's trapped there for ever. I wonder if he will consider me as responsible as I consider myself.

Guilt clouds my thoughts as I skirt the lake. I could swear that its black heart has grown – a splotch of ink spreading, tendrils reaching out.

I push forward, sneaking glances at the water through my peripheral vision, the way I might keep tabs on a wolf at my heel. Expecting to be struck by the Untier or cut down where I stand by the townsfolk, I am surprised to find Heulensee as I left it. The smell of smoke has dissipated, and the fog has lifted.

I stand in the meadow where Mama's real daughter was slain and *listen*. The streets are quiet, but not preternaturally so. I imagined I might find monsters prowling the lanes, or that the cobbles would have disappeared entirely under a pool of blood – but the town is still. Sleeping.

My feet make the winding ascent to our old house before I realize that Thea no longer lives there. Sentimentality causes me to pause. From this vantage point on the hill, I can see all the way to the hay meadows – most of which have been consumed by fire, though none burn actively. Rather than swaying verdant grasses, the landscape is a patchwork of parched earth and ash.

We've never seen wildfires this late in the year. Either the weather took an unprecedented turn while I was in the Hexenwald, or the fires were set intentionally. The scalded sight would make Oma sick. My shoulders droop under the weight of her shattered legacy. Destruction on this scale means the Odenwald family have failed in their duties. Have they simply given up, or have they been prevented from firefighting? And if it's the latter ...

There are few things I can think of that would stop Thea or Mama. I hurry back down the hill and slink past the bakery with my hood drawn close to my face.

The rest of the street lays silent. I dart through the alley by the apothecary and follow it to its end. Thea and Hans's house waits for me. In the front garden, Thea's beloved sunflowers have been decapitated. Yellow heads smatter the ground, mid-decay. The sight makes my eyes burn. I look to the sky and channel my entire consciousness into a simple plea. *Don't let me be too late.*

I knock on the front door. The barest pressure of my fist prompts it to shudder open, as if the house itself is inviting me in. A queasy knot forms in the pit of my stomach. My mind conjures images of blood slicks leading down the hallway – images so visceral they *must* be a premonition. But as the door yawns open, I am greeted with floorboards which are unmarred, if a little dusty. In a home of my own, this would be a typical sight – forgetful, peculiar Ilse – but for Thea, it's unprecedented. She is measured, pristine in all things. My breath is barely a suggestion in my chest as I push into the house.

'Thea?' I call, my voice echoing.

No answer.

I suck in a lungful of stale air and walk through the kitchen. The bedroom door stands ajar, inviting. I pause at the threshold. Nausea reaches a fever pitch in my stomach.

Right here and now, Thea is still alive. I could stay in this moment forever. Thea is just sleeping, tucked beneath the covers, dreaming about Hans. But once I have crossed that threshold, if I find her bloodied and broken, there is no going back.

I step through the door. And I *see* her.

Thea stands with her back to me. My footfalls are clumsy and loud, but she does not register my presence. I swallow; the sound crashes against the walls. Thea stares intently into the mirror propped in the corner of the room. In the reflection, her eyes are wide and glassy.

'Thea.'

There is nothing to suggest that she heard me. I count to ten, then twenty, then thirty. Her chest does not stir, she does not blink. *Wrong*, my brain hollers. Magic pools beneath my fingertips. *Wrong, wrong, wrong.*

I tiptoe across the room, not daring to breathe.

Rabid dog.

I reach out, fingers curled.

Storm about to break.

I graze her shoulder and she screams.

CHAPTER NINETEEN

'ILSE!'

Thea swings around, eyes drawn so wide that they protrude from her skull. I leap back – not with fear, but recognition of a threat, the same way I would duck a fire-hot poker directed at my throat.

'Thea?' I murmur, oh-so gently. Do not disturb the rabid dog.

'You're here,' she breathes, tears welling in her eyes. 'I thought I'd never see you again.'

The tension in her face melts away, and suddenly, I see my *sister*. She opens her arms and I cannot help but throw myself into them. Thea grips me like she'll never let go again. A crisis hug.

'Are you okay?' I murmur into her hair. 'You seemed—'

'Oh, Ilse. Being apart has been torturous.' She pauses, draws in a deep breath. 'As long as you're here, I'm okay.'

I hold her tighter. She has always been a slight little thing, just like Mama – but today, I'm struck by the gentle undulations of her ribcage against my chest.

'Did you do it?' she murmurs, breath hot against my cheek. 'Did you find your fear?'

There is so much hope in her voice that I wish, I *wish* I could say yes. That my mission was linear and successful: enter the forest, find my fear, save my sister.

'I did not.' My words are a murmured admission. Her whole body sags and I can barely hold the featherweight of her frame upright. 'But I'm going to save you, Thea. I found a way.'

Thea looks back at me, her face twisted with concern. 'What do you mean?'

'Do you trust me?'

Her face is open and earnest as she nods yes. I draw her back in, bring my lips to her ear, and whisper, 'I will slay the Saint of Fear.'

Her panic is immediate. She pushes away from me, eyes flashing. One hand twists in her hair, the other clutches at her chest. 'Don't spew such nonsense, Ilse!' I can smell the fear radiating from her, can see the tendrils of shadow spasming as they sprout from her chest. She has spent her entire life nurturing terror for protection, and it washes over her in waves. 'To speak ill of the Saint is sacrilege.'

I step closer; she steps back. 'Listen,' I hiss, my patience evaporating. 'It was never a Saint, Thea. It's a monster. A parasite. We can be free of it. Permanently. No more Rites. No more sacrifice. No more fear.'

A sob builds behind her words. 'No! Ilse, we *need* the Saint. I cannot believe you— '

'That beast ate Oma!' I spit back. 'How can you continue to defend it when it killed her? It will kill *you* next, if I don't stop it.'

Thea starts to hyperventilate, the breaths leaving her body in shuddered gasps. 'You were meant to find your fear! That's all—'

'Wait.' Magic courses through me so violently that I sway where I stand, responding to a threat I cannot yet sense. 'How did you know I went in search of my fear? I told you I was escaping to Flussdorf.'

Her face reddens, then she offers a sheepish smile. 'Mama let it slip.'

I know Mama. She does not let things slip.

Wasps drone inside my ears. 'Where is Mama, Thea?'

Her face contorts for a split second before returning to that serene mask. As she smooths out her features, my bowels twist. There is something foreign about her. Something I do not recognize as my sister. A haunting melody fills my mind, burgeoning from somewhere dark. *Blood spills from veins, skin starts to crack. Ignore the forest; turn back, turn back.*

Voice deeper than usual, Thea says, 'She's fine.'

Sweat beads on my forehead. *Eyes become sockets, flesh melts to bone. The forest is hungry; go home, go home.* 'I didn't ask if she was okay. I asked where she was.'

'Don't be a bore, Ilse,' Thea says, reluctant to meet my gaze.

Realization washes over me in a nauseating wave. *The Hexen won't rest 'til your blood is shed.* 'Look at me, Dorothea.'

She shakes her head. Backs away until she hits the wall. Her hair falls in a shroud around her face. I advance, one hand outstretched.

'Stop it,' she hisses, not once raising her eyes.

'Look at me,' I repeat, my fingers hovering just short of her jaw. *Ignore the warning; you're dead, you're dead.*

Thea's head snaps up. My hand flies to my mouth.

Cold certainty settles in my bones. 'My *sister* has blue eyes.'

Thea stares back at me. Then, hair swinging as she moves, she turns to the mirror to glean her reflection. Green eyes blink back. She runs her tongue across her lip and frets with her hands.

'So close,' she whispers. 'I was so close.'

Her mouth drops open. It's a pose I have seen her adopt so many times before; as children, when the Untier killed Klara Keller; as a young woman, when she passed her Rite. But she does not scream. Her mouth is an abyss, silent yet echoing. Her lips stretch wider, wider—

Thea's jaw dislocates.

Her lower lip sits at her breastbone. The vacant chasm of her throat hangs open, gaping and hungry. Something shudders free of the black. A head. No, a *skull*.

The Untier's skull forces its way through my sister's mouth. Her cheeks split all the way to her ears. The creature's horns unfurl, impaling her eyes. I sink to my knees and heave. The Untier wears Thea, her jaw hanging at the front, the crown of her head hanging limply at the back like a hood. Her once-beautiful countenance acts as a vessel for the unspeakable.

'Little Ilse Odenwald.' The Untier's voice is the crack of thunder, the splitting of logs. 'Back from the Hexenwald again?'

This cannot be real, I pray. *Please, don't let this be real.*

'We had a deal,' I pause, spitting bile onto the bedroom floor. 'You were not to harm her. It's not yet been thirty days.'

'How boldly you speak of deals and their sanctity,' the Untier snarls. 'Were you not conspiring to *kill* me?' The Untier recedes into Thea's body. One of her hands flies to her skull, the other to her jaw. She presses the two halves of her head back together. They heal crooked. It's a poor imitation of Thea's beauty.

The voice which comes next is indisputably Thea. 'Please don't hurt me!' she cries. Tears burst over the ledge of her lids, rolling down her torn cheeks in a torrent. 'If you kill the Saint, you'll kill me too! I don't want to die!' she chokes, shaking her head.

The Untier's voice returns: 'Your sister is still in here. Whatever you do to me, you do to her.'

Calculating, I squint at my sister. Past the crooked angle of her jaw, the colour of her eyes, the blood in the seams of her mouth. There is a distinct absence around her. If I know anything about Thea, it's that she is *fearful*. The creature blinking back at me, half-woman, half-monster, is utterly self-assured. No black cords ripple through the air.

Before I can catch my breath, Thea lunges forward, grasping me by the collar. She drags me close enough that I can smell the coppery tang of flesh on her breath. 'You may not be fearful, but devouring you and your defect will be a pleasure of its own.'

I attempt to wrench her hands away, but she has developed a preternatural strength that my muscles cannot best. Heat itches beneath my fingertips – an ace up my sleeve. I throw my consciousness behind a single thought: *I want her to let me go*. My magic comes to call, racing through my own flesh and then into Thea's. She pulls back, as if stung by a nettle. Her grip loosens for a fraction of a second, but it's enough.

The vile hypocrisy of this moment aches in my heart. I came here to slay this beast. Here it is within reach, presenting itself to me in an unwieldy body. I could rain fire upon its skull or starve the oxygen from its lungs. But I am weak, and I *can't*. I can't slay it. Not while it wears my sister's skin.

So I turn and run.

I push out into the kitchen, into the corridor, into the early morning. The sun stains the sky bloody. Each smack of my soles against the cobbles reverberates through my bones, up to my skull. Covering the distance to the Hexenwald seems like an impossibility.

Doubly so, given what stands between us.

Frau Schmidt looms on the lakeshore, eyes fixed on mine. I do not have time to explain the imminent danger, nor the impossibility of my presence here.

'Run!' I scream. 'Find shelter!'

Women in Heulensee are so shot through with fear they barely feel much else – yet Frau Schmidt does not move. Does not even flinch. She merely stands with her shoulders squared, her mouth set in a grim line.

My eyes snag on her left hand. She clutches a rolling pin in her fist. The end is slick with something scarlet.

Oh *Saints*.

In a split second, I make the decision to double back on myself. I'll zig-zag through the side streets and take a longer route to the lake. Neither Dorothea nor the Untier are anywhere to be seen as I turn to face the street. I make a beeline for the alleyway beside the apothecary—

Johanna Fischer stands at its mouth, arms spread wide. White-knuckled hands curl around a bloody-pronged pitchfork.

Cursing, I flee and attempt the next narrow street but Frau Braun, the woman who taught me how to read, rises up to meet me. She moves to strike, something metallic flashing in her hand.

As I thunder down the road, away from the Hexenwald, a realization settles like sediment in the lake. I am being *herded*.

Footsteps pound behind me, but rather than two beats for each foot, there are four. I turn – Saints forsake me, I *turn* . . .

Dorothea gallops after me on all fours. Her gait is ursine, the roars tearing from her throat even more so. 'Where are you going?' The echoed call is a bastardized mesh of Thea's voice and the Untier's. It is sugar-coated death. 'Don't you want to play with your sister?'

Tears blur my vision. A childish howl builds beneath my lips. The houses on each side of the street blur, and all too quickly, the cobbles give way to sodden earth. The bog looms ahead. I dart along the boardwalk, tall grass and sedge whispering at my steps.

Behind, bones crack and pop. Something wet slides to the floor. I smell rust and metal.

'I'm going to hunt you, Ilse Odenwald.'

I lengthen my stride, pushing until my thighs burn. The Untier's hillock emerges, bulbous and twisted, spitting shadows and screams so visceral they are *visible* – and I throw myself inside it.

Lungs aching, I bolt through the tunnel. The monster's breath moistens my nape. I fumble through the darkness, stone skinning my elbows, leaving any uncovered skin torn and bloody. Behind, I hear the rock shifting and breaking. Shingle clatters from the ceiling, pricking at my eyes and catching in my throat.

'You cannot run,' it booms. 'You cannot hide.'

The tunnel opens ahead, spitting me out into the dank cavern where my Rite fell apart. A fire still burns in the cave's heart, roaring as I intrude. I spin around, hair sticking to the sheen of sweat on my face. The Untier lunges free of the tunnel, having shed Dorothea's mortal coil. Stone shatters in its wake. The tunnel shudders, threatening to collapse.

'We had a bargain,' it slathers, scarlet drool dripping from its maw. 'Find your fear, or I will eat your sister. An Odenwald sister must sate me.'

'What have you done to her?'

'She is alive. Whether she stays that way is up to you.'

Hope sparks dangerously in my chest. 'Where is she?'

A rumble emanates from deep in the Untier's chest. A *laugh*. 'It saddens me to see that you're still embroiled in mortal matters. Sainthood is wasted on you.'

Those words are a bucket of ice water to my hot rage. The Untier is larger than me, stronger than me, but my Sainthood was supposed to be my secret weapon. I thought it believed me weak because it believed me mortal.

'You knew? All this time, you *knew*?'

'I knew you before you were born,' it snarls. 'When the Saint of Sadness came into existence, when your Saint of Love was a babe in her womb, the Saint of Fear already existed – not in flesh, but in potential. An egg, not yet ripe, which would one day complete the triad.

'I sent you to the Hexenwald believing that once you understood your true power, you would forsake your allegiance to this place. That you would understand – as your mother and grandmother do – that humanity is *worthless*. But with power humming beneath your skin, you chose to return. To lower yourself.'

'You stole my identity,' I say, my voice shaking with anger, 'and used it to oppress the women in Heulensee.'

'I have held this identity longer than you,' it spits back, incensed. 'The only reason your name holds weight is because of *me*. Do you see the villagers bowing down to the Saint of Love? The Saint of Sadness?' It whips its head back and forth, antlers mere inches from my face. 'No. I have given you renown. I have given you *power*.'

'Why not kill me, then?' I shout, flinging my arms out wide. 'Why let me live at all?'

'I thought we could reach an armistice.' The Untier grinds its bony jaw. 'One where I need not interfere with the Saints of Pathos.'

The hidden meaning behind his words is clear: he did not kill me because he fears my family. If only they would lend me their power, this could all be over.

'We could be allies,' it says. 'You can return to the Hexenwald while I continue to reap the village's fear.'

'No. Heulensee is my home.' My voice trembles on that final word. 'My sister lives here.'

Steam huffs from the creature's nostrils. 'Your stubborn allegiance to humanity is baffling. What a waste of good magic.'

'And therein lies the fatal flaw in your parasite heart,' I growl. 'You do not understand *love*. You underestimate what I would do to save Thea.'

'Love is a weakness,' the Untier rumbles, 'and *you* cannot see the truth.'

A nagging whine builds in my ears. 'What do you mean?'

'You know where your sister is, Ilse Odenwald. You have known all along.'

CHAPTER TWENTY

Ice crystallizes and bursts in my veins. Time drags. I force down a shaky breath and hold it until my lungs hurt. The dream that struck me during my Rite surges to the surface. I stare at my surroundings. *Really* stare at them. Slowly, surely, a circle of women flickers to life around me, just as they did in the dream. They hang just above the ground, feet dangling. There are hundreds of them, arranged in concentric rings.

Their heads snap up, bleary eyes focused on me. In unison, their jaws drop open – and they howl. Their terror feeds the Untier; it grows, shedding skin to accommodate its new girth. The horns on its head sprout additional prongs; its teeth lengthen and sharpen.

Heat itches beneath my skin. *'Where is she?'*

'Ilse.'

It is a croaked plea, distorted by pain, but I would recognize that voice amidst a hurricane. My head snaps towards the sound.

I find Thea where she hangs, limp and near lifeless. One of her eyes writhes with maggots, but the other – clear and wonderfully *blue* – fixes on me. I rush to her side, my legs barely able to carry my sorrow.

'Thea,' I breathe. 'Thea, *look* at me.'

'You came back,' she chokes. 'To save ... to save me.'

Anger drags serrated claws down my chest. I search for a way to bring her down to the earth. My eyes catch on the silver thread protruding from her skull. It's pulled taut, stretching into the sky, out of sight. I throw myself up and take the thread in my hand, poised to reclaim her, when the Untier suddenly tosses me into the air with its horns, the weight of my body inconsequential. I land hard on my back on the other side of the circle. My spine rattles. Oxygen vacates my lungs in one decisive motion.

'What did you' – I fight to drag air down my windpipe – 'do to her?'

The parasite stands silhouetted against the rising sun. Silver, ephemeral threads drape across its horns like spiderwebs. 'I made her my puppet. Let me show you.'

My mind whirrs. I drag myself to my feet as the Untier swings its head towards another woman, whose body is encased in a silken cocoon. Only the whites of her eyes are visible.

'This one is ripe.'

While the Untier speaks, the cocoon splits at its seams. The woman sucks in air as if she has been held underwater. Detritus falls to the floor, flesh sloughs from her back. Not flesh – a *person*. She is a mirror image of the woman before me, down to each freckle on her cheeks. Her skin glistens like a newborn's, slick with blood and mucus. Vacant eyes stare back at the Untier, who grunts a command beneath its breath.

The clone slinks out of the hillock, leaving her counterpart – the original – behind.

Cold gnaws at my edges; darkness fringes my vision. I clutch at my stomach, desperate to stop the squall of nausea roiling inside me.

I look to my sister, who watches me with tortured eyes. My realization comes at the same time as my tears.

'Thea hasn't been Thea since her Rite.'

The monster laughs. 'Finally, the girl understands.'

I stifle my sobs with a hand clamped over my mouth.

'During the Rite, I serve each girl a feast; they do not realize the flesh they eat is my own. Over several years, they begin to change as I take over their brains and bodies, preparing them to duplicate. The young women are then compelled to return to my den. Once they do, I trap and harvest the host,' it slides its horn down the face of the woman who was just in the cocoon, 'and send the husk back to the village. The puppets aren't perfect, but they're convincing enough, especially to humans in their blindness. Husk and host are connected, just as they are all connected to me. If you peel away the husk's skin, all you'll find is *me*. In their bones, in their flesh, in their blood.'

Grief-stricken, my mind ventures back to the night I found Dorothea emerging from the Untier's den in her nightgown. *She wasn't ready*, she said. The vacant look in her eyes haunted me, but now it makes sense. She wasn't ready for *harvesting*.

All the moments I cursed her for abandoning me in the years following her Rite ... it wasn't *her*. Not entirely. Her body was changing, her mind souring. And rather than cherishing what little recognition she had to offer, I spent the time suspicious, scheming. Shame coaxes fresh heat to my eyes.

The cave walls press in. I need to get out of here. I need to get *Thea* out of here.

'Release her willingly,' I demand, hoping my voice sounds as menacing as my intent, 'or I will make you.'

The Untier advances, drawing its hideous maw level with my face. 'Such fierce words for a Saint who hasn't mastered her own power. The girl is *mine*.'

Heat explodes beneath my skin. Hatred burns like wildfire through my insides. The Untier taunts *me* – the creature who inspired its foul charade.

'You thieving, insidious parasite.' I clench my fists, letting my innate magic rear its head. My vision grows clearer, my hearing more acute. I will flames to my palm and hurl them at the Untier. An infernal noose circles its neck, squeezing, choking. 'You will pay for what you have done.'

It hisses, struggling to draw breath – but then I realize it is speaking. A murmured incantation passes its lips, and suddenly Thea begins to scream. She claws at her throat in desperation. My fists unfurl to soft palms; my magic sputters out.

'Don't you see?' It cackles, bloodied teeth glinting beneath the hazy light. 'I'm a part of your sister now. My will keeps her alive. You cannot conquer me, or even separate us, without killing her.'

My heart gives one anguished beat, and then the Untier is upon me. I roll clumsily to the side, my brain so hazy that I cannot process my surroundings fast enough. Teeth fasten around my leg. I raise a fist to send magic raining down on the beast, but before I can release my power, the Untier tosses me like a rag doll once more.

My back cracks against the stone walls; shingle showers to the ground. My vision fractures into a distorted kaleidoscope.

Copper sours on my tongue. Blood spurts from the puncture wounds. My left thigh bone meets fresh air and I *howl*.

Across the clearing, Thea howls with me. The women around her join in. Their fear bolsters the monster. Terror becomes tangible, radiating from their bodies in waves.

'Stop,' I choke out, watching the Untier drink it in – but my voice is too weak against the backdrop of their horror.

I try to focus on the humming heat at the core of me, to coax my magic into flames and wound this beast, but the pain is all-consuming. The black tendrils of the women's fear lie just out of reach. Bone juts out of my leg, impossibly white against the blinding scarlet of my blood. My shoulder feels dislocated.

How childish of me. How *foolish* to believe that I could slay the monster that has terrorized Heulensee for centuries. The Untier advances, horns lowered. I wonder if it will plunge them through my heart or my skull.

Just above the hulking mass of its left shoulder, I see Thea. Her eyes burn into mine. She curls one crooked hand into a claw, beckoning. If I am to die, let it be by her side. Nails digging into sodden dirt, I use my good arm to haul myself across the ground.

The Untier stalks me, taunting. 'So desperate for mortal comforts.'

I grit my teeth, pressing on despite the droning agony under my ribs. The anguish seeps from my mouth in a muffled scream as I heave myself to my feet, putting all my weight on my right leg. Thea reaches for me with weak, bloodied fingers. I reach up and wrap my arm around her levitating body, pulling her against me as tight as I can. A crisis hug.

I take her warmth, the love in her eyes, and I swallow it. My magic flickers to life, a final gasp. I turn to the Untier and scream.

'Sleep!' I throw all my will behind that word, the same way I did with the Lindwurm in the Hexenwald, desperate to buy myself time.

The Untier's bloody eyes widen a fraction – and then it falls to the floor unconscious.

I turn my attention back to Thea and brush her matted hair over her shoulder. 'We don't have long.'

Thea's fevered lips graze my ear. 'Fight, Ilse.'

'I don't think I can,' I choke, taking stock of my broken body. Even as I cast my will towards healing my fractured bones and torn flesh, the sensation drains from my limbs. The blood loss is too much.

'You are an Odenwald woman,' she says, her voice a grating whisper. 'We *fight*.'

I pull back, allowing myself one look into her unmarred eye. The blue of her iris is tempestuous – dark and roiling. She swallows. That small act causes her to wince. I would take all the pain away in a heartbeat if I could.

'If you cannot fight the fire,' she rasps, 'take away its fuel.'

For a moment I do not understand what she means, but then it clicks. 'No, Thea. I won't.'

'You ... must,' she grinds out, voice full of conviction.

I stare back at her, desperate to conjure a way out of this. What use is Sainthood if I am powerless here? '*No*, Thea. There must be another way.'

'This *is* the way,' my sister whispers.

Raw grief rattles through the corridors of my consciousness. The fragile morsels of hope I had woven disintegrate. Each breath is a battle.

More quietly, pleading, she adds, 'Please, Ilse. It hurts so much.'

I draw back, throat aching with the weight of my grief. Blinking, I clear the tears from my vision and take her in. Inhale a lungful of her scent: star anise, caramel and honeysuckle. Look at her eyes – her *remaining* eye, the one that doesn't writhe with maggots. It is blue and endless. The expanse of a cloudless sky. The impossible vastness of the lake.

If I squint, I can imagine her as she should be: laughing, smiling. I press our foreheads together. 'I love you so much, Thea.' The image of Hans strikes me so suddenly and violently that I let out another sob. 'Hans loves you, too. Saints, Thea. He loves you *so* much.'

A breath rattles between her chapped lips. Her forehead wrinkles against mine, contorted with the effort of speech. 'Love . . . you. Love you both. Always will.'

Behind me, I hear the Untier stir.

'I was meant to save you,' I choke, tears cascading down my cheeks.

Her cold hand finds mine. We entwine our fingers, the way we have a thousand times before, and never will again.

'Saved . . . me,' she splutters. In the next breath, she rallies. Her clear eye turns urgent, the pupil dilating. Her broken hand tightens around mine. '*Sister,*' she urges.

I can only nod back, knowing that our sisterhood is a lie.

'We will defeat it,' I say, my hand shaking as I raise it. 'Together.'

The barest suggestion of a smile curves her lips. 'Together.'

I draw a shuddered breath.

I hold it.

I take Hans's dagger and swipe it across her throat.

CHAPTER TWENTY-ONE

For a blissful moment, nothing happens. I have committed the most abhorrent of sins – the slaughter of a sibling – yet there is no evidence. Thea blinks one blue eye back at me.

Then she swallows.

The line across her throat yawns open. Blood pours from my sister's seams, viscous and impossibly slick. The knife clatters to the ground; I press a hopeless hand against the gaping wound. A river parted, the blood flows around my fingers, finding its course.

I stare into the azure depths of her eye until it turns glassy and unresponsive.

Thea is dead.

Something vital breaks inside me. My guiding star flickers out. Without Thea, what purpose is there? If I cannot save her, what fight do I have left? Thea ceases to levitate. Her limp body is dead weight in my arms. I draw her against me, clutching tighter and tighter as if my love alone can bring her back to life.

My hand catches against the thread attached to her skull. I examine it, spooled around my fingers in the moonlight. As I watch, the malignant gossamer dissolves into particles.

Hands shaking, I lower Thea to the ground. Use my unsteady fingers to close her lids. With her decomposing eye shrouded, she appears to be sleeping.

'What a pretty picture,' the Untier growls, staggering to its feet. 'A dead girl and the Saint who could not save her.'

It shakes its head, as though shaking off the effects of my magic. But I do not look at the beast – do not watch death as it comes for me. I direct my gaze to the women hanging in the clearing. Their eyes flick to meet mine. I count each pair of eyes, each beating heart. Black ribbons of fear tangle in the air around them, stretching from hearts and heads and stomachs.

I beckon the cords and let them come to me. They burn hot and cold against my fingers, frostbitten and scalding at once. Lids fluttering shut, I follow the cords to their origins. It's different, this time. I feel no revulsion. Just pity. Their horror is so heavy.

The tendrils spool around my fingers and twist in my hair. My hands clench to fists, fingers digging into my palms so tightly that they draw blood.

For the first time, I understand: this is how humans fear. How a Saint never will.

Everything snaps into place. *Fear is a gift*, just as Hans said. All I need to do is accept it. Wield it. I tighten my fists, letting their terror channel through me. I want to kill this beast, and I will use these women to do it.

Use them.

My resolve falters. The distinction between myself and the Untier blurs. Eyes pleading, the near-lifeless women watch me.

They cannot consent. There is little difference between a Saint and a monster when both intend to abuse you.

The Untier stalks towards me. The promise of power explodes between my fingertips. Never before have I known intoxication like it. My entire body sings. With their fear, I could be unstoppable ...

'Ilse,' comes a wavering howl. 'Ilse!'

My eyes dart to Johanna Fischer, who stares back at me with desperation.

'Please,' she slurs. Her gaze flits to Thea. 'Finish it off.'

'End it,' echoes Frau Albrecht, her dry lips struggling to form the words.

More pleas rise from the ranks of women. Soon, their voices form a layered chorus. A haunting song of desperation and pain and grief.

'End it,' they shriek. *'End it!'*

The Untier hastens its strides. I exhale. Unfurl my fists. I do not need to wield their fear; I just need them to feel it.

'It's over,' I shout, casting my gaze across the sea of women. 'You are free.'

Women's terror — decades of it — that has pooled in the cords crashes against my veins. I push it back. Back to its source. A tidal wave of fear surges, exploding into each woman's body.

In an instant, their hearts give out.

There is a moment of panic. Eyes widening, mouths dropping open. Johanna Fischer sheds a tear. The women let out a collective sigh. They die quietly, serenely. The silvery cords snaking from their bodies snap and dissolve.

'No!' the Untier bellows, staggering. 'What have you done?'

It draws in a lungful of air, sucking the horror from the

atmosphere before the full supply can dissipate. Its horns grow; it shifts, walking on two legs rather than four; the caverns of its eyes burn white hot.

'You destroyed,' it pants, laboured, 'my stock.'

I bare my teeth. 'I hope you starve to death.'

With what little strength remains in my failing body, I plant my feet against the earth. I can barely see the beast through the halo of black framing my vision. Arm shaking, I scrabble to pick up Hans's dagger from where it rests on the floor. It's still slick with my sister's blood.

'When I rip your head from your spine, you will forget your foolish allegiances. *I* will remain,' the Untier snarls, lumbering towards me. 'In a decade, in a century. I will be here, reaping the girls of Heulensee until the end of time.'

It lunges. Time drops into slow motion. The Untier's jaw snaps open. I stare into the hungry, black abyss of its maw. Teeth inches from my face, I jam my penknife into the gaping socket of its right eye. The beast howls, falters – but not for long enough.

It will consume me, one way or another.

If I die, at least this pain will cease to exist. In the blink of an eye, the anguish of Thea's death will be wiped from my soul. I will forget her, and Oma, and Hans, and Torsten.

I will forget Ash. The green of her eyes; the scent of her hair; the butterfly beat of my heart as her skin grazes mine. There's so much I'll never know. Ordinary things: what does she look like when she's engrossed in a book? Does she sing while she bathes? Worse than that are the *extra*ordinary things I will never experience: the touch of her body, the weight of her embrace, the taste of her lips.

Too late, I realize there is something left worth fighting for.

The earth thrums beneath my feet. Roots burst from the soil. One ensnares my left ankle, the other my right calf. I brace myself, ready to be pulled north or east or south or west – but instead, the roots drag me down. Beneath the soil.

I manage half a lungful of air, and then the earth consumes me whole.

CHAPTER TWENTY-TWO

This is death.

Beneath the earth, darkness is all that exists. Soil presses against my eyelids, my lips, my nostrils. I am moving, but there is no sense of progress. Roots tear at my hair, at Oma's barrette. I dare not – *cannot* – inhale, but the smell of rot and decay seeps into me, nonetheless.

Thea is dead. I will be soon. The Untier still reigns. I failed. Miserably, hopelessly.

I want to open my mouth and let the earth claim me, but I cannot part my lips. The soil hushes me. *Shush now*, it says. *This will all be over soon. You will forget.*

Then, a beacon flashing amidst the darkness. *Hold on, Ilse. I will bring you home.* This voice is soft, familiar. Like slipping into a warm bath after freezing in the lake.

In the dark, my mind separates from the rest of me. I drift away and lay my consciousness beside Thea's broken body. The wound on her throat gapes at me. Soon, the wound will be gone. *She* will be gone. Her flesh will melt from her bones, and her blood will feed the soil. I will forget.

The voice is urgent when it shouts, *Hold on!*

My consciousness stretches like tree sap, roaming further and further away from my body – until it snaps. I am catapulted back into my flesh. Light and air hit me all at once. I am lying on a bed of spruce needles and meadow grass. Blinded by the sun, I cough and heave. Like a babe ejected from the womb, I have to make a conscious decision to live. To clear my lungs and breathe. But what if I don't *want* to live?

Death means forgetting. Catharsis. It's an escape plan. I relinquish my grip on this life. Something warm fastens around my shoulders. The blurry shapes dancing in front of my eyes separate into a nose, lips, eyes ...

Ash.

I vomit dirt, rub my eyes and inhale.

Her mouth is caught between a scream and a sigh as she breathes, 'Ilse.'

And then I collapse.

💀

Light filters through the window. It dances across my skin, illuminating already-fading scars that mark my body like lightning strikes. There is a single, blissful moment – that achingly beautiful point in time between sleeping and waking – where I am unburdened. Then it hits me.

Dorothea is dead.

My chest caves in. The atmosphere grows thick and

suffocating, as if the air itself protests my continued existence. I throw my head back against the pillow and howl. Someone has scrubbed me clean and bound my broken bones. I wish they hadn't. With Thea's blood dried on my arms, at least I knew she existed. At least I still had proof of her.

The fact that I ever believed I could save her seems so infantile. My hopes of emerging victorious, welcomed back to Heulensee with open arms, are enough to make me retch. Triumph cannot exist in the same reality as my dead sister.

My howling turns to a pitiful mewl. The grief is so raw, so intense, that I think it might kill me. I stare at the ceiling and beg it to collapse.

'She's gone, isn't she?' Hans stands in the door frame. The sunlight illuminates the hollows of his gaunt cheeks. Purple bags beneath his eyes accentuate the deathly pallor of his skin. Nothing remains of the boy that entered the Hexenwald with me. The forest's infection has bled him dry.

And I am about to break him beyond repair. I drag in a tortured breath. 'She's gone.'

The bed dips. Hans sits at the foot of it, head in hands, reduced to a faint echo of the man he once was.

'I'm sorry,' I whimper. 'So sorry.'

Arms shaking, I reach out to him. He looks at me, eyes full of hurt he cannot bear to vocalize. The bed shifts again as he moves.

'Where are you going?'

He sighs. 'I don't know. Away.'

'Don't leave,' I cry. 'Please don't leave me, Hans.'

Without Hans, I might convince myself she never existed at all. We both understand this loss. We are her greatest witnesses, left behind.

'Don't worry, Ilse,' he says, voice biting. 'It's not as if I can stray far.'

The accusation in his voice stings. *I* made it so that he could never leave the Hexenwald. *I* couldn't save Thea. The guilt weighs heavy enough – without the slash of his tongue. Scalding tears cascade down my cheeks. 'Please, Hans.'

He spares me one more glance – maybe pitying, maybe loathing. And then he leaves.

Left alone, I ball my fists into the quilt and cry. My body eventually loses the capacity for tears, and I am left with a rotting hurt inside that I cannot purge. Beyond the window, Hexenwald spruces lean across Ash and Torsten's meadow. The trees jeer at me.

'Ilse?' Ash's voice is a gentle breeze across the room, utterly at odds with the tempest raging inside me.

I look to where she stands, hesitating just at the threshold, face caught somewhere between surprise and concern.

'How are you feeling?'

'Did you save me?' My words are an accusation.

'I brought you here. You saved yourself.' She steps tentatively into the room, lowering her voice and eyes in tandem. 'I wasn't sure you would recover.'

'I wish I hadn't,' I say quietly.

I direct my gaze back to the ceiling, knowing it will not judge me. The heat of Ash's gaze burns into my skin. She crosses the room, silent as a wraith, and sits on the bed beside me.

'Don't say that.'

'Why not?'

She pauses. 'Because I do not want you to die, Ilse.'

We sit in silence for a few moments. A gale picks up outside, howling through the cracks in the window.

'I saw what happened,' she admits quietly. 'The trees showed me.'

Shame floods through me like the ice water that melts off glaciers in spring. 'So you know that I slayed my own sister?'

The words carry even more weight in the air than they do inside my chest. Spoken aloud, they draw the scale of my crime into sharp focus. I am for ever tainted by what I have done.

'I know that you gave your sister a final kindness,' she murmurs. 'I know that you liberated those women from a lifetime of pain.'

Her words are a tonic that I cannot swallow. They could soothe me, if only I would let them. 'It was all for nothing. The Untier lives.'

'You made a dent in the Untier's defences. You ended untold suffering.'

My eyes flick to hers. 'You do not have to be kind to me.'

'You *deserve* kindness.' She reaches out, braiding her fingers through mine. 'You deserve to be embraced for who you are, not who you pretend to be.'

I blink back at her, wondering how she knows the exact words I have dreamt of hearing my whole life. She sits before me, all-powerful, and far wiser than I could hope to be, and heals every sour thought I let fester. *She* is the one who deserves kindness.

'I bound you, Ash. You are compelled to help me.'

The words sound even more childish out loud. But the only people who have been kind to me did so out of believed familial obligation. Just once, *once*, I want someone to choose me. I want her to disagree – to tell me that she feels even a *fraction* of what I feel for her. Instead, her face turns cold and unforgiving.

'Is that what you believe? That I sit at your bed and speak in hushed tones out of a sense of duty? Because I am obliged to do so?' A muscle ticks beneath the soft skin of her jaw. 'I thought you *saw* me, Ilse.'

'I do see you,' I argue, petulant, 'and I cannot understand why someone like you would waste time on someone like me.'

'If you think I will sit here and smile while you whip yourself bloody, you are sorely mistaken.' She leans in, dropping her voice to a caustic hiss. 'You are so angry at the world and at yourself that you cannot see what might be right in front of you.'

A bitter laugh scrapes up my throat. 'Leave, then. Just like the rest of them.'

As soon as the words leave my mouth, I realize their consequences. Ash's jaw drops open. Mine follows suit, my own body revulsed by my actions. I try to apologize, but the words will not work their way up my throat. They stay trapped somewhere in my chest, digging their thorns into something vital.

Ash crosses the room and exits without another word.

When I was a child, the Pfarrer delivered a sermon on the importance of suffering. A young girl raised her hand and asked *why* we must suffer. *Saints are borne from suffering*, he told her. *Our own pain brings us closer to the Saints.*

Perhaps it's my Sainthood, then, that condemns me to perpetual anguish. Some pain has been dealt to me; the rest I've delivered unto myself. I was born to an unloving mother, cherished by a sister whom I'd eventually be forced to kill, and seen – *truly* seen – by a Hexe whose kindness I cannot accept.

I find a kernel of magic inside me and use it to seal the door to my room shut. For the rest of the day, I rise only to use the chamber pot as my body demands. Though my flesh wounds are healing, the mental wounds worsen. I picture my brain as a rotting mound of pus, which will only heal if lanced.

Ash comes back to visit the next day at noon. She pushes against the door and, finding it unyielding, knocks relentlessly for a span of twenty minutes. I remain wordless. Defeated, she retreats downstairs. She tries again the following day, insisting that I need to eat. I do not answer.

On the third day, even Torsten comes to coax me from my chamber. Half of me wants to let him in – he knows first-hand the physical pain of recovery, if nothing else – but the seal I welded around the door is sticky and reluctant to shift. I turn to the wall and cover my head with a pillow.

By the fourth day, I can barely move. I am a transitory being, neither human nor Saint, caught halfway through metamorphosis. Rather than emerging evolved and resplendent, I decay in my cocoon. My mind festers.

On the fifth day – I think it's the fifth day, but I no longer care to mark the passing of time – a commotion spurs me into consciousness. When I manage to open my eyelids, Ash's face appears above me. She is talking, but I cannot hear her. Her mouth forms angry shapes.

She vanishes briefly, then returns with a vial held between her fingers. One of her hands fastens around my jaw while the other uncorks the stopper and pours bitter liquid down my throat. As the potion settles in my belly, sensation returns to my limbs. Colour floods back into the world. My ears ring and ring until they make out the frequency of Ash's incensed voice. It makes me wish I remained unhearing.

'Is that it, then?' She spits. 'Is it over?'

'What?' I ask, voice hoarse.

Heavy seconds pass without a response from Ash. I look up to see her studying me, features contorted with rage. 'Your sister is dead, so you're choosing to die with her?'

I grit my teeth, perturbed by the suggestion that I should aspire to *anything* now that Thea is gone. That there is anything worth devoting myself to, now that my course has been permanently altered. Before I left the Hexenwald, possibility hung between Ash and I. Now, with my sister's blood on my hands and a hundred deaths weighing on my conscience, I realize that happy endings don't belong to people like me.

'I am not *choosing* to die,' I snarl. 'There is nothing more for me to do. Thea is dead. I failed.'

Ash raises a brow, questioning. 'You truly believe that – that there's nothing more to do?'

'What else would you have me do?'

'Oh, I don't know, Ilse,' she says, voice dripping with sarcasm. 'Maybe deal with the false Saint that is still very much at large? Or here's a novel idea: you could protect the girls left behind! Would you prefer to let them be slaughtered?'

'I could not defeat it, Ash!' I throw my hands up; she does not flinch. 'There is nothing I can do. I am not strong enough. Perhaps one day, when I have matured into my Sainthood—'

'You have to *live* in order to mature!' She leans in, eyes aflame. 'The Ilse *I* know is not unmoved by suffering. The Ilse *I* know would try – no matter how futile it seems. The Ilse *I* know is not a coward.'

I startle at that. 'You must not know me at all, if that's what you believe.'

'Was it cowardice when you entered the Hexenwald, risking your life to save Thea? Did you end the suffering of those women, of your own *sister*, because you lack compassion? When you met my anger with juniper rather than a blade, tell me: what was in your heart?'

'It is not a matter of cowardice or compassion,' I snap. 'It is a matter of possibility. I cannot kill the Untier. I cannot save the girls that remain.'

Now she flinches. In one fell swoop, I have shattered every good thought she fostered about me. 'I only wish the children in Heulensee had sisters as loyal as you were to Thea. It is a terrible shame there is no one to try and rescue *them* from the Untier's jaws.'

I throw my arms up, exasperated. 'Your image of me does not exist! I am not good, or brave. I do not deserve Sainthood. I do not deserve *you*—'

Her lips silence mine. My muscles coil so tightly that I think I might break. I am a bowstring pulled taut; a deer ready to bolt. This is not a tender kiss. A *loving* kiss. This is a battle declaration. One of her hands fastens around my wrist, pinning me to the bed. The other takes root in my hair. I kiss her back just as fiercely. Our union is fervent, desperate. We claw at each other as if we are starving.

'It is not for you to say what I deserve,' Ash hisses, breath hot against my lips.

She pulls back from me, pupils dilated and cheeks flushed. There is something feral in her expression that makes my heart ricochet against my ribs. Before I can question what just happened between us – before I can beg for *more* – she stalks away and slams the door behind her.

CHAPTER TWENTY-THREE

Mind reeling, I throw my head back onto the pillow. If my lips didn't tingle with the memory of her, I might convince myself that whatever just happened was a hallucination. A wistful figment of my imagination. The way I feel in the wake of our kiss gives me clarity. It's an amplification of how I've always felt around her.

I press the pillow over my face. In the darkness, shapes and colours swirl behind my eyelids into a sequence of fantasies. Ash and I at a market together, laughing as we spend on frivolous little things like roses, and pastries in the shape of hearts; our hands intertwined as we doze in some sun-soaked clearing; a rainy day spent reading books and stoking the fire with each rumble of thunder.

With a grunt, I throw the pillow across the room. Saints do not get to live like that.

Not least because Ash has now seen the most loathsome parts

of me. The awful truth in her words – that my inaction spells more death in Heulensee – leaves a sour taste in my mouth.

'*That is not your concern,*' I tell myself, trying my best to embody the ambivalent detachment of Borbet – my *real* mother. '*We do not interfere with matters beyond the Hexenwald.*'

The longer I sit with those words, the more they needle at my ears. Would it be easier to follow my Saintly family – to concern myself only with Sainthood, and not the lives in Heulensee? Indisputably. But is that what *I* want? Is that the sort of person that Thea and Oma would've been proud of? Is that someone Ash could love?

I heave myself from the bed out of sheer spite. The pain of my wasted muscles is enough to flush Thea's face from my mind. At first, I think I might follow Ash – but the grimacing teeth of the stairs is enough to dissuade me. Instead, I pad down the corridor, one arm braced against the wall, to the ajar door at its end.

Through the open sliver of the doorway, I see Torsten sitting at the desk in his bedroom. His bruises have faded, and his eyes have regained their sunshine glow. At least one of us will recover.

'Torsten?'

He looks up, flustered, and shuts the leather-bound tome he'd been studying. One hand goes to smooth out his hair, while the other braces against the desk as he adjusts his position.

'Ilse,' he says, a smile in his voice. 'I didn't realize you were awake.'

'Are you okay?'

'Divine.' He grins and gestures for me to take a seat on the bed. I stagger in and plop down, exhausted. 'I take it your mission didn't go as planned.'

'I could not save her,' I admit, beneath my breath. 'The Untier still reigns.'

Suddenly sombre, he purses his lips. 'I'm so sorry, Ilse. I know how much you loved her. I'm sure she knew it, too.'

I nod detachedly. My eyes glaze over; I stare at my reflection in one of the many ornate mirrors hanging on the wall. It would be a comfort to find something of Thea in me – but we were never blood-bound. I am the moon, and she was the sun. I merely reflected her light. Without Thea, there is no sense to any of it. The suffering in Heulensee is meaningless.

'A coin for your thoughts?' Torsten asks, peering around my stupor. 'Ash stormed down the stairs. I assume you were involved.'

'Why would you assume that?'

He gives a wry smile. 'Lovers' quarrel?'

My mouth drops open and I turn a ghastly shade of beetroot. What Ash feels for me is closer to loathing than loving. I felt as much in the graze of her teeth against my lips.

'She called me a coward.'

'*Are* you a coward?'

I pause, and on reflection, nod reluctantly.

Torsten sighs and arches a brow. The expression reminds me that he *is* her brother. 'What is there to be angry about, then?'

'I do not *want* to be a coward.'

'Then don't.' I stare back at him blandly, which only serves to widen his grin. 'What I mean to say,' he hurries to add, sensing the irritation building beneath my skin, 'is that – for most people – cowardice is a survival instinct. Their fear instructs them to stay within the lines. To *live*. But you don't have fear to hem you in. What's stopping you from being brave?'

'Logic. I could not defeat the Untier before. There is no reason I would be able to defeat it now. It is a fool's errand.'

Torsten lets out a colossal groan. 'You weakened the beast in your encounter, did you not? You took away its power source.'

I flinch, thinking of the women I slaughtered. 'There are young girls left in Heulensee. It will draw from them as they come of age.'

He looks out of the window across the meadow, eyes narrowed slightly, lips pursed. 'The false Saint imitates *you*, Ilse. Given that the Untier gains power from the women's terror, why can't you do the same?'

I believed my innate magic would have to suffice as the only weapon in my arsenal – that fear would remain a foreign concept, impenetrable and unwieldy. But when I held the women's fear, quivering in my palm, I understood. I think, if I tried, I could wield it now.

The impossibility of this solution settles over me like a blanket of snow. 'The Untier will have the remaining girls close under its watch.'

'What about the men? Can't they be harnessed?'

'The men have never been made to fear the way we have. I'm not sure they know how—'

'There must be a neighbouring settlement,' he says, hopeful. 'A fresh crop?'

I stare myself down in the mirror, searching for inspiration – and then it strikes. A shuddered breath escapes me. 'Torsten Nachtnebel,' I murmur. 'You are a genius.'

💀

I retire to my room and spend the rest of the night plotting. Ash does not return – at least not in physical form. The image of her with flushed cheeks and tousled hair invades my brain often. Not entirely conducive to planning.

When my mind tires, I stretch out my wasted muscles, working life back into my flesh. The shallow hum of my magic grows; I use it to strengthen my once-broken bones, envisioning the fractures melting and fading.

There is a way forward. A way to vanquish the Untier and give the girls of Heulensee the life that was stolen from Thea.

By sunup, hope sparks dangerously in my chest. I dress myself, choosing a blouse and emerald-coloured dress which must be Ash's. It's far too tight and too long, but it's more presentable than my nightgown. The stairs which daunted me yesterday are now child's play. Sainthood has its perks.

Ash and Hans are in the amber-walled sitting room. Some of the tension between them has melted away. In Hans's imprisonment, they have at last found common ground.

'I can still save them.'

Ash and Hans look up in unison. 'Have you changed your mind, then?' Ash asks, voice biting. 'Decided that the girls are worth saving?'

I draw in what I intend to be a calming breath, though it does little to soothe me. 'I found a solution.'

'How fortunate for those people,' Ash says drily, 'that the Saint has decided to descend from her throne.'

Shame forces my gaze to the floor. My decision to help them shouldn't have hinged on Ash. We both know it. I cannot help but feel I have squandered any opportunity that may have existed between us. The bond is the only thing still tying us together – and once this is over . . .

My chest aches.

'Well?' Ash prompts.

Swallowing my disappointment, I say, 'I could not defeat the Untier before, but I only had access to a fraction of my power then. I believe I understand it now – how to wield fear.' My eyes flick to Hans, who watches me warily. 'May I demonstrate?'

He gives a guarded nod, and I turn to one of the cabinets lining the walls. I rifle through its contents and settle on a red-limbed centipede in a glass cage. Not pausing to think, I pick the insect from its confines and drop it onto Hans's lap.

Predictably, he squeals – and then I see it. His fear hangs in the air, an inky cord which originates in his heart. In my mind's eye, I reach out and brush tentative fingers against his terror. It recoils, but I clench my fist around the cord and pull. Just as it was in the Untier's den, the power humming between my fingers makes sense.

Like dry wood to a wildfire, Hans's fear bolsters my magic. Static dances across my body. A gentle breeze rallies around me, filling my limbs with power. I feel as if I could collapse this cabin with a touch of my finger. How must it feel to draw from the fear of not one, but *hundreds*? How far could my power stretch?

I catch my reflection in the cabinet's glass. My eyes are white, the pupils indiscernible. Blue veins vibrate beneath translucent skin. I look terrifying. I look *Saintly*.

As quickly as I grasped it, I drop Hans's fear. He exhales loudly, clutching at his chest. Ash plucks the centipede from Hans's lap just before he brings his fist down to crush it. She places it back in its cage, then the cage back in the cabinet.

Her face is unreadable as she asks, 'We cannot leave the forest. Whose fear will you take?'

'There are untapped women,' I say, and instantly grimace at my choice of words. 'Banished from Heulensee, long ago.'

Hans scoffs, shoulders squaring. 'You do realize one of those "untapped women" is my mother, Ilse?'

Shame rings through me, clear as a bell. In my haste, I had forgotten Hans's mother was banished from Heulensee when he was a child. My cheeks flush. 'I think she'd be eager to help.'

'You don't know her.' He rakes a hand through his hair. 'She is a fully-formed person, Ilse – not just a well for you to draw from.'

'I've never even heard you speak about her,' I snap, embarrassment making me defensive.

'You've hated me since we first met. Did you really think I'd confide in you about how much I miss her? How often I think about her? How I sleep with her journal beneath my pillow because it's the only piece of her I have left?'

His words hang heavy in the air. I suddenly feel very small. Very selfish.

'I don't hate you,' I whisper.

Hans opens and shuts his mouth. 'That's beside the point. It seems backward to make *anyone* lay their fear bare for you to stop the Untier.'

His accusation rips the wind from my sails. 'But I am not doing this for the sake of my own power.' My sideways glance at Ash does not conjure the support I hoped for. 'I am doing this for the future of Heulensee. For the girls with no protectors.'

He bites his tongue, then decides against it. 'You rallied against women's exploitation when it benefited the Untier. Now, when it serves your own strength, you plan to pilfer their fear. What's the difference?'

I think of every Rite in the Untier's den. Those women had no choice. Their fear was torn from them. 'The difference is *consent*.'

'Consent is not given under duress,' he argues. 'Do you truly expect anyone to deny a Saint?'

Heat flares across my cheeks. I silence the part of myself that agrees with him, knowing that this is the only way forward. 'It's a final stand, Hans.'

'Who can say that you won't acquire a taste for it? An appetite for fear?'

My jaw hangs open, disbelief echoing between my temples. 'Is *that* what you think of me? That I am some bloodthirsty predator, no different than the monsters in this forest?'

'I think you came to the Hexenwald with the goal of saving Thea and women like her from the Untier. Now, you expect those same vulnerable women to worship you. To lay their terror at your feet.' He dips his gaze and lowers his voice. 'I don't know who, or what, you are, Ilse.'

My stomach drops. I am too proud to let him see that his words wound me. My skin bristles as I rise to meet him. 'I was a girl, and now I am a Saint. I *am* unrecognisable.' When Hans does not respond, I look to Ash, whose furrowed brow indicates that she is embroiled in a conflict of her own. 'What about you? Can you see the merit of my plan?'

'I see both sides,' she admits. 'Perhaps this is a necessary evil.'

I'm not sure I like the idea of being a necessary evil. 'There is no harm in asking them,' I decide. 'I will not force anyone.'

Thinking this a diplomatic compromise, I look to Hans for his approval. He has retreated into himself, any sense of ire wiped from his expression. I want him to challenge me. To shout at me, to strike me down. I want him to make me suffer for what I did to Thea. The numb expression on his face is worse than any blow he could deliver.

CHAPTER TWENTY-FOUR

I find the image of myself leading an army of howling women intoxicating. That night, when the worst of my doubts rear up, *that* is the image I use to ground myself in the present, in my power. I have seen what epic feats terrified women can achieve. Picturing myself among their ranks makes me believe that this is possible – that the false Saint will fall at the hands of the real one.

The fumes of Hans's fear tell me I *can* wield it, but I must learn to be as skilful and seamless as the Untier. The next morning, Hans says I ought to practise if I plan to ask the women for their fear. He offers himself up as a test subject. Secretly, I think he is desperate to feel *something*. Anything. He spends hours by the window, eyes glazed over. I can barely remember what his smile looks like, nor can I recall the sound of his laughter.

Struck by the memory of his reaction when I held his terror in my hands, I tell him no, I will not use him for practice. He responds with a look of knowing judgement. I cannot bear its weight; I retreat into the meadow, where Ash is curled up in the grass, snoring softly.

She peels open an eye as I approach. 'Good morning.' Her voice is husky with sleep.

'It's the afternoon, Ash.' I'm struck by the urge to brush the stray ringlets away from her face. I wonder what her skin would feel like beneath my fingertips.

'Is it?' She stretches her arms in an arc above her head. 'I was having the most wonderful dream.'

'What was it about?'

Her lips curve into a smile. 'Well, that would be telling.'

Ash has this spectacular ability to make everything else – the Untier, the banished women, the magic I don't fully grasp – fade to background noise. When I'm beside her, we are the only creatures in existence.

'I wondered if you'd come with me to see the banished women,' I say. 'To the edge of the forest, anyway.'

She cocks her head. 'I'm surprised you want my company.'

I swallow thickly, unsteadied by the exposed expanse of her throat. 'I would appreciate it very much.'

'Well,' she pauses to yawn, flashing her teeth, 'it's not as if I'm doing anything else.'

We duck back inside the house, inform the men of our plan, and depart – after taking care to mask my scent from Wilbet and Borbet. The apathy on Hans's face wounds me more than I thought possible. I extend a withered lifeline, asking if he wouldn't like to see his mother; she must still live with the banished women. He tenses for a moment, briefly enamoured, then shrugs his shoulders.

'So I can grow more fond of her before you ask to bleed her dry?' Hans shakes his head. 'No, thank you.'

One thing is clear: Hans no longer cares what happens to me.

The Hexenwald stretches all the way to the meadows east of Heulensee. I am grateful for this fact, because it means that Ash can accompany me for most of the journey. Somehow, I feel more nausea at this endeavour than I did when preparing to face the Untier. Perhaps it's because back then, I had Hans's support. And I still believed I could save Thea. That after everything, we'd be reunited. Sisters once more.

When glimpses of the meadow huts appear between the Hexenwald's boughs, I am half of the mind that I should flee. Ash must sense my flightiness; she holds out a hand, prompting me to stop just short of the forest's edge.

'What's the matter?'

'I can't remember what it's like to be around people,' I admit. 'I'm less human now than I ever was.'

Since we fought – since we *kissed* – Ash has been sharper than usual. Now, she softens. 'I felt the same way when I became a Hexe, and again when I became an Eschenfrau. It felt as if I'd lost something I couldn't get back.' Melancholy fills her eyes. 'When a butterfly emerges from a cocoon, the caterpillar it once was does not cease to exist. Everything that made the caterpillar is still there. It's just . . . arranged differently.' She meets my gaze and I resist the urge to shrink away. 'You have not lost anything, Ilse. Your heart is the same as it always was.'

Unable to hold her eye contact without fainting where I stand, I look at the ground and murmur, 'I'm sorry for the way I treated you. For giving up.'

She reaches out and stops just short of grazing my arm with her fingertips. 'If Torsten had died, I might have done the same.'

Her closeness awakens the memory of our kiss. I'm left feeling light-headed. The sway she holds is nothing short of witchcraft. I force my eyes up to meet hers.

A lazy smile curves her lips. 'What's that look?'

'Why did you kiss me?' The words come out in a tangle before I can stop them. Heat floods my cheeks.

Ash cocks an eyebrow. 'Are you that naive?'

'I didn't mean—'

She leans in unexpectedly. Her breath grazes my face as she whispers, 'Do you know why people tend to kiss each other, Ilse?'

My eyes are drawn to her mouth. *Don't stare, Ilse!* Back to her eyes. But her *lips* . . .

'Is something about my lips interesting to you?'

'Yes,' I breathe, acutely aware of the proximity of our bodies.

Ash drags her thumb across my lower lip. Her other hand curls around the back of my neck. The soft scrape of her nails against my skin is torture. She pulls me closer. Where our bodies meet, a jolt of static surges through my bones – enough to rival my magic.

Her lips hover millimetres from mine. 'Do you prefer them close up?'

My entire body *begs* for me to eliminate the distance between us. To crash my lips against hers and not relent. 'I do.'

We teeter on the precipice. The world narrows down to that singular moment, and time stands still. Her heart beats fiercely against mine; the air grows thick with desire.

Ash's gaze flickers between my eyes and my parted lips, a silent invitation. I feel her words against my mouth as she whispers, 'Then show me.'

The floodgates of my restraint – of my doubt, my self-loathing, my utter disbelief that she could like *me* – fly open. Our mouths come together. Stars burst across my vision. Something warm awakens deep in my belly. Something *hungry.*

Our kiss deepens, a melding not just of mouths but of souls. It's a delicate choreography – unchained fervour, but deeper than that, it's *tenderness*. The dance of two people surrendering to their desires and acknowledging that this is more than just a kiss. Eventually, she pulls away slightly.

'Go,' Ash murmurs against my lips. 'Talk to them.'

The fire dampens, but does not extinguish. '*Ash.*'

I feel her mouth curve into a smile before she pulls away. 'Don't be petulant. *Go.*'

Breaths coming thick and heavy, I reach for her. 'Won't you come with me?'

She shakes her head. 'You know I cannot. Even if I could, it wouldn't be wise. Humans find me strange.'

'They find me strange, too.'

Ash laughs. It's a rare sound. One to treasure. 'Get on with it, Ilse.'

I release a deep sigh and relinquish the shelter of the trees. As soon as my back is turned, I break into a grin. My entire life has been an overcast day. With Ash, the sun shines.

Something needles at me, then. At first, I think it's guilt that I've found happiness even though my sister no longer lives. But when I interrogate the sensation, I realize it's not that. It's regret.

I wish Thea had met Ash. She would've loved her. I can imagine them conspiring, plotting ways to surprise me for my birthday. And Ash's clothes! Gowns of maroon, emerald, sunflower yellow. Thea would've fawned over them. Used them to inspire a whole range of dresses in the village, no doubt.

My eyes prickle. Before I meet the women of the meadow huts,

I must regain my composure. I let the breeze dry my eyes, draw in a deep breath and forge onwards.

I am not sure what I expected to find in the meadows, but I am surprised, nonetheless. The huts stand far away from one another, built specifically to stifle any sense of community – but there are paths worn between the cabins. Lifelines.

Three women exchange produce, swapping corn, butter and a pair of boots. A group of young women gather around a white-haired woman while she teaches them how to work the plough. Another group descends upon a worn-down hut, armed with hammers, nails and planks of wood.

This is the existence outcasts are threatened with?

As I make my way across the women's meadow, heads turn to track me. I raise a wooden arm in greeting. My attempt at cordiality only makes them more suspicious.

One of the elders steps forward, brow furrowed. 'What business do you have here?'

'Heulensee needs your help,' I admit.

'Heulensee needs *our* help?' The woman barks out an incredulous laugh. 'How the mighty have fallen!'

The others join in with a chorus of disbelief. I see them slipping between my fingers, out of reach.

'Please listen.' I will the wind to lift the loose tendrils of hair that have escaped Oma's barrette. I wiggle my toes, feel the earth beneath the sole of my boots, and ask bedrock to imbue my voice with its power. 'My name is Ambet. I am one of the three Saints of Pathos, those Heulensee believed to be Hexen. I am the Saint of Fear, the Daughter Earth, and—'

'What have the Saints ever done for us?'

The question unmoors me. My voice cracks and the wind

dies down. 'You worship the Saints. Many of you were banished because of it.'

A younger woman pipes up, 'Some of us worship them. Others were banished simply for being a nuisance.'

My mouth hangs open. Words form on my tongue and dissolve like spun sugar.

'Men labelled the Saints as Hexen,' the old woman says. 'Some of us simply refused the notion that a powerful woman is an evil one. That was enough to be banished.'

'And besides,' another shouts, 'some of us only saw the truth once we were exiled. I was banished simply for the Pfarrer disliking my fear.'

My gossamer hopes whisk away with the breeze. In their wake, something sour builds. I am a *Saint*. I can force these women to fight with me. Bend them to my will. Draw on their fear and use it to kill the Untier.

I cast a long look over my shoulder to where Ash waits in the trees. Will she be disappointed? Will she be *proud*?

'Where did you get that barrette?'

My heart swings with me as I turn back to face the crowd. One of them – a dark-haired woman with rosy cheeks – steps forward from the crowd. My hand drifts to the back of my skull. I trace the familiar lines of the barrette Oma gave me. It is such a permanent fixture in my hair that I barely register its presence anymore. 'It was a gift.'

'I made that barrette in my forge,' the woman replies, voice cool, 'and gave it to a dear friend of mine.'

My skin itches with the accusation. 'It was given to *me* by my Oma Margitte.'

'Margitte Odenwald?'

'You knew my Oma?'

Her hand flies to her chest. *Knew*, past tense. Hushed whispers roll across the crowd. 'I feared something had befallen her.'

'How could Margitte be your Oma if you were born a Saint?' the old woman asks.

I swallow around the lump in my throat. 'We belong to each other by love, not by blood.'

The dark-haired woman murmurs, 'What happened to her?'

I cannot soften the blow of my Oma's murder. I will tell her story frankly. 'The Untier ate her.'

A collective gasp rises from the women. They clutch hands against hearts, cover their mouths with their fingers. To see Oma's loss shared almost moves me to tears.

The woman with dark hair pales. 'I'm ... I'm so sorry.'

I nod numbly, the grief of losing Oma still fresh despite all that has passed. Heat prickles at my eyes, reminding me that despite my Sainthood, I was raised a human.

The older woman presses a hand against her chest. 'She deserved better.'

'She did,' I agree.

I watch as the women form a circle, discussing something in hushed whispers. Their eyes occasionally dart my way – some judging, some pitying. Eventually, they part. The younger woman steps to the front of the crowd and says, 'I think you ought to come inside.'

Inside one of the meadow huts, I am ushered into a chair by the fireplace. Julia, the dark-haired woman, prepares a cup of herbal tea. The white-haired woman, Esther, scowls at me from the corner of the room.

Once my hands are wrapped around the warm mug, Julia clears her throat. 'Tell us what happened.'

I drag down a sip of tea. It scalds my tongue, but I am careful not to wince. I tell the women my story: a girl born unfearing, failing to sate the Untier, Oma's death. Not willing to sob in front of these stoic women, I refrain from sharing Thea's demise.

'Your Oma was formidable,' Julia whispers.

'How did you know her?'

'She used to visit, even though she knew she'd be banished along with us if word got out. She'd bring us gifts, provisions – things we can't easily make here.' My heart rings in my chest as I remember the mornings Oma slipped out of the house without me, which I'd assumed a slight. 'But most importantly, she brought us *stories*. She kept close to my boy. Being torn from him was unbearable, but she made it feel like he wasn't so far away.'

The puzzle pieces slot together. The hammered barrette, forged in fire; her dark hair, the sparkle of her eyes. 'Are you Hans's mother?'

'I am,' she says, beaming at the mention of his name. 'Do you know him well? What's he like?'

'He is brave and kind beyond measure.' I falter, wondering whether I should disclose Hans's true affliction – the fact that no matter what happens next, he will never be able to leave the Hexenwald. 'He is . . . hurting. But he will pull through.'

Tears cling to Julia's eyelashes. She squeezes my hand. Of course Hans comes from a woman who is kind of heart and pure of intention.

'What will you ask of us?' Esther says, voice abrasive.

'What do you mean?'

'Don't be coy,' Esther says. 'You came here a beggar. Out with it.'

I take a long sip of my tea. When I swallow, it gets lodged in my throat. Guilt will do that.

I relay all that has come to pass in Heulensee. Julia purses her lips. Esther's expression does not change, though I notice her fingers curling around the table, knuckles turning white.

'I was unable to defeat the Untier on my own, but with your help I believe it can be conquered.'

'Your Oma was our lifeline,' Julia says, voice turning wistful. 'And we hate that Saints-forsaken creature. We have desired its death for many moons. Tell us what you need.'

On the surface, her response is an acceptance – but I get the sense that a warning lies below. *We will help you, but do not abuse this opportunity.* I blink back at the women in front of me. Black cords flicker around their throats. Saint of Fear or not, their apprehension is plain to see. Julia's lips pucker; Esther's brow furrows. They still cling to each other's hands, wondering, *what next?* How will I exploit them?

I think of all the times Heulensee demanded a taste of my fear. Of Thea as a child, screaming until veins in her eyes popped – because that's what was expected. Of the men beyond the church windows, carrying on, as women broke themselves again and again offering up their fear. The Pfarrer and the Untier rooting around inside my soul for horror, salivating.

It is harrowing to be lacking, to feel less than human and to be shunned. But to have your humanity torn from you without consent or consideration is its own sort of torture.

Any thought I had of asking these women for their fear

disappears. Hans was right all along. So was Ash. Harvesting their fear is evil. Whether it's necessary or not is up to me.

I look around at them. 'The girls will need you,' I say. 'Once this is all over. They need to be nurtured. To be *loved*. Will you see to it that they are?'

The distrust drains from Esther's face. It's replaced by an indiscernible mixture of regret and surprise. The women exchange a tense glance.

'I will not ask you to go back there,' I add, wondering if that is the root of their apprehension. 'But will you welcome them here?'

'Of course,' Julia stutters. 'Of course we will.'

'I need to come up with a plan.' I do not tell them that *they* were my plan. 'Expect them in a week or so.' I sink the remainder of my tea. The detritus in the bottom of the mug forms a dark mass, studded with two rosehip rinds for eyes. 'Thank you for the tea.'

I push away from the table and open the door.

'Ambet,' Esther calls. I pause in the doorway, half-turning to face her. 'Ilse. Saint. Whatever your name truly is.' She shakes her head, grey strands brushing her forehead. 'If you can slay this beast, I will worship you for the rest of my days. I swear it.'

I turn back, staring out across the meadow to the dark fringes of the Hexenwald. 'I will not slay it for your worship. I will slay it for your freedom.'

CHAPTER TWENTY-FIVE

'You didn't ask them, did you?'

Ash sees the truth written on my face as I re-enter the forest. The first time I pushed into the Hexenwald, it felt like plunging into a pool of ice water. Now, it's like stepping out of the smoke and into fresh air. The line between worlds blurs.

'It is not for me to decide whether evil is necessary.'

She smiles; my heart skips a beat. 'I'm glad.'

I push her shoulder playfully, hoping it might even the tempo inside my chest. 'I wish you had told me that you have a preference.'

'What do my preferences matter to you?'

'A great deal,' I murmur. 'They matter a great deal.'

Ash wrestles with her brows to keep a composed expression. She takes a breath and says, 'I wanted you to decide on your own. You need to choose your own path as a Saint. As a woman.'

Her words ignite my awareness that whatever I do now will

leave a legacy. This is my origin story. I do not want to be a wrathful, blood-soaked Saint.

I laugh out loud before I can stop myself.

'What's so funny?'

'My entire life, I have wanted to be fearful. My desire to be like the others has always defined my existence. And now – just now – when I pondered what I want, I realized I want to be kind. Like Thea. Like Hans. Not fearful, but *kind*.'

All of a sudden, Ash throws her arms around me. She smells like spruce needles underfoot, like petrichor and spring shoots as they burst through the soil. The shock of her embrace sends butterflies fluttering across my ribs. I lean into her. The pressure of her arms around me is warmth and safety.

'There is power in letting go,' she murmurs into my hair, 'and there are so many better things to be than ordinary.'

She pulls back, cheeks flushed. Her eyes are dew-kissed grass, all sparkle and light. The mischievous edge returns with a devilish grin at her lips. 'Besides, were you ordinary, you would be awfully boring.'

I rein in my breaths, not quite understanding the effect she has on me. 'I cannot think of a worse torture for you than to be *bored*.'

'Nor can I.'

A delightful tension lingers between us. We take a lackadaisical approach to traversing the Hexenwald, as if we were just two women, not a Saint and an Eschenfrau. Ash shows me toads that glow like coals; a pool of ether that ripples with each of our breaths; a burrow of *Wolpertinger* – hares with the antlers of roe deer and wings of a pheasant. I wish they'd shed their velvet horns; how I'd love to add them to my collection.

I scoop up handfuls of the ether, drinking long and deep at

Ash's command. The ether burns its way down my throat, like a potent liquor. In my stomach, it continues its charade – both unsteadying and steeling me, somehow all at once.

'We rarely stumble upon these pools. It must be a good omen,' Ash says, observing me with a strange curiosity. As I draw breath, she kneels beside me and takes a swig of the ether.

By the time the ether reaches my belly, magic is bursting from my seams. I feel it oozing from my every pore, shimmering across my very soul. When I look into the mirror surface of the pool, halos of white surround my pupils. It is not the pupil-less white of the Saints, nor is it the eye of a human. It's somewhere in between. *Different.*

I used to spend hours wondering why I didn't look like Thea. I wished for her blue eyes, her fair hair, her willowy frame. A visual testament to the fact that I belonged to my family. But I always belonged to Thea, and she to me. Even if our sisterhood was fabricated.

'I wish you had met her.' I clear my throat as if it might dislodge the emotion gathering there. 'Thea, I mean.'

'I wish I'd met her, too,' Ash says thoughtfully. Her reflection shimmers beside mine. 'But just because I didn't get to meet her in life, that doesn't mean I can't get to know her. I'd love you to tell me about her, when you're ready.'

'Thank you.' My voice trembles.

Ash dips her eyes, no longer willing to meet mine in the reflection. 'What will you do when this is done?'

My mind whirrs. I have been so focused on the task at hand that I haven't paused to examine what happens afterwards. There is no place for me in Heulensee, that much is certain.

'I'd like to stay here,' I murmur. 'If you'll have me.'

'I would like that very much.'

I can't help but think of the fight ahead of me. If sheer will could serve as a shield during battle, mine would be more than sufficient. Though I am a Saint, I can break. If the Untier wounds me fatally, I won't return to Ash – at least not the version of me she knows, that knows her in return. We study each other, silence carving a rift between our bodies. A confession lingers like medicine on my tongue. Now is the time I should speak it. On the precipice of death, I should tell this magical force of a woman that I've been enchanted by her since the day we met.

But I've never done this before. I don't know how to tell her, or *what* to tell her. A thousand clichés run through my head: that sunsets remind me of her, that my heart rabbit-kicks at each word she speaks.

I attempt to blend them into one meaningful declaration but instead, I blurt out, 'You remind me of a rabbit.'

Ash snorts. 'Is it my twitching nose? My long ears?'

Heat rises to my cheeks. I take a moment to compose myself before clarifying, 'What I meant to say was that I am very lucky to know you. And no matter what happens . . .'

'Let's make this day unforgettable.'

Before I can properly respond, Ash stands and sheds her clothes, undressing until she's wearing nothing but a gauzy chemise. She prompts me to do the same. I'm so spellbound by her that I do it without thinking. Ash takes my hand and pulls me into the pool. It's not deep enough to submerge me entirely; it rises just to my breasts, lighting up my body with the sensation of pins and needles, but *pleasant*. Inch by inch, my skin rings. When Ash dives in all the way, freckles of magic stipple my cheeks.

She vanishes briefly below the surface, emerging with ether

clinging to her eyelashes. A swollen sun peers between the trees, illuminating motes of pollen and fluffy seed heads as they dance around Ash's face. A breeze stirs the pool, causing it to shimmer, iridescent and smoke-like.

'Open,' Ash says, gesturing at my mouth.

When I oblige, she cups her hands and pours more ether down my throat. I splutter and swat her hands away. 'Are you trying to poison me?'

'Wouldn't dream of it.' She grins, showing sharp teeth.

The ether breeds hyper-awareness in my bones – of each pore on my skin, each strand of hair. Moreover, it makes me hyper-aware of *her*. Of the way the ether laps hungrily at her midriff, just as bewitched by her body as I am.

Flesh humming, I head back onto the grass and lie flat on my back to recentre myself. Blissfully unaware of the effect she has on me, Ash follows suit.

'I never thought I would drink ether with a Saint,' she says, staring up at the mosaic of sky between branches.

'Nor did I think I would lie with a Hexe-turned-Eschenfrau,' I pause, considering the implication of my words. 'Lie *down*, I mean. Not the other sort.'

Ash laughs and rolls onto her side, facing me. Her eyes sparkle with mischief. 'Saint of Fear, can I tell you my sins?'

I am too dumbstruck by her beauty, by the proximity of her body, to do anything other than nod.

'I've been having most impure thoughts,' she whispers, her breath cool against my lips, a smile playing on her own, 'and worst of all, I covet a Saint.'

My heart clenches, and then seems to stop entirely. Tiny stars burst across my vision. I drag in three measured breaths before

I regain enough coherency to respond. 'Without knowing the nature of these thoughts, I cannot decide a fitting punishment.'

She pauses, drawing her bottom lip between her teeth. 'Perhaps it's easier to show than it is to tell.'

Ash pulls us both to our feet. Her left hand grazes my lower back, her right cups my jaw. Pulse fluttering at her throat, her gaze darts between my lips and my eyes.

'How beautiful you look in the setting sun,' she breathes.

'Show me,' I press a finger to her lips; she parts them slightly. It makes me ache. 'How you dream of sinning.'

'It's something of a role reversal.' Her eyes capture mine. I could not tear away our gazes, even if I wanted to. 'I want you to get on your knees, Ilse.'

I stare back at her, my entire consciousness thrown behind *yearning*.

When I do not obey, she removes my hand from her lips, pins it by my side, and hisses, 'Kneel.'

Without thinking, without even stopping to breathe, I drop to kneel before her. I can only stare at the grass grazing her ankles while my heart riots inside my chest. Ash bends at the waist and hooks one finger beneath my chin.

'Now look at me, Ilse.'

As she straightens, I let my eyes ascend the endless expanse of her legs. Her skin – the colour of autumn leaves – is impossibly smooth, and it's all I can do to stop myself reaching out and running my hands across it.

My gaze snags on her bare midriff. The sharp lines of her hip bones, skimmed only by her translucent shift, rob my ability to breathe. I force my eyes upwards, but cannot prevent them from lingering on the swell of her breasts beneath her chemise.

Her collarbones, the soft curve of her throat, her jaw, her lips, her eyes.

The woman before me is an artist's life work. A masterpiece. Yet for every sumptuous curve of her muscled body, it is her *eyes* that undo me.

'Tell me what you want,' I breathe.

Her lips curl at the edges. She leans down and tucks a strand of hair behind my ear. Each part of my body heats, quaking with desire. If she draws this out any longer, I swear I will combust.

'I want you to *worship* me.'

Several hours later, we return to the meadow. My gait is haphazard, my hair mussed beyond fixing, my breaths still coming thick and fast between parted lips. Ash winds one arm around the small of my back as we walk.

'Okay?' she murmurs as we take the steps up onto the porch.

Okay doesn't even begin to cover it. It feels as if I've spent my whole life in black and white, only to discover that colour exists. I squeeze her hand as I say, 'More than okay.'

Ash insists that I sit on the fainting couch while she fetches me water. My eyelids drift shut. When I open them, the light has fled the room. A full moon hangs beyond the window.

At the foot of the couch, Ash snores softly. I study the soft expanse of her cheeks, the way her eyelashes flutter in her sleep. Contentedness swells inside me.

'Ilse?'

Hans stands in the doorway. He looks worse than he did before entering the Hexenwald; better than he did last time I saw him. My body tenses at the sound of his voice, ready to receive whatever punishment he has decided fits.

'Will you accompany me into the meadow?'

Perhaps he simply doesn't want Ash to witness this. I raise myself from the couch, cringing at each groan of the springs. Fortunately, Ash is a deep sleeper. I follow Hans outdoors, where he sits on the porch stairs.

We spend minutes in silence, watching the moon sail across the sky. The meadow grass still glows with fading tangerine light, undulating like waves of molten gold. Tomorrow, I will formulate a plan to slay the beast that nearly killed me. But tonight, the breeze is warm, Ash sleeps softly indoors, and Hans sits willingly by my side. Tonight, we are safe.

Hans eventually speaks. 'I wanted to apologize. You are in an impossible situation. I understand that now.'

The urge to sob rips through me. *He* wants to apologize? He should hate me for failing to save Thea. I certainly do.

'It should be me apologizing.' Sorrow sticks in my throat like wood smoke. 'I couldn't save her. But I really, *really* tried.' Tears well in my eyes.

He does not look up, but places a warm hand on my shoulder. 'If anyone could have saved her, I know it would have been you.'

'The monster took her a long time ago.' I choose to spare him from the most macabre details, but I explain how the Untier steals girls away during their Rite. How it creates strange marionettes, almost indiscernible from the real thing. His face pales even further.

'So when you fought the Untier, she was still alive?'

'Yes. Barely. She was in a lot of pain.'

'Did you,' Hans stutters, voice trepidatious, as if he's not sure he really wants the answer. 'Did you kill her?'

'Yes,' I confess with a sob. 'I am sorry. *So* sorry.'

Hans grits his teeth. Tears spring to his eyes. He looks to the sky and lets out a shaky sigh. I want him to shout at me. To strike me. To leave me bloody and bruised and broken, the way I left Thea.

All he says is, 'You ended her suffering. That was your final act of love towards her. She was lucky to have you. *I'm* lucky to have you.'

Hans's hand finds mine. We interlock fingers and squeeze so tightly that I hear my knuckles pop. A cuckoo lets out a mournful cry. The clouds shift and the sky darkens.

'She knew,' Hans says quietly, after a while.

I look up at him. Gentle sadness weighs on his face. 'What?'

'Thea.' He swallows, shifting uneasily. 'She knew she wasn't your sister.'

My chest deflates. It takes me a moment to remember how to breathe. 'She *knew*?'

'I thought she would tell you when she was ready. But now . . .' Hans's jaw strains; he shakes his head. He draws in four deep breaths before he's able to continue. 'Thea told me one day over tea. She said it like she was commenting on the weather – like it was nothing. I still remember her face when I asked how she knew.' His face crumples with bittersweet nostalgia – his mouth smiling, his eyes mourning. '"Isn't it obvious?", she said. But it didn't matter to her. She loved you all the same. You weren't the sister she was given; you're the one she chose.'

I purse my lips but cannot stop the quivering breath that passes between them. Thea's loss is not something I will ever reconcile. It is a mountain I cannot summit, an island to which I cannot swim. But she died knowing that she and I were never blood sisters at all. And she loved me anyway. A fraction of the guilt lifts from my shoulders.

'She chose me.'

'And she would do it again,' Hans murmurs. 'If only she had the chance.'

'Dear Saints,' I choke out, losing the battle against the tears which fall. 'I miss her.'

'We will spend the rest of our days missing her.'

Silence stretches between us. There is comfort in knowing our grief is shared.

'I'm sorry,' I say again.

'It wasn't your fault,' he insists.

'For that, and for what happened to you. If I had known the Hexenwald wouldn't let you leave, I would have stopped you from coming with me.'

'Now that Thea is . . .' he trails off, unwilling to verbally acknowledge that Thea has passed beyond our reach. 'Without her, there is little for me in Heulensee.'

'Your mother,' I say. 'I spoke to her. She's alive and well. Happy, even. She thinks of you all the time.'

He smiles, though there is more hurt than happiness in his eyes. 'Perhaps one day, you can bring her to me.'

'You are more gracious than I could ever be to my own absent mothers.'

Hans laughs darkly. 'You are quite literally a Saint, Ilse.'

Only Hans could find a light in this aphotic dark. I smile back at him. 'I am glad to have you.'

'I'm glad to have you, too.' He pauses, pondering. 'Once you learn how to wield those Saintly powers of yours, perhaps you can rid me of this curse.'

It's the least he deserves. I nod sagely, the way I think a Saint might. He stands, retreating into the cabin. The stairs creak with the weight of his body, and then I'm alone.

I draw in five blissful breaths. One for Oma and her endless strength. One for Hans and his unwavering grace. One for Torsten and his reckless bravery. One for Ash and her unending loyalty. One for Thea, my first and forever keeper.

Always, one for Thea.

CHAPTER TWENTY-SIX

We spend the next day gathered in Torsten's study, planning how to summit the mountain ahead of us. It feels as if we just need to twist the problem – look at it from a different angle – and suddenly, the perfect solution will spark to life. We never quite manage it, though. There *is* no miracle answer. It all comes down to me.

I renew my training with vigour. My innate magic feels paltry now that I know the power of wielding fear – but it has to be enough. *Has* to be. To bolster me, Torsten teaches me about alchemy. He makes me watch as he brews potions and tinctures, then shows me how to administer them.

Three days pass. I cannot tell if my innate magic is getting stronger, or if my memory of the heft of my fear-based magic has faded. I choose to believe it's the former.

I will wind into existence, draw water from blades of grass, spark fire into life without kindling or fuel. It begins to feel as natural as breathing. Reflexive. I weave practical magic into something fanciful. If I can will a gust to blow, why can't I make it smell of honey? If I can conjure water from the earth around me, can't I turn it into ice that melts on the tongue?

I'm doing exactly that – chilling water to ice – when Ash staggers across the border of the meadow. Her cheeks are flushed; her hair clings to her forehead in damp strands.

'Ash,' I call out, 'Let me show you—'

'Ilse . . .' The intonation of her voice tells me this is not the time for fantastical magic. I loosen my grip on the ice; it melts back to water, scattering to the earth in a handful of droplets. 'What's the matter?'

She opens her mouth. Closes it again. Runs a hand through her hair. 'Torsten sent me to the edge of the Hexenwald. There are mushrooms that grow just on the boundary between the forest and Heulensee, and . . . ' Ash breaks off, shaking her head. 'It's stealing more girls, Ilse. The Untier. I saw it leading them away. They looked really young.'

My blood turns cold. Sluggish. It creeps through my veins. 'How many?'

'I don't know. Ten? Twenty?'

Time stretches interminably. A sour feeling builds and bursts in my stomach, unsteadying my knees.

'I thought we had more time,' I say. It sounds weak.

Ash nods, her pupils constricted by fear. 'If you want to save them, you can't wait any longer. You have to go now.'

A breath hisses between my teeth. 'I don't think I'm ready.'

There is a break in Ash's apprehension. She closes the distance between us and takes my hands between her own. 'Would you ever feel ready?' Her gaze softens, lashes lowering over emerald eyes. 'You are stronger than you think, Ilse. And for what it's worth, I believe in you.'

My heart lurches in my chest. Before I can thank her, or hug her, or kiss her, she ferries me inside the house to Torsten's study. In a hushed voice, she tells him that it's now or never. He nods curtly and stuffs tinctures into a rucksack while Ash darts out of the room to find Hans.

Torsten rallies off explanations of each potion. I listen half-heartedly. The cavern of my brain is filled with the red-hot glow of the Untier's eyes.

'This one stems bleeding, that one will steady your mind, this one cures poisoning, that one can mend bones, and this one – Ilse?' Torsten clicks his fingers in front of my face. 'Are you listening, Ilse?'

My gaze tracks back to his. 'I'm listening.'

'Then repeat the list of salves to me.' Heat creeps to my cheeks. I offer an apologetic smile; Torsten rolls his eyes. 'I'll just label them, shall I?' He mutters to himself, rifling through the desk drawers. There is affection in the way he frantically scrawls notes on bits of parchment and fastens them to each bottleneck.

'Thank you,' I murmur.

My words ease his mania. He pauses and looks me in the eye. 'You are most welcome.'

'Not just for this,' I say, dipping my gaze. 'For saving me from the Saints. For everything.'

'You would've done the same for me.'

My instinct is to refute him. To say that being unable to fear is not the same as being brave. But now, I realize, I *would* do the same for him. For Hans, for Ash. They are my people. The family that I choose, just as Thea chose me.

Torsten carefully wraps each bottle in muslin and tucks them into my rucksack. 'You'll be careful, won't you?'

'Careful as I can be.'

He pauses, face turning serious. 'I mean it. Don't be reckless. Don't be like me.'

'Do not tell me you have a *soft spot* for the Saint of Fear, Torsten,' I tease, pulling at the sleeve of his tunic.

A half-smile tugs at his lips. 'You make good company. And . . . she needs you.'

'Your sister?' I scoff, a touch of hysteria to my voice. 'I don't think Ash needs anyone.'

'You're right,' he concedes. 'To *need* is a practicality. Perhaps "want" is better. *Want* is a choice.'

We exchange a long look – him knowing, me hoping.

CHAPTER TWENTY-SEVEN

Our departure from the meadow feels like the closing of a book. All three of my companions insist on accompanying me. When I tell them I don't need all the fuss, Torsten pulls a face.

'We'll hold off the Saints and any other unpleasantness the forest produces,' he says. 'It's for your safety.'

Hans snorts. 'Because you've done such a stellar job protecting us so far.'

We all laugh. There's a quiet melancholy in it. A finality, knowing this might be the last time we all stand together.

But I cannot fixate on that. I have to believe I will survive.

We exit the meadow, scents masked to stave off my family. Torsten leads us confidently through the forest, instilling me with his bravery; Hans is quiet and contemplative, reminding me to be gentle; Ash is strategic, discussing every eventuality as it may play out, spoon-feeding me hope. I study their faces, knowing that I will need each of their strengths in the battle ahead.

The edge of the Hexenwald comes all too quickly. Hans meets my gaze, hesitates for three of his panicked breaths, then throws his arms around me. Tears threaten to spill over. My sister may be gone, but she left me a brother in Hans.

'Be safe,' he whispers. 'Fight well.'

'You be safe,' I reply. We peel away from each other. I look to Torsten and say, 'Look after him.'

Torsten nods and flashes me his signature smile. 'Show that parasite what it means to fear, Ilse.'

Ash gestures for the boys to leave without her. 'I'll meet you back at the meadow.'

After a moment of hesitation, Torsten and Hans disappear into the Hexenwald. Ash and I are left alone, caught in each other's orbit – two stars, drawn together across the vastness of the universe.

'I wanted to give you this,' Ash says, soft-spoken. In her palm sits an intricate wooden ring, shaped to look like interwoven twigs. Minuscule leaves bud from each branch. She continues, not quite able to meet my eye, 'It's a piece of me. I might not be able to come with you, but I hope . . . I hope this will *feel* like I'm there.'

The ring slides easily onto my finger, as if it's an extension of my body. I inspect my gift under dappled sunlight. Ash watches me expectantly, hopefully.

'It's beautiful,' I whisper, dipping my head so she will not see the tears beading at my lashes. Her gesture reminds me that we're on the precipice of the one thing that ties us together dissolving entirely. 'If I defeat the Untier, our bond,' – my voice rattles, and I take a breath to compose myself – 'our bond will be dissolved.'

Her brow furrows, just slightly, and only for a split second. She dips her gaze. It catches me off guard; it's so *human*, so unlike her.

'What was that?'

Ash feigns ignorance with a tilt of her head. 'What do you mean?'

'You made a face.'

Her chest rises and falls with the effort of a deep sigh. She appears torn, her mouth closing and opening, the words she wants to say never quite making it past her lips.

I push her shoulder playfully. She is wooden and unyielding beneath my fingers. 'Talk to me, Ash.'

'I need to confess something,' she says, extricating her fingers from mine. 'I haven't been entirely honest with you, Ilse.'

A pit opens in my stomach. 'What do you mean?'

'We haven't been bound for a long time, Ilse. Torsten dissolved the bond the first night we all spent in the Hexenwald, after leaving the meadow.'

My heart flutters, half-inclined to take flight. 'I don't understand.'

Her throat bobs as she swallows. She fastens soft fingers around my wrist. 'I thought if you believed I were still bound, my following you would make sense.'

The fluttering turns into a pounding so fierce that I feel it in my bones. Pressure bursts beneath my forehead, leaving me dizzied. 'What are you saying, Ash?'

Ash falters. She draws her bottom lip between her teeth, gnawing at it until I reach out and place my hand over hers.

'I am not bound,' she pauses, lips fluttering around words until she is able to form them, 'but still, I choose you. It means I trust you enough to follow you, but respect you enough to tell you when you are wrong. It means I will stand with you and fight. It means your happiness is my happiness.' Ash dips her gaze to the ground; tears roll down the swell of her cheeks. 'It means that I love you, Ilse.'

I press my lips to hers. It's as if our mouths were made for each other. My heart beats out a staccato rhythm as we meld into one. She tastes – *Saints*, she tastes like honey and citrus. Her hands tangle in my hair; mine wind around the small of her back.

'I love you,' I whisper, pained to part from her even for a second.

She clutches me tighter, pressing our foreheads together. 'Promise you will come back to me.'

'Not even death could separate us.' I count the freckles on her cheeks, memorize the shade of her eyes, and inhale a lungful of her scent. 'I *will* find you. In every lifetime.'

She exhales unsteadily, not yet willing to leave. 'We will read poetry together, won't we? Take afternoon naps together? Arrange flowers together and wake up beside each other each morning?'

'All of that and more.' I look to the clouds, which are growing more crimson by the second. 'I'll come back to you, Ash.'

Ash presses one more kiss to my lips, one to my forehead, and then she's gone. I watch her slink away into the trees. My eyes begin to sting. I force myself to turn and walk to the Hexenwald's fringes, lingering there on the precipice between worlds.

I reach into my rucksack and unstopper the bottle which Torsten has labelled 'focus'. The contents are bitter, like over-steeped tea. I pour it down my gullet and twist Ash's ring round and round my finger until I start to feel balanced again.

Coaxing unsteady legs into action, I skirt the lake as I have so many times before. The broken bodies of the women I killed still lie on Heulensee's cobbled streets. These false husks are flimsy, a poor imitation. They crumple, shedding hair and skin with each whispered breeze. With their real hosts decaying in the Untier's den, they have nothing to draw from. The silver threads protruding from each of their heads are broken. A connection severed; their lifeline doused.

A scattering of children wander the streets with horror etched across their faces. Their fear is not groomed or manufactured. It is raw. *Visceral.* I move to comfort a girl crouched over a body in the street, but my intrusion only serves to disturb her more.

'Where are the men?' I ask one of the girls as she drifts aimlessly across the cobbles.

'Gone,' she murmurs, her eyes a thousand miles away. 'All gone.'

'What do you mean?'

'When the Saint took more girls, some of the men went to challenge it. To take them back. They never returned.' She swallows, a wooden motion. 'Others left for the mountains when the women broke. Said they would fetch help. They haven't come back, neither.'

I swallow my anger on the girl's behalf. 'It's okay,' I lie. 'Perhaps they'll be back soon.'

Unconvinced, she wanders away from me. She and the other children drift about the street like dandelion seeds. My heart aches for them. Stripped of all familiarity, their female relatives crumpled like vacant sacks of grain.

Among the children, a few women still stand. One tries to lift a husk onto a stretcher, while another soothes a grousing baby. Others are attempting to distract the children—to make them forget the horrors they've witnessed. The chiming bells and straw dolls in their hands are not enough. It does not make sense that these women persist despite my annihilation of the Untier's captive women. But if *they* have survived …

Before I understand that my legs are moving, I arrive at my childhood home. It's a puerile thing for a Saint to do, but I want one last charade. One more chance to sit in my childhood bedroom. To pretend that Thea is about to burst through the door, and that we will make Lebkuchen in the kitchen with Oma.

Seeing the house shatters my play before it has begun. Perched on the hill, it has always evoked a falcon about to take flight. Today, there is something sad about it. It's the vacant shell of a snail, weathered by time, bleached by the sun. As I approach, the scent of death seeps through the rotting window frames. I suck in a breath of fresh air and push through the door.

What's left of my three Tanten lies on the kitchen floor, limbs held at strange angles. Their eyes are glassy and lifeless. Grief swells inside me, but it quickly dissipates. There is nothing worth grieving here. It's strange to think that I never truly knew two of them. They took their Rite before my birth. The women who taught me to braid hair, to sew princess seams, to bake *Pfeffernüsse* – they were husks. The whole time, they were husks.

I continue down the hallway and into my bedroom. Everything is as I left it, my belongings still scattered in the wake of my hasty exit. I ease open my chest of drawers, running my finger across the treasures I so painstakingly gathered: the feathers, the bones, the shells. They seem so dull compared to the bizarre contents of the Hexenwald. I can't understand why I ever thought them worth cataloguing.

As I'm about to leave the room, something catches my eye.

A lump beneath the bedcovers. I cease to breathe, standing perfectly still, *daring* that lump to move. A minute passes. The floorboards creak as I cross the room. I take the corner of the quilt between my thumb and forefinger and throw it to the ground.

Mama screams.

CHAPTER TWENTY-EIGHT

Seeing her curled in the foetal position, I am almost unsure that she is alive. But then she screams again, and there is no disputing the way she bolts upright.

'Ilse,' she says, each word tremulous. 'You came back.'

My jaw hangs open with the impossibility of her living. 'Impossible,' I hiss. 'The husks are all dead. Your sisters, Thea—'

'Thea?'

Mama blinks back at me, eyes turning glassy. She clutches her hands together.

I cannot carry her grief as well as my own. The reminder of Thea's death wrenches the strength from my legs. I sink onto the bed beside Mama, nausea building in my belly. 'She's gone.'

A desperate cry escapes Mama's lips, an outpouring of pain that reverberates throughout the room. She slaps her hand over her lips to stifle the sound. I would've done it for her if she hadn't. The last thing I need is for her to draw the Untier to us.

'I thought so,' she whispers, wiping her eyes with her sleeves. 'The minute your Tanten dropped, I knew what that meant for Thea. I have been hiding here ever since.'

I cannot see her through the cloud of tears settling over my pupils. My eyes narrow, forcing tears onto my cheeks. 'What do you mean you *knew*?'

She cannot meet my gaze. Each of her features scream guilt. 'I had a ... sense.' Mama pauses, swallowing so loudly that I think to admonish her. 'I do not know the intricacies, but I knew that the Rite changed women. They came back different; Thea was no exception.'

Anger simmers beneath my skin. I do not give her the satisfaction of letting it overspill. 'But you are just the same. You passed your Rite.'

Mama folds the blanket back over herself. 'I entered the Saint's den, but before I could offer up my fear,' – she pauses, shaking her head – 'it interrupted me. Said I had a different purpose. When I left, the Pfarrer behaved as if I had passed and I ... let him believe it. Let *everyone* believe it.'

My jaw twitches. A cracking sound rattles through my brain with how tightly I grit my teeth. Every time I fretted over Thea's Rite, Mama was the first to belittle me. To make me feel stranger than I already did. She did that while *knowing* she had never passed her own Rite.

My slumbering anger flares up; I quench it with the image of Ash's face. Expending energy on Mama is pointless. She matters less than what is to come.

A question springs up in place of my rage. 'Did Oma know you didn't take your Rite?'

'I didn't dare tell her – but you know how mothers are,' she says, expecting me to nod in agreement. I don't know how mothers are; only how *she* is. 'I suspect she knew anyway. Sometimes, we'd have conversations that came *so close* to discussing what actually happened inside the Saint's den. I wonder if it told her the same thing – that she had another purpose.'

'What other purpose?' I urge. 'What else could it want from you?'

'I don't know,' she admits. 'Not for certain. But the infertility that gripped your Tanten did not affect me, nor was it something they inherited from your Oma.'

Understanding settles over me. The emaciated women kept captive in the Untier's den could hardly carry a pregnancy to term – and the Untier described the husks as imperfect. In order to perpetuate the cycle, the Untier would need to set some fertile women aside. Allow them to have children.

'You were breeding stock,' I whisper.

Before she can respond, a realization washes over me in a sea of blood and broken bones. Of maggot-filled eyes and chapped lips.

'If you knew the Rite was perverse,' I say, my voice shaking with anger, 'why did you let Thea take it?'

My accusation wounds her. She flinches and her brow draws tight. Memories seem to flit through her eyes, sparking sorrow and pain and regret.

'I have not had an easy life, Ilse. Your papa was not always kind. He died a slow and terrible death while I watched, feeling that I was responsible. I thought ... I thought that the ills that befell me were a result of me not passing my Rite as planned. I believed that if Thea had the Saint's approval, she might fare better.'

I grit my teeth. 'Would you like to know the worst part of all this?' I do not draw breath for her to respond; willing or not, she will learn that her choice for Thea damned her. 'That beast was never a Saint at all.'

Her chest stills. 'What?'

I will my voice to stay cool and detached. 'It's a false Saint, impersonating the true Saint of Fear. A parasite. A monster.'

'A parasite.' She lets out a rattled breath. 'No. I cannot have sacrificed my daughter to a parasite.'

I twist the knife. 'The only Saint in Heulensee is me. But you already knew that.'

Panicked eyes rise to meet mine. 'You are a Saint?'

'*The* Saint,' I correct her. 'The Saint of Fear.'

She frets with her hands, staring numbly at the wall behind me. Ten seconds, or perhaps thirty, pass without a word between us. For a moment, I convince myself something has snapped in her brain – that she will stay rooted in this spot for ever, eyes fixed to the wall, unspeaking and unfeeling.

Then, her voice barely audible, she whispers, 'My baby had blue eyes.'

'What do you mean?'

'She had blue eyes,' Mama repeats. 'Just like her big sister.' Mama pauses, working around something that seems to be lodged in her throat. 'The next morning, when I went to feed her, those blue eyes had turned white. It wasn't the same baby. I *knew* it wasn't the same baby. But by the time I fetched someone, her eyes had turned green.

'They said I must've been imagining things. That the lack of sleep was making me see things that weren't there. But she was *my baby*. I knew her like I know my own reflection. Nobody believed me, Ilse. Nobody except Julia.'

My heartbeat slows as I recall what Hans told me about his mother – that she was banished after being reported as a heretic.

'What did you do?'

Mama sinks her head into her hands. A hurried breath hisses between her fingertips. 'She told me that my baby had been replaced by a powerful creature of the Hexenwald, in its infancy. That the *real* mother had performed the swap and fled to the forest. She is the one who gave me the map. I thought she was mocking me.' When Mama lifts her head, her eyes are glassy. 'I told your Tante Lena, in confidence, what Hans's mother said. Lena told the Pfarrer. Julia drowned a few days later.'

I do not tell Mama that Hans's mother is alive and well. I prefer for her to stew in the guilt.

'I always had this idea – this silly, *foolish* idea – that I'd use the map to find my baby. That I'd bring her back home. But I was too late. She died without ever knowing how loved she was.'

Her lip wobbles. My mother has never seemed vulnerable, but as I look at her, I'm struck by the grief etched into her face. She seems so small, so defeated. It has taken me this long to realize that there is no joy, no justice, in striking an injured animal. I could break her down to her base components, but who will it serve? It will not erase the trauma of my childhood, and it will not bring Thea back.

Detached, I murmur, 'I would advise you to leave Heulensee for a few days. Upon your return, the false Saint will be gone. So will I.'

Mama leans forward, fingers curled, as if she is about to hold me for the first time in our lives.

I cross the expanse of my childhood bedroom towards the door. 'I do not forgive the way you treated me,' I whisper, voice thick with emotion I cannot let spill, 'but I understand it.'

'You do not understand,' Mama says, voice hoarse.

Caught halfway through the door, I pause.

'Even though they told me she was mad, I knew there must be some truth in what Julia said. You weren't mine – not really. But there were moments where you'd laugh, and my heart would *ache* with how much I wanted you to be.

'I knew that if Julia was right, there was no way a creature of the forest would leave their babe behind forever. I always had a feeling they would come back. That you would be taken from me.' She draws in a shaky breath. 'Not loving you was a battle, Ilse.'

A sob pounds against my chest, demanding to be let loose. If I let it out, I might never stop. 'If you love me,' – my voice hitches in a way most unbecoming of a Saint, reminding me that at my core, I am caught between worlds – 'if you love me, will you help me?'

'Anything.'

I divulge my plan; she accepts it with grace. We head for the church, as we have so many times before. Thea and I used to skip along this route, hand in hand. Today, Mama and I walk at arm's length. But my head is held high. My breaths are measured. I am fearless and brave. I am a woman and a Saint. I am not ordinary, nor do I wish to be.

'Gather the remaining women and girls,' I say. 'Ring the church bell to alert them. Take them to the meadow huts. As quickly as you can.'

Mama nods and disappears inside the church. Even now, I do not dare cross its threshold. The bell drones out an unusual rhythm. Girls flock to it, moths to a flame. Some hold their younger siblings in their arms, struggling beneath the weight of babes they weren't supposed to raise. They are battle-worn and exhausted – but they are *alive*. I intend to keep them that way.

Mama re-emerges. She barks instructions at the girls, who follow her words with silent agreement. They begin to stream out of Heulensee, bound for the meadow huts. Before following them, she falters. 'What will you do, Ilse?'

'End this cruel cycle. Once and for all.' At the horror which leaps to her face, I add, 'I am a Saint. I will be okay.'

'You may be a Saint, but you are still my daughter.'

My tongue rises to inflict some vicious wound – but I remind myself of the fact that she is human. Flawed. Just as I was. Just as I still am. 'I will be okay, Mama.'

Sensing my conviction, Mama smiles sadly. She reaches out to brush my cheek with her forefinger, but seems to think better of it.

The church doors fly open, the snapping jaws of a wolf. The Pfarrer – of *course* that slimy, pious man persists – flings himself at Mama. He must think she is an easy target – that she will be beaten into submission, strong-armed into aiding *him* rather than me. He snatches at her blouse and hair, bald head glinting in the sun.

'Pfarrer,' I snarl. My voice is the toll of a bell, echoing all the way across Heulensee. The Pfarrer flinches; his eyes snap to mine. Tendrils of fear unfurl from his body. 'If you must lay your hands on a woman, I invite you to lay them on me.' My eyes dart to Mama's. 'Go. Look after the girls.'

Mama wrestles between obeying my command – listening to her fear – and following the protective maternal instinct that has flickered to life inside her.

'*Go*, Mama.'

For the second time in my short life, I turn my back on

Mama. The Pfarrer rushes after me, trailing my steps down the cobbled street to the lake. His vicious words fade to background noise.

I shed my shoes as I reach the shore. The pressure of the pebbles against my feet grounds me. I wriggle my toes against the stone, feeling the ties that bind me to this earth.

The Pfarrer directs his ire at me, full of misplaced confidence. His jaw is set; his brow furrowed. 'You were exiled from this place for a reason, Ilse Odenwald. Do not think you are forgiven.'

I smile back at him, nauseatingly sweet. 'I would never seek forgiveness, Pfarrer.'

There is something in him that senses the threat humming beneath my skin. Black cords ensnare his throat. His eyes are wild, his forehead slick with sweat. He *knows*, deep down, that I am an apex predator – but he cannot equate it with my physical form. To him, I will never be more than a pawn. A commodity.

Underestimating me will be his downfall. I gesture to the carnage behind him – the fallen husks, the disarray. 'Even rats flee sinking ships, Pfarrer,' I say. 'What keeps you here?'

'This is *my* village,' he hisses, spittle gathering at the corners of his mouth, 'and they are my flock. I will not have them taken from me.'

'Whose authority do you act upon? Whose grace gives you such an inflated sense of self-worth?'

He bristles, squaring weak shoulders as if that should frighten me. As if I have *ever* been afraid. 'I act on the will of the Saint of Fear.'

'I'm curious, Pfarrer. Did you know what it was doing?' I ask, a snarl barely caged beneath my lips. 'Reaping the women, keeping them in its burrow?'

He pauses. 'It was a necessary evil. The Saint of Fear demanded my compliance. *Our* compliance.'

'And what is the Saint of Fear to me, Pfarrer?'

'It is a *Saint*. It is holy.' He grasps me by the front of my blouse, wrenching me towards him until I feel his spittle on my face. 'You would do well to remember that.'

'Oh,' I say, my voice pitiful, mewling. False tears turn my eyes glossy. 'Please, Pfarrer, forgive me.'

A twisted grin plays at his lips. My suffering is his tonic. 'What will you offer in exchange?'

'There is nothing I could not offer you.'

At first, he is pleased by my acquiescence – but then it all *clicks*. I see the pieces falling into place in his head: the cool smirk at my lips, the wind which stirs around us, the static in the air, the light flickering behind my eyes. Too late, he realizes his misstep. He has asked a wolf to a game of teeth and claws.

The Pfarrer's mouth drops open. White light bleaches his skin. Power dances through my body.

'Who – what *are* you?'

I let the wind lift me. My feet leave the ground. '*I* am the Saint of Fear. My name is Ambet. I am the third of the Saints of Pathos, the daughter earth. I have existed for eighteen years; I will persist for a thousand more. When you are dead and rotting in the ground, *I* will endure. When Heulensee is nothing but a memory spoken in ancient tongue, *I* will endure. When the false Saint lays bloodied and broken, *I* will endure. I am the constant; I am eternal; I am *power*.'

The Pfarrer drops to his knees, hands clasped in front of him. The wind rallies, lifting my hair. Black cords whip around him in a frenzy. I pinch one between my fingers, squeezing, *testing*.

He does not know that I hold his life in my hands. One small movement and his heart will give out.

'I am sorry, oh Saint,' he sobs. 'I did not know – I was fooled! To see true power is to understand. I will forsake the false Saint, and worship only you, if you just let me live.'

'You *will* worship me,' I purr, lifting his chin with my power. 'I am your Saint now. You are my disciple. My follower.'

'Of course,' he murmurs, chapped lips fluttering. 'What will you have me do? How can I prove my devotion?'

'Retribution is not mine to deal.' I force a sympathetic smile between bared teeth. 'The girls will decide your fate.'

His face crumples. 'Please, Saint of Fear. The girls are vengeful. They will—'

'The girls will decide your fate,' I reiterate. 'And if they allow you to live, you will spend the rest of your days seeking penance. You will be a benefactor of women. You will devote your time and wealth to helping them escape abuse and mistreatment. And if you do not,' I pause, cocking my head at a strange angle, letting my voice echo from the church tower to the Hexenwald, 'I will devour you whole.'

The Pfarrer sways on his knees. His eyes dart between me and the lake at my back. I suspect what he's planning, but do not move to stop him. He staggers to his feet and launches himself into the water, dragging his body deeper and deeper into its inky heart. Fear surges from him as the shock of the cold water sets in. Perhaps a death by the lake's hands seems like a mercy compared to what the girls might do with him.

His bald head dips beneath the water. A stream of weak bubbles rise to the surface. The Pfarrer's reign of hatred and fear comes to an end not with a scream, but with a whimper.

As the final bubbles burst, heat surges beneath my skin. My head snaps back to the village. The few willows fringing the wetland at the other end of Heulensee have shed their leaves. The skeletal prongs of their branches extend into the sky.

No – not just branches. *Antlers.*

The Untier stalks free of the mire. Tendrils of vapour curl from its cavernous nostrils. It is more terrible than I remember; flesh has begun to slough from bone. Its ribs have pierced through its sides, creating a bone cage surrounding the monster.

'Little Ilse Odenwald,' it hisses. 'Have you come to play?'

CHAPTER TWENTY-NINE

The battleground – the long, cobbled street I played hop-scotch on as a child – yawns open before us. Static crackles in the air.

I glide forward, hands loosely held at my side. 'I will give you one chance to flee.'

'I have bested you before,' the Untier bellows. 'I will do it again. Your powers are as weak now as they were when I last gored you. Saints cannot be made in a day.'

'Nor can they be mimicked.'

The Untier's bony jaw twitches. 'Now, let me offer *you* a chance. Leave – forget about this place. You have your domain and I have mine. These girls mean nothing to you; there is no reason for you to interfere. To me, they are *survival*. Let me feed, the way I've always fed.'

I wrinkle my nose. 'I'm afraid you'll have to starve.'

The air turns thick. It suffocates. Each breath cloys in my

throat. The Untier grimaces at me, showing bloodstained teeth. The tension in the atmosphere is pulled so taut that when it snaps ...

It will be fatal.

My magic comes to a boil. I grip the dregs of the Pfarrer's fear between my nails. The Untier's hollow eyes track to my fists just as I clench them. I will clouds to form overhead, envision lightning forking down – and it *does*. A scar splits the sky. The jagged fork strikes the Untier's flesh. It groans; the smell of singed hair fills the street.

Behind me, the lake roars.

The false Saint closes the distance between us in a span of seconds. Jaws pulled wide, it lunges. I sidestep deftly, moving like the dancer I dreamed of being as a child. The wind guides my movements. Again, I call on lightning – and it comes. Thunder reverberates through the streets. The Untier buckles, legs splaying beneath its hulking form.

I will flames to my palms, wielding them like dual swords in front of me. When the Untier charges again, I do not cower. I stand resolute and plunge my twin flames into its chest. Rancid, steaming blood pours from the wounds. I ask for the strength of a team of oxen, and the universe grants it. The flames give me the leverage I need to manoeuvre around the beast, driving it towards the lake.

'Giving up so soon, beast? Do not tell me you are *scared*.'

Its hot-coal eyes are frantic with bloodlust. Something about its expression needles at me. I *know* that look. All too late, I recognize the look of an animal caught in a trap. And as a woman who spent her formative years trailing her papa as he laid snares and pitfalls, there is one thing I know to be true.

A trapped animal is a dangerous one.

I fling my weight backwards, leaping away from the Untier. It moves faster, more decisively. Teeth scrape my arm, gouging great ribbons of skin.

'I will bleed you the way I bled your sister,' it snarls, flecks of my blood spraying from its mouth. 'I will hurt you the way I hurt her.'

Thea's face fills my mind. Not as she lived – smiling, happy – but as she died. Her chapped lips, blood-slick skin, her anguished brow. My rage froths over as it has so many times before, caustic and scalding. The flames at my hands burn white-hot. I lash out wildly, sometimes striking flesh, but more often bone or thin air.

The Untier is more calculated in its fury. It tears my blouse to tatters, slicing into my flesh and exposing a sliver of my collarbone in the process. The pain is blinding. Stars bloom and explode across my vision. I stagger backwards and it strikes *again*, this time with teeth. My thigh gushes blood.

Colour flees my sight. My wounded leg buckles, sending me to the ground. I roll down the shore until I am half-submerged in frigid water. My fingernails tear as I claw my way out of the lake. I reach for my satchel, torn from my back in the fight.

The Untier's shadow falls over me. It crushes my rucksack – the potions that might've saved my life – beneath its paw. That action seems to spark an idea in its foul mind. It takes its other colossal paw and slams it on my head, pinning me in place. Weight bears down. Harder and harder and *harder*.

My jaw pops. Pain bursts through my skull. I lose the vision in one eye as it ruptures.

My next exhale is a futile sob. It's happening again. *Is this it?* Am I damned to suffer this defeat for the rest of my Saintly existence? Is this my penance – my origin story?

In a moment, it will all be over. My heart rends in half as I realize what that means. I will lose them *all*. My memories of Oma, of Thea, of Hans and Torsten and Ash. Frantic, I scrabble against the Untier's weight. My mind fights, but my flesh is weak. I imagine Ash waiting on the fringe of the Hexenwald. Waiting, and waiting, and waiting, until she realizes the Saint is not coming home. At least not the one she knows.

'You will *rot*, Ilse Odenwald.' The Untier's claws pierce my scalp, scratching at my skull—

'Stop!'

The Untier falters. It lifts its paw, relieving the pressure on my skull. I turn my head to the side. Blood spills from my mouth like wine from a chalice.

Mama stands at the foot of the street. The sight of her makes a sob build in my throat. It is a terrible scene: a mother watching the last of her daughters, the one she never asked for, dying in the street.

I swallow a mouthful of blood and hiss, '*Run*, Mama.' Every inch of her shakes as she stares down at me. Tears overflow, cresting the curve of her cheek and landing in splotches on her blouse. 'If you do not run,' I wheeze, 'it will kill you.'

Something changes in Mama. Her face hardens; her hands clench to fists. Her eyes leave me and fix instead on the Untier.

And then she screams.

'No, Mama,' I whimper.

Mama does not hear me above the perfect falsetto of her scream. She stares at me, eyes filled with urgency. I will not *take*. I will not feed on her terror. If I am to die, I will die true to myself. To Hans and Thea. To Ash.

The Untier rumbles approvingly. What a terrible thing – to

have my Mama inadvertently give the beast the strength it will need to slay me. Bolstered by her terror, I can only hope that the false Saint will deliver me a swift, decisive death.

'Goodbye, Ash,' I whisper, praying that somewhere, *somehow*, she can hear me. That she will feel the force of my love as I implode.

But then ... From the corner of my working eye, I notice something peculiar. The cords unfurling from Mama's body are not black. They are gold. The Untier falters. So do I.

I study Mama's face – the hard line of her shoulders, the anguish in her eyes, the rage behind her bared teeth.

Mama is not scared. She is *brave*.

Her scream is not one of terror, but a battle cry. The courage radiates from her in waves, spilling across the cobbles. I reach out with broken fingers and grasp a tiny cord of her bravery. It burns against my fingers.

'You killed two of my daughters,' she screams, staring down the Untier, 'but you will not kill a third.'

The Untier lunges at her. Mama rolls away, narrowly escaping its teeth. Her courage settles over me, and I am transformed. My broken bones knit back together; my torn flesh reunites. The vision in my injured eye clears, and the blood I have spilled rushes back into my veins.

Wielding Mama's bravery like a sword, I slash a hand through the air. The Untier *bleeds*. It bellows, so startled by my imposition that it misses Mama slipping away. It turns on me, slathering and ravenous. I strike out with my hand again, but this time, the cut is blunt.

Mama's cords turn black. Her bravery is overridden by fear. The Untier draws in a deep breath, using Mama's terror to bolster it. It grows, rearing to walk on two legs.

'Be brave, Mama!' I shout – but my words are robbed by the Untier barrelling into my chest.

It gores me with its antlers. The pain is so intense I cannot think around it. Mama screams – this terrible, raw sound that scrapes all the way up her throat. I think I might be screaming, too. The Untier tosses its head and shakes me loose. I slide from its antlers onto the cobbles, blood oozing from my chest.

My efforts to escape, to place at least a fraction of air between myself and the beast, are fruitless. Each move is agonizing. Steam curls from the Untier's nostrils. I blink, and when I open my eyes, its antlers are once again plunging towards me – this time, aimed straight for my eyes.

This will be the fatal blow. This is my end.

But then, mere inches from bisecting my brain, the Untier pauses. Enraged, it blasts hot air across my face. It has the upper hand. The chance to kill me is presented to the beast on a pedestal – yet it hasn't seized it.

Two memories come to me in rapid succession. Wilbet, her face cold, telling me, 'The parasite would not have killed you', and the Untier's tense expression when I asked why it hadn't slaughtered me already. Everything slots into place.

'You can't kill me.' A hysterical laugh bursts past my lips, paired with a spatter of blood. 'You *need* me.'

The Untier's teeth grind within its bony jaw. 'Every parasite needs a host. I adopted your image. You are the Saint of Fear in name only; *I* made your identity matter. I am the one people worship. I am the true Saint.'

'None of that matters.' I wince, each word tugging at the wound on my chest. 'You *cannot kill me.*'

'Perhaps not,' the Untier growls. 'But I can kill her.'

Before I can react, the Untier switches course. It heads straight for Mama, claws outstretched. Mama darts away, aiming for an alleyway or an open door – but the beast is too quick. Too vengeful.

I try to hoist myself up, but without Mama's bravery, my body cannot heal – at least not as fast as I need it to. I'm left to watch, propped up on my elbows, as the monster chases her down. As it prepares to deliver her death, just as it did to Oma.

Then I hear a cry at the end of the street.

The Untier falters. It swings its brutish head to the side, our gazes following the sound to its source.

Julia – my dear Hans's mother – musters all the courage she has and lets it out into the atmosphere. Beside her, Esther shakes and shakes but she *does not yield*. Her mouth drops open and she bellows, her rage and anguish becoming a tangible force.

My sobs return with a vengeance as I notice what's behind them. Or rather, *who* is behind them.

Lines upon lines of women and girls. They march forward, tears in their eyes, heads held high. A blanket of gold light settles over them and I draw from it – feeding not from their fear, but their *courage*. They willingly channel it through me.

Like a marionette given new life, I rise.

Suddenly, it all makes sense. Why would I ask them for an emotion I do not understand? I have spent my life trying to carve fear into my bones. It never stuck. Not because I am a heretic, a blasphemer – but because I was *born* to be unafraid. That is as much a part of me as the colour of my eyes or the sound of my voice or the fact that Thea *was* my sister, blood-bound or not.

Fear means nothing to me. But courage – *courage* I know all too well. I saw it in Oma fighting fires others ran from; in Mama when she watched her own daughter slain; in Hans when he followed me into the Hexenwald; in Thea when she looked me in the eye and asked me to end her life; in Ash when she told me she *loved me*.

The women scream for their exile, for the friends and family they have lost to the Untier's bloodlust. The girls scream for the unfairness of it all – for seeing their sisters and aunts collapse, reduced to vacant shells. The weight of their emotion almost topples me. It billows from them, spooling at my feet and draping across my arms. I clutch it in my fists and let it steel me.

'You brought me a feast,' the Untier bellows. 'Fresh fear.'

Esther levels her finger at the beast and cries, 'We are not afraid!'

The Untier stalks towards her. I ask the wind for its carriage; it whisks me across the cobbled street, placing me between the beast and the women. I curl my fist around a tendril of their courage and inhale deeply. My skin glows; my eyes burn gold.

I think of every Saints-forsaken wildfire I spied from my bedroom and channel their power through my palms until the flames burn white hot. When I hurl meteoric fire at the beast, I will it to ravage the way wildfires do. To rage and consume and burn until there is nothing left.

An anguished howl tears free of the Untier's throat. Its evil eyes dart between me and the women, searching for fear it cannot find. Amidst its fury, something else spreads across its countenance. For the first time in its life, the Untier is *scared*.

'Impossible,' it screeches. 'They have no fear.'

'No,' I agree. 'They have something better.'

We advance, an army of howling women. For the very first

time, the Untier looks small. We stalk it down the street, into the meadow. It cowers against the backdrop of the Hexenwald.

'I have a riddle for you, beast,' I shout. 'If there is a rat in your cellar and it will not be starved or poisoned, what do you do?'

The Untier snarls, spit flying from its mouth. 'I have no time for your games, girl.'

I smile sweetly. Feet barely grazing the ground, I close the distance between myself and the monster. I tether its jaws shut with a thick cord of bravery, stand on tiptoes, and whisper into its ear. 'You *drown* it.'

The women scream, and I scream with them. We drive the Untier back. Its rear paw hisses and sizzles as it touches the water. Jaw grinding, it pries apart the cords sealing its mouth.

'I cannot be killed,' the monster roars. 'You will pay for this. I swear it, you will.'

The Untier's words are lost to a pained growl. Flesh melts from its rear legs. Its red eyes stutter inside that cavernous skull.

'For a creature that claims it cannot be killed,' I hiss through gritted teeth, 'you look awfully scared, false Saint.'

Panicked, the Untier lunges for me. Its teeth fasten around thin air, jaws snapping. The women reach a crescendo that makes my heart flutter. I call on everything they have – everything *I* have – and use it to push the Untier further into the lake. The water rises to its hocks, then to its shoulders, then to its jaw.

'May you die with your heart full of fear. May you die *alone*.' I part my lips and *scream*. The sound echoes from the street to the forest to the mountains, haunting. The women and girls cry with me. It is catharsis.

The Untier's horns disappear beneath the lake. Heat hisses to the surface, the water frothing and bubbling . . .

And then it is gone.

Silence falls over Heulensee. We study the water with bated breath.

'It's dead,' Mama says. 'It's really—'

Pain explodes across my ankle. The lake sucks me in like a tornado. Water so cold that it takes my breath away washes over my head. I thrash and writhe, desperate to escape. Beneath me, the Untier's eyes glow red. Even with my leg clamped between its teeth, it *smiles*.

I try to spark fire at my hands, but the flames sputter out. I cannot call lightning, for it will wound me just as it does the beast. The women's courage grows fainter, more distant. Bubbles leave my mouth as I scream for them to be brave. The lake swallows my pleas.

Water invades my lungs. The light disappears. I ache to my bones with cold, and I am tired. *So* tired.

The Untier's voice invades my mind. *To the depths with you, Ilse Odenwald.*

The lake sings me a lullaby. Giving up would be a relief. I can barely feel the Untier's teeth around my ankle. Numbness is a beautiful, haunting thing.

Pressure builds around my finger. I lift my hand above me, examining it in what's left of the surface light. Just as darkness envelops us, I see it. Ash's ring has sprouted, winding around my wrist and fingers and . . .

At my knuckle, the wood sharpens into a dagger.

My veins turn to steel, my ears whine. In the darkness, I reach down and *strike*. Fast, determined. The Untier's red eyes widen with fear. I smile back at it, bloodthirsty, and slit its throat.

Black blood billows into the water. Silent screams echo from the creature's mouth. Its grip on my leg loosens, and as it sinks to the depths, I rise. The water rallies around me, because after all this, the lake is my *friend*. It knows me as I know it. It refused to kill me before, and it will not kill me now.

The lake spits me out onto its shore. I cough and splutter as the dark rings around my vision ebb. The women drop to their knees in worship, hands clasped in front of them. I move to tell them *no*, do not worship me – but the words do not come. Tears stream down my face, mingling with the lake water.

My triumph is bittersweet. I've saved the girls, but not my dear sister. But while I could not save her, I've avenged her. Spilled blood for all the women the Untier took. And I did it all as Ilse. The strange, unfearing girl who was secretly a Saint.

Mama kneels beside me, clasping my cold hand between hers. With the women's bravery lingering in the air, it doesn't take long for the warmth to return to my body. My weary muscles reawaken; my lungs strengthen.

'Let's go home,' Mama says, her eyes hopeful.

We spend a moment in time together, lingering together at the lake's edge. A breeze picks up, and with it comes a peppering of sleet. The glistening flakes melt as soon as they touch down. Chatter begins to fill the air. Laughter, even. Long-lost aunts reunite with their nieces; banished sisters find their kin.

When Mama looks at me, I see Thea reflected in her eyes. I could do it, I think. Spend a lifetime with her. Pretend to be an ordinary mother and daughter. Watch for fires and bake Lebkuchen over winter. Make visits to Thea's grave, sharing stories and leaving her bunches of wildflowers.

But I am not meant for Heulensee. I never was.

Mama senses me pulling away. Her mouth sets in a hard line. Tears glisten at her eyes. 'You have to leave, don't you?'

I offer her a melancholy smile. 'Will you be okay?'

'I think so.' She reaches for me, but falters. It is the first time she has ever been compelled to hug me, but she stops herself long enough to realize that I do not *want* to be hugged. That realization is more meaningful than any embrace.

'I will visit,' I say.

Mama smiles softly, knowing that I will never return. We play our parts, continuing the charade that I am just a girl, and she is my mother. We braid our hands together.

A tear rolls down her cheek. 'I am proud of you, Ilse.'

'And I of you.'

She helps me to my feet, hangs my tattered backpack on my shoulder, and turns me towards the woods.

My walk back to the Hexenwald is bittersweet. I ache with nostalgia. Each awful, beautiful moment replays in my head. Thea and I on the lake shore, building pyres from the pebbles. Me, as a girl, wading out into the lake with rocks tied to my feet. Klara Keller's head between the Untier's jaws. Oma praying to her Saints. Hans and Thea admiring the sunflowers in their front garden.

I take one last look at the town that shaped me and shunned me – and then I leave it behind.

CHAPTER THIRTY

Ash meets me on the boundary between our worlds.

I collapse into her arms. She holds me together as I fall apart. Grief and exhaustion and relief flood through my body at once. Ash trails kisses across my forehead, my cheeks, the hollow of my throat.

'I did it,' I sob, my fingers curling around the contours of her waist.

'My girl,' she whispers, 'my brave girl.' She pulls back, studying me as if she wants to commit each part of my face to memory. 'Let's go home.'

The Hexenwald is pliant and permitting. I feel a cold presence following us through the trees, but it merely lingers, refusing to make itself known. Ash carries me most of the way back to the meadow, my head resting against her shoulder. The even tempo of her breaths is like a hymn. I stare at her pulse as it flutters against her throat. It's the most beautiful thing I've ever seen.

In the meadow, Torsten and Hans sit on the top step of the porch, heads in hands. When they see me, it's like the sun breaks over their faces. Ash sets me down gingerly; the boys leap up, racing across the grass to greet us. Hans collides with me so fiercely that it knocks the air from my lungs. I burrow my face into his chest.

'I knew you could do it,' he tells me, voice tight. 'I *knew* it, Ils.'

Torsten and Ash share an embrace so poignant it brings fresh tears to my eyes. We all walk back inside the house, where Hans begins cooking frantically, and Torsten asks me to relay the details of the battle. I tell them all about Mama's help, about the women's bravery, about the Untier's death. Ash brings out bottles of aged wine. We sink them as the sleet peters out, leaving the meadow dusted in crystalline droplets.

Many hours later, Hans and Torsten retire to their beds. Ash watches me as if I'm the only thing in the world that matters. Armed with blankets, we venture to a hidden part of the meadow; a dip in the earth, shrouded by meadow grass and clusters of edelweiss. I spark a fire to keep us warm. She shows me exactly what I mean to her, in glorious detail.

We lie in the furrow for the rest of the night, tracing constellations with our fingertips – both those in the sky, and those formed by the freckles on her skin. She takes me into her arms and for the first time in my life, I do not wonder where I belong. This is it. I belong with Ash.

When the sun rises over the meadow, I push – reluctantly – to my feet. 'There's something I need to do.'

'So soon?' She pulls a face. 'What is it?'

'Unfinished business,' I tell her. 'Half an hour, and then I'm yours for ever.'

She smiles as she beckons me down to kiss her. 'For ever sounds like heaven.'

💀

The Hexenwald seems to sigh as I cross the boundary from the meadow. That cool presence I felt earlier returns. My breaths leave my mouth in plumes of steam. Ether snakes in between the trees, caressing the exposed skin of my cheeks.

'Mother,' I say.

She materializes just to the side of me. I do not look at her; I do not need to. White light scalds my right side.

'Ambet,' she drones. 'You have been hiding from me.'

'I have.'

'You went against my guidance. You interfered with human matters.'

'You saved Hans,' I tell her. 'What would you call that, if not interfering with human matters?'

Borbet is quiet. I feel her milky eyes boring into the side of my face. 'I did not save him. Merely gave him the opportunity to save himself.'

The white light fades. My next glimpse at her reveals that she has shed her Saintly appearance. Instead, she is a mirror of me, if slightly older.

'I was like you, once.'

'We are not alike,' I say, my words clipped.

'Not yet,' she says. 'But we will be, one day. All that will remain are echoes of what you once were. Once you feel the power of the triad, you will not want anything else. It is time for you to join us, Ambet. We will ascend. This forest will bow to us.'

I shake my head. 'Why do you need *more* power?'

She tilts her head. 'I do not understand your meaning.'

'You are the strongest creatures in this forest,' I say, 'yet you still want to bleed it dry. *Why?*'

Borbet pauses before responding, 'Why does the squirrel hoard acorns? Why does the honeybee's hive overflow?'

'But if the squirrel hoarded *all* the acorns, there would be no oak trees left. There would be no forest at all. The squirrel can gorge itself for a year or two, but what happens after that?'

'After,' Borbet muses, as if she's never dared to think beyond the completion of the triad. 'After, after, after.'

Before I can change my mind, I reach out and take her hand between mine. It is cold, stiff, as if rigor mortis has set in. 'What if we could be different, Mother? What if we could draw magic from an infinite well, instead of drying up what remains beneath the Hexenwald?'

Borbet cocks her head, listening.

'You saw my power grow yesterday. You know how humans can feed a Saint's magic. What if *I* protect Heulensee from the creatures of the Hexenwald? With the Untier dead, the village will grow. Once word spreads of my presence, people will flock to the valley. Imagine, Mother: a supply of magic which grows year by year.' I squeeze her stiff hand between mine. 'Humans and Saints can live in symbiosis.'

'Symbiosis,' she says, her tongue licking across each of the four syllables. Darkness passes across her face. 'Wilbet will not like this.'

'But do *you* like it?' I ask, my voice lowered. 'It's not just about Wilbet. Not anymore.'

Borbet wets her papery lips. She looks at me with glassy eyes, mouth opening and shutting as if she has never been permitted to think on her own before. Something rustles in the undergrowth behind us. The line of Borbet's shoulders tightens; her eyes widen, if only by a fraction. She drops my hand.

'Watching you yesterday, Ambet, I felt something foreign,' she whispers, each word hurried. 'I believe humans call it pride.'

Before I can respond, Wilbet surges into the clearing. Her nostrils flare, white eyes darting between Borbet and I.

'The cuckoo child,' she hisses. Her total detachment makes Borbet seem warm. 'Slayed the false Saint, did you?'

'I did,' I tell her. 'Without your help.'

'Help.' A cruel laugh forces past her lips. 'It is time for you to join us, Ambet.'

I shake my head. 'I have other plans.'

She bristles, her eyes emitting searing light. Her hands curl into fists at her sides. I feel the ache of her magic, manipulating my not-quite-human sadness. Reflexively, I reach out for the fear that I know must exist inside her. It's there, buried deep beneath layers and layers of apathy – a fossil beneath rock. Teeth gritted, I unearth those withered remnants of terror. Clutch them between my fingers.

Wilbet's eyes widen. A trace of emotion – of *fear* – flits across her face. 'Do not challenge me.'

Borbet winces as I bite back, 'I am not a weapon to be wielded.'

'If it were not for me, you would not exist,' she hisses, wincing. 'You came from me. Both of you—'

My grip tightens. I barely even mean to do it, but suddenly, the terror explodes from Wilbet. A breath whistles between her crooked teeth. It feels as if my magic has grown, almost ungovernable. Wilbet rises, feet dangling, until she looks down on me.

'You are trapped with me for eternity,' Wilbet drones. She hooks her cold fingers beneath my chin, dragging my gaze to meet hers. Her eyes burn white. She stares back at me, somehow unfeeling yet knowing – seeing right to my very core, past flesh and bone and pretence. 'Play your games, little cuckoo. You will grow towards us one day. We will be waiting.'

With that, she turns and glides away between the trees. The leaves whisper in her wake. Borbet casts her now-white eyes towards me. There's something in her gaze I haven't seen before. Conflict.

'She will not adhere to your plan,' Borbet murmurs. 'She will bend you to her will.'

Slowly, slowly, I search Borbet's consciousness. A tiny glimmer of gold slips between my fingers, elusive as a minnow. Borbet must feel something swell inside her – not quite bravery, but its precursor – for a gasp slips between her lips. She turns, fleeing in the same path Wilbet took.

I don't think it's the last I'll see of her.

☠

My conversation with the Saints is not the closure I wanted. I do not know if I have scared Wilbet, or if she is simply biding her time. Either way, she does not dog my steps as I walk through the forest the next day. Maybe Borbet reasoned with her; maybe they know something I do not.

I do not let my family's strangeness plague me; I have plenty else to attend to. The next day, that comes in the form of a trip to Heulensee. I leave Ash with instructions to bring Hans and meet me at the forest's edge at midday. She kisses me before I leave. It's such a small gesture – the barest grazing of our lips – but it feels like everything I've ever wanted.

Heulensee hums, alight with women digging graves, fixing buildings damaged in the skirmish, scrubbing the cobbles clean. There is also the mundane; annual rituals of winter, which now seem so extraordinary. The scent of candied fruit and sweet pastry herald freshly baked *Stollen;* pines taken from the edge of the mountain are being sized for their suitability as the village *Tannenbaum*; I pass a group of women debating the perfect ratio of aromatics for spiced wine.

I find Julia in the church, which she explains is being used to house the banished women until their new homes are ready. She's sewing little flowers out of fabric, ready to hang on the Tannenbaum. When I tell her there's something I need to show her, she follows me willingly.

Julia talks animatedly as we skirt the lake. Only when she sees a figure on the edge of the trees does she fall silent. Her little boy, all grown up. I do not move to stop her as she sprints past me, colliding with Hans so forcefully it knocks the air from both their lungs.

'Mama,' he whispers, voice breaking. 'I've missed you.'

Their reunion heals a wound I did not know Hans bore. The moment is so poignant that even Ash begins to cry, though she pretends she is unaffected. We stand just to the side, staring out across the lake while mother and son catch up on years apart.

Hans and Julia agree to meet each other every other evening. I cannot help but feel it's a poor compromise, compared to what he could've had. But it is something.

That night, when Hans asks me to spark a fire in the hearth, I nearly set the entire cabin alight. Once I've doused the flames, helped not a jot by Torsten's shrieking, I realize I was right: my magic *has* burgeoned. Torsten sets aside his irritation long enough to hypothesize that with the parasite no longer leaching from my identity, my strength has multiplied.

Hans offers me a hand from where I'm planted on the floor, swatting at the last embers. When I take his palm, I realize I can sense a darkness inside him. I draw it out, like venom from a wound.

The next time Hans embraces his mother, he does so in Heulensee.

A new sort of normal settles over the village. Hans's father returns, accompanied by a handful of the other men who went in search of help. The villages across the mountains either did not believe them, or did believe them, and wanted nothing to do with it. Some of the men dislike what Heulensee has become. Their opinion matters less than it used to.

Hans becomes a liaison between the Hexenwald and the village. Each time the sky above Heulensee reddens, he comes to the forest's edge and calls for me. Reassured by my presence, the townsfolk meet the Hexenwald's tide with steely resolve. Their courage is all I need to cut down monsters where they stand.

Sometimes, I think I catch Borbet on the edge of the forest, watching.

EPILOGUE

Heulensee continued to change while I stayed the same. I was a boulder in a stream – unchanging, despite all that moved around me. Ash and Torsten aged slowly enough that they at least appeared constant. Hans... well, Hans was a different matter.

I hoped the forest might leave him with some of its vigour, but it didn't take long for me to realize that Hans was, above all, human. Impermanent. When I first saw the signs of ageing on his face, I spiralled. I instructed Torsten to mix tinctures and ointments to keep him youthful. Hans shunned them. For a time, I believed that he was keeping his fear tamped down – but one morning, I realized that he had not been afraid of death for a very long time.

Hans slipped away peacefully at the age of seventy-four. It was serene. It tore me in half. I sat by his bedside and watched as he opened his eyes for the last time. His pupils focused beyond the window. The last word he said was my sister's name.

Wherever Hans is – whether that's as matter in the soil, or as a spirit in some golden realm ... I hope he and Thea are together.

Torsten, Ash, and I shared many more blissful years. I lost count after one hundred and ten. One morning, Ash and I woke to find a note passed beneath our bedroom door. In an elegant scrawl, Torsten wrote that he had left. That he didn't know where he was going, and he loved us very much, but he needed to spread his wings.

We cried. Ash raged that he didn't say goodbye in person. We drank wine – *copious* amounts of wine – and remembered every reckless thing he ever did, every beautiful moment of honesty and bravery.

And then, my dear Ash. I spent my whole mortal life in search of a home, and I found it in her. She saw me at my best, my worst, and loved me through it all. To see her fading before my eyes was a rare sort of torture – so all-consuming, so painful that it was almost a relief when she tipped over the precipice.

I buried her in the meadow, where the most beautiful ash tree grew from her bones. I spent hours talking to that tree, hoping that somewhere, somehow, she could hear me. In death, she deals me the greatest wound I will ever suffer – but I would do it all again.

In every lifetime, I would choose her. Even knowing how it ends.

My family waits for me in the forest. When I step into the Hexenwald, the trees do not loom. They beckon.

Acknowledgements

People speak of writing as a solitary career, and it often is – but I was never alone on this journey. There are so many people without whom this book wouldn't exist, and I'd like to thank a few of them.

 Thank you to my mum, who inspired my love of writing by feeding my insatiable reading habit. You believed in me before I believed in myself, and moulded me into the woman I am today. This book is dedicated to you. Thank you to my dad, who thinks I'm the best at everything I do. Thank you for being my most enthusiastic supporter not just in writing, but in life. Thank you to my brother, who I'm not sure will ever read this book, but shows his support in other ways – like leaving stupid comments in my first drafts, most of which I manage to delete. Thank you to Maple, the sweetest, silliest spaniel in the world. Half of this book was written with you at my side, and I wouldn't have it any other way.

 This is a book about sisters and the love between them. I don't have a sister, but I *do* have the most incredible group of girlfriends. Eresha, Katie, and Emily: you taught me the meaning of sisterhood. It's cheering for each other's achievements, howling at the moon, wearing matching denim jackets without meaning to. Thank you for your unwavering support. I'm so lucky to have you all.

Thank you to Gab, my platonic soulmate; to Tori, whose friendship I wouldn't have survived university without; to Becca, who inspires me every day; to Ryan and Elouise, for always indulging my delusional behaviour; to Benito, for being an icon and never failing to get the party started; to Cesca, for being my best writing buddy and lifeline.

To my agent, Chloe Seager: thank you for taking a chance on me. You saw the heart of this book, and helped me excavate it. I'll never be able to thank you enough for everything you've done for me. To my incredible editors, Charlotte Trumble in the UK and Jessica Anderson in the US: thank you for helping shape *Season of Fear* into the best book it could be, and for loving Ilse as much as I do. I'm a better writer because of you both.

Thank you also to the authors who have helped me on this journey. Thank you to everyone who read early versions of this book – especially Javin, Kaela, and Emily, whose feedback was instrumental. To Erin A. Craig, one of the kindest people I've had the pleasure of meeting. I felt (and sometimes still feel) like such an imposter. I cannot tell you how much it means to have an author I've admired for so long welcome me with open arms. To the incredible authors who read and blurbed this book – Kathryn Foxfield, Logan-Ashley Kisner, Elle Tesch, Lyndall Clipstone, Jamison Shea, Erin A. Craig, Alexandria Warwick, Adrienne Tooley, and Ava Reid – thank you from the bottom of my heart. I will spend the rest of my days telling everyone I know to buy your books. Your kindness will live with me forever.

Thank you to everyone at both my UK and US publishing houses for the colossal collective effort required to make this manuscript into a real book. At Little, Brown Young Readers, thank you to Managing Editor Jen Graham; Associate Art Director Jenny Kimura; Copyeditor Starr Baer; Production Manager Kimberly Stella; Marketers Christie Michel, Andie Divelbiss, and Savannah Kennelly; and Publicist Hannah Klein. Thank you also to Chris Mrozik for my hauntingly beautiful US cover.

At Simon & Schuster UK, thank you to Karin Seifried and Isabelle Gray in Production; Wilhelmina Asaam for freelance copyediting; Editorial Assistant Aneesha Angris; Sarah Jeffcoate in Marketing; Laurie McShea in Publicity; and Pip Watkins for designing my gorgeous, moody UK cover.

And finally, to Phillip. Anyone who knows me knows that I would *never* attribute my accomplishments to a man, but I couldn't have done this without you. When I felt like giving up, you were there to put me back on course. Thank you for your ceaseless patience, your empathy, and your steadfast support. I've never had someone believe in me so fiercely. I cannot understand what I did to deserve you and your love, but I thank my lucky stars for it. I love you endlessly (don't be weird about it).

And finally, thank you to *you* – the reader. I'm so grateful you picked up *Season of Fear*. I hope you loved it as much as I do.